JAW

PRISONER OF DESIRE

"You're fascinated with me because you think I'm savage, rather than civilized." The half-breed's fingers lightly brushed against Zoe's scalp, sending erotic tremors down her spine. "I can feel your body trembling to my touch. You like the primitive, don't you, Zoe Randolph? Then let me give you another taste of what you so desire."

The brave's hands dropped to his captive's shoulders and he dragged her into his embrace. With a feral growl he lowered his head, his lips touching hers, her breasts pressed against his chest. Zoe shivered and wrapped her arms around him. He was right; she was glad he was a Comanche, glad she was his slave. She wanted him to overpower her.

Her mouth moved against his and she welcomed the sensual exploration of his kiss. She asked — no, begged — for her own seduction.

COMANCHE BRIDE

EMMA MERRITT

ZEBRA BOOKS
KENSINGTON PUBLISHING CORP.

ZEBRA BOOKS

are published by

Kensington Publishing Corp.
475 Park Avenue South
New York, NY 10016

First printing: January, 1989

Printed in the United States of America

Chapter 1

In the heat of the day, a small caravan of five mounted horses and five heavily laden mules trudged single-file up the steep and perilous mountain. Zoe Randolph was frightened and made no secret of her fear. The trail was incredibly narrow.

"Careful, Dusty," she murmured, patting the sorrel's neck.

Higher they went. A boulder, wedged precariously in the outer rim of the canyon, crumbled beneath Dusty's weight. As the sorrel felt herself slipping down the side of the mountain, her eyes dilated in fear; she whinnied and stumbled forward. Fighting for survival, she thrashed her hooves against the glass-smooth surface. Zoe, hanging onto the saddle pommel, lurched back and forth.

Pebbles clinked down the sheer incline, their echo a warning. Zoe sucked in her breath. Dusty regained her balance, moved closer in toward the mountain, and continued to trudge up the steep trail. Zoe exhaled slowly, but didn't completely relax. No matter how many times she traveled over these mountains, she didn't think she'd ever get over her fear.

"Dr. Randolph!" The masculine shout, originating from much higher up, grew louder as the caravan guide approached Zoe. "Are you all right?"

"I'm fine, Mr. Snyder," she answered without anything in her voice to betray her anxiety. Patting the sorrel's neck, she said, "And Dusty seems to be fine as well."

"Won't get no worse," Digory Snyder announced as he wiped his forehead with his arm. "Move on up to that ridge up there and catch your breath while you wait for the mules to catch up with you. I'm gonna ride ahead. Think there's a place big enough up ahead where we can all make camp and rest, but I want to be sure that we're alone."

"Indians?" Zoe asked.

Exposing tobacco-stained teeth, Digory smiled his slow and infrequent smile. "Anybody, ma'am. Out here you don't share until you're absolutely sure you're sharing with friends." His weathered hand patted her shoulder. "Now, don't you go to worrying. That's what you hired me to do. I'll be back."

"All right," Zoe murmured. She was grateful that Digory had reminded her that it was his responsibility to worry about the trip; that gave her more time to worry about arriving safely. Her concern really wasn't Indians, unsavory company, or even reaching the ledge ahead; it was remaining on a trail that seemed to decrease in size the higher they traveled. She was an excellent horsewoman, but these mountains tried the expertise of the best.

When she finally reached the ridge, Zoe pulled Dusty to a halt and sighed in relief. She felt safer than she had for four hours. At last her mount was standing on more than the outer trail. As Zoe's gaze swept across the fire-glazed horizon, she encountered more of the treacherous mountains, their

6

craggy and stoic faces lifted to the blistering heat of the afternoon sun. Like the Indians who had so recently claimed the land, the mountains seemed to want to prove their ability to withstand all elements—especially the fiercest of all, the sun.

Zoe removed her hat and ran her fingertips over moist, honey-blond hair that was deliberately combed back from her face, braided, and twisted into a coil on top of her head. Normally she would have gone for a softer look, an elegant chignon with short tendrils around her face, but not for the trip into Mexico. It was much cooler this way and more manageable. Also—a smile twitched at the corners of Zoe's lips—Digory had told her in his gruff way before they departed Chandlerville, *If'en it's hid under your hat, Doc, we're less likely to entice scalp-hungry or wife-hunting Indians.*

The hat looped over her saddle horn, Zoe untied the bandanna from her throat and wiped the grit and perspiration from her face as best she could, pushing damp strands of hair from her forehead. When she dabbed the kerchief inside her opened neckline, she looked down at her clothes and grimaced. She was covered with dust. Perspiration ringed the underarms and neck of her ecru blouse. Her brown riding skirt, having caught on the cactus and prickly bushes of the desert, was snagged beyond repair, her boots deeply scarred. At a glance, she thought, no one would know that her outfit was brand-new, the pride and joy of Halstead's Emporium in Chandlerville. Hearing the tentative clop of hooves above her, Zoe looked up Digory rounding the mountain.

He pulled his horse to a halt next to her, his gaze taking in the string of mules and five drivers who were still climbing behind them. "We're making good

7

time today," he announced, dropping his head to spit, tobacco juice splattering on the rocky surface with a wet thud. "And the trail's good all the way down the other side."

When Zoe had first met Snyder at the Dry-as-a-Whistle Saloon in Chandlerville and hired him to guide her into Mexico, she could hardly understand what he was saying. His mouth was always full of tobacco, and because of his low, guttural voice, his words came out in snorts and growls. Now, after two days on the trail with him, she was accustomed to his speech patterns and had no problem making out what he said.

Nodding her head in acknowledgment, she quickly retied the bandanna around her throat and plopped her hat on her head. "How soon before we reach Candaleria?"

Snyder scratched his head, mussing his thin gray hair and knocking his hat askew. He thought for a few minutes and stared into space as if he expected to find an answer there. Finally he mumbled, "Another day, I reckon."

Zoe nodded her acknowledgment and said as she turned her head slowly, "I have a feeling we're being watched. Have you seen any sign of Indians?"

"Yep." Snyder lowered his head and spat again. "Signs of 'em everywhere, but I ain't seen nary a one."

Zoe wasn't irritated by the man's curtness; during the three days that they'd been traveling together, she'd learned to communicate quite well with her guide and to trust his judgment even more. "Should we be worried?"

"Yep." He wiped the faded red sleeve across his sweaty face again before he crossed his arms in front of him and squinted into the distance. "If'n you

8

want to be alive in this-here country, it pays to be worried about Indians. The way they look at it, this here's their land. These-here are their trails we be traveling on."

"If these are their trails, Mr. Snyder, why *are* we traveling on them?" Having lived in the west for only nine months, Zoe didn't pretend to fathom the frontier mind. At times it defied all reason and logic.

The man chuckled quietly. "Because these are the only trails through these-here mountains, ma'am. Comanches either found or made 'em hundreds of years ago and have been traveling 'em ever since. They got the way clearly marked and know every water hole in the country."

"Weber . . . Mr. Fielding hates the Comanches," Zoe said, thinking about her fiancé.

"Reckon Mr. Fielding has a right to hate 'em," Snyder said. If anyone knew the whole story behind Fielding's hatred of Comanches, Dr. Randolph would, Digory thought. After all, she was engaged to the man. Quiet for a long time, the guide finally ventured curiously, "Heard tell that one of them Comanches, a half-breed, got his sister with child about fifteen or twenty years ago."

"So I've been told," Zoe returned noncommittally, not wishing to discuss Weber's past with her guide. She was also resentful because Weber shared so little of himself with her, especially his past. She wouldn't have learned about Veronica's pregnancy had it not been for her best friend, Myra Halstead, who insisted on telling her when she learned that Zoe was seriously interested in Weber. Later, when Zoe had confronted Weber with the facts, she could tell that he was displeased that she asked, but reluctantly admitted the incident and curtly explained to her what had happened.

Uriah Chandler's half-breed grandson, Matt, had gotten his younger sister pregnant and had refused to marry her. More Comanche in his blood than white, Weber had declared. Before the baby was born, Veronica became ill and Weber quietly took her to some of their family back east. The baby died at birth, and Veronica soon afterwards. The half-breed had joined the Comanches and persuaded them to go on the warpath against all whites. Led by Matt Chandler, they had attacked a group of innocent whites, brutally massacring all five of them. Only one, horribly maimed, lived to tell the story.

"Heard tell the poor girl went crazy and had to be put in one of them sanitariums back east," Digory said, breaking the silence. "Heard tell them's mighty horrible places to put people."

Although Zoe shared the same sentiment, she was defensive of Weber and said rather sharply, "I'm sure Mr. Fielding had his reasons for doing what he did, Mr. Snyder."

"I'm sure he thinks so."

"—and I'm also sure he wouldn't appreciate our passing the time of day gossiping about his sister."

"Don't reckon it's gossip, Dr. Randolph," Snyder replied. "We ain't judging the man or figuring out the reason why he did what he did. Just simply recalling the facts."

"Then it's a fact we don't need to be talking about, Mr. Snyder." Zoe's voice snapped with authority. "From what I understand, the guilty parties are dead now. At least, we can let them rest in peace."

"Yep, reckon all of 'em are dead," he drawled, as if the thought had never occurred to him. Tilting his head, he rubbed the bottom of his chin. "Heard tell, Miss Veronica and the baby died back east during

10

childbirth, and Matt Chandler was killed during the recent War between the States."

"Yes," she said, remembering the day that some former Confederate soldiers had ridden into town with the news that Captain Matt Chandler had been killed in the line of duty, "that's what I've heard also."

The soldiers who served with Matt, unlike Weber, had liked their commanding officer. They painted a picture of a man entirely different from the Matt Chandler she had heard Myra and Weber describe. When later she attended Matt's memorial service with Myra and Greg Halstead, she was surprised to see so few people gathered. She was even more surprised at his half-brother's officiating over the service, rather than a minister. Conspicuously missing was Uriah Chandler, the man who had disowned his half-breed grandson fourteen years ago, refusing him his half of La Candela de Oro. Zoe couldn't understand a man like Uriah Chandler — a man who had tamed this land, established one of the largest ranches in Texas, 500,000 acres, and built a town as a lasting memorial to his name. Yet he had disowned and disinherited his own grandson and refused to pay his last respects to a Confederate war hero.

Myra had told Zoe that Uriah disowned Matt because he'd gotten involved with a Fielding, and Uriah hated the Fieldings, whom he considered deadly parasites. Others said Uriah had never cared for Matt because he was half-Indian; Bryan had always been his pride and joy. Zoe didn't know the real reason, but her heart hurt for the man. Though he had chosen to be a Comanche and had murdered white people, he had died without a family. Since then, she'd been assailed with insatiable curiosity about this man whom Weber hated so intently.

During the nine months she'd lived in Chander-ville, she had infrequently seen Uriah Chandler or Bryan, but for some reason she couldn't visualize Matt Chandler as being like either one. Although she and Bryan were the same age, she thought of him as being younger. He was an extremely sensitive man who reminded her of a little boy, with his big blue eyes, and golden blond hair that curled around his face. He found the courage to stand up to his grandfather in extreme situations—as in having the memorial for his brother—but generally found it more comfortable to go along with Uriah's wishes.

Zoe could like Uriah Chandler, but he didn't want to be liked. He was a tall, wiry man with a thick moustache and a deep, authoritative voice. In fact, he was a man who expected his word to be law and order. He wore his hatred of Weber Fielding on his sleeve for everyone to see. Until the war changed things, he had been the prime mover in the commu-nity. Now Weber was, and Uriah hated him even more.

The founder of Chandlerville could forgive the banker of anything but being a scalawag and found it degrading and humiliating to be beholden to a Fielding for anything, much less existence. Money was hard to come by in the South, and the war had taken its toll, leaving the Texas ranchers broke. Three months ago, Uriah, swallowing his pride, had come to Fielding for a loan. The collateral was a 50,000-acre parcel of La Candela de Oro chosen by Fielding himself.

Greg Halstead, owner of the local emporium, was upset when he heard which section of land Weber had selected; he knew the choice had been quite deliberate and premeditated, a sort of revenge against the dead Matt Chandler. The 50,000 acres should have been part of Matt's inheritance. Greg constantly fretted about Chandlerville's safety should Weber foreclose on the property. Although Greg was vocal in his grumbling, he wasn't a man of action, and like the majority of Chandlerville, he was content to sit back and let Weber run the town. Zoe quickly recognized that Greg and Myra were weak people who were much more comfortable when responsibility rested on someone else's shoulders, thus shifting decisions and consequences to them, and ultimately guilt or glory. Still Zoe liked the Halsteads and accepted them as they were.

Zoe soon learned that Weber controlled and concealed his feelings, except when it came to Matt Chandler — a man he hated. Greg told Zoe that when Matt left Chandlerville, Weber had transferred his hatred to all Comanches. If Weber should ever become the owner of that 50,000 acres, he would drive the Comanches off, and they, having lived here for more than a hundred years, would take unkindly to the idea. They would fight before they moved.

"If Matt were here," Greg told Zoe, "Weber wouldn't be doing this. Matt Chandler is the only man who could make Weber toe the line, the only man Weber feared!" Naturally the talk she'd heard about this half-breed had aroused Zoe's curiosity. She didn't doubt that Matt Chandler was a strong man, because people either loved or hated him. None were indifferent.

"Did you know Matt Chandler, Mr. Snyder?" Zoe asked, unaware that she had put her curiosity into words until she heard herself speak.

Digory looked at her for a few minutes before he shrugged his shoulders as he leaned over to spit. Wiping his hand across his mouth, he said, "That'd be about fourteen or fifteen years ago, I recollect. Yep, I kinda remember Matt Chandler. Right nice boy, he was. Looked more Indian than white."

"Why do you think he refused to marry Veronica and to give his child a name?" For a woman who had so sharply reprimanded Digory Snyder a few minutes ago, Zoe was now ferreting for information.

After a lengthy silence in which he stared into the distance, he said, "Some says it weren't his child. Reckon we'll never know for sure."

Zoe knew for sure! Her best friend Myra Halstead swore on a stack of Bibles that the baby was Matt's. She knew, Myra insisted, because Veronica herself had confided in her. Greg was Matt's best friend and refused to believe he was the father of the child. To the end he had stood up and proclaimed Matt's innocence.

"I think Matt Chandler proved his guilt," Zoe said, a small self-righteous lilt to her voice as she parroted Weber's words, "when he ran off and gathered a war party of Comanches and massacred innocent white people. I believe Weber said he was responsible for the death of five or six upright citizens of Chandlerville."

"Weren't upright by the time them Comanches got through with 'em," Digory drawled, his lips twitching into a grin.

"I don't find death a suitable topic for levity, Mr. Snyder."

"Reckon in every fight, ma'am, there be those who claim each side is innocent."

"Yes, Mr. Snyder, that's true," Zoe replied. "I just happen to believe Mr. Fielding." Feeling as if she were losing control of the conversation, Zoe smiled and changed the subject. "Back home in Charleston, Mr. Snyder, we used to read accounts about the

Indians. Some of the journalist said the Comanches were the worst of all the Plains Indians. Do you agree?"

Digory snorted. "Don't figure they're that much worse, ma'am. Just figure they're about that much better. Guess they're just about the best warriors among the Indians. A Comanche and his horse is a powerful sight to see—pretty, and at the same time frightening. Reckon anybody in his right mind would respect him and, in fact, be kinda scared of him." He paused for breath. "I know you don't want to do no more stopping than we have to, ma'am," Snyder said, "but I figure we ought to take a break now. If we don't, we might not reach Mexico a'tall. Mighty hot to be pushing the horses and the mules."

"Where?" Zoe nodded, her eyes scaling the horizon through the undulating heat waves. A novice when it came to surviving in the West Texas desert, she trusted Digory Snyder, but saw no place that was any more protected or any cooler than where they were. And this ridge, wider than most they had been over during their journey, was hardly wide enough to accommodate more than three animals and their riders.

Snyder pointed. "I found a mountain stream right up there and a shallow cave that'll offer us some cool."

"Good!" Zoe exclaimed. Water and shade were all the encouragement she needed to move forward again. "I'm ready, and I know the men must be." Turning at the same time that Snyder did, she looked at the five heavily laden mules steadily ambling up the steep incline behind them. "It's a wonder they don't fall over the sides of these mountains," she remarked with a twinge of compassion for the beasts.

15

"Ornery as the devil," Digory snorted, "and you gotta talk to 'em like they was one, but they're sure-footed, Doc. More durable than oxen and less enticing to the Indians. Yep—" he nodded his head vigorously and pulled his hat lower over his face "—reckon I'd rather be traveling with mules any day. Don't you worry none, ma'am." His voice softened perceptibly, as did the weathered face. "We'll get your medicine to them Mexicans so's you can treat them, and we'll get you there in time to stop an epidemic if there really is one. I promise you, it ain't a'gonna reach Chandlerville. You paid us to git you there in record time, and we're gonna see that you get your money's worth."

Zoe smiled gratefully. "Thank you, Mr. Snyder."

As if he were uncomfortable with the compliment, the man curtly nodded and lifted his hand to the brim of his hat, tipping it in acknowledgment. He eased his gray around Zoe and moved on out, shouting orders for their midday stop as his hand waved the men and mule forward. Zoe fairly raced to the place Digory Snyder chose for camp. As he'd promised, gushing out of the mountain to pool in a natural reservoir of rocks was a thin, crystal clear spring, not big enough to bathe in, but big enough for her to drink freely. When Zoe knelt beside the pool, she knew there were times in her life when she was bound to have been as happy, if not happier, but she wasn't sure when. As soon as she was through, she filled her hat with water and retreated into the shade of the shallow cave in order to give the men and animals room.

Using her bandanna, she washed her face and neck and arms. Then she ate a cold biscuit and a slice of fatback with the men. After the horses and mules had drunk their fill and grazed, one of the

16

drivers led them to the back of the cave. Fairly content herself, Zoe sought a spot away from them, spread a blanket, and lay down for a nap. The men, filling their mouths with a fresh cud of chewing tobacco, gathered at the mouth of the cave to exchange yarns and to spit. As Zoe grew drowsy, she heard above the low buzz of conversation Snyder's growl as he stationed the guard. Yes, she thought, he was taking care of her. She could rest easy. Neither her father nor Weber had anything to worry about. She would reach Mexico and be back home before they even missed her.

Zoe squirmed into a more comfortable position and thought about her coming marriage to Weber Fielding. She had been assured by more than one of Chandlerville's citizens that he was quite a catch. And he was. Zoe didn't delude herself into believing she was in love with him or he with her, but she liked him and wanted to marry him. She admired his ambition. She was proud that he was Chandlerville's most influential citizen and was even happier that he was wealthy and could offer her what she wanted out of life.

Zoe was not an avaricious person, and these were not the only reasons she wanted to marry the man. At twenty-nine, she was a mature woman looking for more out of life than youthful passion and romance. She was looking for stability and security . . . things Weber could provide for her.

She and he shared many interests which bonded them together. She honestly believed that once they were married, she would come to love him. Even if she didn't love him, she was sure that the two of them could have a happy marriage. Marriage to him would make her happy, and she promised herself that she would make him happy. She would never give him cause for regret.

At first her father had disapproved of her seeing Weber because he was twenty years her senior. Old enough to be your father, Quintan Randolph had pointed out, and not too kindly. But Zoe didn't mind Weber's being older. In fact, she rather liked it. He was a distinguished man, tall and slender, with silver temples that glistened in his black hair. Their friends frequently commented on how beautifully she and Weber complemented one another. Quintan had snorted disdainfully when he heard the comment.

Later, when he learned about some of Weber's postwar schemes for progress for Chandlerville—namely the ridiculous irrigation canal that would run from the Rio Grande to some point in New Mexico—Quintan had warned Zoe that the man was after their property. Zoe agreed that her father did own most of the acreage that surrounded the town, and expansion had increased its value until he was land-rich; she also agreed with him that of the choice acres, she owned the choicest—the ones he had deeded over to her as a site for her future hospital. But Zoe scoffed at the idea that Weber wanted to marry her because of their property; he was wealthy enough to purchase it, if he wanted it that much. Furthermore, the canal wasn't coming within a mile of either her property or Quintan's.

In addition to their sharing common interests, Zoe admitted that she was as ambitious as Weber. While some faulted ambition and charged that it went hand-in-hand with ruthlessness, Zoe didn't agree. Ambitious people had goals and were not easily distracted. Weber was such a man. In the fifteen years since he had come to Chandlerville to open a bank, he had become a multimillionare, a

18

respected and powerful voice in the community. He was the vision and force behind the city's growth, the visionary behind the Trans-Pecos Irrigation Canal that would transform the area from a semiarid desert into fertile farmlands. Since the ending of the War between the States, he had reestablished the stage route through town and was planning ahead to the laying of the first railroad, which would ensure Chandlerville's future as the prime city of West Texas.

Although Zoe's conscience bothered her when she thought of Weber's moving the Comanches off their land should Uriah not be able to repay his loan, she could understand Weber's position. He had explained it to her when she voiced her misgivings. When Uriah had come to him for the loan, he had been quite honest about which property he wanted as collateral — the 50,000 acres on which the Comanches lived — and his reasons for wanting it: because that was his first choice route for the Trans-Pecos Irrigation Canal. He had patiently explained how short he was of cash and that he could not extend payment beyond the maturation date. Understanding this, Uriah had signed the papers. As Weber had pointed out to her, this was business, nothing personal against Uriah Chandler or the Comanches.

Zoe wanted more than anything to see Weber's plans come to fruition, and she hoped to be a part of those plans. She wanted Chandlerville to grow into a bustling city. Herself a visionary, she dreamed of the day a huge hospital complex would sit in the middle of the metropolis on the property that she and her father had chosen and that he had already given to her. The Zoe Ellen Randolph . . . Fielding Hospital. Because of its research center and its modern equipment, it would attract doctors from all over the world. All people, regardless of race or economic status, would receive the best treatment. Zoe and her father were already talking about establishing an endowment that would guarantee this.

Yes, she and Weber were farsighted leaders of the community. Together they made a striking couple and a formidable team.

Snyder's call, "Time to get going," roused Zoe from her fanciful dreams. She opened her eyes but didn't immediately move. She lay there watching the men as they led the animals out of the cave to water one last time before they started traveling again. Sitting up, she yawned and stretched. Then she heard an agonizing scream, then a shout: "Indians! Indians out here! They got Williams!"

Glad she was wearing the divided riding skirt, Zoe rolled over, grabbed her rifle, and raced to one of the huge boulders at the entrance. An arrow-riddled body lay in the clearing; the other four men, unable to reach the safety of the cave, were scattered and hidden outside.

"Don't you come out, ma'am," Snyder yelled. "Don't want them redskins to see a woman." A pause, then came the flat pronouncement: "Reckon you know to save that last bullet, ma'am, in case something happens to all us menfolks?"

"Yes," Zoe called, "I know, Mr. Snyder."

"If it comes to that, don't hesitate to use it, ma'am. Dying by your own hand will be much quicker and more merciful than dying by the hands of them murdering savages, and much better than living with them." When Zoe didn't immediately answer, Snyder demanded curtly, "You hear me, ma'am?"

"Yes, Mr. Snyder, I hear."

Then a stillness, fraught with fear and uncertainty,

settled over Zoe. She waited, perspiration beading up in her palms—perspiration that had nothing to do with the heat of the late spring day—and ran down her forehead to sting her eyes. She dropped first one hand, then the other, laid her rifle aside, and took off her hat. Untying the damp bandanna from around her neck, she retied it around her forehead to form a headband. After she had put her hat back on, she picked up her rifle and clutched the stock more closely to her chest, her finger curling around the trigger.

She heard her first Indian ululation, and it caused a shiver of fear to wrack her entire body. She had heard about savage battle cries, but the description didn't begin to compare to the horrible sound that ripped her very soul. She broke out in a cold sweat. One of her men screamed out, and in a moment she saw a young brave atop a rock shouting and waving a bloody scalp in the air; she saw the thin trickle of blood run down his uplifted arm. Two were dead. Only five of them were left.

Shots peppered from all directions, but the Indian was untouched. As if drugged on his own invincibility, he leaped even higher in open sight, taunting the white men with his battle cries. More shots; then another cry—that of a white man screaming out—pierced the air. A second scalp atop a lance was whisked through the air; a second Indian danced his victory; a third member of Zoe's escort died.

Zoe was more frightened than she'd ever been in her life, more frightened than she'd been when she was nursing the wounded on the battle front during the recent War between the States. At least she had known her enemies then—their way of thinking, their moral codes, their possible reactions to a given situation.

21

About the Indians she knew nothing save what she had read in the newspapers and dime novels and what the white settlers in Chandlerville had told her, and none of that had been good. According to them, Indians were savages who killed and plundered without provocation. No white man would be safe until all Indians were removed from the face of the earth. The only good Indian was a dead one. This attack on her caravan reinforced all that Zoe had been taught about Indians during the nine months she'd lived in West Texas.

She wanted to call out; she wanted to be convinced that some of her men were still alive; but she didn't. Instinct warned her that she would give her position away, if not theirs. If they were alive, she couldn't betray them. The quietness stretched beyond endurance. Zoe was tense, her body leaden; she felt as if she were carved of stone. Yet she was alive. She felt each beat of her heart at the base of her throat; her chest hurt with each breath of air she took; and her entire body was clammy with pure fear.

Zoe heard loose rock clank down the side of the mountain. She whirled around and pulled the stock of the rifle more closely against her chest, her finger curling tightly around the trigger. Someone was coming. She waited; she watched; she listened. She heard only more silence. Then a great whoop filled the air and an Indian, seeming to appear from nowhere, leaped into the clearing where only an hour before Zoe and the men had been eating their meal. Before she could pull the trigger, a shot rang out.

In surprise the Indian looked toward the huge boulder behind which Snyder hid; he clutched his chest, blood oozing through his fingers. Then he crumpled to the ground in death.

Zoe was watching the Indian so intently that she didn't see Digory leap from his hiding place and run to where she hid. Only when she felt his strong fingers dig into her arm did she look up.

"We gotta get out of here," he grunted, his eyes darting around. "Them Indians cut us off from the water. Can't last long in this cave. Figure we can make a better stand back the trail a-ways. I'm gonna get the horses."

"The other men—" Zoe's fingers dug into Snyder's arm. "What about them?"

"Don't know." Snyder bruskly patted Zoe's hand, then moved it. His eyes never left the clearing; he crouched and rocked forward on his toes. "If they ain't dead, they'll see me heading for the horses and they'll give me some cover. Now, in case we're by ourselves, you gotta give me cover, and plenty of it. Don't know how many of them devils are out there."

Zoe nodded and watched Digory run across the clearing. She scanned the cliffs around them and saw no movement, no sign of life. Digory reached the horses and grabbed the reins. Suddenly five braves, screaming at the top of their lungs, stood up as if they were an extension of the unholy rocks themselves, as craggy and indomitable as the land around her. Zoe pushed from behind her boulder and raised the rifle. Before she could fire, a hand clamped over her mouth and an arm banded around her upper arms and chest. Her rifle fell to the ground.

The arm around her was like a band of steel cutting off her air. She gasped and struggled, her fingers clawing at the human manacle. She kicked her assailant, but he seemed impervious to the heels of her boots that flayed against his shins. Tears flooded her eyes and she screamed—the sound muf-

23

fled by the hand over her mouth—as she watched one of the Indians leap on Snyder's back and grab a handful of hair; the red man pulled the caravan master's head back and with one deft flick of the knife, slit his throat. Snyder was still alive and squirming when the brave with another swipe of his bloodied knife whisked the hair from his head and held it up, blood running down his arm.

Zoe's captor released his hold on her so abruptly she staggered backward but regained her equilibrium and stumbled toward Digory.

"Mr. Snyder," she called, too frightened and panic-stricken for tears, "I'm here. I'm going to help you."

"Doc?" Snyder's hoarse whisper barely reached Zoe's ears. "Doc Randolph, don't—don't let 'em take you . . . alive."

Before Zoe reached the dying man, another Indian jumped in front of her and blocked her way. She bumped into him, her face slamming against a chest that seemed to be made of pure iron. Her hat flew to the ground, and his arms banded around her. Dazed, she pulled back and looked up to see the brave staring at her head in wonderment. In horror she watched his hand move toward her hair. *Oh, my Lord, he's going to scalp me!* She jerked her head away and struggled to free herself from his grasp.

He grinned and released her, laughing aloud when she stumbled and fell forward to land on top of Snyder, who no longer moved. Her face fell against his chest, her cheeks rubbing against the bloody shirt. Zoe lifted herself, her hand brushing the wagon master's shirt; she felt for his heartbeat . . . none. She caught the lapels of his shirt in both fists and pulled her head to his chest. She listened for his breath; she watched for movement in his chest. She

24

prayed for life. . . .

"Mr. Snyder," she called, shaking him. "Mr. Snyder, answer me!"

When Digory's head lolled forward, Zoe could only stare at him, at the blood on her hands. She couldn't believe he was dead and she was alone. Gently she laid him down, and for a few seconds she sat there in shocked silence. Then she heard a noise and turned her head. The Indians were tossing her medical supplies down the side of the mountain. Furious, she leaped to her feet and charged at them.

"Leave those alone," she yelled with such force they actually turned to stare at in her in amazement. She placed herself between the provisions and the Indians, her breasts heaving with her exertion. Defiantly she planted both hands on her hips and glared. "These are mine, and I'll kill you before I let you damage them."

The Indians laughed at the foolish but brave white woman. One of them grabbed her by the blouse, ripping the flimsy material as he jerked her out of the way. When she kicked him, he pulled back his hand and slapped her across the face, blood trickling from the corner of her mouth. As she reeled from the blow and stumbled to the ground, her hand brushed over a large round stone. Her fingers curling around it, she lifted and whirled it through the air. The Indian saw it coming and ducked to miss the blow, but he was angry. His eyes narrowing, his face contorted with his fury, he moved toward the white woman with intent to punish . . . just short of death. The knife whisked out of the belt, the slick metal blade glinting in the sunlight as he pulled his hand back to slash her face. A furious Comanche command boomed through the air to stop him, but his eyes never left Zoe's face.

Zoe looked in the direction from which the sound came to see another Indian—the first one that she had seen, the first one to wave a scalp through the air. His countenance and black eyes were filled with the same hatred and hostility of the other braves, but for some reason Zoe didn't understand, he had saved her life. He nudged his horse through the opening, speaking in Comanche and gesturing. The two braves argued, the one refusing to sheath his knife, his gaze moving back and forth between Zoe and the newcomer. Finally, muttering under his breath, he returned his knife to his belt and stomped off to his horse.

The brave who'd saved Zoe's life rode to where she stood, leaned over, and wrapped an arm around her waist, easily lifting and depositing her in front of him. His arm digging into her waist affirmed her captivity. Over his shoulders she watched the Indians string her mules and horses together. As they rode down the mountain, she looked at her precious medical supplies being left behind, exposed to the elements.

Tears pricked her eyes. Since the ending of the War between the States, United States currency was scarce and Confederate money good for nothing but fire-starter. Because her patients needed medicine that cost money and money came only through the Union, Zoe tolerated the newly formed Unionist government of Chandlerville and used them to secure what she needed for her practice. Her toleration caused some of the diehard rebels to label her a scalawag. For the good of the people she bore the derisive label; she had borne worse in her twenty-nine years.

Four months ago, when she traveled to Boston for the physicians' seminar, she had exchanged the last

26

of her mother's jewelry for Union currency, some of which had purchased these supplies. The remainder had gone to her endowment for the hospital. The pain of leaving her medical supplies was so great that Zoe turned her head, straightened her shoulders, and stared blankly ahead, refusing to touch her Indian captor any more than was absolutely necessary, but as the afternoon turned into evening, she didn't know if she could keep her resolve.

Through the night the Comanches rode hard, stopping infrequently and erasing their tracks. Zoe had no idea how far they had journeyed; nor was she sure in what direction they traveled. She kept her body rigid and concentrated her thoughts on plans of escape.

By evening the next day, Zoe was numb. She had been deprived of her hat, and her face was sunburned, her lips so dry they were cracking. At first she kept her hopes up by imagining her rescue, but these thoughts soon paled. Neither her father nor Weber would miss her for days. By the time they realized she hadn't reached Mexico, all traces of her capture would be eradicated. The Indians had wrapped pieces of deerskin around the hooves of the horses and mules, leaving no trail behind them. Her rescuers might find her medical supplies and the decomposed bodies of her escort, but little else. Zoe Randolph would become nothing more than a memory.

She remembered how adamantly opposed her father and Weber had been to her going to Mexico. When the messenger from Candaleria had first arrived asking for her help, both men had warned her of the dangers in traveling to Mexico, especially with the Comanches riled up and on the verge of war because of the way Weber's men had been harassing

27

them, promising that soon they would be driven off their land.

But Zoe couldn't believe the Comanches would bother her. When she had first arrived in Chandlerville, she and her father had traveled to Candaleria and hadn't been harmed. She had done nothing since then to incur their wrath. Besides, the plight of the Mexicans tugged at Zoe's heart. In their time of greatest need, she couldn't abandon them. She must go and find out if they were suffering an epidemic of cholera. In the best interests of her patients, she refused to harken to Weber's warning.

Secretly she had packed her supplies, hired Digory Snyder as wagon master, and waited until her father was miles away delivering Mrs. Ginnison's baby and Weber was in El Paso presenting his Trans-Pecos Irrigation project to the business leaders of the community. By the time her father and Weber returned to Chandlerville and read the notes she had left each of them, she would be well on her way to Mexico. She had planned so well that while both would be irritated with her, neither would be in a hurry to come after her.

Chapter 2

On the third morning of Zoe's captivity, the Comanches rode into a large village, where tepees stretched along the creek for several miles. The crowd that rushed to greet the returning warriors was so great that Zoe thought the entire population of the village must have turned out. The young braves, basking in their moment of glory, whooped their victory and waved their lances in the air, the scalps dancing with the motion. A black hair fell from one of them to wrap around Zoe's fingers. Her stomach tightened as memories of mutilated bodies swam in her mind.

Without warning, Zoe was shoved to the ground; then her captor leaped off the horse to lean down and grab her by the arm. After jerking her to her feet, he dragged her through the corridor of laughing and shouting people to the chief's tepee at the end of the village. Here he thrust her to the ground in front of several older men who sat around the campfire. When Zoe pushed herself up on her hands, he kicked her down, her face landing in the dirt, pebbles and twigs digging into her burned flesh.

Although she was in excruciating pain, her muscles aching, her face burning, Zoe rolled away from him and leaped to her feet, glaring into the Indian's face. The people, quickly assembling in a semicircle around her, grunted their approval. A spirited prisoner made the torture even better, giving the Indians more pleasure. Zoe brushed the dirt and pebbles from her eyes and face; she dodged Bright Knife's seeking hand. Again a grunt of admiration ran through the crowd. Bright Knife's face twisted in anger, but deep down he, too, appreciated her defiance. He was going to enjoy taming this white woman. Moving past her, he stood before the village council, who sat on either side of the chief, their expressions bland, giving away none of their feelings. The young warriors gathered to sit around them. Then came the women and children.

"Soaring Eagle," Zoe's captor said in Comanche, "my braves and I have fought the white man twice in battle today and have been victorious both times. I, Bright Knife, am an honored war chief. All my braves have returned unharmed to tell our stories of valor. We bring our trophies of war with us."

The young brave walked around the circle looking into the face of each elder; Zoe's eyes brimmed with hatred, and although she couldn't understand a word he said, she heard the arrogance in his voice and saw it in his strut. He reminded her of a bantam rooster.

Soaring Eagle, his expression never changing, looked from the brave, to Zoe, to the scalps, and back to Zoe. His predominantly white hair was parted down the middle and hung down his shoulders in two braids. His chest was bare and he wore buckskin leggings and moccasins. When Zoe looked into his black eyes, she saw none of the hostility that

30

was resident in her captor's eyes, but neither did she see friendship.

Before she could identify his emotion, the glint of gold in the sunlight caught her attention and her gaze dropped to the cross that gleamed on his broad chest . . . a Christian cross!

Hope soared. Perhaps he *was* a Christian. If so, he would. . . . Swiftly her eyes lifted to encounter his briefly, but long enough to know that he wouldn't help her. He was not hostile, but neither was he friendly. She understood the emotion she saw stirring in his eyes. He was indifferent. Her fate mattured not one jot to this man. As quickly as her hope had arisen, it died.

Soaring Eagle waited a long time after Bright Knife was silent before he spoke, waving his hand toward Zoe. When he did speak, his voice was strong and full of authority; it was also heavy with censure. "Look at our herds. We are wealthy in horses and mules, and we have no need of slaves. You speak to me and your people of valiant behavior. You call capturing a white woman and a few horses and mules valiant behavior? I call it stupidity."

Zoe looked in confusion from Soaring Eagle to Bright Knife. From the pointing, she knew they were discussing her. From the tone of their voices and the expressions on their faces, she could tell that neither was pleased. Perspiration beaded in her palms, and she inched forward, wishing she could understand their conversation, wishing she knew what fate awaited her.

"We are not stupid," Bright Eagle declared angrily, stomping around the circle. "Nor do we call capturing one white woman valor. Look at our lances." He thrust his own through the air and motioned his

31

braves to do the same. "This is what we call valor." Flags of human hair waved through the sky.

As she listened to the guttural sounds of the young war chief, Zoe's gaze moved from one scalp to the other until she was staring at Digory's. Recalling the horrible mutilation, she was filled with renewed anger. She hated the murdering devils.

"Today we killed ten-and-five white men; each of us has a white scalp to prove our bravery. Some have more than one."

"And what have we gained from the deaths of these white men?" Soaring Eagle demanded, ignoring the scalps as if they were of no importance. "A temporary victory that is sure to end in a great battle that we cannot hope to win. In the end, will we not lose more scalps than the white men?"

"No," Bright Knife shouted defiantly. "The Great Spirit has smiled on us today. We have won the first of many victories over the white man." He straightened and thrust his fist through the air many times. As he called for total decimation of the white man, he led his people in great shouts of victory. "Now we can push him off our lands. No longer will we be at his mercy, but he at ours. We will join with the other tribes who are journeying to our land for a great *taquoip*. Not only will we meet at the great talk with them, but we will join our numbers together."

Zoe heard the impassioned speech and watched the spectators; they were all caught up in whatever it was the young brave said. They nodded their heads in assent, and their eyes glittered. An old woman rose to her feet, her movement serving to quiet the crowd.

Zoe stared at the Indian woman in fascination. She wore no blouse, only a loose buckskin skirt tied about her waist with a drawstring. Tattooed on her right breast and cheek were black stars; a bright red-orange circle decorated her left cheek. Her coarse black hair was cropped rather unevenly and needed combing; the part line was traced with vermilion. Broad red lines zigzagged around her eyes, and the insides of her ears were painted red. She wore many bracelets and necklaces, most of which were made of bones and beads.

"You have done well, Bright Knife," the Indian said slowly in Comanche. "Buffalo Woman is proud of you. You have acted like a Comanche warrior. Your medicine is strong. You have brought honor back to the Comanches."

"Thank you, medicine woman," Bright Knife replied. "Your words of wisdom fill my heart with gratitude."

"Even if Soaring Eagle does not listen to the talk of other tribes when they come to the great talk, the council and young chiefs will. We will join all the Comanches together to be strong, our numbers so great the white man cannot count them."

"Sit, Buffalo Woman, and be silent," Soaring Eagle ordered. "I have consented to the great talk. I will listen to what these other tribes have to say, but I will judge their words. Then I will make a decision. Now, do not interrupt the council again. I have not finished speaking with Bright Knife."

Buffalo Woman nodded and returned to her place. As she sat down, she turned to see Zoe staring. Their eyes met and held. Zoe started and drew back from the burning hatred in the Indian's eyes. The woman had spoken only Comanche, but Zoe read her hostility as clearly as if she'd spoken it in English. Zoe couldn't remember when she'd witnessed such strong emotion directed entirely at her, and for no apparent reason other than because she was white.

"Speak, Bright Knife," Soaring Eagle commanded. "Tell us of your battle with the white man today."

"Battles," the chieftain corrected, holding up two fingers. He slowly pivoted to look into all the faces that circled him. Then he began to talk. "First, my chief, we encountered the white men, who have stopped hunting the buffalo and are hunting the Indian for his scalp, and who in turn sell these scalps to their white chiefs. We killed nine of them."

In unison the people clapped their hands, their rasping shouts of "Here! Here!" filling the air. They were delighted with Bright Bear's report. They hated the men who hunted them as if they were animals and who sold their scalps for money. These men had no honor themselves and took all honor out of death for the Indian.

Swelling with pride and a little carried away with an inflated sense of his own importance, Bright Knife said, "We were riding home from that battle, my chief, when we encountered the small trade caravan—six men and the woman. Our luck was good; the Great Spirit had blessed us." Amidst shouts of praise and encouragement, Bright Knife continued to recount his story to Soaring Eagle and the villagers who thronged around them.

The afternoon sun was unbearably hot, and Zoe felt as if the crowd was closing in on her; she felt as if she were suffocating. She untied her kerchief and reached up to wipe her forehead. As she gingerly touched the stinging skin, she wished she had some ointment to relieve the burn. She threw back her head and looked up at the blue sky, ungraced by a single white cloud. The sun had already begun its descent in the west. Night would soon be here. Three long and harrowing days since she had been captured. How many more before she saw her people again?

Retying her bandanna around her neck, she crossed her legs and sat back. Unable to understand a word the Comanches were saying and bored by their orations and arguments, she passed the time by gazing curiously at each of them. Inadvertently her gaze moved beyond Soaring Eagle and the old men to the brave sitting immediately to his right. He was much younger than the chief, Zoe decided, but older than the bantam rooster who was still crowing and strutting around the circle.

She studied this new warrior intently. He wasn't an Indian . . . at least, not a full-blooded one. He had features like an Indian all right—jet-black hair, brown eyes, and an aquiline nose—and with the exception of his shorter hair, was dressed much like the other braves. He wore long buckskin trousers with knee-high moccasins. He had to be either a half-breed or a captive reared by the Comanches, Zoe decided. During the short time she'd been out here, she'd learned that these white Indians and half-breeds were not uncommon. Indians raided white settlements for the specific purpose of taking women and children. The children they adopted; the women they wanted simply for childbearing.

The Indian moved his hand and the gleaming metal on his wrist caught her attention. She leaned forward to stare at a beautifully engraved gold bracelet—a white man's bracelet. She grimaced . . . no doubt a white man had been murdered for it.

When the hand lifted to brush an errant lock of hair from his forehead, Zoe followed the movement until she found herself staring into his insolent dark brown eyes. So great were his anger and contempt,

Zoe felt as if she had been struck; she flinched as she imagined the blow against her tender, sunburned skin. She glared across the campfire, and when his lips curled into a derisive smile, she wished she was close enough to slap the smugness from his face.

No matter how much she despised the man, Zoe couldn't escape him, nor could she break eye contact with him. She felt his searing gaze move over every inch of her face, down her neck, to linger on the rip in the yoke of her blouse. Blushing furiously, she lifted her hand and laid it over the eyelet material, covering the tear as best she could. Those despicable lips smiled even more. Zoe dropped her face, refusing to be insulted any longer.

Then she heard Soaring Eagle speak and looked up to see the cocky young brave finally sit down beside the old woman with the star tattoos.

"Many suns ago, when we were the warriors of the plains, we would have considered that a sign of bravery and we would have been proud of our young braves, but not today, Bright Knife. For the past fifty winters, we have lived in peace with the white man."

"Ever since your daughter, Wind-over-the-River, married a white man." Bright Knife spat the words at the old chief. "You have become soft, like a white man. Where once you feared no man, animal, or thing, you now shake with fear. When the white men came bringing a sheet of paper to tell you that we have lost our lands, you gave up. You tell us to pack up our tepees and prepare to move. You don't have the stomach to fight them anymore or to drive them from our land."

"You are right, my son," Soaring Eagle admitted, his words carrying no shame, "I do not have the stomach to see my women and children killed needlessly. We cannot drive the white man from our country; he has come to stay. We can only hope to learn to live by his side in peace."

"I won't live by his side in peace." Bright Knife spat on the ground to demonstrate his contempt for the white men. "I will fight until I have no life left with which to fight. And there are other red men who agree with me."

Her eyes on Bright Knife, the impassioned tones of his speech still ringing in her ears, Zoe heard another brave speak.

"It is good that you have such determination."

The voice was deep and resonant, and filled with quiet authority; his words were unhurried and lacked the gravelly tone of the other Comanches. Zoe's eyes had been averted from all this, but intuitively she knew it was the warrior who sat to the right of the chief, the one who had been mentally undressing her, who now spoke. Although his words were strange to her ear, his tones were caressing and compelling. Slowly she turned her head to see him rise with all the grace and agility of a tiger and move around the circle until he stood in front of Bright Eagle and was staring down at the young brave.

Now Zoe could study the man at her leisure without fear of being discovered. He was younger than she had first supposed, but much older than Bright Knife; she judged him to be in his late thirties. He was tall, at least six feet, five inches. His bronze frame was lean, tough, and muscular. Although he was at least partially white, Zoe judged him to be the more primitive of the two warriors. He was strength personified and exuded a raw virility that frightened yet captivated her.

"You are going to need more than good medicine and more than determination when the white men

37

learn that you have taken one of their women," the tall Indian promised. "They already want your land; now they will have an excuse to come in force to drive you out. They will wipe out the entire village."

Bright Knife, laughing derisively, leaped to his feet. "You are soft like your grandfather, Ma-ta-mon-yahu. These fourteen years of living in the white man's world have made you more white than Indian. Your name calls you Treasure -of-the-Great-Spirit, but that you are not. You are Shame-to-the-Great-Spirit. A Comanche warrior you are not, even though you wear the coveted arm band of valor."

Ma-ta-mon-yahu looked at the bracelet on his wrist and remembered the day his grandfather, Soaring Eagle, had bestowed it upon him—the day he proved he was a Comanche warrior. He smiled, refusing to be baited by the younger man. "By blood, Bright Knife, I am half-white and half-Indian. I am proud of my mother and my father. I am proud that both bloods flow through my veins. I am not soft; I am wise."

"Wise, bah!" Bright Knife spat. "You are full of false promises. Your grandfather and then your father promised us land to live on for as long as we wished. Yet the white man comes with papers signed by his government that say we must leave. He claims our village land, our hunting grounds, and our Sacred Mountain will soon belong to him. When they do, we must move to the west."

"No one is going to put you off your property," Ma-ta-mon-yahu said, wondering at his own audacity in making such a promise. Fourten years ago he had been disowned by Uriah Chandler. His half of the ranch had then been promised to his younger half-brother. Ironic, that the disinherited was making such a vow.

Because of Uriah Chandler's and his son Charles's efforts, the Comanches had peacefully coexisted with the white man for the past fifty years. For twenty years it was without a guarantee of any sort, then thirty years ago, Charles Chandler had persuaded his father to give 50,000 acres of their 500,000-acre ranch to Soaring Eagle and the Comanches. Uriah Chandler, not one to like or accept Indians, did so because it was a strategic move for Chandlerville and La Candela de Oro. The Comanches would be a buffer between him and other hostile forces. Better to fight the known enemy than the unknown.

Charles had not been unduly worried about the arrangement. He knew that once his father gave his word, he would not go back on it. He also knew that one day he would inherit all his father's domain, and at his death La Candela de Oro would be divided between his two sons. The land on which the Comanches lived would go to Matt; thus they would be protected and no one could take their land away from them. With Matt's inheritance of the Comanche property would come the guardianship of his people. He, like his father, would promise Soaring Eagle and his people a home which the encroaching white people could not take away from them.

Although Charles had never convinced the Indians to trust or to like the white men, he'd taught them the value of existing peacefully side by side. Since returning from the war, Matt was realizing that toleration was too thin a string to bind two cultures together in permanent peace. Weber Fielding had used his absence to his advantage. According to the message he had given Soaring Eagle, Uriah had used the 50,000 acres the Comanches lived on as collateral for a loan which matured in sixty days. If payment were not made on time—and Fielding seemed confident that it wouldn't—the land belonged to him. He was giving the Comanches fair warning that if they wanted to avoid bloodshed, they were to be off the land the day it became his property.

Matt had returned to Texas after having been gone fourteen years for the explicit purpose of visiting both his grandfathers, Soaring Eagle and Uriah Chandler. After learning about the loan and the removal of the Comanches, he was even more eager to see Uriah. But thanks to this stupid woman, he had a large obstacle to dispense with—one that would take up precious time and a great deal of effort. As soon as he returned Zoe to her people, he must go directly to La Candela de Oro and talk with Uriah to find out why Fielding was already acting as if the land were his. Matt would never inherit the ranch, but he sure as hell wouldn't stand by and see Weber Fielding get one single acre of La Candela de Oro.

"My grandfather and my father promised you that this lands is yours. Now I, Ma-ta-mon-yahu, make this promise. Only the Comanches had a legal—and moral—claim to the land. We must return the white woman to her people before they retaliate. We can settle this land dispute without bloodshed."

"No!" His face contorted with anger, Bright Knife leaped to his feet, shaking his head. "I will not return her. She is mine, and I am keeping her." He looked down at Soaring Eagle. "Even *you* cannot make me give her up or return her. Comanche law declares that it's my right to have her."

Zoe didn't understand a word they had spoken, but she was caught up in the intensity of the argument. Her gaze turning to Soaring Eagle, she watched the expressions play across his face.

40

"Yes, Bright Knife," the chief finally agreed, "Comanche law says that the woman is yours." The voice was old now, the shoulders sagging a little. "Even I cannot change the law . . . so be it. It is—"

"No, my grandfather," Ma-ta-mon-yahu said in Comanche, his angry gaze locked to Zoe.

She blanched under such overt fury, knowing that the men argued over her.

"It is not so. I challenge Bright Knife for the white woman."

"No!" Bright Eagle exclaimed as if he hadn't heard Ma-ta-mon-yahu correctly.

"Why not?" Mat-ta-mon-yahu taunted softly, his words barely audible. "At one time such a custom was considered honorable among us. Perhaps the little boy who jumps up and down and shouts about valor isn't so courageous, after all."

The crowd gasped, and Zoe stared curiously at the two men. Each was beyond mere anger; they were furious.

Bright Knife's features twisted into pure hatred. "I am brave and honorable, and I have no fear of you. I do not wish to fight you because you have no right to challenge me for possession of the white woman."

Ma-ta-mon-yahu smiled menacingly. "By Comanche law, the same law that you are quoting, Bright Knife, I have a right." Now he laughed softly. "Yes, I think you are afraid to fight me. But why should you be? You're a young warrior, a *tao-yo-vis-se*. I am an older warrior; I have seen three-tens-and-six winters."

Bright Knife's eyes ran the length of Ma-ta-mon-yahu's lean, muscular frame, and he, too, laughed. "No, I'm not afraid of the challenge. You are right. I am a *tao-yo-vis-se*. I have seen ten-and-eight winters. Not only have you see three-tens-and-six win-

41

ters, you have been with the white men for the past ten-and-four winters and are no longer called Ma-ta-mon-yahu. Now you are called—"

"Do not call me by my white name," Ma-ta-mon-yahu said, still using that quiet tone. "If I am to help the Comanche retain their property, I do not want my identity revealed until I choose to do so. I do not want the white woman to know who I am."

"I don't know that you ever were a Comanche." Bright Knife grinned but he didn't call Ma-ta-mon-yahu by his Christian name. "Even if you were, you have forgotten how to fight like one."

Ma-ta-mon-yahu's eyes narrowed and silently he agreed. For fourteen years he had been separated from the Comanches and the Chandlers—from the day his grandfather had disowned him and he'd become a man without a family, a man who didn't want his past. Before the War between the States, he was one of New Orleans' most illustrious riverboat gamblers, and during the war he had served the Confederacy as a colonel in the cavalry.

Now he was coming home, a broken and weary man, first to see his Comanche grandfather, Soaring Eagle, then to see his white grandfather, Uriah Chandler. When he lay in the hospital on the verge of death, he realized stubbornness and pride were no substitute for love. He promised himself that he would come home and make things right between him and Uriah . . . no matter what it took.

"Then again, maybe you never knew how to fight like a Comanche," Bright Knife taunted when Matt didn't answer.

A smile pulled one corner of Matt's lips. "I know, and I haven't forgotten." His gaze swept over to the chief, and for a minute the brown eyes softened. "My grandfather, Soaring Eagle, taught me well."

Bright Knife paused for a long while before he slowly said, "I do not wish to fight you, Ma-ta-mon-yahu, but I must; otherwise, I lose my honor among my people. But . . . since you have challenged me without just cause, I will set the rules."

Matt stared at his opponent for a long minute before he said, *"To-quet."*

"It is well," Soaring Eagle nodded his head and repeated his grandson's words, the tribe repeating it in unison after their chief.

"If I win, the woman is clearly mine. If I lose, the woman is yours —" Bright Knife hesitated, a strange smile playing around his mouth as he looked down at Zoe.

"To-quet."

Bright Knife lifted his hand to indicate that he had finished his statement. "If I lose, the woman is yours, but in order to keep her, you must make her your woman. The entire village must be assured that she is your *mah-cou-ah*." His gaze swept the group of Comanches, finally lighting on the medicine woman. "Buffalo Woman will determine if she is truly yours or not."

Matt settled a hard gaze on Zoe. Bright Knife was smitten with the idea of possessing her, and Matt decided it was because she was white and had such beautiful blond hair. She had nothing else going for her. Her face was sunburned, and she was in her late twenties, well past the prime age of childbearing. Matt was furious with Bright Knife, but he was more furious with the woman who had caused the young pup to behave so irrationally. Matt well remembered the last time he'd been so angry, and that anger had been directed toward a white woman. All women were good for was trouble.

This one ought to have known better than to

travel through hostile territory with such a small caravan, especially with scalp hunters roving at will, their own lust for scalps greater than that of the hostile Indians who wanted scalps as a coup of valor; the scalp hunters sold theirs to the highest bidder — which now were the French.

Surely she knew better than to travel through Comanche territory now that Weber Fielding had issued an eviction notice to them!

Why was she going to Mexico, anyway? he wondered. Wasn't she aware that the political scene was a powder keg ready to explode? Mexican rebels, called Juaristas, continued to fight against the established but foreign French government of Maximilian.

If the situation hadn't been so grave, Matt would have found it ludicrous. His eyes roved contemptuously over her face. He wondered what she looked like when she wasn't beet-red. His gaze lingered on her hair, gleaming golden in the sunlight. He had visions of it washed and brushed and hanging down her back in silken waves. He didn't bother to hide the smile that played at the corners of his mouth: here he was, fighting for a woman with whom he was furiously angry and for whom he had no sexual interest, yet in the presence of a witness he *must* possess her. What would the prisoner's reaction be if she knew of this? he wondered. He didn't suppress the small chuckle of amusement that slipped through his lips.

"Also, Ma-ta-mon-yahu, if I win —" Bright Knife's gaze fell to Matt's wrist "—I shall receive the gold band of valor."

The announcement jarred Matt from his reverie. His gaze quickly swept from Zoe to the young warrior. A boy, he had called him a minute ago! No,

Matt quickly reevaluated, he wasn't a mere boy . . . he might be only eighteen, but he was well versed in warfare. Those five scalps on his lance testified to his prowess as a Comanche warrior. A chill ran along Matt's flesh when he encountered Bright Knife's cold, glittering eyes and scornful smile.

Matt lifted his arm and looked at the bracelet he'd worn since he was seventeen — just about Bright Knife's age. Soaring Eagle had placed it on his arm himself after he had fought and single-handedly killed a mountain lion.

"I shall receive the gold band if I win," Bright Knife iterated.

Matt looked up and quietly said, *"To-quet."*

A satisfied smile gleamed on Bright Knife's face. "I choose to fight with the white man's hatchet at the going down of the sun. My back will be to the west," he shouted and pulled the hatchet from his belt. Before anyone knew his intention, he threw it across the clearing.

Zoe didn't understand a word Bright Knife shouted, but she gasped, her hand inadvertently going to her mouth, when the metal head bit into the dirt at the tip of Matt's moccasin, the shaft twanging in the air.

The two men stared at each other for what seemed like an eternity. Zoe hardly dared breath. She saw the taller of the two men, the older brave, lean down to pick up the hatchet. He ran his fingers over the edge, cleaning off particles of dirt. Then he rubbed the ball of his thumb over the cutting edge to test the sharpness. He transferred the hatchet to his right hand, gripped the handle, and balanced it. Then, with a fluid grace and speed that awed Zoe, he lifted and pulled back his arm. With a flex and twist of his wrist, the hatchet sang through the air to graze

45

Bright's Knife's temple and sliver the ornament that decorated the top of his braid.

"The hatchet at the going down of the sun with your back to the west," Matt announced softly, his eyes lighting on the feather and piece of leather thong that fluttered to Bright Knife's feet. "So be it." His brown eyes mocked the young brave.

Chapter 3

"So be it!" The words echoed into silence as Matt dropped his arm, mockery slowly moving from his eyes to his lips.

Zoe closed her eyes and felt the breath as it whooshed out of her body, leaving her as limp as the bandanna around her forehead. Nothing in her medical career had prepared her for such primitive barbarianism as this. The horrors and atrocities she witnessed in the war seemed to pale before the actuality of Indian warfare. She excused the North and the South; at least each side felt as if it had a goal to attain or the status quo to maintain. She could attach no purpose to this Indian behavior at all.

The Comanche completely puzzled and frightened her. Why the two men were angry and throwing hatchets at one another she couldn't fathom . . . unless it was male pride. Even less could she determine her role in the scheme of things.

The one thing of which Zoe was aware, of which she was absolutely conscious, was the hatred that emanated between these two warriors — not a simple competitiveness, but overt hatred and hostility — and her fear of these people. She remembered every tale of horror she'd heard about their treatment of prisoners; she couldn't get it out of her mind.

Zoe also remembered a woman whom the Mescalero Apaches had returned to Chandlerville recently in exchange for two of their braves. Two years with the Indians had taken their toll on Inez Patterson. Although she was only twenty years of age, she looked forty. The bottoms of her feet were nothing but scar tissue; the Apaches had burned them to prevent her from escaping.

The memories were so vivid that Zoe trembled. She raised her hand to her lips. *Dear Lord,* she prayed silently, *please help me escape. I must get away from here.* Having the eerie feeling that she was being watched, she opened her eyes to find Matt staring at her. Against her will, despite all effort to ignore him, Zoe's gaze locked to his, and she was drawn into the depth of those solemn brown eyes . . . those mocking brown eyes that had the uncanny ability to read her soul. Zoe sensed that he thoroughly enjoyed reading hers.

The summer breeze gently ruffled the black hair burnished to a high sheen. She watched in fascination as he reached up to brush a lock from his forehead, the agile movements, the ripple of taut muscle deceptively concealed beneath smooth bronze skin. Her lips twitched when the recalcitrant lock of hair refused to obey and lopped across his face once more. His eyes seemed to soften into a smile, but just as quickly they hardened. She must have imagined it.

His hands dropped to his side, the movement compelling Zoe to look at his entire body, the smooth, broad chest that tapered into narrow hips and legs, their lean muscularity clearly visible in the tight leather trousers he wore. When her gaze returned to his face, she again saw the mockery gleaming in the depth of his eyes. Then she realized that he had subtly manipulated her into becoming physically aware—sexually aware—of him as a man and was now enjoying her discomfort.

The man was despicable!

Matt was angry at the woman; at the same time he was fascinated by her, almost drawn to her by an invisible force he couldn't explain, a bonding that he'd never felt before in his life. He'd wanted women before; he'd taken them—had taken his choice. But his attraction to Zoe was different and puzzling. Thick blond braids were wound together into a chignon at the crown of her head, but beautiful soft golden curls framed her face. Her eyes were blue—the color of Texas bluebonnets. Enchanted, he stared at her hand lightly poised over her dry, cracked lips. Although her fingers were slender and delicate, he knew they were strong. How easily he could lie with this woman! How easily she would fit into his bed!

Matt muttered an oath under his breath and cursed himself for the fool he was; he cursed Bright Knife as well. The crazy young buck, out to gain glory, had landed him in a fine mess. This wasn't a whore or the kind of woman a man casually bedded one night and left the next morning. If Matt was any judge of character, this woman was someone important enough to bring down upon the Comanches the wrath of the entire white population in West Texas.

When Matt turned to speak to one of the Indian maidens nearby, Zoe stared at the scars crisscrossing his back. Old ones, she judged by their paleness.

"The sun is high overhead," he said, irritated because of the predicament he was in over Zoe, "which means we have many hours before the contest. Since

49

I have preparations to make, I want you to take the white woman to my tepee and see that her burns are tended to. If she's going to be my woman, I want her to look presentable."

The young Comanche girl giggled, casting a contemptuous glance at the prisoner. She would try her best to please Ma-ta-mon-yahu, but she didn't know that the white woman would ever look presentable.

Buffalo Woman brushed past Matt to stand in front of Zoe. "The prisoner has been entrusted to me, Ma-ta-mon-yahu. I shall take care of her." Reaching down, she caught Zoe by her hair and yanked her up, pins spilling to the ground and the braids coming loose from their chignon.

Zoe yelped and her eyes smarted, her hand flying to claw at the Indian's painful grip. When she had freed her hair, Zoe tossed her head defiantly, the golden braids swinging around her face. She glared at Buffalo Woman. "I'll walk on my own two feet, thank you."

Matt bit back a smile. The woman had spirit and dignity, that much he could say for her. Defeated but not destroyed: one swift look took in the limp bandanna that now ringed her neck, the torn blouse, and the snagged riding skirt. Wash some of that dirt off her, treat her face for sunburn, and she'd probably be a nice-looking woman. Again his eyes touched the honey-colored tendrils that fell loose from her braids. It was his weakness; he'd always liked blond hair.

He felt a pleasurable tingle in the lower part of his body. Tonight's work could turn out to be most enjoyable, after all.

The camp was in a frenzy as Buffalo Woman herded Zoe down the road fronting the small stream that ran through the village. A group of women

50

followed to taunt and torment Zoe. They yanked on her braids and pinched at the material of her blouse, tearing it even more, the upper swell of her breast now exposed. They spit and threw sand on her. Children, laughing and jeering, ran behind, tossing pebbles at her. Buffalo Woman made no attempt to stop the harassment; rather, she seemed to enjoy it.

Zoe was glad when they finally reached a tepee on the outer edge of the village and the crowd fell back. The old woman picked up the stiff pelt door that was attached to the top of the hole in the tepee and shoved Zoe through inside the dwelling. She stumbled across the dirt floor to fall on her hands and knees. When she looked over her shoulder, Buffalo Woman had dropped the pelt and it swung into place by means of the weight attached to the bottom. She heard the woman outside talking with a brave, and realized a guard was being posted.

Not knowing what was coming next, only thankful that she hadn't been molested and tortured any worse than she had, Zoe sat up and brushed the loose dirt from her blouse. Glad for the shade and coolness, glad for a moment to compose herself and to think, she looked at her surroundings. Directly opposite the opening was a thick mattress made of buffalo robes. On top of them were several pillows made from skins and stuffed with grass. Fluffing them together, Zoe stretched out on the thick mattress and was surprised at the softness.

The door of the tepee, Zoe noticed, opened to the east, to the rising sun; therefore, the glaring rays of the afternoon sun were deflected by the back wall of the leather dwelling. The floor looked to be about fifteen feet in diameter, the height from the center of the floor to the peak about the same. In the center of the room was the fire-hole. Suspended on ropes that extended from one frame pole to the other were clothes, cooking utensils, weapons, and torches used at night for light.

Exhaustion catching up with her, Zoe's eyes slowly closed and she dozed, the noises of the village receding into the distance. Almost asleep when she heard the swish of the leather flap, she opened her sluggish lids and turned her head to see Buffalo Woman. After the Comanche woman reached the center of the room, she hunched a shoulder to allow a leather strap to slide down her arm and a pouch to land on the ground. Next to this she set a tin basin filled with water. Cross-legged, she sat down beside her paraphernalia and began to work.

Curious, Zoe rolled over to see the woman open the pouch and withdraw some roots, which she pulverized in a stone bowl and mixed with an oily substance to make a paste. Setting that aside, she picked up another plant — one that looked similar to cactus — and broke the thick stalk in two, thick green sap oozing out. The medicine woman squeezed the sap onto a small piece of wet deerskin draped over her hand. Zoe stared as the deerskin covered in the slimy mixture came straight for her face.

Although the old woman's eyes were venomous and looked weird outlined in bright red circles, her hands were as skilled. First she gently cleaned Zoe's face, then she smeared the blackish salve over the blistered skin.

The ointment was soothing and Zoe wondered what it was. "Thank you," she murmured appreciatively, her eyes catching the old woman's.

Buffalo Woman dropped her hand and pulled away from Zoe as if she had been hurt. She understood enough English to know what the prisoner was saying, but she wouldn't let on that she did. Neither would she let herself like the prisoner—white people were her enemies. Without uttering one word, Buffalo Woman quickly gathered her herbs and returned them to the pouch. Slinging the strap over her shoulder, she stood and walked out of the tepee, leaving Zoe alone again.

Rested now, her sunburn numbed, Zoe untied her bandanna and dropped it into the basin. Then she unbuttoned and slipped out of her blouse, washing as much of the dust and perspiration off her upper body as she could. When she redressed, she picked up the torn piece of material and adjusted it across her shoulder, but it fell down again. Several times she tried; several times the material fell. Imprisonment didn't rob Zoe of her humor. She smiled, glad the tear hadn't been any lower, or she would have been indecently exposed.

As her hand lay over her breast, she remembered the way the Indian, the brave wearing the gold bracelet, had stared at her. Again her skin burned, though this time the burning had nothing to do with the sun. She recalled the intensity of those brown eyes as vividly as if she were staring into them now. She detested him, yet she couldn't forget him. His expression danced through her mind, mocking her with his soft laughter. His slim, muscled body beckoned to her and created a yearning.

Zoe was irritated with herself; she never felt this way when Weber looked at her. He never stirred any deep emotion in her . . . none at all. They were extremely comfortable together, and that's the way she liked it. She wanted her life to be comfortable. She smiled as she thought of the evenings she and Weber had sat in the parlor, quietly discussing their future together, most of which centered on plans for Chandlerville. Of course, Zoe reasoned, she wasn't a person to be at the mercy of her emotions. She prided herself on her rational, analytical nature. That's why she and Weber made such a perfect couple; he felt the same way about life as she did. Both of them controlled their lives and their destinies.

She wouldn't want to be around a man like the Comanche for long. He made her feel extremely ill-at-ease; he was draining. From him emanated an intensity that touched everyone he came in contact with, and to them he transmitted a part of his tremendous energy. No, she thought, he wasn't the kind of man she would want in her life. She could easily lose her control where the warrior was concerned, and that would be a disadvantage. She liked Weber; he was safe and dependable. He would never arouse any emotional response from her that she wasn't ready to give. She would always be in control; the thought gave her strength.

Zoe closed her eyes, willing herself to think pleasant thoughts, willing herself to think of Weber . . . the man who was going to become her husband. She tried to remember the color of his eyes and the sound of his voice, but she couldn't . . . she absolutely could not. Another face swam through her mind, mocking her with soft, caressing laughter. She could see the texture of the skin as clearly as if she were looking at him, the hard lines and angles of his face, the contempt in the depth of those beautiful eyes.

Zoe heard someone lift the pelt. Her eyes flew open and she jumped. Buffalo Woman appeared at the door again, her gnarled hand beckoning Zoe to follow her. Thankful to escape her thoughts — thoughts over which she had no control — Zoe crawled out of the tent to squint at the brightness of the sun. She had expected her face to hurt when the heat and glare touched it and was surprised to feel no discomfort. She wished the Indian woman spoke English; she would like to ask her about the herb.

Zoe looked about for her tormenters, but none was to be found. Whereas moments ago the camp had been a flurry of activity, it was now vacated. Only a few dogs ran up and down the streets barking. Weaving through the tepees, Zoe raced after the Indian woman to keep up with her. She didn't have long to wonder where they were headed. The entire village was congregated at the east end of the village. Buffalo Woman elbowed her way through the crowd, Zoe following, until they stood at the edge of a large clearing. The Comanche woman's hand clamped on Zoe's shoulder and pushed her to the ground.

As Zoe landed painfully on her knees, she stared at the circular clearing in front of her. In the center was a log, a hatchet head deeply embedded within it. The sunlight reflected off the metal. A combat circle! As innocent of Indian customs as she was, Zoe knew that much. Bright Knife and Matt stood at opposite ends of the field, a hand bound behind each. Save for the bands which they wore around their foreheads, neither had changed clothing. Bright Knife wore his breechclout and Matt his trousers. From having seen each wield the knife earlier with his right hand, Zoe knew both were fighting at a disadvantage with their left.

As her gaze returned to the hatchet, a chill of fear ran up her spine. Now she knew what had happened . . . what was happening. These two men were fighting over her . . . as if she were nothing more than chattel. She belonged to the man who won. The thought tasted bitter.

Leaving Zoe, Buffalo Woman moved to take her place beside Soaring Eagle and the village elders. She lowered her head and quietly mumbled her own prayer as the chief raised both hands, blessed the warriors, and asked the blessing of the Sun. When Soaring Eagle sat down, a brave, separated from the crowd, threw back his head and opened his mouth, an ululation ringing out at the same time that a crescendo of drumbeats echoed through the air. The combat had begun.

Horrified, Zoe watched. Each man dashed from his end of the circle to the log, hoping to be the first one to get the weapon. Bright Knife was the smaller of the two, the younger, and the fleeter. His hand curled around the shaft, but the head was sunk in too deeply for him to yank it loose with one jerk. Before he could straighten with the weapon, a shadow fell across him and out of the corner of his eye he saw Matt's looming figure. Bright Knife reared up, his back and shoulder catching Matt in the stomach and pitching him away from the log. Matt grunted, his arms flailing through the air like a windmill as he staggered backward several feet, yet he kept his balance. He breathed deeply, and although the sun was bright and directly in his eyes, he never lost sight of his adversary.

With a loud shout of pleasure, Bright Knife yanked the hatchet from its resting place and brandished it through the air, the sunlight sparkling off the gleaming, lethal blade.

Unconsciously Zoe rounded her dry lips with her tongue, and her eyes went to Matt. His chest was rising and falling as he sucked air into his lungs; perspiration gleamed on his golden brown skin, the muscles flexed, the veins dilated. Down he went into a crouch and began slowly to circle Bright Knife.

The young brave, exalted at having first possession of the hatchet, laughed in Matt's face and followed his every step.

"You're an old man, Ma-ta-mon-yahu," he jeered. "Too old to fight a young buck like me. You're a white man, Ma-ta-mon-yahu. Too white to fight a Comanche." The taunt grew louder and louder until many of the spectators were chanting with Bright Knife.

Matt's expression never changed and his gaze never left Bright Knife's face. *The eyes,* Soaring Eagle had taught him. *Watch the eyes! They are the windows to a man's soul; by looking into them you can read a man's very thoughts and anticipate his every action.*

Bright Knife swung the blade through the air, back and forth. Matt nimbly jumped out of the way. He had known the blow was coming. He felt the adrenaline flowing through his body; he was more alive and alert than he had been in a long time. He was walking on the very edge of danger and enjoying every minute of it. He had to act quickly, to think even quicker. He advanced.

Laughing, Bright Knife lithely danced back, always a step beyond Matt, once again lifting and circling the hatchet above his head. Then he rushed forward, the arm darting out, the sharp metal targeted for a chest swipe. His face glowed; he had the half-breed warrior. One clean cut would draw blood and the woman would be his. He would be one of the most honored braves in the village; he would have defeated the mighty Ma-ta-mon-yahu. He would also receive the gold band of valor! Then the women would sing and dance in his honor. Then the braves would be ready to follow him on the warpath against the white man.

Matt gauged the depth of the swing and instead of retreating, he surprised Bright Knife by rushing forward to greet the blade. He threw up his arm to deflect the descending arm, and his fingers locked around the young warrior's. They twisted and jerked Bright Knife toward him. Matt's leg bent and shot out, catching the Comanche in the chest with his knee and knocking the wind out of him. Bright Knife grunted and fell to the ground; Matt grabbed the shaft of the ax and yanked it from his limp grasp.

His eyes gleaming with hatred for Soaring Eagle's half-breed grandson, Bright Knife lay in the dirt and breathed deeply. He spat blood out of his mouth, and as he watched Matt brandish the ax in the air, the young warrior grabbed a handful of dust and pebbles and rolled away from Matt. He took advantage of his opponent's momentary distraction to throw the dirt and pebbles into Matt's face. Bright Knife laughed when Matt squinted his eyes in pain and staggered backward.

In an instant Bright Knife tensed his body and flipped through the air. His feet hit the ground running; his head jammed into Matt's stomach and he knocked the wind out of him. Reeling from the blow and blinded by the dirt, Matt gasped. Bright Knife, knocking Matt off-balance, fell to the ground on top of him, his victory cry echoing through the air. Bright Knife shoved up on his knees, his eyes desperately seeking the ax which had fallen from Matt's opened hand to slide across the dirt and out of the circle.

He saw it. Climbing over Matt, he grabbed the hatchet and leaped to his feet. Sure of his victory, he waved it through the air and did a few steps of his victory dance. He laughed as he watched Matt slowly roll over and push up on his hands and knees.

"This time I have you, old man," Bright Knife taunted, slowly moving closer to Matt. "The white woman will be mine to do with as I choose. I shall wear the gold armband of valor."

Matt slung his head back and blinked his eyes, still gritty and burning from the sand. "Don't brag, little boy," he gasped between breaths, "until you've drawn first blood. That's when the contest has been settled. Until then, we know no victory."

Matt's gaze swept from Bright Knife's extended hand to the crouched legs. He judged the distance between him and Bright Knife; then his gaze swept to the young man's face, to those black eyes gleaming with undisguised hatred. With a low whine that escalated into a growl, Matt leaped forward, his arms circling Bright Knife's legs, making him topple over. In one continuous movement, Matt rolled until he was on his feet, the Comanche sprawling ingloriously in the dirt. As Bright Knife struggled to stand, Matt rushed forward and kicked him in the chest; his ribs cracked under the blow. . . .

Bright Knife's legs swung through the air; he rolled over and was pushing up on his knees, growling anger and hatred, when Matt kicked him in the face. The force of the blow sent the young Comanche reeling backward, his back full against the log. Matt's fingers curled around the shaft of the ax, and he sent it sailing through the air to swipe lightly against Bright Knife's upper arm. Blood trickled down the young brave's arm to drop on the log.

Matt lifted his arm in the air to accept the praise of the tribe members, to claim his victory. Then he turned and walked to his grandfather to have his right hand untied. Stepping away from Soaring Eagle, Matt brought the hand in front of his body and rubbed the wrist where the thongs had cut into the flesh. Zoe's gaze slowly moved from Matt to Bright Knife, who had risen now and was holding the hatchet in his right hand, someone having already untied it for him. She watched as he drew back his arm and the hatchet flew through the air, the blade sailing directly toward Matt's back. Her eyes rounded in horror, and her hands flew to her mouth, a scream already echoing through her throat.

Chapter 4

Above Zoe's scream, Matt heard his grandfather's shout, "Watch out, my grandson!" He spun around and ducked, but not in time to deflect the weapon. The blade sliced into his upper arm, the flesh gaping and bright red blood spurting down his arm to drip off his fingertips. In silence he gazed at the wound, then lifted his face to stare at Bright Knife. Evincing no pain whatsoever, he walked to where the hatchet lay, bent, and picked it up.

"Bright Knife," Soaring Eagle accused, pointing a bony finger at the young brave, "you have brought dishonor upon your name."

"No," the young warrior exclaimed angrily, his followers gathering protectively around him, "you and your grandson have brought dishonor upon all of us. I call you an old man—too old to be our leader. I challenge you."

The air was fraught with tension as a hush fell over the people, their eyes settled on Soaring Eagle. His back straight, the old man walked to where his grandson stood. Without saying a word, he took the hatchet from Matt, his fingers circling the bloody shank, and swished it through the air a time or two.

"I have seen seven-tens winters, Bright Knife," Soaring Eagle said, his voice deceptively soft. "I have lived longer than my father or my grandfather because we have not been warring with the white people. I am not white and do not wish to be white, but I wish to be alive. I wish my people to be alive. You are a brave warrior, but a foolish young man." With a fluid motion Soaring Eagle pulled the hatchet back and sent it sailing through the air, the blade slicing into the ground inches from Bright Knife's foot. "I remember your bravery and forget your foolishness. I wish you to know, Bright Knife, I am the one who taught my grandson to throw the hatchet, and you can be thankful that my eyesight is good. What is the punishment you desire to see inflicted on Bright Knife for his dishonorable behavior?"

"None," Matt said, his hands on his hips, his gaze on the young warrior, the brown eyes slicing through him. "But the next time you throw a hatchet at me, Bright Knife, don't miss, or I'll kill you. I have beaten you fairly; the woman is mine. The gold bracelet remains mine."

"The next time I will not miss, Ma-ta-mon-yahu," the young Comanche buck promised. "And the white woman is not yours yet. Not until you take her like a Comanche warrior."

"You will appear before the council tomorrow," Soaring Eagle said to Bright Knife. "We will determine your punishment."

"I will be there," he replied, then called to Matt, "Remember my words, half-breed. The woman is not yours until you have taken her according to my conditions."

Bright Knife's warning ringing in his ears, Matt turned and walked to where Zoe lay sprawling in the dirt. His chest heaving, he stood for a moment and stared down at her, his blood splattering onto her blouse. Above his grandfather's warning he had heard her scream. He dared not think of his fate if the two of them had not given a warning; yet she was the reason why the young buck hated him anyway. Matt leaned down and grabbed her arm, yanking her to her feet. He dragged her down the road toward his tepee.

Angry at the way he was treating her and humiliated by the jeering crowd that was following them, Zoe squirmed and flailed until she broke free of his grasp, stumbled back, and fell to the ground.

Matt was tired; his arm hurt, and he needed quiet so he could devise a plan to return her to civilization without her learning who he was, without offending the customs of the Comanches any more than was necessary, and without having to make love to her. So much to think about . . . he shook his head; he had too much on his mind to contend with an obnoxious woman. His patience was at an end. When he spun around and planted his hands on his hips, the crowd closed in. His stance betraying the full depth of his anger, Matt glared at Zoe. She seemed determined to get herself raped or killed or both before he could save her!

Matt studied the eyes that glared at him through splotches of black salve. Under her defiant gaze, his anger began to evaporate. He grinned because he had to admire her spunk. Besides, she couldn't help the situation in which she found herself, nor could she be blamed for trying to escape. He would have done the same if he were in her situation. If only he could speak to her in English!

Opening his mouth, he thought of doing so, but decided not to. He wasn't sure the outcome would be good. His speaking English didn't guarantee that the woman would trust him, nor that she would be assured he didn't mean to harm her. It would mean explanations which at the moment he wasn't prepared to give. Also, it would destroy the tenuous thread of trust that bound him to his people. One slip, and they would swing to Bright Knife's side and to open hostility with the white communities. Matt knew he must tread softly for both their sakes.

Unable to stop himself, he allowed his gaze to wander lower to encounter the soft swell of her upper breast exposed by the tear in the material. He felt the familiar pangs of sexual desire and realized how long he'd been without a woman. Under other circumstances . . . hell, it didn't matter what the circumstances were, he didn't have time to think about sex. He had to get this woman out of here.

Zoe slowly pushed to her feet and returned Matt's stare. She lifted a hand to tuck tendrils of hair behind her ears and wiped her palms down the sides of her skirt. When she saw Matt's gaze lingering on her breast, she straightened her back and squared her shoulders, not realizing that she had thrust her breasts tighter against the blouse until she felt them swell and pull against the material. The mockery in the depth of those dark brown eyes sent a hot rush of blood to her cheeks, but she didn't lift her hands to cover herself as she so desperately wanted to and was glad her face was covered in the black ointment.

When she saw the grin tugging those sensual lips and the laughter in the recesses of those brown eyes, her flagging spirit soared. She hadn't fought her way through a man's university for an education or fought in a male-oriented society for a career as a physician to be intimidated by a half-breed savage. Tilting her chin, she brazenly returned his stare. She'd let him know how it felt to be leered at — in a sexual way — by the opposite sex.

Overtly her eyes moved over his features, lingering on the full lips that smiled even wider, down the thick neck to his chest. She stared at his bronzed muscles, then at the diagonal scar that jutted into his shoulder, probably a battle scar. Evidently he spent his life fighting over women!

Her fascination with his body amused Matt. His grin turned into a smile and he moved closer to her. The movement startled Zoe and she hastily stepped back until she bumped into a tepee. Matt stood only inches from her. Her breathing labored, her heartbeat accelerating, she looked in surprise from the smile-softened features of his face to the smoldering eyes.

Spellbound, she watched his hand move to her face, and with a touch ever so gentle, he smoothed the salve over her cheeks and across the bridge of her nose. Zoe felt as if she were warm butter melting to the ground and wondered if it was fear or passion that made her feel this weak, that caused her legs to tremble and buckle under.

Matt saw the expression in her eyes change from anger to inquisitiveness. A man accustomed to taking what he wanted, his hand moved to cup the back of Zoe's head and he spread his fingers in the silken strands of golden hair and tugged. Zoe resisted, but Matt was too strong; he pulled her close enough that he felt her warm breath against his skin, the length of her soft body next to his.

For a moment the two of them stared at each other. He lowered his face and his lips touched hers — nothing else but her lips — in an infinitely soft kiss meant to be a mere brushing of flesh, yet a promise of passion to come. But once Matt tasted her sweetness, he wasn't satisfied with such a tiny morsel. He wanted, and took, more. His mouth covered hers, and he forced her lips apart with insistent pressure of his tongue, teasing shivers of reaction from Zoe.

Overwhelmed with emotion, she forgot who Matt was and where they were; she closed her eyes and swayed against him, her breasts brushing his chest. She was only aware of the man who held her, who seemed to be drawing her will from her body with his demanding kiss. Her hands against his chest, she felt the slow thudding of his heart and wondered why his was calm and steady and hers was pounding so fast. Her eyes flew open and she stared at him, then at the laughing and taunting Comanches who circled them. She couldn't have been more startled if he had seduced her . . . she couldn't have been more humiliated. Her entire body was burning, her blood boiling in her veins.

She jerked her head out of his grasp, drew back her arm, and slapped him soundly across the face. "Don't you ever touch me again, you savage!" She was so angry—at herself—that she was hissing the words. "I'm a white woman, and don't you ever forget it!"

"I won't," Matt said in Comanche for the benefit of the spectators, his hand darting out to slap Zoe's cheek lightly before she was aware of his intention, "and don't you ever forget that I'm a Comanche warrior. Never strike me again."

Tears stung her eyes, and though he had only tapped her, startling her more than hurting her, she covered her cheek with her hand. "No one," she whispered, fighting valiantly to control her feelings,

"absolutely no one takes his liberty with my person."
She drew up to her full five feet, seven inches. "I'm a
lady."

"You're a fool," Matt corrected, sorry that he had
to be so harsh with her, "hell-bent on self-destruc-
tion!" His hand darted out to clutch her blouse at
the nape of her neck, and he herded her across the
village and shoved her into a tepee. "You had better
be glad that I'm not a Comanche, woman, or I'd
beat you for hitting me in public and for humiliating
me in front of my grandfather's people. Be thankful
I only tapped your cheek."

When Matt turned her loose, Zoe staggered
around the room for a minute before she regained
her balance. On the opposite side from the door,
standing in front of the second bed, she stared at
him.

"I've brought your things." Still speaking in Comanche, he waved his hand and pointed at the black
medical satchel, the valise, and her saddlebags sitting on the floor.

Zoe dropped to her knees, and like a child receiving a long-coveted gift, she touched each of the
objects, reassuring herself that they were really here,
unharmed. Now the tears wouldn't be stopped. Embarrassed, she turned her back on Matt and reached
up to wipe the escaping tears from her cheeks. She
wouldn't allow him to see her crying.

Only hours ago Matt had wondered what Bright
Knife saw in Zoe; now he knew. He was caught in
the magic of her spell. He wanted to take her into
his arms and kiss her, ointment and all. He struggled
to keep his face devoid of expression; he struggled to
keep from reaching out and taking her into his arms.
He wanted to console her, to assure her that she was
going to be all right. Most of all, he wanted to make

love to her.

Again he pondered speaking to her in English, but quickly decided it would be foolish. He didn't want anyone to know that Matthew Barnabas Chandler had returned to Chandlerville, and until he discovered what was going on, he wanted to remain anonymous. He didn't know if he could trust this woman to keep his identity secret. He had another reason for keeping his silence. If his name were connected in any way with this woman, he knew the good citizens of Chandlerville, especially Weber Fielding, would accuse him of abducting her, and it would only stir up Uriah's ire that much more. Matt had enough to face without new accusations. No, it was best for him that she didn't know who he was until later . . . much later.

Zoe had regained her aplomb. She stood, waved her hand toward the door, and said in her most professional tone of voice, "I would like for you to leave now. I want to go to sleep."

Totally enthralled by the woman who stood so fearlessly in front of him, calmly ordering him out of his own tepee, Matt folded his arms across his chest and grinned.

Zoe could tell by his stance, the way his feet dug into the floor, that he wasn't about to move. She turned her back to him and pretended a thorough perusal of the room. His grin growing wider, Matt moved to where she stood, clamped his hands on her shoulders, and turned her around. He pointed to the cut on his arm.

"Take care of my wound," he said, careful to speak only in Comanche.

Understanding his gestures, even his command, Zoe stared at the cut, but made no effort to help him. "If you want it taken care of, get one of your

Indians to do it."

At her announcement, Matt looked at the scratch that ran the inside of his upper arm. Pointing to it a second time, he ordered in a harsher tone, "Take care of this!"

Zoe didn't understand the words, but she fully comprehended the order; she felt the full impact of his anger. Her cool blue eyes met his furious brown ones. She knew he wanted her to doctor his cut. While a part of her chose to defy him, the physician in her refused to ignore his wound.

Eventually she gave in. "If I'm going to treat your arm, I'm going to need some clean water. Wa . . . ter." She slowly enunciated each syllable several times as she knelt and splashed her hand in the basin, water dripping from her fingers. Then she motioned as if she were wringing out a washcloth and wiping Matt's arm. "If I'm going to clean your arm, I need fresh water."

Matt wanted to smile but he didn't. He had a grudging respect for the woman. Despite her prejudices, she was brave. Any other white woman would be in a fit of vapors, or hysterical. Not this one! *She's a good Samaritan, doing what she can for humanity . . . even for those who aren't so blessed as to be within the fold of accepted humanity. And I'm one of those who is outside the fold.*

With no change in his demeanor, Matt leaned down and picked up the basin, then disappeared through the tepee opening. When he returned with water, Zoe was sitting on the mat waiting for him. He placed the bowl on the floor and sat down beside her.

When Matt jumped as she probed the area around the wound, she said, "Sorry. I didn't mean to hurt you."

You didn't, Matt silently answered, irritated because her touch unnerved him. Now he reached out to run his fingers lightly over the bruise on her cheek where she had fallen when she warned him. He felt Zoe shiver as he laid his callused palm against her satiny flesh. Then she jerked her face away from his touch and glared defiantly at him.

"Leave me alone," she gritted.

For the next few minutes Matt did. Silently he watched her clean the wound. Then she shoved the bandanna up her face and onto her forehead to form a sweatband; he watched the steady hand thread the needle and stitch the long gash.

"I'm Dr. Randolph," she said, her eyes on her work. "Zoe Randolph, from Chandlerville, Texas."

No wonder she's so calm and collected! She's a doctor, he thought.

"I was on my way to Candaleria, Mexico, with provisions and medical supplies when your villagers attacked my caravan." She sat back to rest a minute and wiped the back of her hand across her sweatband. "It was quite a harrowing experience." She paused. "Gold Bracelet—I think I shall call you that for lack of a name—I watched them kill and scalp the men who were escorting me. Well," she added sarcastically, "I can't in truth say I saw them kill and scalp *all* the men who were with me. I only saw them kill and scalp Digory Snyder, my guide. However, this afternoon I saw flying from the lances scalps that belonged to my escort. What bothered me the most was that they scalped Mr. Snyder before he was dead."

Matt's gaze moved from the crown of her head to the dark stain on the sleeve of her blouse, the bloodied imprint of his hand. His eyes strayed to the rip in her blouse and the satiny flesh that peaked so entic-

70

ingly through the tear.

"I must return for my provisions," Zoe continued in that same dead voice. "I don't know when I'll get another shipment, and even if I should receive one soon, I don't know that I would have the money to pay for them. You see, Gold Bracelet, I sold all of my mother's jewelry for enough U.S. currency to buy the medicine. Besides—" Zoe knotted off the thread and leaned back to better inspect her surgery—"the people in Candalería need me desperately. If what the messenger told me is true, they may have an epidemic of cholera, and I must stop it before it reaches Chandlerville."

When Zoe laid the needle and thread aside, she looked at Matt's chest. She leaned over him, so close that tendrils of hair tickled his chest and touched the puffy scar. She heard his quick intake of breath and lifted her head. His hands caught hers, and he pushed her away from him so roughly that she fell to the ground.

"You've been burned, haven't you?" She remembered the scars on his back. "And beaten?"

Matt leaped to his feet and rushed out of the room. He had to get away from the woman; she was driving him insane. When he stood outside the tepee, he raked his hand through his hair. He had to get her back to civilization before he did make her *mau-cou-ah,* before he made her his woman in the fullest sense of the word. How tempting the idea was, and how willing the woman was, though little did she know it!

After Matt was gone, the minutes slowly turned into an hour and Zoe paced the tepee. She had to get away. She *had* to. She glanced at the door. She dared not leave that way; a guard was posted there. She knelt and opened her medical satchel. With-

71

drawing her scalpel, she crawled to the back of the tepee and slit the hide. Deliberately pushing back any thoughts of the consequences, should she be caught, she quietly squirmed through the opening, and in the fading light of dusk, she sat a moment to get her bearings. She had one chance and must make it count.

She looked around until she found the corral. A horse! She must have a horse. In a crouch, she slipped through the tepees until she arrived at the pen. To her relief it wasn't being guarded. She opened the gate, then careful not to frighten the horses, moved through the herd until she reached her sorrel. Grabbing the mane, she lifted her body and swung onto Dusty's back.

Briskly nudging the sorrel with her boots, Zoe slapped several of the other horses on their flanks and sent the herd stampeding through the gate. In the flurry she galloped in the opposite direction, her braids flying behind her. Looking over her shoulder at the pandemonium, she laughed exultantly.

She was free.

She hadn't ridden far before she heard the thunder of hooves behind her. She hunched over her horse. Her hands began to sweat and her heart beat so furiously she thought her chest would explode. Her head sang, her blood was coursing through her body fast.

Closer and closer the pursuers came.

Zoe crouched lower, hanging onto Dusty's mane. She had to get away from the Comanches; she couldn't let them recapture her. They hadn't really tormented her before . . . but then they hadn't been angry. If they captured her a second time, they would be furious; she had scattered their horses and had dared to escape. She remembered Inez Patterson's burned feet and wondered if that would be her fate should they recapture her.

Then she no longer heard the sound of following hooves. At first she was elated; then the silence began to torment her. Around her it lay like a heavy wool blanket in the heat of summer. The Comanches wouldn't have given up so easily. Where were they? She looked over her shoulder and in the first shadows of night could see no one behind her. Still, she didn't get careless. She continued to move Dusty at a fast pace, putting as much distance between her and the Indian village as possible. When she reached a group of boulders that offered her protection, she eased the sorrel between them and stopped long enough to listen. She heard nothing that sounded like approaching horses.

Running her hand down Dusty's neck, she waited longer, hardly daring to breathe lest she not detect a warning sound. Finally, when she was convinced that she was being followed no longer, she breathed in deeply and threw her back her head, soft laughter filling the still night air. For now, she refused to accept that she was lost and didn't know how to get back to Chandlerville.

She was free.

For a moment she reveled in admiration for her ingenuity and daring in escaping the Comanches. How easily she had slit the tepee and slipped undetected through the village and into the corral! She chuckled softly when she remembered the thundering of hooves as the horses stampeded through the open gate. Zoe thoroughly enjoyed her freedom.

She nudged Dusty and was moving out of the narrow corridor of rocks when a rider slid onto the horse behind her. Strong arms circled her waist and bound her to a hard masculine body that pressed

73

hotly against her from buttocks to shoulders; warm breath stirred the tendrils of hair at the nape of her neck.

For a moment Zoe sat in paralyzed silence. Slowly she turned her head and stared into Gold Bracelet's shadowed face glowing sinisterly in the moonlight.

"No, you're not taking me back," she screamed, twisting in his arms. She couldn't return to the Indian village now, not after she had tried to escape and turned their horses loose. They would burn her feet to ensure that she wouldn't do it a second time.

Her writhing took Matt by surprise and toppled him from the horse. Because his arms were wrapped around her, she tumbled with him. As they landed, Matt's grip loosened, and Zoe was on her feet, running among the boulders, away from him. A cloud slipped over the moon, cloaking her in darkness.

"Oh, no," he muttered, quickly leaping to his feet and following her. He had ridden as if he were dogged by the devil himself to reach her before Bright Knife did. Now he had to catch her before she became lost in the maze of boulders. He cursed his clumsiness in not holding onto her. He should have figured she would resist.

He moved quietly through the rocks, stopping every now and then to listen, hoping he could hear a twig break, or a pebble chink, or even the soft sound of her breathing. He couldn't leave her, that was for sure; he was the only thing standing between her and death. Dear God in heaven above, why had she spooked the horses?

He heard something!

The moccasined feet moved in the direction of the sound, and the clouds passed over the moon, silvery light beaming down on the rocks. He saw the shadow and felt that it was Zoe. Trusting his instincts, he moved closer and closer; then he leaped, his arms closing around warm flesh.

"Turn me loose," Zoe screamed, her legs kicking, her arms flailing through the air.

"Not on your life," he answered in Comanche, refusing to turn her loose, no matter how much she thrashed. Slowly he made his way back to his stallion, and bracing her against the top of a large boulder, tied her with his rope so he could swing her onto the saddle in front of him more easily.

"Please, don't take me back there," she begged, shaking her head. "Take me to my house." She repeated the words slowly.

"I wish it were that simple, woman," Matt answered in Comanche, "because I have things I want to tend to. But it isn't. You have made that impossible, now that you scattered the horses and ran away. You'd better be thankful that it was me rather than Bright Knife who found you first."

Although Matt was irritated with Zoe, he couldn't help but smile when he looked into her face, the oil in the ointment reflecting the moonlight. He caught her into his arms and situated her on the stallion in front of him, pulling the rope off once he had his arm around her waist.

Still speaking in Comanche, he said, "You've pushed both of us into a corner, and there's only one way out. Whether you like it or not, you are going to have to become my woman. But I have a feeling, *mah-cou-ah,* that you are going to thoroughly enjoy it." Matt laughed aloud and Zoe felt his chest move against her back. He pulled her tighter against him, liking the gentle pressure of her body against his.

Yes, ma'am, Dr. Zoe Randolph, you've asked for this, and you're going to get exactly what you asked for. Tonight I'm going to show you the difference

75

between being a lady and a woman. And I think in the long run you're going to prefer being a woman to a lady. You won't believe the pleasures that accompany a defrocking.

Chapter 5

By the time Zoe and Matt were close enough to the village to see the light from the campfire arcing high in the night sky, she had encased herself in a cocoon of numbness and created a vacuum in her mind. She neither cared nor worried about what happened to her. She had long since relaxed her weary body and leaned back against Matt. Her world was the warmth and strength of the Indian who held her, and time was marked by the steady cadence of the stallion's gait. Zoe had completely erased all thoughts from her mind and didn't believe she had an emotion left in her body. Even when the villagers crowded around to shout and laugh at her, she felt nothing — not even fear. With lackluster eyes she scanned the sea of faces that swam before her, then lifted her blank gaze to the star-studded sky.

Matt was worried about Zoe's passivity. She was too spirited to be docile for long, and too intelligent for the cogs of her mind not to be turning at a rapid pace. He had been glad when her taut body sagged against him and she had ceased her vitriolic tirade and her struggling. That made the journey easier.

But he wanted her to be a little more alert than she was. He feared this was one of her strategies to get him to relax his guard so that when he least expected it, she could bolt.

Taking no chances on her escaping from him into an even worse fate, Matt dismounted and pulled her into his arms. One slip on her part—she was certainly aiding and abetting her enemy at every turn—and she would belong to Bright Knife. Neither Matt nor anyone else would be able to do anything to save her.

Because of the dark Matt couldn't see the faces of the Indians who crowded around him, but he felt their resentment and hatred. He knew the majority of them eagerly awaited the time when delegates from different tribes would meet at the Sacred Mountain to discuss an alliance made up of the many Plains Indians, an alliance so numerous and strong they could drive the white man out of their land forever.

In the village, tension mounted higher each day that passed from the time Fielding and his men had ridden into the village with the eviction notice. With young bucks like Bright Knife having a few successful raids, and with the old, venerated women like Buffalo Woman singing the valor of warriorhood, Soaring Eagle's Comanches would soon join with the alliance and be on the warpath. Matt had to protect his people.

He looked up to see Bright Knife elbowing his way through the crowd, and his grip on Zoe tightened perceptibly. He resolved that if any one of them were going to take her, he would be the one. At least, he assured her a pleasant seduction, not rape and torture. He knew only too well what ignominies the young brave would heap on her. As a child around the evening campfire and in the tepees during the winter, Matt had heard the old braves recounting their stories; he had seen fellow warriors at work on other Indian captives. Matt took a step but the braves didn't give way. The feelings of antagonism directed toward him and Zoe were so strong, they seemed an impenetrable barrier.

A young woman swaggered to where Matt stood. "Let me have the white woman, Ma-ta-mon-yahu," she said, dropping her torch until the tip was just inches away from the soles of Zoe's boots. "I know how to treat her so she won't run away again."

In the light of the flames that lapped greedily at the bottom of her feet, Zoe saw the face of Inez Patterson; she saw the scarred feet and the battered body; nothing had kept that woman from getting back to her people. Resolve and determination overcame Zoe. If nothing had stopped Inez Patterson, nothing was going to stop her.

"Put me down," she grunted, pulling at the fingers that bit painfully into her flesh.

Matt was glad that the spark had returned to his captive, but as usual, her timing was off.

Bright Knife planted himself directly in front of Matt. Taking a firm stance, he folded his arms across his chest and glared straight ahead. "It's good that you found the white woman before I did," he said. "I would not have been so lenient as you."

Zoe was most uncomfortable. Bright Knife had blocked Matt's progress, and they were unable to move through the crowd. Neither had the woman moved. The torch was still burning close to Zoe's boots; she could feel the heat through the leather. Matt's arms cut into her arms, and her face itched unbearably. She tried to free a hand, but Matt's grip tightened even more. Finally she rubbed her cheek against Matt's chest.

"If the captive belonged to me, she would know who her master is." Bright Knife balled his hand into a fist and held it against his chest. "I am a *taoyo-vis-se*. I am a Comanche warrior. I know how to make a woman mine."

"It appears, my young warrior, that I too know how to make a woman mine." Matt smiled and said to Bright Knife, "Look how the woman nuzzles me, like a mare nuzzling her stallion. Tell me, boy, that she doesn't know who her master is."

Bright Knife was angry. "That is not enough, Mata-mon-yahu. We must have proof that you took her like a Comanche. If you don't, you will return her to me in the morning."

"No one tells me how to take my women, certainly not a boy," Matt quietly returned. "I'm old enough and man enough to know how to do that. Now get out of my way."

The villagers moved aside to allow Matt to walk to his tepee, but Buffalo Woman followed him. When Matt set Zoe down inside the dwelling, he turned to see the medicine woman and a guard standing their vigil outside the door. In order to save Zoe, he knew what he must do; yet he stalled. For the first time in his life, circumstances had taken the pleasure out of sex and made it a chore. He paced around the room for a few minutes, wondering what he could do.

"Buffalo Woman," he finally called, moving out the door, the stiff pelt closing with a thud behind him, "this white woman is dirty; the ointment on her face stinks. I want you to prepare her for me. I want her thoroughly cleansed, but I do not want her harmed. I do not want to find one mark to mar the beauty of her body. No matter who might harm her, I shall punish *you*."

80

Buffalo Woman stared at Matt for a long time before she said, "I will see that she is bathed in the river. That will be enough."

"That will not be enough," Matt returned. "I want her to have a vapor bath."

"Then you will bathe her," Buffalo Woman declared, folding her arms over her sagging breasts. "She is a white woman, and when she bathes in the vapor house, she will stink."

Matt nodded; he knew the Comanches thought white people had an offensive odor when they perspired. As a child when he had taken a vapor bath, he had been teased because he smelled different from the Comanches. "I'll construct her a bathhouse while you take her to the river. Bring her to me when she finishes her bath."

Matt was already walking away when he heard the medicine woman grunt. Taking his time, he located eight slender poles and stuck them in the ground in pairs, twisting the tops around each at the right height above the ground to hold a blanket above them. He laid a buffalo robe on the ground for Zoe to lie on; then he built a fire and surrounded it with stones. He figured by the time Zoe was through in the river, the fire would have burned out and the stones would be red-hot. He set a water jug and gourd dipper next to the rocks.

He was standing here, his head lowered, watching the fire when he heard Buffalo Woman and Zoe approaching. As soon as he turned, Buffalo Woman disappeared into the darkness and left Zoe with him. The Comanche would witness the consummation, but not the vapor bath.

Matt watched Zoe, clad only in moccasins and an Indian shirt that hung to mid-thigh, walk out of the darkness. Her face was clean of ointment, and the firelight glistened in her freshly washed hair. The length of it hung down her back in ringlets, but tiny curls brushed against her cheeks and temples. Slowly Matt's gaze moved down the shirt to the long, slender legs.

Zoe's gaze darted to the buffalo robe that lay beside the fire. She turned to look at him with panic-stricken eyes. He was going to rape her out here. That's why he had given her the bath and stripped her of her clothes. He was going to rape her. She saw the fire and the red-hot rocks. And torture her. He was going to torture her!

She turned to run, but Matt anticipated her action. His hand darted out to band around her arm, and he tugged her to the pallet. His hands going to her shoulders, he eased her down and draped another blanket over the wooden frame.

Zoe lay on the buckskin pallet too exhausted to move. She heard the splatter of water against the hot stones and the sizzle of the steam before she realized she was in a sweat bath and the Comanche was outside the shelter. Confused with his actions, Zoe stayed under the blankets as long as she could. Finally, however, the heat was too much; her chest hurt and her head was swimming. Dizzy, she scampered from beneath the temporary structure.

"No more," she begged, shaking her head. "No more."

Matt scooped her into his arms and carried her back to the tepee, ignoring Buffalo Woman, who stood outside the door. When he set Zoe on her feet, she weakly teetered back and forth for a few minutes before she regained her equilibrium. Wide-eyed, she watched Matt sit down on the mat and take off his moccasins. His hands went to the belt around his waist.

"No!" Zoe cried, running toward the door and grabbing a club that hung from one of the ropes. "I'm not going to let you rape me!"

Matt leaped to his feet, and before she hit him with the club, he caught her by the shoulders and dragged her into his arms. Knowing that Buffalo Woman was watching and what fate awaited Zoe if he didn't take her, he lowered his mouth to hers. Her arms pinned to her side, Zoe ineffectively fought him. She twisted her head, kicked her feet against his shins, and twisted her shoulders within the circle of his arms. Matt's hand tangled in her hair and he raised her face to receive his kiss. When his mouth touched hers, Zoe bit his lips.

"Ouch!" Matt bellowed, turning her loose.

The club dropped from her hand and Zoe stumbled backward to fall against her medical case. Automatically her hand closed over the grip, and when Matt, his face thunderous, advanced toward her, she swung it through the air. Matt grabbed it out of her hand and tossed it down with such force the fastener came undone and her instruments clattered across the ground.

"Now, lady," Matt muttered in Comanche. "We're through playing games. It's time for you to pay for your transgressions."

Never taking her eyes off Matt, Zoe's hand began a frantic sweep of the hardened dirt around her. She touched the scalpel; she scooped it into her hand. "I'll kill you before I let you take me," she said, throwing back her head, her mane of tangled curls swirling around her face. "I won't have a savage making love to me."

Love, Matt silently repeated. *Nobody said anything about love? This is sex, lady. Pure sex and nothing else!*

83

For a moment Matt and Zoe circled the tepee, then Matt grabbed her wrist and wrenched the knife from her fist. Without releasing his grip, he dragged her into his embrace, his arms once again pinning hers to her side, and he kissed her, tasting the saltiness of his blood as it mingled with the sweetness of her mouth.

He kept telling himself he was doing this because he wanted to save her from Bright Knife, from a much worse fate, but the deeper the kiss became and the more he touched her, the less he thought of Bright Knife. He was kissing Zoe because he wanted to; he was making love to her because he wanted her for himself.

His conscience smote him. He ought to tell Zoe who he was; he ought to allay her fears by speaking to her in English. But again he pushed the thought from his mind. His speaking English wouldn't convince her of his good intentions. No matter what language he spoke, he would never convince her that taking her body was *good intentions*. No, his remaining a Comanche was better for all concerned — Zoe, his people, and himself. When he returned her to civilization, she could forget what happened to her more easily if she thought of him as a Comanche and not as a white man.

His hands slid down the smooth buckskin on Zoe's back to curve around her buttocks, and he urged her closer to his body. The movement of his hand ignited fire down her spine and instilled a new surge of resistance. Zoe twisted, but was unable to break free of his embrace. Her foot touched something cold, something that slithered noisily on the floor. Zoe tensed and Matt released his grip. Both of them saw a bottle spinning around at the foot of the pallet.

"Whiskey," Zoe murmured when Matt lifted surprised eyebrows. She was so excited that she could hardly keep her smile to herself. She had been told that Indians couldn't hold their liquor. If she could get him drunk, perhaps he would leave her alone. She'd have to be careful, because she couldn't hold her liquor either. But then, she wouldn't be drinking . . . she would merely entice him. Looking from the bottle to Matt, she decided it was worth the effort. She bolted up and reached for the bottle.

"Although it's for medicinal purposes, it can be used for celebrating and for drowning your sorrows." Holding the bottle to her mouth, she yanked the cork out with her teeth and tilted her head back to take a long swig of the whiskey, coughing and sputtering as she swallowed. She handed the bottle to Matt. "Now it's your turn."

Matt laughed and shook his head, but didn't stop her from drinking. Perhaps a little liquor might make it easier for her.

After she had taken several swigs—actually drinking considerably less than what she wanted Matt to think she had—she handed him the bottle. "Go ahead," she said, squirming into a comfortable position. "It's good for what ails you. I know Indians are supposed to leave firewater alone, but you're half-white, judging by your looks, so your white side should be able to hold your liquor."

Lady, Matt silently said, *you're what ails me, and whiskey isn't going to help one bit, and if you think you're going to get me stinking drunk so I don't know what I'm doing, you're crazy! But I'm having fun, so we'll play your game a little longer.* That secret smile lifting his lips, he took the bottle and tipped it to his mouth. It was good whiskey, fiery to the taste and smooth going down. He took a second and a third swallow.

"Now it's your turn," he said in Comanche and held the bottle to Zoe's lips.

She tried to take it from him, but he held on, tipping it high and pressing against her lips. She fought to push it away, but Matt held it there. Her lips finally opened, and she took a large gulp. Zoe was heady. She laughed with him and they exchanged the bottle several times. By now she had drunk more liquor than she had in her entire life. Inebriated, she grasped the neck of the bottle with her hand and braced the bottom against her leg. She looked at Matt in the light of the glowing embers.

"Thank you, Gold Bracelet—" she stopped and leaned closer to slur, "You don't mind my calling you Gold Bracelet, do you? You know, everybody needs a name, and that one seems to fit you." She took another swallow of whiskey and when she lowered the bottle, she said, "Thank you for everything. I know in your way that you've saved me." She picked up the tail of the leather shirt. "Certainly you've cleaned me. I don't know that I've ever been so clean before, two baths in one night."

Completely enthralled with Zoe, Matt grinned. He had been with prettier women before, but never had he been with one who was more desirable. Unable to help himself, he leaned closer and laid his lips against hers, lightly and evocatively.

"You certainly know how to kiss," Zoe murmured, her lips moving against his. "I don't know that I've ever been kissed like this before." She laughed shakily. "To be honest, I've *never* been kissed like this before." She dropped the bottle to the ground and turned to wrap her arms around him. Her fingers dug into the muscles of his shoulders, and she opened her mouth and pressed her lips

86

against his, sighing softly as he slid her down the pallet and stretched out beside her. Her mouth opened beneath his and welcomed the thrust of his tongue. She quivered when his hands, warm and callused, slipped beneath the shirt to touch her bare skin.

Their kisses were long and drugging; his hands discovered all her sweet curves, hers beginning a tentative exploration of his back. Tenderly her fingers traced the swell of scar tissue long since healed. When he finally lifted his mouth, Zoe opened her eyes and looked at his face, shadowed from the glowing embers. She looked at the puffy scar that jagged across his chest. So many battle wounds . . .

"You've been burned here, haven't you?" she asked, her arms still circling his torso, her palms resting on his shoulders. Then she raised her head and kissed the scar. "How did it happen?" Her whiskey-scented mouth moved against his warm flesh.

Matt inhaled deeply and pulled away from Zoe to look at the scar, a scar he had borne for the past fourteen years, a constant reminder that he was a half-breed—neither white nor Comanche—not really accepted by either race.

"A battle, I suppose," Zoe hypothesized. "Or maybe it was a wound that had to be cauterized." She was quiet for a moment, then said, "And your back . . . where you a captive who was beaten?" Zoe lay down on her back, the moonlight playing across her features, and looked up into Matt's face. She locked her hands around the nape of his neck and pulled his head close to her. "You're going to make love to me, aren't you?" she whispered. "I—I suppose if any one of you Comanches is going to do it, I'm—I'm glad that it's you, but I—don't know how Weber is going to feel about it. Weber . . ."

Matt stiffened in her arms and pulled away from her, but Zoe didn't notice. She was puzzled with her own reaction to Weber's name. It sounded hollow to her; she wondered who Weber Fielding was; she couldn't even draw a mental picture of the man. She wrinkled her brow in an effort to envision him.

"Weber . . . Weber Fielding . . ." Her face relaxed and she licked her lips. "He's my fiancé, and he hates you Comanches. I'm sure he isn't going to like this, and I don't know how he'll feel about me afterwards . . . but . . ." she giggled ". . . I think I'm going to enjoy it." She stretched out a hand and ran teasing fingers down Matt's chest to his navel.

Matt smiled at Zoe and caught her hand in his. So she was engaged to Weber Fielding . . . his hand automatically rose to touch the scar. A slow smile played on the hard, stern lips. Yes, he thought, Weber Fielding hated the Comanches, but not nearly so much as he was going to hate them when he learned that his fiancé had bedded one—in particular, the half-breed Matthew Chandler.

Matt released Zoe's hand and stood to walk out of the tepee, saying to Buffalo Woman, "Stay with her and see that she doesn't escape. I'm going to talk with my grandfather. I have a request to make of him."

Although Buffalo Woman wasn't happy with her task and wondered why it was taking Ma-ta-mon-yahu so long to make the captive his, she slipped inside the tepee and sat down to stare across the dwelling at the white woman. Zoe was too drunk to wonder about Matt's strange behavior; nor did she care about Buffalo Woman sharing her tepee. At the moment she hadn't a care in the world. She curled up on the pallet and was sound asleep within seconds.

Matt walked to the huge campfire in the center of the village, around which the villagers still sat. When Soaring Eagle saw Matt approach, he lifted his hand. "Have you come to tell us that the white woman is now your woman?" he asked.

"No, my grandfather," he said, "I have not taken her yet. I have come to make a request."

"What would you ask, my grandson?"

"I ask you to perform the special marriage ritual for me and the white woman. I would have her be more than my *mah-cou-ah*. I would have her be my *mah-ocu-ah*." As was customary, he repeated his request. "I want her to be more than my woman; I want her to be my wife."

The request was met with silence and blank stares. Eventually Soaring Eagle said, "This is a strange request."

"But a request all the same," Matt returned.

"Do you love her?"

"No."

"Is this Ma-ta-mon-yahu or Matt Chandler speaking?" Soaring Eagle demanded.

"Both, but it is Matt Chandler who wants to bind her to his side with marriage, my grandfather."

Matt's winning the woman and having her for his whore bothered Bright Knife, but not nearly so much as his making her his wife. When the white woman became Ma-ta-mon-yahu's wife, no other brave stood a chance of ever getting her into his tepee. His face contorted in anger, Bright Knife jumped to his feet to protest, but Soaring Eagle with a wave of his hand commanded the warrior to be seated and to be quiet. He admired the young warrior, but he'd endured enough of his impertinence for one day. Now he was concerned about his grandson.

Matt spoke again. "Matt Chandler and Ma-ta-mon-yahu wants the white woman in order to save his peoples' lives, in order that they may continue to walk the road of peace and—"

"You speak lies," Bright Knife shouted.

Ignoring the interruption, Matt continued, "—to have his revenge on the man called Weber Fielding."

"Ah," the Comanches breathed, verbally giving their sanction for revenge as they vigorously nodded their heads. Revenge was a point of honor that time never erased, one they could understand.

Matt's hand went to the jagged scar. "Weber Fielding did not inflict the wound himself, my chief, but he is responsible for it. The men who beat and branded me were following his orders."

Soaring Eagle, holding his pipe by the shank, filled the bowl with tobacco, then reached for a burning twig from the fire. "How will you be getting revenge if you marry the white woman?"

"The white woman is to be married to Weber Fielding," Matt explained. "I want to marry her myself."

"That will be revenge?"

"Not only the marriage," Matt confessed, "but the child that will come with the marriage—the child that will belong to Matt Chandler."

90

Chapter 6

Matt's request still hovered over the stunned crowd, and they, as he, watched Soaring Eagle puff on his pipe. While Soaring Eagle pretended indifference, Matt knew better. His grandfather was nearly seventy-one, but he was an astute man, keenly aware of what was going on in the world about him. Matt also knew from Soaring Eagle's reaction that he did not like the request at all.

But fourteen years of bitterness and hurt wiped out all rational thinking for Matt. He was possessed with the idea of getting even with Weber Fielding, the man who had branded him emotionally as well as physically. The entire community of Chandlerville had branded him a seducer of innocent women and a murderer. Had it not been for the influence of his grandfather Uriah Chandler, Weber would have seen that charges of murder were pressed against Matt and that he hanged.

Now Matt had within his grasp the means of getting even with Weber Fielding. He was so caught up in his own plan and scheme, he never thought to consider Zoe's feelings or the consequences of his marrying and making love to her. But he had no reason to think of consequences. He had always had his choice of women and had never found one that he wanted on a permanent basis. He wanted one in his bed, but not one to clutter his life. He wanted no emotional entanglements with a woman . . . absolutely none.

Soaring Eagle puffed on the pipe for a long time and stared into the red-orange flames. Eventually he said, "I have always been proud of you, Ma-ta-mon-yahu. You are a good Comanche and a brave warrior; you are a good grandson."

"Thank you, my grandfather."

Soaring Eagle's black eyes rested on his only grandson. "I love you as if you were my own son."

"And I love you, Grandfather."

"I think Ma-ta-mon-yahu, that you have a Comanche body and his blood flows through your veins, but your soul is white. You love your Indian brothers and will do all within your power to help us keep our lands and way of life, yet you have chosen to walk the white man's road. How will your revenge affect your life as Matthew Barnabas Chandler?"

"I want the woman for my wife as long as I shall live, grandfather. I want her to bear Matt Chandler a child. Forever she and the child will be mine. The man called Weber Fielding can want her but cannot have her. Always he will be haunted by the knowledge that I have what he wants."

"Do you love this white woman?" the chief persisted.

"I find her good to look at and soft to hold."

Soaring Eagle nodded his head. "For some that is enough."

"I will be satisfied with it," Matt promised. "It will make me happy to know that I have something

Weber Fielding wants. He accused me of putting my seed into a white woman; let me turn his lies into truth."

"Tell us your story, Ma-ta-mon-yahu," Bright Knife said, still chaffing from the whipping he had received from Matt first, then his grandfather. "Tell us and the village council why you behaved like a coward and ran away from the man called Weber Fielding ten-and-four winters ago. Tell us why you did not seek revenge then." The chieftain laughed mockingly. If he could prove Ma-ta-mon-yahu was a coward and dishonorable, he would be exonerated and would not have to face the council on the coming sun. "Why did you tuck your tail between your legs and run away like a dog?"

The young war chief made no effort to hide his hostility toward Matt. Until yesterday, until Ma-ta-mon-yahu had ridden into camp, Bright Knife was one of Soaring Eagle's favorite warriors and had entertained hopes of becoming the next chief. Now he was a disgrace and would have to go through purification. Ma-ta-mon-yahu was Soaring Eagle's grandson and he was a Comanche warrior. Bright Knife's eyes gazed covetously at the gold wrist band.

"Bright Knife wants to know why Ma-ta-mon-yahu tucked his tail between his legs like a dog and ran away," Matt said. "I will tell you if Chief Soaring Eagle grants me permission to speak." After receiving recognition from his grandfather, Matt walked around the fire and looked into the stoic faces of the people who had gathered there. The elders sat immediately around and beside Soaring Eagle; behind them were the young warriors. The women and children made up the outside of the circle.

Following Comanche custom, Matt took an oath that what he was about to say was true. "Sun, Father, you saw me do it. Earth, Mother, you saw me do it. Do not permit me to live until another season, if I speak falsely." Then he said, "Most of you remember what Weber Fielding did ten-and-four years ago when Ma-ta-mon-yahu had only seen two-tens-and-two winters. You, Running Horse—" he pointed to one of the warriors, an old friend of his "—you were one of the hunting party that saved me."

Running Horse nodded his head.

"For those of you who are too young to know Ma-ta-mon-yahu's story, let me tell you," Matt said, laying his hand against his chest. "For those of you who have heard Ma-ta-mon-yahu's story, let him tell you himself."

Silence settled upon the Comanches and they leaned forward to listen. No matter how many times they had heard the story—and heard it they had—they listened again. This time was special. Ma-ta-mon-yahu was telling it himself.

"I am half-Comanche and half-white, the eldest and only son of Comanche princess Wind-over-the-Water and the eldest son of Charles Chandler. My Comanche grandfather is He-Who-Soars-Like-an-Eagle; my mother was his only daughter, Wind-over-the-Water; and my white grandfather is Uriah Barnabas Chandler. Both are chiefs, men of great power and authority."

The firelight played against Matt's six-foot frame as he slowly moved around the circle, careful never to break eye contact with his listeners.

"Charles Chandler loved his Comanche wife and her people; he became blood brothers to the Comanche. To make sure they could never be pushed off their land, Uriah and Charles Chandler agreed that they could live on La Candela de Oro. When Ma-ta-

94

mon-yahu had seen only four winters, his mother died and a year later his father, Charles Chandler, remarried—a white woman this time. When Ma-ta-mon-yahu had seen six winters, his second mother presented his father with another son, Bryan Chandler. Three winters later Charles Chandler was gored to death by a bull.

"Ma-ta-mon-yahu's second mother was not unkind, but she was a harsh woman," Matt continued. "She wanted to make sure Ma-ta-mon-yahu grew up to be a white man and to be accepted in the white man's world. Soaring Eagle was also a harsh taskmaster. He wanted his only grandson to become a Comanche warrior. And I am," Matt yelled, waving his arm in the air, the firelight glinting off the gold bracelet.

"This armband proves that I am a Comanche warrior, and today I again proved my ability by defeating one of your bravest warriors and war chief, Bright Knife."

The Comanches were delighted with their entertainment for the evening. They nodded their heads and grunted their approval; they recognized Matt's prowess as a Comanche warrior. Now they were learning his ability to tell a story. Bright Knife's eyes glittered with hatred and his lips curled in contempt. Someday he would get even with Ma-ta-mon-yahu; he would have his revenge.

"Matthew Barnabas Chandler was sent to the east to attend the white man's school called William and Mary University. When he returned home during the summers, he threw aside the white man's world and lived with his Comanche brothers as Ma-ta-mon-yahu. The Comanches welcomed him into their tepees and into their hearts. The summer after he had seen two-tens-and-two winters, Ma-ta-mon-yahu learned that the white man would never welcome him into their homes or their hearts. They hated him because he had Comanche blood."

"Matt Chandler wanted to court and to marry a white woman called Veronica Fielding, but she scorned him because he was half-Comanche. Six moons later this same woman came to see Matt Chandler and told him that she had changed her mind. She wanted to marry him. But Matt Chandler had changed his mind; he no longer wanted to marry this woman who despised his Comanche blood and heritage."

"Yes! Yes!" some of the people cried out.

"Soon Matt learned the reason why Veronica Fielding wanted to marry him. She was pregnant with another man's child and did not want to carry the shame for her deed."

Heat swept Matt's body as he relived the humiliating events, first to be turned down and scorned by the woman, next to be selected as a pawn in her fight for respectability, then to be cited as the scapegoat in her quest for revenge.

"The woman pointed a finger at Matt Chandler; she accused him of being the father to her child. The majority of the people of Chandlerville, including Matt's grandfather, Uriah Chandler, and Weber Fielding, believed the lies the white woman told. Only Bryan Chandler and Gregory Halstead believed in his innocence. Weber Fielding insisted that Matt marry this woman and give her child a name. Matt Chandler refused."

"Hear! Hear!" the people shouted, the cries quickly dying out as they leaned forward to hear Ma-ta-mon-yahu tell the rest of his story.

"Seven suns after Matt Chandler refused to marry Veronica Fielding, he was alone and working on the far reaches of his grandfather's ranch."

Matt's voice became distant as he remembered that summer fourteen years ago.

The August day had been exceedingly dry and hot, the temperatures well above the hundred mark. The blue sky was without cloud; no rain was in sight. Matt was riding the bottom fifty acres looking for strays when he spotted the cow and knew from her bawling that she was in trouble. He dismounted, tied his horse to a low hanging limb, and ran to her. She was in labor and needed help.

Unbuckling his gun belt, he slung it over the saddle and, returning to the cow, rolled up his sleeves. The calf was born about an hour later. He was stepping away when he heard horses and looked up to see six riders approaching. He recognized Dudley Smith and knew they were Fielding's henchmen come for him. He wasn't surprised; during the past week since he had refused to marry Veronica, mob lunacy was rampant in Chandlerville. Matt made a dash for his revolvers, but the men surrounded him before he could reach them.

"Howdy, Matt," Smith drawled through tobacco-stained teeth as he looked at the calf. "Really seems strange that you can be kinder to a cow having a baby than you can to the woman who's bearing your child."

Hiding his anxiety, Matt slowly unbuttoned his shirt and took it off. Using it as a cloth, he wiped the blood and afterbirth from his arms and chest. "The woman isn't bearing my child."

Harlan Innes, a thin, shifty man who rode with Smith, nudged his horse forward and leaned down to whine into Matt's face, "Are you saying Miss Veronica don't know who she was sleeping with?"

Even at that distance Matt could smell the man's

97

foul breath. "I said what I mean, and you heard what I said." The brown eyes never wavered; Harlan's did. His face dropped to the ground. "I'm sure Veronica Fielding knows who she's been sleeping with, Innes," Matt added softly. "And so do I."

"She said you was the papa of her baby," Smith insisted.

"So she said, but people have been known to lie before." Matt didn't move his head, but his gaze swept the circle, taking in each of the men as they slowly moved in closer. He wished he had his revolvers because these were a hardened and dirty lot, the filth of mankind.

"Way Mr. Fielding sees it, his sister weren't lying."

"Seems like Mr. Fielding and I are looking at this in a totally different light," Matt returned.

Smith was irritated because Matt refused to be ruffled. "Well, half-breed, we come to teach you a lesson you ain't never gonna forget," he drawled, a sinister smile tugging his shapeless lips. "We gonna teach you never to mess with a white woman again."

Matt darted a glance at his bay, but escape was impossible. He saw one of the men swirling his lasso in the air; then it looped over his shoulders and slid to his ankles.

"Drag him for a few miles, Luther," Smith ordered, "but don't kill him. We'll save the best for last. We want him to know what we do to Indians whey they touch our womenfolk."

Luther Ugger giggled as he tightened the rope and jerked Matt off his feet. Spurring his horse into a gallop, the henchman rode in ever-increasing circles, dragging Matt behind him.

Matt grabbed the rope as his body bounced painfully across the rocky terrain, the cactus and mesquite shrubs cutting into his face and body and shredding his clothes. His eyes and mouth were filled with dirt; he couldn't see and he was gasping for breath. His hands were rope-burned and bleeding.

"That's enough, Luther," Smith finally called out. "We don't want to spoil our fun, now do we?"

A cloud of dust swirling around him, Matt lay there a minute in excruciating pain, regaining his breath and spitting blood and dirt out of his mouth. As he struggled to his feet, he grimaced and gently touched his fingers to his face. Fielding's men circled him again.

"Now git on your horse, half-breed, and don't give us no trouble," Smith ordered, "or we'll drag you the rest of the way."

Matt's eyes were burning and watering; he blinked to see better. Breathing deeply, he said, "My grandfather will kill you for this. He thinks I'm the father of Veronica's baby, but he'll kill you for doing this to a Chandler."

"You ain't no Chandler, boy." Smith's leg shot out, the toe of his boot catching Matt under the chin to send him sprawling. "You're a stinking Comanche, the likes of which we don't want around Chandlerville and decent people. Now git on that horse."

Rather than taunting Matt, Smith's words gave him determination. He saw the gleam of his bracelet in the sunlight. The man was right: he was a Comanche warrior. Although his ribs were broken and hurt so bad he didn't think he could move, he did move, and without one murmur of pain. He pushed up on his hands and knees and spit the blood out of his mouth. He climbed onto the bay and the men circled him on their horses, one of them catching the reins and leading him. They rode until they were miles away from Chandlerville and La Candela de

Oro, until Smith raised his hand and pulled his horse to a stop.

"This place looks as good as any," he said, glancing around the deserted clearing. "Nobody will find him for days. Luther, you gather the wood and get the fire going. Orville, you know what to do with the brand. The rest of us are going to *talk* with Mr. Chandler here." Grabbing Matt by the belt, Smith yanked him from the horse to the ground and repeatedly kicked him in the ribs. He grinned when Matt's face wrinkled in pain and he finally bent double, grabbing his stomach. "We gonna show him the consequences of ruining a decent white girl."

One of them stood behind Matt and held him up; the others jabbed their fists into his face and stomach time and again; his eyes were bruised and swollen shut; blood trickled down his face. They kicked and spit on him, but he refused to cry aloud. He hated them; he despised them; but he wouldn't let them know how much they were hurting him.

A Comanche, they called him; well, he was a Comanche. He chanted his death song, and the more they beat him, the angrier they became, the louder he sang. When they tied him to a tree and whipped his back until it was a bloody pulp, he still sang. Inside he was racked with pain and cried but outside he was singing. Surely God would hear him! Surely!

Fielding's men were furious. Matt wasn't playing their game. They wanted him to beg for mercy, but he seemed to have withdrawn into a world of his own—that damned Indian world. They untied him and threw him on the ground, close to the fire. Harlan Innes saw the firelight gleaming off Matt's bracelet and he leaned over to peer at it more closely.

"Well, boy, this here is mighty pretty." His dirty fingers traced the etching. "Reckon it belonged to some decent white folks at one time."

Summoning all his strength, Matt lunged at Innes, spitting in his face. He twisted his arm, but couldn't free it from the man's grasp.

"You dirty Injun!" Innes jammed his fist into Matt's face and knocked him to the ground again, a fresh spurt of blood running down to mix with the dirt on Matt's chin. "Don't you never spit on a white man again." Innes pulled the bracelet off Matt's arm and slid it over his wrist, then stood and rubbed it down the side of his pants. "Yes, sir," he said, "I reckon I'll just keep this for me. Call it a good-luck charm."

"Put that damned bracelet up," Smith called out. "We got to get finished here, Harlan."

Innes laughed. "Yes, sir, Mr. Smith, I reckon we do. We're gonna make this Injun cry like a baby yet." He looked at Matt and laughed. "Just you wait and see. Orville, is it ready yet?" He ran to the fire and came back waving a branding iron through the air.

Matt couldn't focus. He saw something coming toward his face, but it was fuzzy and red. Then he felt the heat and knew it was a branding iron.

"We're gonna brand you right here on the cheek," Harlan said and threw back his head to laugh. "You're gonna be so ugly, you ain't never gonna entice another white woman in your bed. Couple of you fellows hold him down. I want to make sure we do it good. Want to give him a pretty brand."

Two of the men caught the writhing Matt and held him down as Innes lowered the brand to his face. Closer and closer it came until Matt felt the heat on his cheek. With a sudden surge of power, he broke away from the two men and lurched forward to knock Innes off balance. The brand missed his face but seared into his chest. The pain was so intense Matt's stomach churned; his heart seemed to explode; his head spun until he was so dizzy he passed out.

That happened fourteen years ago, but Matt had never forgotten.

He walked around the circle of people. "Look at my back," he said. "See the scars of that beating? Look at my chest. See the white man's brand? Now can you understand why Matt Chandler wants revenge? The white men want no part of Matt Chandler, the half-breed Comanche. They kicked him out of Chandlerville and told him never to come back."

Knowing the people of Chandlerville believed Weber hurt Matt, but not nearly as much as he hurt when he learned that Uriah believed the Comanches under his leadership had initiated such atrocities against white men. No one, absolutely no one but Matt knew what happened on that late spring day when Uriah had disowned him.

Uriah had refused to share Matt with his Indian family or culture. He had issued an ultimatum: Choose to be a Chandler or a Comanche. If you choose to be a Chandler, you forever forget you're part-Comanche and your Indian heritage. If you choose to be a Comanche, you give up your Chandler birthright — your name and La Candela de Oro.

Refusing to give his grandfather the satisfaction of an answer, Matt turned, walked out of the house, and mounted his horse. Without turning his head once, he rode away from La Candela de Oro, tears running down the cheeks of the hardened half-breed who was recovering from a close call with death. He had never returned.

After a while, when he was over the bitterness, he wrote to Uriah, but his grandfather had never answered. Bryan did, and through the years they had corresponded sporadically, the younger brother always begging the older to return. For fourteen years Matt nursed his hatred and his grief. A close scrape with death of which the family was unaware brought him home; it was past time for old wounds to heal. As the nation had to get on with living, so did he, and he couldn't have a future until he made peace with his past. Now he was coming home.

Matt didn't write to let them know he was coming home. He wanted to surprise them. Perhaps deep down he didn't tell them because he feared that Uriah had never changed and would vehemently oppose his return. This way his grandfather would have no previous warning and would be totally unprepared. Matt would see an unrehearsed reaction, an honest one, maybe a joyful reunion of grandfather and grandson.

Matt returned to Chandlerville to work with Uriah and Bryan at La Candela de Oro, as a hired hand if Uriah had too much pride to forgive and let bygones be bygones. Matt planned to save his money and to buy his own property so he could build his own ranch. Uriah's was the Golden Candle; Matt's would be the Golden Bracelet—El Brazalete de Oro. How fitting, he thought. In Spanish the word for candle was feminine in gender; *brazalete* was masculine. One was soft; the other hard. Maybe the Chandlers would never be bound together with love, but at least they would once again be united, the one complimenting the other.

Running Horse rose and moved to where Matt stood; he laid his hand on his friend's shoulder. After he received recognition from Soaring Eagle, he

103

said, "I have seen three-tens-and-six winters like Ma-ta-mon-yahu, and we have been friends for as many winters. He and I learned to be Comanche braves together, and we attended the white man's school together. Like Ma-ta-mon-yahu, I speak and write English. Unlike Ma-ta-mon-yahu, I have chosen to walk with the Comanches rather than the whites."

He walked around the circle, staring into the elder's faces. "On the day the white men were branding Ma-ta-mon-yahu, I was leading a hunting party. We thought he was dead and wanted to get his body for Soaring Eagle. A horrible wound ran across his chest. The white men, thinking we were coming after them, started firing at us. We fought and killed all but one of them who escaped and made it back to Chandlerville. We brought Ma-ta-mon-yahu back to the village where Buffalo Woman treated his wounds and the burn. We killed the white man who took his bracelet, but Ma-ta-mon-yahu won back his bracelet when the white man called Smith tried to kill him the second time." He picked up Matt's arm and held it for the people to see.

When Running Horse sat down, Matt spoke again. "The white man who escaped told the people of Chandlerville that I and my murdering Comanche braves innocently attacked and killed five outstanding citizens and would have killed him had he not escaped. Weber Fielding pressured this man to bring charges of murder against Matt Chandler so that he could be hanged, but Uriah was much too influential for Fielding to do this."

Matt had to give Uriah credit. The old man had drawn the line at murder. Much better to let him live and suffer than to end it all! Through disowning Matt, he made sure no one inherited his property but Bryan. He was taking no chances on an illegiti-

mate Fielding claiming it at some future date.

"Uriah rode into town and told Fielding that his grandson may be the father of Veronica's baby, but he wasn't a murderer. If Matt died, Uriah promised the same to Fielding. Because of Fielding's lies, the white people turned against Matt Chandler. I did not fear what Fielding would do to me, but what he would do to both my families. I fled my home and have been gone these ten-and-four winters. Sun, Father, you saw me do it. Earth, Mother, you saw me do it. Do not permit me to live until another season, if I have spoken falsely."

When Matt was finished, the Comanches whooped and clapped their hands.

"My grandfather," Matt yelled above the ovation, and immediately they quieted and turned to look at the chief. Eagerly they awaited his answer. "I now ask for my revenge."

Soaring Eagle closed his eyes and sat quietly, rocking back and forth, smoking and pondering his decision. Patiently the people waited. Soaring Eagle was a reputed leader among his people, a revered patriarch; his wisdom and knowledge eagerly sought by young and old. Today he had proved that he was still a warrior. None disputed his claim to leadership.

Finally he stood and spoke. "You have a right to ask for revenge, my grandson. I give you permission to marry the white woman in a Comanche ceremony which I will perform myself. You must hunt and kill the animal that is to be used in the ceremony. We now prepare for the marriage of my grandson Mata-mon-yahu to the white woman."

Matt thanked his grandfather and turned to walk back to the tepee. He was irritated with himself. He should have been exultant that his grandfather had granted his request and that after all these years he was going to get even with Fielding, but his conscience was niggling him. He was thinking about the white woman and what he was doing to her.

But, he argued with himself, *you're making an honest woman out of her. You're going to marry her before you make love to her, and you're going to make sure she enjoys her sexual experience. That's more than what many husbands give to their wives. What more could she want?*

At the tepee Matt lifted the pelt, stooped and entered the dwelling. Across the room he saw Zoe curled up on the pallet, sleeping soundly. His gaze inadvertently brushed the whiskey bottle and he smiled. Her sedative. Buffalo Woman sat on the other side of the fire and glared at him. Pushing his conscience aside, Matt grinned.

"You may leave now, Buffalo Woman. Tomorrow I will marry the white woman. I go now to kill the deer."

"Hrumph!" the old woman grunted. "Do you wish me to return in the morning to prepare her for the wedding?"

"No," Matt answered. "I want you to find a maiden to come dress her." He walked to the rope and lifted the quiver which he settled over his shoulder. He reached for the bow. "I want the captive to dress as a Comanche for the wedding. I'm sure you can find someone here who is her size and will barter a dress."

With another grunt the old woman stood and left the tepee, leaving Matt alone with Zoe. He moved to the pallet and knelt over her. She was curled up like a little girl, her hands tucked under her chin. He remembered her drunken confession and smiled.

106

"You weren't quite sure to what occasion we were drinking, little one, and at the time I didn't know either," he whispered in English, reaching out to twist a golden curl around his index finger. "Now I do. We were celebrating our marriage." He lowered his head and kissed her lightly on the lips. "I promise that you're going to enjoy your wedding night and your husband."

Chapter 7

Zoe sat on the mattress of buffalo robes, oblivious to the warm sunshine that fell on her face. Her mouth tasted horrible and felt as if it were stuffed with cotton. She would swear one of the Indian musicians was in her head, beating his drums fast and furiously. When she had first awakened, for one blissful moment she had thought she was home in her bedroom, but as her gaze wandered around the dwelling—the leather hides stitched together to form the outer wall, the frame poles, and the fire pit in the center of the dirt floor, realization came quickly and with a jolt. She was in an Indian tepee.

She glanced up to look through the smoke hole. From the position of the sun, it was past noon, but Zoe didn't mind. She had nothing pressing to do and nowhere to go.

She moved and the soft buckskin garment rubbed against her skin to jog her memory even more. Remembering she was in a tepee in a Comanche village was the mildest of the returning memories. She recalled the wizened old woman with the long, sagging breasts and the star tattoos, Buffalo Woman, who had taken her to the river and allowed her to bathe.

The drumming in her head was driving Zoe crazy; she reached out and dipped her hand into the basin, pressing wet fingers to her forehead. The cool moisture brought back more memories. She had bathed. Yes, she had taken two baths. She remembered the cool creek water; she remembered the steambath. Her hand dropped from her forehead to the yoke of the shirt, and as she absently fingered the soft leather, she looked up to see her clothes draped over one of the ropes that stretched from one frame pole to the other.

Slowly, carefully, she slid down onto the mattresses again to nurse her aching head. Running the soles of her feet over the skins, she stretched her legs out, enjoying the freedom and coolness of the Indian garment. Perhaps being a captive of this particular Comanche wasn't going to be such a grueling ordeal after all. *This particular Comanche! Where had that thought come from?* she wondered. Unbidden came the face with the mocking eyes and grin, the gaunt, indomitable features framed in thick, black hair. In spite of her misery, she smiled. He had fought for her. Maybe, just maybe, he was smitten with her.

She giggled and squirmed into a more comfortable position. The tips of her toes touched something cold. Disregarding the headache, she bolted up. At the end of the pallet a whiskey bottle was rocking back and forth on its side. Zoe's hand flew to her face to brush the hair from her temples as more memories came tumbling back brutally to haunt her. Dear Lord, the baths were only the beginning.

Her headache abruptly disappeared in the wake of full memory. Zoe's entire body burned with humiliation as she remembered her shameless behavior with the Comanche warrior. She knew beyond a shadow of a doubt that he had been laughing at her all the while. He had known she was trying to get him drunk, and he had turned the tables on her. He had deliberately gotten her drunk. Him smitten with her! How stupid could she be? She had been smitten with him, and the whiskey had wiped out all her inhibitions. She wasn't so drunk that she couldn't remember clearly every detail of the evening.

Instead of his raping her, she had almost raped him!

Castigating herself for having been so foolish, she fell back, her hands on her temples. But her traitorous body refused to let her be too harsh with herself. She delighted in the mere recall of the Comanche's drugging touch. The thought of his caresses set Zoe's heart aflutter and created an unfamiliar and acute ache in the depth of her stomach. She wanted his callused hand again to cup her bare buttocks and to pull her virgin body against his hardness. She yearned for the taste of his lips on hers and the gentle, erotic thrust of his tongue in her mouth. Her breasts tightened as she remembered how they felt pressed against the muscular wall of his chest.

Had Zoe Randolph really behaved like this with a stranger, with an Indian! She covered her face with her hands as if the action would serve to cover her shame. In all her twenty-nine years she had never behaved like this before . . . never! So why now, and with this uncivilized man? She couldn't say.

Why hadn't Weber aroused these primitive emotions in her? She accused him silently. After all, he *was* her fiancé. When Zoe compared Weber to the Indian, he paled in insignificance. This angered her even more. He was her choice, a reflection of her judgment. Now she wondered if she had any judgment. She certainly wasn't discriminating, else she wouldn't be infatuated with the Indian. She smiled . . . yes, that's it—she was infatuated with the man, nothing more. She was drawn to him because he was something forbidden and foreign.

Now that she clearly understood her attraction to the man, she knew how to handle it. Up she bounded, standing for only a moment as the room quit spinning about her, and marched across the tepee to the rope where her clothes hung. In quick motions she jerked the buckskin garment over her head and dropped it at her feet; as quickly she redressed in her clothes. They were dusty and torn, and of flimsy material, but she felt safer in them. They were her armor. Somehow, she felt as if she had put her integrity and identity back on with them, and they served to remind her of the difference between her and the Comanche . . . Gold Bracelet.

She was a lady, he a savage.

Zoe heard a noise outside the tepee and turned to see the pelt lift. A short, plump Indian girl in her early teens entered the dwelling carrying an envelope-shaped case of rawhide under her arm. Unlike Buffalo Woman, she was fully dressed and smiling. Her obsidian eyes, accented with yellow lines above and below the lids that extended and crossed beyond the corners, glittered with undisguised curiosity. Like the other Indian women whom Zoe had observed, her hair was cut short, the center part line traced with vermilion, and her ears were painted red on the inside. Both cheeks were daubed with a solid red-orange triangle, and she wore many necklaces and bracelets.

"Me Voice of the Sunrise," the girl said in a low husky voice. "Who you?"

111

Zoe was so surprised she stood there a moment in absolute silence, staring at the woman. Then she screeched, "You speak English!"

"Me speak white." Voice of the Sunrise nodded, her full lips turning into a beautiful smile. "Who you?"

"I'm Zoe Randolph." She could hardly contain her excitement. It had been four days since she'd heard another word of English. Although the woman was a Comanche, Zoe felt as if she were her dearest friend.

"Bring you dress." Kneeling, Voice of the Sunrise set the rawhide case on the floor and opened the flap to withdraw a lemon-colored buckskin dress which she held up by the shoulders.

The gesture was so sweet, the dress so beautiful, that Zoe was overcome with gratitude. "Thank you very much," she murmured, her eyes admiring the dress. "This is kind of you."

"You like?" Voice of the Sunrise asked.

"Oh, yes. Yes, I do. It's beautiful."

The skirt, decorated in alternate rows of fringe and intricate beadwork, was slightly flared. Lacing the loose, poncho-styled bodice to the skirt was an ornamental skin peplum that hung in deep points to mid-thigh. Geometric medallions were sewn across the peplum in a band, and medallions of varied size and color were sewn across the front and back of the bodice.

"Me do all," Voice of the Sunrise said proudly, pointing to the beadwork.

The neckline, a horizontal slit in the center of the bodice, was high and straight, and brilliantly banded with colorful beading that extended across the shoulder to the elbow-length, butterfly sleeves. Zoe reached out to touch first the soft leather, then the colorful beads scattered along the edge of the deep fringe that finished the sleeves.

"It's more than beautiful," she breathed. "It's truly exquisite."

"You take," the Indian maiden said.

Zoe dropped her hand and shook her head. "Oh, no, I couldn't take your dress. I don't have anything to give you in return."

"No give. Ma-ta-mon-yahu give. You put on," she insisted.

"Who is this Ma . . . ta . . . mon . . . yahu?" Zoe asked, although she had a suspicion he was her captor, and her eyes strayed to the empty bottle, gleaming brightly in the sunshine.

"Him *Coth-cho Teja*." Voice of the Sunrise beamed. "Him Comanche warrior."

What a description, Zoe thought. She was in a village of nothing but Comanche warriors! "He wears a gold bracelet," she said dryly, pointing to her left wrist to make sure the girl knew what she meant.

"That Ma-ta-mon-yahu." Voice of the Sunrise nodded her head. "Wear band. Him want dress."

"Then let him have it. I don't want it."

The gleam went out of Voice of the Sunrise's eyes. "Him like heap. Give me this." She raised her hand to show Zoe the ring on her index finger.

Zoe looked at the cheap copper trinket that had already turned the girl's fingers a brackish green color and was outraged. "That's all he gave you for the dress?" she exclaimed. "That's all he thought this dress was worth?" *That's all he thought I was worth!* she thought indignantly.

"You slave," Voice of the Sunrise answered practically. "He said you no worth horse. Horse heap valuable. Slave worth this. My mother want horse.

113

She mad at ring. I like." She touched the ring lovingly.

Fury surged through Zoe. She thought she had been discriminated against by the best, but she had been mistaken. In this society she was considered a slave whose worth was being calculated in such base terms as copper rings and horses. After the passionate interlude with him last night, she was even more furious that her *owner* didn't think she was worth at least a horse. If only she could get her hands on him, she'd show him how much she was worth—and how little he was worth!

"You wear," the Indian woman pleaded, pushing the dress toward Zoe. "Heap pretty."

"Thank you for the dress," Zoe replied calmly, taking the buckskin and folding it up. She didn't want to hurt the girl's feelings, but she wasn't going to let this Indian order her around like she was his slave. "It's truly beautiful, and the decoration—" she smiled as she pointed to the bands of beads and the fringes "—is truly a work of art. I appreciate it but cannot accept it." She replaced it in the garment bag and fastened the flap. "You keep."

Voice of the Sunrise, afraid Matt would take his ring back if the white woman didn't accept the dress, said, "Have more." She grabbed the case, unfastened the flap, and dug through until she held two beaded moccasins and designed braid wrappers for the hair. She pressed them into Zoe's hands. "You have now?"

Zoe saw the pleading in the girl's eyes and wanted to accept the garments because Voice of the Sunrise so wanted her to, but she would not accept anything from a man who considered her his slave, a man who would stoop so low as to get her drunk deliberately. Zoe conveniently forgot that she had planned

114

to do the same to him. After all, she had her dignity to maintain then and now.

"I cannot accept these," she replied firmly, the wave of her hand including her blouse and skirt. "I have my own clothes. I'll wear them."

"No," Voice of the Sunrise said, shaking her head, "Ma-ta-mon-yahu no want white woman. Want *Coth-cho Teja*. Want Comanche."

Oh, he does, does he? "I don't give a damn what he wants," Zoe muttered angrily, tapping her foot against the floor. "Just let me find him and I'll—" She stopped in mid-sentence. "Take me to this Ma-ta-mon-yahu."

The girl's eyes widened; shaking her head, she backed up. "No can do. Ma-ta-mon-yahu be mad at Voice of the Sunrise. Him come get slave when he want slave."

"Then I'll go find him," Zoe declared. She charged across the tepee, hit the pelt with the flat of her palm, and bolted through the opening. Before she had taken two steps down the path, two hands caught and bit into her upper arms to drag her back. She turned to look into the fierce countenance of a Comanche warrior. She had forgotten about the guard.

"No find Ma-ta-mon-yahu," Voice of the Sunrise said as the guard unceremoniously propelled Zoe through the small opening and she tottered across the floor. "Ma-ta-mon-yahu no want you go." She knelt to pick up the buckskin dress and held it up to Zoe. "Heap pretty. Give you. Put on. No want Ma-ta-mon-yahu angry."

"Oh yes I do," Zoe answered, throwing caution away again without so much as a second thought. Let him beat her or burn her or rape her. Nothing he could do frightened her at the moment, she was so

115

consumed with anger. She had had enough of this arrogant Comanche. She had to draw the line somewhere, and this was it. She refused to put on the Indian costume. How *dare* he equate her with a cheap copper ring, or call her a slave, or be ashamed of her because she was white. How dare he!

As Zoe furiously marched in a circle around the dwelling, Voice of the Sunrise begged her to change into the buckskin dress, reverting back and forth from broken English to Comanche, but Zoe wouldn't relent. Her American-made clothes represented her identity and integrity. She'd be damned if she'd let anyone strip her of that. Why, her clothes were her only bridge to sanity. She looked down at the ragged blouse and skirt, a melancholy smile crossing her lips—if they truly represented her bridge to sanity, it was tenuous indeed.

Because she was so deep in thought, Zoe wasn't aware that Voice of the Sunrise had ceased talking. She was thinking of a way to escape this dreadful place; she wanted to get to Mexico to find out if the villagers really were sick with cholera and if so, to stop a full-scale epidemic. She wanted to get away from here before she broke her moral code for this half-breed. She had to have her horse, and Dusty was in the corral. That's where she would go, but first she must get past the guard. A slow smile spread across her face as an idea occurred to her. The creek ran through the corral.

"Voice of the Sunrise—" she stopped her pacing and turned to face the Comanche girl "—I think I will change clothes. Will you take me to bathe first?"

"You wear?" Voice of the Sunrise exclaimed happily and held up the dress. "You wear?"

"I wear," Zoe returned, smiling into the girl's

round face.

Elated that Zoe was going to change clothes, Voice of the Sunrise leaped to her feet and nodded her head, her coarse black hair brushing against her round cheeks. "I bring water. You wash."

Zoe shook her head. "No, you take me to water. I wash."

Voice of the Sunrise cocked her head and stared dubiously at Zoe for a long while before she finally nodded. "I take."

Zoe could hardly contain her excitement. Her heart beat so loudly she was afraid Voice of the Sunrise would hear it, but the Indian woman was busily packing the necessary clothes into the garment bag.

After she fastened the flap, Voice of the Sunrise rose. "Come," she said and moved toward the stiffened pelt over the door. "We go." Outside the door, she turned to the guard and said in Comanche, "I am taking Ma-ta-mon-yahu's slave to the creek so she can bathe and change into her wedding dress. You may let her go with me."

Zoe waited until the guard nodded his head, then she moved out the opening to follow Voice of the Sunrise down the street beyond the corral to a secluded area where she could bathe. As Zoe slowly unbuttoned her blouse, she looked around, memorizing everything around her, the layout of the village, the terrain, and the best possible route of escape.

That's when a group of women huddling together, talking loudly and clapping their hands, caught her attention. They stepped aside to break the circle, and one woman pirouetted in front of them. Over her buckskin dress she wore a beautiful white lace chemise—*Zoe's beautiful white lace chemise.*

All thoughts of escape forgotten, Zoe stared at the woman as she proudly paraded in front of the others. Zoe lost all control . . . she was angry beyond thought. That woman had no right to be wearing her clothes! Her eyes blazing fury, she marched away from the creek down the road to the tepee. Voice of the Sunrise watched Zoe in surprise, then leaped to her feet and ran behind, begging the captive to return to the creek. Zoe heard nothing but the anger as it pounded in her head; she reacted to nothing but the injustice of being a slave and having her belongings stolen, of being a slave whose worth wasn't even that of a horse. The Indian women were astonished to see the white woman. Surprise caused them to drop back when Zoe pushed through to stand in front of the woman who wore her undergarment. Hands planted on hips, anger visibly imprinted on her countenance, Zoe glared into the woman's bewildered face.

"I want my clothes," she said, her tone matching the fire in her eyes, "and I want them right now. If you don't give them to me willingly, I'll rip them off."

Chapter 8

"No," Voice of the Sunrise shouted, running to Zoe, grabbing her by the arm and tugging, "you no have. Ma-ta-mon-yahu gave my mother. He no give horse. He give white woman clothes. They worth slave. He say."

Zoe was so furious that she didn't feel an ounce of fear. She didn't hear a word Voice of the Sunrise said. Nor did she think. She shook the young girl's hands off her arm, reached out, and grabbed the chemise by the shoulders, ripping it off the Comanche woman. She'd show this savage that no Comanche was going to be dictating her life . . . or giving her clothes away without her permission. Breathing heavily, she stood there holding the pieces of material in her hands.

The surprise in the Comanche's eyes turned to violent anger and hatred. The white captive had dishonored her in front of her friends. She had destroyed the white woman's dress Ma-ta-mon-yahu had bartered to her for the buckskin wedding dress.

In Comanche, she shouted for those around her to hear, "I, Woman Who Sews Well, do not allow slaves to treat me dishonorably. I will punish her."

The women clapped their hands and yelled, "Hear! Hear!"

"No," Voice of the Sunrise yelled in Comanche, running to stand between her and Zoe, "do not punish the slave, my mother. She is not your property. She belongs to Ma-ta-mon-yahu."

"According to our custom, my daughter," Sews Well answered, "I have the right to punish the slave because she has stepped out of her place. She has dishonored me. If Ma-ta-mon-yahu had watched his slave more carefully, this would not have happened."

By now men and children had gathered around Zoe and Sews Well. Her anger was quickly dissipating, and she felt clammy with fear.

"My husband," Sews Well called to one of the braves, "take the white woman to the chief. Speak my grievance and tell him I wish to punish the slave."

Before Zoe knew what had happened, the man moved through the crowd and his hand bit into her shoulders. She looked into his face and such venomous ugliness frightened her. She twisted her shoulder, but couldn't loosen his grip. Inwardly quaking and wishing she could shrink away from him, Zoe fought her fear and glared at him. His fingers dug into her tender skin, and he yanked her down the road toward Soaring Eagle's tepee.

"My father," Voice of the Sunrise called out, "turn her loose. She belongs to Ma-ta-mon-yahu. You know what he'll do to you if he finds that you've harmed his slave."

"The white woman will be punished," he shouted.

"Yes," the Indian maiden answered, "she will be punished, but Ma-ta-mon-yahu should be the one to punish her."

"We shall let the council make that decision," the

man answered. "Ma-ta-mon-yahu doesn't know how to treat a slave. If he did, she would be shaking in fear rather than attacking a woman of the village. She would be subdued and docile."

Voice of the Sunrise didn't tarry. Frightened of what her mother and father would do to Zoe, the young maiden raced through the village in search of Matt. She didn't really care about the fate of the white woman, but she cared about what happened to herself. If anything happened to the slave he had entrusted to her keeping, he would punish her. Voice of the Sunrise hoped Ma-ta-mon-yahu had returned from the hunt. He would know how to handle her parents and the slave. Finally she came to the large clearing in front of Soaring Eagle's tepee. To her relief, Matt was skinning and cleaning a deer that hung on a large frame in front of him.

"Ma-ta-mon-yahu," she called, "come quick. Your slave dishonored my mother when she tore the pretty white dress off her, and my father is taking her before the council for punishment." The words tumbling out, the girl repeated all that had happened.

"Damn!" Matt muttered, picking up a piece of deerskin to wipe off his hands. The woman was determined to get into trouble despite all he could do. Here he was, trying to save her life, and she was raising a ruckus over a piece of underwear. Where was her sense of priorities? Damned senseless woman! She probably didn't have any.

Furious with both Zoe and Sews Well, he turned and strode toward the creek. Before he had gone far, he saw Curved Bow dragging Zoe down the road. Since Zoe's blouse was unbuttoned, the material flapped to the side, exposing the fullness of her breasts above the scooped neckline and showing the imprint of her nipples against the cotton chemise.

121

Matt's anger turned to fury. He stopped in the middle of the thoroughfare, took a firm stance, and folded his arms across his chest to await their approach.

Curved Bow threw Zoe to the ground between him and Matt. His eyes locked with Matt's. "Your slave has dishonored my wife. She Who Sews Well demands satisfaction."

Although he was angry at the callous way the Indian treated Zoe, Matt evinced no emotion. In that brief instant before he met Curved Bow's gaze, Matt had ascertained that Zoe was not physically harmed. From the Indians he had learned many important lessons, one of which was never to let his opponent know his thoughts or weaknesses, or they would be used against him.

Zoe, landing on her hands and knees, welcomed Matt, even though his face was set in angry lines. For a moment she wondered at her own curious behavior and glanced down at the piece of gauzy white material she still clutched in her fist. She had risked so much for so little; yet at the moment it had seemed important to do.

Without taking his eyes off Curved Bow, Matt stepped over Zoe, silently announcing his ownership of the white woman.

Curved Bow said, "You bartered the white woman's dress to Sews Well for one of Voice of the Sunrise's dresses."

"I did," Matt answered, his eyes straying to the woman who knelt at his side. Although he was furious at Curved Bow for mistreating Zoe, at the moment he wanted nothing more than to shake some sense into that beautiful head of hers. She was hell-bent on destruction.

"Look at the dress you gave me," Sews Well

shouted, moving from behind her husband, waving the frayed pieces of material in the air. "She ripped it from my body."

"According to custom, your slave must be punished," Curved Bow said, his voice becoming louder, his demands increasing with the size of the gathering crowd.

"Yes," Matt answered, "that is so." A murmur passed through the people then rose into a buzz of whispers. Matt raised his hand for silence. "I apologize to you, Sews Well. My slave has insulted you, and you have the right to ask for her punishment."

Sews Well crossed her arms over her breasts and smiled smugly.

"But," Matt continued, "if you take her to the council, they will decide only on the way she should be punished. You would not receive anything in place of the garment which she has destroyed."

"That is true," Sews Well muttered.

"I would like to punish my slave myself," Matt said, "and I will give you another gift. Think on what I have said and let me know if this will restore your honor."

"How will you punish the white woman?" Sews Well asked. She was intrigued with Matt's suggestion. While she would enjoy seeing the slave punished, the Indian woman also wanted another gift.

"I will whip her," Matt answered.

"What gift will you give me?"

"You wanted a horse," Matt answered. "I shall give you one of mine."

"Punish her," Sews Well said.

Matt shook his head. "Not until you agree to my suggestion."

Sews Well thought for a moment. Ma-ta-mon-yahu was promising her a horse, a far better gift

123

than the dress. The people in the village would really look up to her now. She was a wealthy woman. This would give her five horses in her own herd.

"I will take the horse and you will punish your slave. I shall choose the horse which you're to give me, Ma-ta-mon-yahu," she said. After Matt's curt nod, she said, "I want the black stallion."

Matt drew in a sharp, painful breath. His prize possession . . . the only thing he truly owned when the War between the States was over. Matt felt Zoe brush against his legs as she stood. She moved to his side and tossed her head, the riotous mane of hair flying out of her face. His eyes lowered to the gentle swell of breasts exposed by the low-cut undergarment, and he was angry because she was exposing herself in front of all these leering braves, angrier still because he desired her. His hand circled her wrist.

"So be it," he muttered, the quietness of his voice a contrast to the fury that thundered through his bloodstream. "The stallion is yours."

Bright Knife pushed through the crowd until he stood in front of Matt, his lips curling into a contemptuous smile. "You have demonstrated that you are unable to tame the white woman, Ma-ta-mon-yahu, when she is a slave. How much less will you be able to control her when she is your wife?"

Those listening joined in the raucous laughter.

"She is my slave," Matt answered. "She will be my wife. How she treats me is my business, not yours."

"Perhaps you ought to take a lesson from the women," the young buck taunted in an effort to humiliate Matt. "Let them teach you how to control your slave."

His gaze darting to Zoe, Matt found it extremely tempting for him to believe his earlier Sunday

124

School lessons, which taught that women had intro-
duced all problems into the world — and if Eve
hadn't, Zoe seemed to be doing a pretty good job of
it.

"Thank you for your worthy advice," Matt answered smoothly, "but I shall take care of my property, Bright Knife."

"We have all seen how you take care of it."

Again laughter taunted Matt. Still he refused to
punish Zoe in front of the Indians. With her in tow,
he pushed through the crowd, walking toward his
tepee. Zoe didn't mind that Matt's hand was digging
into her wrist or that he was dragging her along with
him. She was happy to be rescued. Grinning, she
turned her head to see Sews Well, Curved Bow, and
Bright Knife still standing in the middle of the road,
glaring at them. Their expressions were so ludicrous
that Zoe actually chuckled.

The soft laughter was Matt's undoing. He stopped
walking so abruptly that Zoe bumped into his chest.
"What the hell's so funny?" he demanded as her
hands inadvertently climbed his chest.

Zoe was so shocked she could only stare at him.

"Tell me. I'd like to laugh with you."

Zoe still couldn't speak.

"For the past two days, I've been trying to protect
you, and you've done everything in your power to
undermine me. I was out of my mind to rescue you
from Bright Knife. You deserve someone like him.
I've half a mind to turn you over to him. You're sure
as hell not worth my stallion."

Before she could reply, Matt turned and with long,
purposeful strides headed for his tepee, dragging
Zoe behind. By this time her shock and surprise had
been replaced with anger. He'd understood English
all along. He'd known everything she was saying. He

125

could have talked to her and explained what was happening.

"You speak English!" Zoe ran, dodging from side to side in her attempt to get in front of him, but he walked all the faster. No longer did she try to free her hand from his clasp. "You speak English."

Matt didn't answer, nor did he slacken his pace.

"You son-of-a-bitch," Zoe screamed, not caring that everyone in the village was privy to their argument. She wondered whether the whole damned village spoke English. "You lowdown son-of-a-bitch! All this time . . . all this time . . . and you spoke English but didn't utter one word to me. You could have talked to me."

Still Matt ignored her.

She grew angrier. "Go ahead," she goaded, "give me to Bright Knife."

"Lady, right now that's one dangerous request to make of me," he said. "He wants you, and giving you to him would be the simplest answer to the entire situation." But he was lying and he knew it. He wasn't about to give her to Bright Knife, and he'd kill any man who tried to take her away from him. How could he have become so involved with a woman? He'd fought for her and suffered a wound in his arm, and now he had given up his prized stallion. A knight in shining armor on a white charger may have fought for her and suffered a wound in the process, but he sure as hell wouldn't give up his horse. What kind of fool was he?

"Take me home, please," she asked him, twisting her arm, trying to free it from his iron grip. "Please take me home. I'll see that you get a reward for it." She remembered the ring he'd given to Voice of the Sunrise and how proud of it she'd been. "I'll give you a ring like the one you gave to Voice of the

Sunrise."

Although he was so angry he felt he'd explode any minute, Matt couldn't suppress the grin that tugged at his lips. She was offering him one of those cheap copper rings.

"Or another bracelet," Zoe said, when Matt didn't answer. "One you can wear on your right arm. You'll be the best dressed and richest Indian in camp. Everyone will envy you."

"Everyone in the village envies me now," he told her. "All of them would like to have a slave like you."

"I'm not your slave," she shouted, her fingers clawing at his. "I'm not anybody's property, and if I were, I'd be worth more than a cheap copper ring. I'm worth more than a horse, too."

"Not just a horse," Matt informed her dryly, "but a stallion. An Arabian stallion. And let me tell you something, lady, you're gonna have to be one hell of a woman to be worth more than my stallion."

Matt stepped in front of the tepee, lifted the pelt, and shoved Zoe through the opening. She stumbled across the room, teetering before she regained her balance. By the time she turned to face him, he was standing with his legs apart, his hands on his hips.

"You think you're worth more than a horse, yet you were bargaining for your life with a cheap copper ring," he taunted, watching the heaving of her breasts.

Zoe felt uncomfortable under his gaze. She pulled her blouse together and buttoned it, wishing her breathing would slacken so that her breasts weren't thrusting against the material of the blouse. "What are you going to do with me?"

"A lot of things," Matt said.

Zoe's head jerked up and she saw that his gaze

was still on her breasts. "Please take me home," she said. "I'll pay you handsomely. Just name your price."

"I'll take you home in due time," he promised.

"Thank you," Zoe murmured. "Thank you so much. You'll not regret this."

"No," Matt drawled, "I think not."

Zoe was extremely uncomfortable; the man was altogether disconcerting. She had the feeling that his words veiled subtler meanings. Yet she had no alternative but to accept them at face value. "What do you want as a reward?"

His lips slowly curled into a sensuous smile. "I'll tell you later."

"All right," Zoe answered, excitement swirling through her body. "I'll give you some time to think about it . . . and remember, *anything*."

"*Anything*," he drawled as if savoring the word. "I'll remember."

"Why did you wait until now to speak to me in English?" Zoe asked.

"There was no need to before."

"No need!" she exploded. "I've been frightened out of my wits thinking I was a captive of savages and you didn't think you needed to speak to me in English?"

Matt regarded Zoe's rising anger with amusement. "My speaking English wouldn't have changed anything. You are a captive of the savages, as you put it . . . of one savage in particular—me. Remember, lady, I fought for you. My arm is sliced because of you, and in order to save you from a punishment worse than death, I just gave away my prize black stallion."

"And I suppose you're going to throw this up to me the rest of my life!" Zoe exclaimed angrily, un-

128

aware of her unconscious slip.

Matt's gaze softened as he continued to stare at her, wondering what she would look like twenty or thirty years from now. Pretty, he thought. She would always be pretty. The golden hair would turn silver, and laugh lines would form around her eyes and mouth, but she wouldn't be old or ugly. Her bone structure assured him of that. Zoe Ellen Randolph would never be anything but beautiful.

"Why did you?" Zoe asked, wetting her dry lips with her tongue. Although his eyes were no longer leering at her, she was uncomfortable beneath his gaze; she wondered what he was thinking.

"Why did I what?" Matt asked, having lost himself in his thoughts.

"Why did you fight and trade your stallion for me?"

"I wanted you," Matt said simply, his brown eyes blatantly roaming her body. "More than I wanted the stallion."

Zoe felt herself growing hot and flustered. "You said you were going to take me home." She lifted her hand and placed it protectively over her breasts. Although her blouse was buttoned, she felt as if she were standing in front of him naked.

Matt grinned. "I said in due time. Right now, we have some formalities to which we must attend."

"Such as?"

Matt leaned down and picked up the buckskin dress and held it up. "Getting you ready for the feast."

Zoe shook her head. "Please, I'd rather not wear that dress."

"At the moment, your wishes aren't being considered," Matt told her. "You'll wear this dress and go to the feast with me."

129

Zoe's gaze traveled over Matt's hard and unyielding face, and she tilted her head a mere jot in a show of defiance. "If I go, I'll wear my own dress."

"No," Matt returned, "you won't wear your dress. For one thing, it's filthy. I wouldn't allow you to even if it weren't filthy."

"What do you mean, you won't allow me to wear my own clothes?" Zoe shouted indignantly, forgetting her status in the Comanche community. "Do you think you . . own me?" her voice faded into a whisper.

"Yes, ma'am," he said, "I do own you. I fought Bright Knife for you and you belong to me." He held the buckskin garment out to her. "Now put the dress on, or I shall put it on you myself."

Zoe didn't take the dress. "What are you celebrating tonight?"

"A wedding."

She hiked her brows quizzically. "I didn't know Indians married. I thought they just lived together."

"I don't see the difference myself," Matt answered. "Don't white people live together when they get married?"

Zoe ignored the question and suggested, "Let's compromise. I'll go to the wedding with you, but not dressed as an Indian. I'll wear my own clothes."

Matt shook his head. "No compromise. You'll attend the wedding in the Indian dress."

"I won't! You may like Indian women better than you do white ones, but I'm not going to become a squaw to satisfy your whims."

In two strides Matt closed the distance between them. "Becoming a *squaw* takes more than putting on a dress," he said. "It means a change of heart, and lady, I'm not sure you have one. I know for certain you have no brain. Now it's time to get dressed." His hands caught the lapels of her shirt, and he ripped it from her body as if it were a piece of paper. Angrily Zoe clawed at his face, her fingernails leaving slender red lines where they raked his chest. She stumbled back, but he caught her.

"Put the dress on."

"Never," she muttered. "You can beat me, even kill me, but I won't put that dress on voluntarily." Before the words had echoed into silence, Matt caught the straps of the thin chemise and tore it from her shoulders.

Stripped of her blouse and undergarment, Zoe stood for a moment in paralyzed silence. Her first inclination was to raise her hands and to cover her nudity, but she didn't. The Indian would like that, and she wouldn't give him that satisfaction. She would show no shame in front of this beast. Fighting back the mortification that burned through her body, she straightened her back, unconsciously thrusting her breasts forward and giving a proud lift to the nipples. Her arms hung at her sides.

Matt's hands dropped, the shredded material dangling from his fists. He could only stare at her breasts, beautifully rounded and supple. Her skin, smooth as ivory, begged to be possessed. His loins tightened, and desire surged through his body.

"Take your skirt off," he said in a thick voice.

"No." Zoe stood her ground, her eyes never leaving his face.

"Do you want me to rip it off, too?" he asked in a dangerously quiet voice.

"No, but my desires don't seem to matter."

"Then take it off!" Matt threw the chemise to the floor.

Zoe shook her head, her hair tumbling over her shoulders, golden tendrils shimmering over the satin smoothness of her breasts.

"You really want me to rip your clothes from your body, don't you?" Matt emitted a harsh oath. "You're begging me to."

He stepped so close Zoe felt his breath on her face, the warmth of his body against her breasts. His very proximity caused them to swell and the nipples to grow taut. The fight was slowly oozing out of her to be replaced with heated desire. She realized the foolishness of her position. If she continued to fight this man, she might end up in direr straits: in his exasperation, he might give her to Bright Knife. Only moments ago she had foolishly demanded that he do just that, but she didn't really want him to. At least this one was part-white, and perhaps she could reason with him . . . with him she stood a chance of being returned to her people.

Quickly Zoe accepted the wisdom of her arguments and enjoyed the new and exciting emotions that were rushing through her body. Giving herself up to the heat of passion, she looked at Matt anew. Still she didn't offer to dress herself. A part of her, a new and dangerous part of her, wanted to push this man to the end of his patience. She experienced the same about-to-fall-off-the-edge excitement that she had felt last night. Always a cautious woman, she couldn't understand this sudden fascination she had with danger, in this situation, with this man.

"You're a strong, obstinate woman who wants a primitive man, one who is strong enough to possess you fully. I shouldn't wonder, with the fiancé you have."

Zoe was so mesmerized by the nearness of the man that she barely heard his murmur. She was so caught up in the magic of his spell that she blatantly disregarded the warnings of her conscience. She knew she was racing headlong into calamity, possibly destruction, but she didn't care. Her only desire was to know fully the touch of this savage. She closed her eyes when his hands caught her face, then slid through her temples to tangle in her hair. His touch set her on fire; the heel of his hand rested against her chin, the callused palms against her temple. His fingers cupped her skull.

"You're fascinated with me because you think I'm savage, rather than civilized." His fingers lightly brushed against her scalp, sending erotic tremors down her spine. "I can feel your body trembling to my touch. You like the primitive, don't you, Dr. Randolph? Then let me give you another taste of what you desire so much."

His hands dropped to her shoulders, and he dragged her into his embrace. With a feral growl, he lowered his head, his lips touching hers, her breasts pressed against his chest. His lips opened hers to the driving force of his tongue, and his hands moved all over her back.

His hands glided down her midriff to the material at her waist, and his fingers slipped beneath the skirt band. Zoe shivered and wrapped her arms around him. He was right; she was fascinated with his primitiveness. She *did* want to be possessed by him. She was glad he was a Comanche and she was his slave; he would have no compunction about taking her. She wanted him to overpower her. Her mouth moved against his and she welcomed the sensual exploration of his kiss. She asked—no, begged—for her own seduction.

Matt broke the kiss, but didn't lift his lips from hers. He was at the point of no return. Zoe's body, her response, set him aflame with desire. It reminded him of his long abstinence. Yet he held back; he wouldn't take her until she was his wife.

"You want me to force you so you can have a clear conscience. So you can tell yourself that I raped you and there was nothing you could do about it. You think I'm a savage, Dr. Randolph. I say you're a hypocrite."

Zoe opened her mouth to protest, but his lips captured hers in another brutal assault. He caught the waistband of her skirt to rip it apart and to push it and her pantalettes over her hips and down her legs. His hands brushed over her naked skin to cup her buttocks. He held the trembling woman tighter as she instinctively pressed her lower body against him, innocently seeking and searching for fulfillment to the desire that he had stirred within her.

Zoe's hands, with a will of their own, investigated the muscular terrain of Matt's back; they swept up the indentation of his spine, across the flexed muscles of his shoulders, over the ridged scar tissue, and down to the small of his back. Her fingers slipped beneath his britches and she felt the swell of his muscle-hard buttocks.

As Zoe gave herself to his possessive touch, as she gave herself to the pleasure of exploring his body, their kiss deepened. She moaned softly and raked her fingers through his thick black hair. She trembled anew when Matt's hands slipped around her body and cupped her throbbing breasts. His thumbs stroked the nipples until Zoe emitted a hoarse, impassioned cry. The hand journeyed over her flat stomach to the downy triangle at the juncture of her thighs. The tips of his fingers teased the point of highest sensitivity.

Zoe pressed even closer, the touch of his fingers sending sensual tremors through her body, making her one mass of emotion. Her mouth opened beneath his, and her tongue began a quest of its own. Her hand gripped his shoulders and she gently rotated her hips, begging for more than a promise.

But Matt didn't give her more. He finally lifted his mouth from hers and stepped back. He looked at her with smoldering eyes as he drew air deeply into his lungs. He went into that familiar stance, hands on hips, legs slightly apart, and smiled at her.

"No, Dr. Randolph, I'm not going to make love to you. I'm going to the feast, and so are you. You can go as you are now, or you can wear the buckskin dress." He shrugged nonchalantly. "The decision is yours."

Only moments ago Zoe had been afire with passion; now her entire body burned with shame. She no longer wanted the Comanche to look at her with those sultry brown eyes; she wanted to run and hide. She was mortified that she'd begged him to caress her body, that she wanted him to. . . . She looked at her clothes strewn across the dirt floor, her last vestige of modesty savagely ripped from her body by this arrogant Comanche . . . but she had given him permission. That was her shame!

Matt smiled even wider. "What's it going to be, Doctor? If you're going to wear the buckskin, you'd better get started dressing. We're going to be leaving in just a few minutes."

She despised the insolent man who stood there issuing her an ultimatum, who could turn his emotions on and off at will. He was totally indifferent to the intimacy they'd just shared. In an effort to appear as casual as the Comanche, Zoe tossed her head and walked to where the buckskin garment lay. She picked it up and dropped it over her head; then she sat on the pallet and slipped into the beautifully beaded moccasins. When she was fully clothed, she stood, the heavily fringed hem of the dress hanging to her ankles. The leather was soft and caressing against her skin. She pirouetted around the tepee, enjoying the freedom of movement the garment allowed.

Sashaying up to Matt, she asked, "How do I look, my lord?"

"Beautiful," Matt murmured.

"I notice that Comanche women don't comb their hair," Zoe said caustically, "but I would like to do so. May I?"

Matt chuckled. "Be my guest."

Zoe in motion was a graceful sight. The soft fringes swayed with her every movement and the brilliant patterns of beading glittered in the sunlight that spilled into the tepee from the smoke-hole. When Zoe had finished brushing her hair, she turned to Matt. "I'm ready."

"Braid your hair," Matt said. "You'll find the braid wrappers in the wardrobe case Voice of the Sunrise brought."

"I don't want to braid it."

"I didn't ask you what you wanted," Matt returned. "I told you I wanted it braided, and it'll be braided."

He walked over and lifted the flap of the rawhide envelope. Pulling out two decorated thongs, he moved across the tepee and handed them to her.

Zoe refused them. With an arrogant tilt of her head, she returned her comb and brush to the saddlebags and moved to the door. "I've consented to wear the dress," she announced, "but I will not wear my hair in braids."

"I'll give you one more chance to braid your hair," he said in that softly dangerous voice she'd heard him use on Bright Knife. "If you don't, I'm going to call Voice of the Sunrise and let *her* braid it for you. And when she does, I'll let her transform you outwardly into a Comanche. She'll smear vermilion down your part line and put makeup on your face."

Zoe didn't move. She could be as obstinate as he.

"As you've seen, the Comanche women like to wear either red or yellow lines above and below her eyes. Some even want it to extend and cross beyond the corners," Matt taunted, and visions of Voice of the Sunrise's made-up face swam before Zoe's eyes. "She's extremely fond of painting the inside of her ears a bright red. And she paints a red-orange triangle or circle on both cheeks. Quite a masterpiece of beauty, wouldn't you say, Doctor?" He waited only a moment before he added, "Which do you like best? Triangles or circles? Or perhaps you'd like to have your breast or your face or both tattooed?"

Matt smiled when Zoe stamped across the tepee and knelt beside her saddlebags to withdraw her comb and brush. He watched as she deftly parted her hair and braided it, the ends secured with the decorated thongs. When she finished, she rose.

"Now you're ready for the wedding," Matt announced.

Again Zoe had the feeling that Matt's words held a double meaning. Finally she asked, "Is this a special wedding?"

"Quite special." He smiled, and his eyes sparkled. "It's my wedding."

"Oh," Zoe breathed limply, dropping back a step. "Who are you marrying?"

"You."

"Me!" Zoe whispered.

"You and I are getting married," Matt announced.

"No!" she exclaimed, her voice a scratchy whisper of disbelief. "I'll not marry you."

"Yes, Zoe Randolph," Matt drawled, "you'll marry me, because that's the price you're going to pay to get me to return you to civilization."

Bewildered, Zoe could only stare at him and shake her head.

Clasping her elbow in the palm of his hand, he led her to the doorway. "Remember, you said *anything*." He paused, then said, "I can have all the copper rings I want, and I have all the gold bracelets that I want. Now I want marriage."

"Surely—" The tip of Zoe's tongue moistened her lips, which had suddenly gone dry. "You'd be happier with one of your Indian women."

Matt smiled mockingly. "If I thought I'd be happier with one of them, I wouldn't be marrying you."

"You won't be happy with me," Zoe said and added, "You really won't. I shall never conform to your wild and barbaric ways, and I shall escape the first chance I get."

"I don't want you to conform," Matt informed her, "and I won't let you escape." His smile broadened and settled in his eyes as he grasped her arm again. "After you've had a taste of your primitive husband, Doctor Randolph, I don't think you'll be too eager to escape."

"You—you insufferable bas—"

Matt laid a silencing finger over Zoe's lips. "You must learn to guard that tongue of yours. I would be disappointed to think the names you've been calling me are part of your professional vocabulary." He chuckled at her outraged expression. "It's certainly not the language a lady would use."

Chapter 9

Zoe's eyes sparked fire, and she jerked her head away from the warm touch of Matt's fingers. "I won't marry you, and you can't make me. Beat me. Torture me. But I won't become your wife."

"Yes," Matt answered with deceptive softness, his head lowering and his gaze fastening on the empty whiskey bottle. "I can make you and without resorting to violence. Remember last night."

Flushing, Zoe quickly realized she was getting nowhere. The more she was around him, the more she realized *he* controlled the situation . . . and her.

"Remember only moments ago," he mocked.

Evocative shivers raced up Zoe's spine, but she pushed them aside. She would appeal to his ego; men enjoyed a woman's begging. "Please," she said, "understand my position. I can't marry you. I'm already engaged. I have a fiancé waiting for me in Chandlerville." Zoe scanned the hard, implacable face for some sign of relenting, but found none.

"I understand your position full well," he answered. "You're the one who doesn't understand the predicament you're in. You have a choice: marry me, or be raped, beaten, and tortured by Bright Knife."

The flat tone was a slap to Zoe's sensibilities, but she never allowed her discomfort to show. "You could help me escape."

"I could, but I won't. There's a lot you don't understand, and I don't have the time to explain . . . even if I wanted to."

Zoe couldn't believe he would be so obstinate. Frantically she struggled to find an argument that would convince him to return her to her people. Whatever she did or said, she must remain calm and assured. She mustn't let him know that she was frightened. . . . She straightened her shoulders and said firmly, "To speak English as well as you do, you must have spent a great deal of time around civilization."

Matt made no comment.

Before her composure could slip, Zoe continued, "Surely you must understand what it means to be engaged. I'm promised to another man."

Zoe's argument fell on deaf ears. Matt was too caught up in his scheme of revenge to listen. He shrugged. "It seems to me you have a dilemma to solve: if you marry me, I'll free you and eventually return you to your people. If you don't marry me, you'll remain a Comanche slave. After I'm through with you, you'll be passed on to one man after the other as each one tires of you. Treatment from your other owners won't be so nice. If they're married, their wives will torture you, and you'll be subjected to hard labor." He waited a moment for the words to digest before he smiled and added, "You'll have a better chance of returning to your fiancé if you marry me."

"A marriage in name only," Zoe said hopefully.

Matt laughed aloud, then said, "To quote you, ma'am, we Comanches solemnize a marriage by sleeping together, and I'll remind you that we have only first names. We never bother with two. You see, we believe it's the living together that makes a marriage, not words uttered in some ceremony."

"I can't," Zoe affirmed. "I really can't. Weber would never, never be able to forget that I —" Her head jerked up and she looked pleadingly into Matt's eyes. "Don't make me do this."

"I'm not going to force you," Matt replied silkily. "The decision is yours. I've told you the consequences. I'll also warn you that you're being watched every minute, so you'll never make it back to civilization without my help."

"But that help comes only if I marry you," Zoe said, maintaining her aplomb and blinking back the tears that burned her eyes.

"That's right."

Determined not to let him see her weakness and use it against her, she turned her back to Matt. She breathed deeply and calmed her shaking. During the years she'd studied to become a physician, she learned to discipline her emotions, to use them to both her and her patients' advantage for healing. She had toughened herself to suffering and pain. Pity she discarded; compassion she used in her relentless desire to heal. And Zoe reckoned herself to be among the best of physicians. Someday she would have a memorial, not only to herself, but to all women. Her hospital would be a testimonial to her pioneering the way for other women physicians. In spite of this man, she would achieve that!

Where matters of the heart were concerned, matters of *her* heart, Zoe was unschooled. She didn't understand the conflicting emotions that raged within her, each struggling for dominance. She wanted to return to Chandlerville and to Weber and to pick up her life where she had left it, but in the deepest recesses of her heart, she was excited about the idea of becoming this man's wife—in every sense of the word. Her own ambivalence angered her. How could a man like this stir up such strong emotions within her? She couldn't allow him to make love to her. *She couldn't.* She had to think of her reputation, her integrity as a doctor.

Then her gaze strayed to the whiskey bottle, and she remembered how wonderful she'd felt in his arms last night, and her feelings had nothing to do with the amount of liquor she had had. Her resolve weakened. After all, she told herself, this is only a Comanche ceremony. It's not binding. She turned, her head lifted, her gaze encountering the man who stood in front of her. He wouldn't relent . . . he was determined to have her, and one way or the other, he would. The one way promised pain and perpetual slavery, the other freedom.

Zoe smiled at Matt, an icy regard. She would marry him; she'd gain her freedom, but she'd fight every inch of the way. She'd make him rue the day he took Zoe Ellen Randolph for his bride. She walked to the door and slapped the pelt with her hand. "I'm ready," she announced, moving through the opening. "Let's go."

Now that she'd made the decision to marry him, Zoe was more relaxed. Her resolve filled her with renewed courage and optimism. As they walked down the street, she asked, "What do I call you?"

"The Comanches call me Ma-ta-mon-yahu."

"I didn't ask you what the Comanches called you," Zoe returned, smiling when out of the corner of her eye she saw Matt give her a quizzical look.

"I want to know what I'm to call you. In other words, I want to know what the whites call you."

"What makes you think the whites call me anything?" Matt asked.

Zoe cast him a superior smile. "After listening to you talk, it's not difficult to deduce that you've spent as much of your time around whites as Indians. You speak English too fluently. In fact," she added, "your English is quite sophisticated."

"My father was white," Matt explained. "When I was old enough to go to school, he sent me to his family back east. I stayed with them until my education was completed."

Zoe wasn't surprised to know that he had been educated in the east, but she was surprised that he had chosen to return to a life among the Indians. "Why did you come back here?"

"There's something to be said about the simplicity of Indian culture," he evaded.

"And the barbarism," Zoe added.

"Barbarism isn't uniquely Indian," Matt retorted. "If memory serves me right, all races have ably and frequently demonstrated their barbaric tendencies. I believe the whites recently concluded a war between themselves over the question of slavery."

"That—that wasn't barbarism," Zoe loftily disagreed. "That was war, Ma . . . ta . . . ma . . ." She groped for his name.

"Ma-ta-mon-yahu," Matt supplied.

"That was war," Zoe reiterated, refusing to stumble over his name again. "A matter of principle."

Matt laughed. "Wars are usually fought over matters of principle, Miss Randolph."

"What was the principle involved in your people's attack against my caravan?"

"Your fiancé is taking their land."

143

"Oh, no," Zoe said, turning to stop in front of Matt, "he isn't taking the land. Uriah Chandler used it as collateral for a recent loan. If he can't repay the loan, then Weber will have no recourse but to foreclose. Naturally, the property will become his. Surely you can make your people see that Weber's only taking what is rightfully his."

"Rightfully his!" Matt exclaimed, furious with both his grandfather and Fielding. Curbing his anger, he said, "Even if Weber gets this land legally through default of payment, this land will never be rightfully his. My people will never understand how property can be owned by one man. How can I explain that their possession of this land for hundreds of years means nothing?"

"Ma . . . ta . . . Ma-ta-mon-yahu," Zoe said, her heart going out to this man. She saw the pain in the depths of those dark brown eyes, and curiously she wanted to touch him, to reassure him. "I don't understand why your people are so angry that they have to kill innocent men, scalp them, and take women captive. There's plenty of land out here," she said, parroting Weber's arguments. "They're nomadic. I don't see why they don't just pack up their tents and move on to another place that would serve their purposes just as well, if not better."

Matt could hold his tongue, but he couldn't keep the anger from blazing in his eyes. "Why should the Comanches be the ones to pack up and move? This is *their* land." He gestured to encompass the surrounding terrain. "This is the land of the *Choto Teja*. Canyons and arroyos with breaks for protection. Water and abundant grass for the large herds of horses, for the buffalo and antelope. Here we have food and water for ourselves. And over there—" he pointed "—is the Sacred Mountain,

144

which is very important to my people. And you say we should move because one man wants our property."

"You don't understand," Zoe began.

"No, lady, I don't," Matt replied, "and I don't *want* to understand."

"Chandlerville needs the land," Zoe said. "Weber and several other civic leaders have come up with a wonderful idea that will make the land more fertile and will diversify its uses. He wants to build a trans-Pecos irrigation canal from the Rio Grande into New Mexico."

Matt laughed. "He wants all this land in order to dig a ditch from the Mexican border into New Mexico."

"It's more than a ditch," Zoe replied. "With the irrigation canal, Chandlerville will become the hub of civilization out here in West Texas and will automatically attract the railroad. This particular piece of property is the vital link which we need; the Indians don't."

Too angry to speak, Matt gazed at the Sacred Mountain in the distance.

"They're going to have to move," Zoe said gently. "If you want to help them, you could explain that they must move, and the reasons why. You could also persuade them not to resort to violence."

"Believe me, Miss Randolph," Matt said, "I'm going to help them."

"If you'll . . . take me back to Chandlerville before the marriage, before you . . . before you . . ." Zoe's face flamed with embarrassment as Matt's head turned and his gaze again encountered hers; she cleared her throat and wanted to slap the smirk off his face "—I'll introduce you to my fiancé, and he can explain the importance of this irrigation

145

canal to you. Perhaps the two of you can work together to make a peaceful move out of this."

"I'll be sure to talk with your fiancé, but I don't guarantee that we'll come up with a peaceful solution." He reached out and laid his hand on her shoulder to guide her off the road up to one of four tepees that faced and semicircled around a much larger one. "Here we are," he said. "You'll stay here. Voice of the Sunrise will bring you to the wedding."

"Where are you going?" Zoe asked, her fingers gripping into Matt's lower arm.

He laid his hand over hers and laughed. "Miss me already?"

"Not the way you're thinking!" Zoe drew back. "You're the only one with whom I can communicate in this place. I'm afraid of most of the Indians."

"I'm going to take a bath and change clothes," Matt said gently. "Don't worry. No one is going to hurt you. You belong to me." When Zoe slowly nodded her head, he called out in Comanche, "Voice of the Sunrise."

The girl came rushing out of the tepee, her face wreathed in a smile that grew even wider when she saw Zoe wearing the dress she had sewn. "Oh, Ma-ta-mon-yahu," she breathed, "the white woman is pretty."

"Yes," Matt agreed, "she is. The dress is pretty also."

"Thank you," Voice of the Sunrise said. She clasped her hands together, tilted her head to the side, and studied Zoe. "All she needs to be beautiful, Ma-ta-mon-yahu, is paint on her face. Then she won't look pale."

Matt laughed. "The white woman likes to look

pale. I must go now and prepare for the feast. In appreciation for your taking care of my slave today and warning me about what your parents were going to do, I shall give you another present."

"Oh, no," Voice of the Sunrise said, immediately wrapping her right hand around her left to hide her ring. "I don't want another present. I want to keep the ring."

"You can keep the ring," Matt said, the brown eyes unusually kind. "I'm going to give you a horse as an extra gift."

"Will this mar my mother's honor?" the Indian asked anxiously, not willing for her parent to lose favor in the eyes of the villagers because of her actions.

"I have already talked with your father," Matt explained. "Now that I'm going to marry the woman, her status changes from that of slave to wife. A wife is worthy of a gift that is bartered for a horse. The horse your mother received—" Matt shuddered when he thought of his black stallion belonging to Sews Well "—is a retribution gift and has nothing to do with you."

Voice of the Sunrise squealed and clapped her hands. "I will indeed be a rich woman. The villagers will envy me." She rushed to Zoe's side. "I already like the white woman, Ma-ta-mon-yahu, but I promise you that I'll take very good care of her. I'll bring her to the ceremony myself. Do not worry about her."

"I won't," Matt answered. He turned and walked away.

"Come," Voice of the Sunrise said to Zoe, leading her into the tepee. She sat down on one of the pallets and pointed to the mirror and an array of various containers that sat on the floor. "Me paint

147

face. You want face pretty?"

"No, thank you," Zoe replied hastily, shaking her head. She sat down across from the Indian and watched as Voice of the Sunrise meticulously applied her makeup.

When the girl was through, she looked up and smiled at Zoe. "Like 'em?"

"Yes," Zoe answered with a smile, "I really do like it." Now that she was over her shock, she realized that the lines accentuated the girl's glittering eyes. "You're very beautiful."

The girl bobbed her head. "You pretty."

"Thank you," Zoe replied, reaching out to clasp Voice of the Sunrise's hands. "And thank you for the lovely dress. I know Ma-ta-mon-yahu has paid you for it already, but I would like to give you something else."

"No gift," the maiden said. "Ma-ta-mon-yahu give 'em me horses. You wife now. Worth horse. Me can take." She gathered her cosmetics and tucked them under the bed that was on a raised platform. "Now we go feast."

The sun was low in the sky by the time Zoe and Voice of the Sunrise arrived at Soaring Eagle's tepee, and the crowd had already begun assembling. While the Comanches were friendly with Voice of the Sunrise, they were overtly hostile to Zoe. The women and children had ceased tormenting her, but they cast her hateful glances. The Indian girl, after sitting Zoe on a mat to the right of the chief, disappeared into the crowd to sit with her family.

Soon Bright Knife entered and crossed the clearing to take his place behind the chief. Because of Ma-ta-mon-yahu's wedding, his meeting with the council had been postponed. When he saw the white woman, his blood boiled. The minute he'd seen that caravan, he'd wanted her. That was the reason for the attack. If only he hadn't been so quick to rush back to share his good news with the camp! If only he'd known that Ma-ta-mon-yahu had returned home!

He stopped directly in front of Zoe and looked into her face, but she never dropped her head or quailed before his hard stare. Finally he turned his head to speak to Soaring Eagle and several of the older warriors who sat close to the chief; then he sat on the second row, just behind Zoe. He stared at the beautiful golden braids that hung down her back and rested against the muted color of the buckskin. He would have his turn with her; that he promised himself. And someday he would kill Ma-ta-mon-yahu.

Zoe felt Bright Knife's eyes boring a hole through her, and although she was uncomfortable, she kept her back straight and held her head high. She occupied herself with watching the villagers as they circled the blazing fire. In the center of the clearing sat the musicians beating their small drums. Men and women stood in two separate lines a short distance apart, facing each other. When the music began, each man selected a dancing partner by placing his hands around her waist; the women clasped him in similar fashion. To the accompaniment of the rhythmic beat of the drum, they chanted their songs and danced, their movements vivid and natural.

Dusk slowly turned into night and the celebration continued. The Comanches danced and played games. Zoe watched the festivities with interest, but she missed Matt. She didn't feel comfortable sitting among people who hated her and didn't mind her knowing it. She was so uncomfortable that she kept squirming and looking about. When she saw Voice of the Sunrise and a young warrior slipping off from the crowd, she smiled. Some customs didn't change from one culture to another. Zoe noticed that the rhythm of the drums changed. She turned her head. Standing in the center of the circle was Ma-ta-mon-yahu, looking so handsome she caught her breath. He was clothed in the most beautiful blue buckskin clothes she'd ever seen.

His short black hair, gleaming like polished onyx in the flickering light of the campfire, was held out of his face by a headband, the trailing ends glittering with metal that caught and reflected the light. His lips were curled into a smile; the brown eyes, focused on Zoe, were inscrutable. Holding out his hands, he walked toward Zoe, but she didn't move.

She was mesmerized by this man who was about to become her husband. The tunic, extending below Matt's buttocks, was exquisitely made. From the v-shaped collar and sleeves hung thick, heavy fringe into which were woven pieces of silver. His close-fitting leggings, the same dark blue as the shirt, were beaded and silver was woven into the fringed outseam.

Matt walked to where Zoe sat and held his hands down to her. "It's time now for you and me to dance."

"But I can't." She laid her hands in his and looked into the shadowed face. "I don't know how."

"I will teach you." He tugged her gently to her feet and led her to the center of the clearing. Both were silhouetted by the huge bonfire. When she stood facing him, he said, "I'll have them beat the drums slowly until you learn the steps. Just watch my feet." His hands clasped her waist on either side. "Do the same to me," he said.

150

The drums began to beat slowly as Matt had promised, and standing in place, he moved his feet while he showed her the steps. Then, when she had mastered them, he grinned at her and the two of them slowly moved around the circle. Matt nodded his head to the musicians, who began to beat the drums faster. He and Zoe danced around the circle, moving faster and faster until Zoe thought she was spinning through the heavens. Exhilarated, she threw back her head and laughed aloud.

For the moment she forgot civilization; she forgot that she was Weber Fielding's fiancée, or that she was one of Chandlerville's most esteemed citizens and its physician. She was a woman right now, Ma-ta-mon-yahu's woman, and she thrilled in the knowledge that she belonged to him, that soon she would be his wife.

For a moment Matt forgot, too. All bitterness and his quest for revenge was pushed aside; he was glad that Zoe was his woman, that she would become his wife tonight. She was indeed beautiful. He loved the way the firelight caught and glistened in her hair; he liked the sparkle in her fiery blue eyes. She belonged to him.

The music ended, but Zoe and Matt, united in their emotions, continued to stand in the circle. Only when the crowd quieted did Zoe realize Soaring Eagle had risen. At the gentle tap of Matt's hand on her elbow, she walked beside him to stand in front of the chief.

"Ma-ta-mon-yahu and this woman are now married. I say this is so according to the Law. She is no longer his slave but his wife. *To-quet*." Soaring Eagle walked to the huge fire and cut a morsel of meat from the roasted deer. He held it up toward the sky. "I thank you, Great Spirit, for providing us with food and shelter. Now I give it back to Mother Earth, because she has so freely provided for us." He then stooped, dug a hole, and buried the piece of meat.

Soaring Eagle remained in the center of the circle while Matt guided Zoe to her place. Then he returned to the fire to cut a huge slice of roasted venison, which he impaled on a sharp stick about four feet long. He brought it back to where Zoe sat. He stuck the handle end of the serving stick into the ground. From this he cut off two smaller servings of the venison and placed it in the thick piece of hardened hide that served as a plate. From a huge skin container, he poured honey into an indentation in the edge of the dish. He picked up the plate and moved to sit directly in front of Zoe.

"This is the deer I killed today," he said. "According to one of our marriage customs, the bridegroom must hunt and kill the animal that is to be used for the feasting after the wedding. This is honey for which we traded goods. Now I will feed you a bite; afterward, you will feed me." He dipped the meat into the honey and held it up to Zoe's mouth.

The odor of the cooked meat was tantalizing to Zoe. She hungrily bit into it, savoring the taste of venison and sweet honey. When she had eaten and swallowed, she picked up the other morsel, dipped it in honey, and fed it to Matt. She went to remove her hand, but he held her fingertips against his lips as he ate. A shiver of delight slid down her spine to settle in her stomach.

"Now we eat," Soaring Eagle said and returned to his seat amidst great shouting and laughter. The marriage was concluded, the feasting about to begin.

After Matt and Zoe finished eating, Matt laid the dish aside. "Now it's time for us to go," he said.

"Must we?" Zoe asked nervously, wanting to postpone the consummation of their marriage as long as possible. She glanced at the couples who were lining up in front of the fire. "I . . . would like to watch them dance some more."

"No," Matt told her quietly but firmly, "we must go now. It is expected of us. I must make you mine. We cannot put off the inevitable any longer."

He stood and reached down to clasp her hands, tugging her to her feet. In silence Zoe walked down the road beside him. Nothing in her education or career as a doctor had prepared her for marriage to a Comanche brave. She wasn't sure what to expect. Many of her women patients had told her the sexual experience was something the man enjoyed and the woman endured, but she knew her experience with Matt was going to be different. Last night his touch had enflamed her body. She had begged him for more than mere touches then.

When they reached the tepee, Matt pulled the door aside and Zoe entered. Moonlight streamed into the room from the smoke-hole to illuminate the dwelling. Stepping over her torn clothes that lay on the floor, she moved to the other side of the bed. Matt watched as she nervously pulled at the fringe on her dress. He smiled.

"I don't suppose you have any more of that medicinal whiskey in your medical supplies, do you?"

Zoe shook her head, her eyes going to the empty bottle. "Why?" Her voice trembled.

"I was going to propose a toast to my beautiful bride," he said and moved closer.

Zoe backed up. "Don't," she begged. "Don't do this to me."

153

"You seemed to like it well enough last night." Matt took another step. "You completely forgot your fiancé and were willing to consummate our relationship without the formality of a wedding ceremony."

"That was the liquor talking," Zoe said, "not me. That's one of the reasons why I don't drink; I don't hold my liquor very well."

"I prefer a woman who can't handle her whiskey. She's much more desirable. That's the way I want you tonight. It'll make it so much better for both of us, especially you." Matt reached out to catch her shoulders with his hands and to pull her against him. "I haven't been able to get you out of my mind," he whispered, laying his cheek against her head. "All I could think about was the sweet and wonderful way you fit into my arms."

Her own plight making her forget Matt's wound, Zoe brought her arms up between them and pushed against his chest. "No," she cried.

Matt winced from the pain, but his arms circled her to pin her body to his. "Yes," he murmured, his head lowering. "Don't fight me, Zoe. Enjoy it."

"Never," Zoe said, twisting and squirming. "If you make love to me, you'll have to force me."

"I won't use force," Matt said as he dropped to the pallet, bringing Zoe down with him. Using his body, he pinned her thrashing body to the pallet and stilled her head with his hand. "But I will make love to you." He sealed his promise with a kiss. Then he felt her tears against his face and lifted his head. He wiped them from her cheeks. "I'm sorry," he whispered, "but this is the way it's got to be."

"You may make love to me," Zoe said, hating herself because she was crying, "but you won't keep

154

me here. Weber will come and find me. When he does, he'll kill you." Matt moved slightly and Zoe freed her arms. Doubling up her fists, she beat them against his chest. "Do you hear me? He'll kill you."

"No, he won't," Matt replied, grabbing her fists in his hands to stop the painful barrage, "but now is not the time to discuss Weber Fielding. Now is the time for you and me to complete our wedding vows." His hand slid down her body to catch the hem of the buckskin.

"We . . . really . . . aren't married," Zoe whispered, his touch unnerving her. The warmth of his body fused through the layers of buckskin to remind her that he was a man, she a woman. The nearness of his body made her forget their quarrel.

"As married as we'll ever be." His fingers, pulling the dress up her body, brushed lightly against her flesh, up her ankles and then her calves, their touch a whisper behind her knees and on her thighs . . . over her head.

Zoe heard the rustle of the buckskin as it landed somewhere behind her, but her body was burning so, she could hardly think. She turned her head and lifted her face as Matt lowered his lips to hers for a long, warm kiss. Then his lips traveled over her face, sending tremors of delight through her body.

"Am I the first man to have lain with you?" Matt whispered, his lips lowering to her neck and collarbone, his tongue gently licking the vulnerable place where her pulse throbbed.

"I'm—very much—a free woman," Zoe said between breaths. She was glad that she hid in the soft, silvered shadows of the night and that he couldn't see her embarrassment to know that she

155

was a novice when it came to lovemaking. "Men don't wait until they are married to sleep with women. Why should a woman?"

Matt chuckled; he knew Zoe was an innocent hiding behind a façade of braggadocio. But he was unsure of her feelings for Weber, and for some reason he was disturbed by the thought of her wanting marriage with the man. His lips toyed with the throbbing pulse at the base of her throat. "How does your fiancé feel about such liberal views?" he asked as his hand slid up her thigh.

"Don't you dare bring up my fiancé!" Zoe cried, ashamed because she was feeling desire rather than revulsion, because her fury was directed at herself, not at him. Savagely her fists pummelled Matt's chest, and only when she heard him grunt his pain did she remember his wound. She ceased her fighting.

"According to your customs, we may be married, but you'll have to fight to take me," she promised. "I'll never come to you willingly."

Matt chuckled, his berry-scented breath warm against her heated flesh. His laughter was rich and mellow, a sedative to Zoe's ragged nerves. "Yes, my wife," he agreed, "you will fight and you will try to escape. That's your nature. But you will also love me. That I promise."

"No . . ." Zoe cried, but Matt's warm lips claimed her with an intensity that drained her of all energy. His hand cupped the back of her head, forcing her mouth against his; his tongue demanded entrance, craving the sweetness which he remembered all too well.

When he finally broke the kiss, he said, "I am glad you have never known another man."

Breathless from the emotion that blazed through

156

her body, but determined to keep him at bay, Zoe said, "Perhaps I have never made love to another man and you shall be the first to take my body, but you will never take my heart. That alone belongs to me and to the man whom I choose to love. You will make love to me, but you will never be my husband."

When Matt's lips captured hers in a hard demanding kiss, revenge was not his motive. His desire was to be one with Zoe Randolph, to make her his wife. She would never escape him; she would never think of Weber Fielding again. Matt shifted his weight and intertwined his leg with hers. He was half lying over her, his dark eyes smoldering with a naked desire that was hidden by the soft curtain of night.

"I'm your husband. Don't ever forget it." Matt moved so that Zoe could feel the hardness of his body.

His words echoed through her mind as his hands traveled tormentingly over her hips and up the sides of her torso, causing her to move sinuously beneath his weight. Her stomach was tied in knots; her body clamored for him. She was starved for his love. She lifted her lashes and gazed at Matt. Darkness veiled the intense passion that gleamed in the fevered depths of his brown eyes, but Zoe felt the intensity of his emotions, and they ignited feelings in her that she had never experienced before. Her breasts rose and fell with each shallow breath.

Matt's slow smile turned into beautiful warm laughter that was husky and resonant; its vitality filled the tepee. "Already, my wife, I have made you want me. And soon I will make you fall in love with me as well."

Matt spoke with a calmness and a certainty that

he was far from feeling. The more he was around Zoe Randolph Chandler, the less he knew or understood about her, and the more he wanted to know and understand.

"No," Zoe whispered, a tear sliding down her cheek, "you'll not make me love you, Ma-ta-mon-yahu. I won't give you that much power over me. You may possess me; you may arouse passion in me; but you'll never force me to love you. Love flourishes only when it is freely given."

He lifted a hand and gently grazed his knuckles across her cheeks and the bridge of her nose. Feeling the moisture on his fingers, he lowered her head and tenderly kissed the tear tracks. Then he sat up and rolled over to take off his moccasins and strip off his tunic.

He stood and Zoe watched his hands move across his flat stomach as he unfastened the belt, then drop to his sides as the buckskin garment slid down his legs. She had seen naked bodies before, many of them, but never had one stirred her senses as this one did. Under the circumstances, she should have been embarrassed, but she wasn't. The moonlight pouring through the smoke-hole sculpted him in silver. Muscles rippled from his chest to his feet. Zoe's eyes touched every feature discernible on his face, the chest, the thin, hard line of stomach.

Color and warmth flooded her face as she hastily dropped her eyes below his manhood to gaze at his muscular legs. He knelt beside her, naked body touching naked body. All her professionalism deserted her; her bravado vanished. Large tears ran down her face.

"Please," she begged.

Matt straightened his lean body along the length of hers, the bronzed beauty of his masculinity com-

158

plimenting the ivory whiteness of her femininity. His lips closed over hers, and his desperation made him less than gentle, frightening Zoe. She balled her hands and crammed them between their bodies, pushing against him, fighting. She would never willingly give in to him. She wriggled beneath him, but Matt would not be stopped. Neither her pleas nor the pain from his wound would stop him. For days he had wanted this woman; he had fought for her, and had almost been killed because of her, and he would take her now.

His long legs covered both of hers, and he stopped her movements; then he heaved his body up and over, his chest touching her breasts. He pulled her hands above her head, clamping her wrists together in an iron-banded fist, and brushed his lips down her throat, across the collarbone, back and forth in whisper-soft motions that teased and tormented her. His mouth, hot and moist, claimed the creamy whiteness of her breasts. His tongue sought the pink tip that had hardened with desire. When he felt her quiver beneath his caresses, he murmured. His other hand brushed over her breasts, down her stomach, around her navel. Then his fingers touched the downy-soft triangle.

Sensing her surrender, Matt loosened his grasp, and Zoe slipped her hands down, raking them through his thick hair. She arched until she felt him flatten his body against hers, the smoothness of his chest rubbing her nipples. She began to move her hips as she felt the hardness of his arousal. His fingers touched her in preparation. They slipped in and out of the moist portal, touching her most intimately.

Zoe unconsciously whimpered her pleasure, lifting her body to his when he removed his hand. She cried out to him, begging for his touch. Then he lowered the weight of his body over hers, his knee spreading her legs apart, his hand stroking the inner line of her thighs. She felt his hardness as it touched the gate of her maidenhood and she tensed. But his hands lovingly reassured her before he sheathed his masculinity in the warm folds of her femininity. He felt the tightness, the moist warmth. He sighed his joy.

Zoe gasped as she felt his bigness, the strangeness of him in her, and she began to cry. But Matt would have no tears. He caught her chin and pulled her face up, his lips touching hers, tasting the salt of her tears. He kissed her and moved within her; his hand kneaded her breast.

Zoe moved, trying to jerk her body from his touch, but instead found that the movement brought her pleasure that could not be denied. Her arms closed around his body and her fingers dug into his back. Locked in combative oneness, she clung to him and he moved faster and deeper, murmuring sweetly to her.

Matt brought her to the realm of womanhood, gently, caringly. He was in no hurry; time had ceased to exist. His hands, his lips—they spoke to her of his needs and his wants. They told her of his pleasure in touching her and in loving her. Unselfishly he gave, a new experience for him. His lovemaking was different from that which he had shared with any other woman. He made love to Zoe more softly, more gently; his every gesture was filled with meaning. Always before he had taken; he had given of himself physically, but never emotionally. Now his utmost thought was to give of himself as he had never done before. His making love to Zoe transcended mere sex and became a sharing.

At last Zoe tore her lips from Matt's, her head rolling to the side. Her body drew taut as she reached the pinnacle of fulfillment. In that moment of explosive joy, the moment when lovers become one, she gasped her pleasure, then moaned softly. Her body shuddered and her arms tightened around him. She turned her face to his shoulder, her teeth softly biting into his burning flesh, her fingers digging into him. She felt the small beads of moisture that had formed on Matt's hot skin, and she rubbed her cheek against the dampness of his chest.

"Oh, Ma-ta-mon-yahu," she softly cried, "what have we done?"

"Matt," he said quietly as he rolled to his side and gathered her into his arms. "Call me Matt."

"Do you realize what you've done to me?" she asked, still hiding her face against his chest.

"Yes," he answered, sitting up to brush damp tendrils of hair from her face. His lips covered her eyes, her cheeks, her lips with soft, quick caresses. "Do you?"

"Tell me," Zoe whispered.

"I've created a woman and made you my wife."

Zoe laughed quietly. "When we return to the white community, am I to call myself Mrs. Matt?"

"How about Mrs. Ma-ta-mon-yahu?" he said, laughing with her, the husky sound filling the te-pee. Eventually he picked Zoe's tiny hand up in his and intertwined them. "When we get back to the white community, I promise you a lovely last name."

"Shall we think up one together?"

"Someone else has already thought up one," Matt answered, his head turning so that they were gazing

161

into each other's shadowed faces. "The whites call me Matthew Barnabas."

Charles had named his first son after both grandfathers: Matthew because it meant "gift of God" and sounded quite similar to the Comanche name chosen by Soaring Eagle, and Barnabas because it was Uriah's middle name. But Uriah still hadn't been happy. Ever since Matt could remember, the old man had grumbled because he refused to be called Barnabas.

"Do you mind going by a name someone else gave you?" she asked compassionately, her heart truly going out to this man who was now her husband.

Matt chuckled. "You sound more like an Indian than you know. Indians get to choose their names, but most whites I know go by names given to them by someone else, namely their parents."

Zoe grinned. "That's not what I meant."

"I know," Matt murmured, enjoying the color that softened her cheeks. "I just wanted to tease you, and no, I don't mind going by Matt Barnabas. In fact, I rather like it. The man who gave it to me gave me a proud name, a name that suggested the duality of my heritage."

"Yet you have chosen to live with the Indians rather than the whites," Zoe murmured, snuggling up to him.

"No, as you've already surmised, I've spent many years of my life among the whites."

"Tell me something about yourself," Zoe said.

"Someday," Matt promised, "when we know each other better."

Zoe was disappointed with his answer, but at the same time content . . . during her career as a physician, she'd learned to measure people's veracity, and

162

she heard a ring of truth in Matt's promise. She suddenly bolted up to lean over him.

"Come back to Chandlerville with me," she suggested. "It's a growing city, Matt, and Weber and I are growing with it . . ." Her words trailed into an awkward silence.

Matt didn't say anything, but his facial muscles tightened and his mouth thinned. Before he met Zoe, his hatred for Fielding had diminished somewhat. Now it was intensifying, to a degree that was greater than before. He toppled her over as he stood and tied his breechclout about his waist. "I'm going to the creek to bathe," he said. "Do you want to come with me?" When Zoe nodded and stood, he grabbed a deerskin robe from the rope and threw it over her shoulders.

"Matt," Zoe said tentatively as they moved down the deserted road, "when are you going to take me home?"

"This is home," he said.

Zoe turned on him. She knew a moment ago she had blundered when she'd mentioned Weber's name. Matt had reverted to his primitive aloofness; once again he was hiding behind the implacable mask of Indianhood. "You were lying to me, weren't you? You don't intend to take me back to Chandlerville."

"In time."

Zoe caught his arm. "I don't have time. You've got to take me home so I can get a new guide and gather what few supplies I have left. I must get to Candaleria before we have a full-blown epidemic on our hands. Oh, Lord, I wish Bright Knife and his braves hadn't dumped my—"

Zoe's words trailed into silence, and her face brightened visibly. "Matt, you can help me! Take

163

me back to where he attacked my caravan and help me get my things; then you can take me to Mexico."

His hands on his hips, Matt studied her for a long while.

"Please," she begged.

Thinking about his grandfather's loan payment which was due in sixty days, he eventually said, "I have things I must do."

"Then take me as far as my supplies and I'll handle things from there. You don't have to go with me. I'll go by myself. Just show me the way."

She was serious! But he didn't dare let her start out for Mexico by herself; it was far too dangerous. "You don't stand a chance out there by yourself." Matt's voice softened perceptibly as his opinion of the woman rose.

"Neither do the people in Candaleria. I'm their only hope."

"How long are you going to stay?" he asked.

"As long as necessary," she answered.

He figured he'd have time to take care of the debt when they returned from Mexico. As close as Candaleria was to the border, they couldn't risk cholera sweeping through the border communities. "I'll take you," Matt said. "We'll leave early in the morning."

"What's going to happen to me when we return from Candaleria?" Zoe asked.

"We'll worry about that when the time comes."

Chapter 10

Bright Knife's promise of revenge and his report of scalp hunters in the area caused the ride from the Comanche village to Candaleria to be a swift one, with no overnight camping and infrequent stops for water and rest. Zoe had thought the route Digory Snyder had chosen was a dangerous one, but its danger didn't begin to compare with the one Matt now led them over. Many times, when the trail looked to be no more than a hair's-breadth wide and the fall straight down the side of a cliff into a bed of sharply pointed rock formations, Zoe closed her eyes and prayed that Dusty be sure-footed, shortsighted, and free of the fears of her mistress.

During the trip Zoe learned to eat and to relish pemmican — Indian bread, Matt had called it — a sausage-like mixture of pulverized dried fruits and nuts, meat, tallow, and marrow fat. Zoe particularly enjoyed eating pemmican when she could dip it into honey. Most of the time, however, they ate as they rode and the sweet had to be bypassed. Although the trip was grueling for Zoe and often frightening, she didn't complain about the hardships or voice her fears. If Matt and the three braves who accompanied them could travel without complaint, so could she. She was grateful that Matt had consented to bring her along.

Thoughts of Matt brought Zoe's head up and she skimmed the line of mules directly ahead of her to see him riding in front, setting the pace and selecting the path they would travel. Like all the Comanches she'd observed, Matt sat easily and gracefully on the horse; it seemed that man and beast were one, so synchronized were their movements. For the journey he wore his leather breeches, knee-high moccasins, and headband, but there the resemblance to Indian attire ceased. He wore a buff-colored linen shirt, and fastened around his waist was his gun belt with two holsters.

Three other braves journeyed with them; two rode with Zoe, Running Horse slightly ahead, Keen Eyes directly behind her; another followed, leading the string of mules. At the moment Zoe was irritated with Matt. She had asked that she be allowed to ride up front with him, so they could talk. Without any explanation, he'd positioned her in the center of the caravan.

She was also puzzled by Matt's attitude. He had made no sexual overtures to her since their wedding night. While she didn't want to become any more intimate with Matt than she already had—so she kept telling herself—she didn't like his avoiding her. No, she thought, he was doing worse than merely avoiding her . . . he was deliberately ignoring her, treating her as if she didn't exist. He was polite, as one is to a stranger, when she spoke to him, but otherwise he was reserved, almost aloof.

Matt didn't stop frequently, but even when he did, Zoe had little opportunity to talk with him. They drank water, ate, and tended to their personal needs, all of which had to be done briefly and in order. Zoe learned after the first stop that she had to do all these things before she indulged in conversation or the trip could become miserable. Matt was rather cold to her: it was as though someone had taken out his heart and replaced it with a stone.

Of course, she had to admit he wasn't being disagreeable. When she insisted on wearing her own clothes—a riding outfit she'd recently acquired at Halstead's, in preference to her buckskin dress, he'd given in with a shrug of indifference. After her eloquent argument, his easy acquiescence galled her. He'd gone farther by insisting that she twist her hair into a chignon and hide it beneath a hat he supplied for her. Although the hat had to be secured to her head because it was much too large, it protected her from the sun. This new, aloof Matt bothered Zoe and piqued her curiosity. He compelled her to get to know him better, to find out who and what he really was beneath that veneer of barbarism.

When she laughingly complained that the brown hat didn't match her blue skirt and blouse, he laid his hand against her cheek. "You may think a red face would match your clothes better, but I prefer the peaches-and-cream complexion, so wear the hat."

Zoe had reached up to lay her hand over Matt's, and for endless seconds they gazed into one another's eyes. Even now, Zoe could feel the warmth of his hand on her face and the intensity of his searching gaze. As she remembered the gentle abrasiveness of his callused knuckles on her cheeks, she trembled and desired him all over again.

The man to whom she was married was an enigma; Zoe didn't know that she would ever really understand him. She knew that in getting close to him she risked getting hurt deeply . . . even if she were willing to take the risk, she didn't know that he would permit her closeness. Sleeping with her had been simply a physical gratification for both of them, and anything beyond that fringed on the heart's territory. Zoe was certain that Matt had allowed no woman the liberty of stealing his heart. She wondered if either of them was ready for that. Grateful that Matt had found the hat for her, she pulled the brim lower over her face and squirmed into a more comfortable position in the saddle, staring straight ahead at the swaying broad shoulders of her Indian husband . . . her first lover.

On the fourth day of their journey, Matt and Zoe rode into the small village of Candaleria. A crowd was gathered around a vendor's *carreta,* a long, narrow cart that was parked in the middle of the plaza. When the people saw the riders approaching, they scattered in all directions. The women gathered the children and hastened into their houses to peer curiously out the windows. The vendor quickly piled his goods onto his cart and led the burro out of the plaza into a side street, peering over his shoulder at the visitors. The men, pulling their sombreros low over their faces, withdrew to the shadowed porches that lined the streets and stared at the strange caravan: the Indians, the big *Americano* in the leather trousers and moccasins, the *Americana* with the large hat that was tied to her

168

head and covered her face.

Having expected people to recognize her immediately and to come running with their joyous greetings as they had on each of her previous visits, Zoe was disappointed when they scattered. Matt, also puzzled about the reception, stopped the caravan and waited and watched. He was very much aware of the anxiety that permeated the air; he watched the *carreta* rumble out of sight. He felt the tension and saw it in the villagers' stances. They were expecting someone, but it wasn't Zoe. Eventually one of the men moved to the center of the plaza.

Cautiously he neared the riders until he was close enough to recognize Zoe beneath the flopping hat brim. His face burst into a smile, and he yelled, *"La doctora! Es la doctora!"*

As quickly as the plaza had emptied, it now filled with people who quickly swarmed around Zoe, their faces radiating love and devotion. All of them talked at once as they greeted her. A portly man dressed in white with a brightly colored poncho thrown over his shoulder bustled through the crowd. He swept the large sombrero off his head and bowed deeply. Blue-black hair belying his fifty years fell across his forehead.

"Señora doctora," Raul Mora said, the corners of his eyes crinkling in a friendly way, "we are so glad to see you." He moved closer, his hands circling Zoe's waist as he helped her dismount.

"What about the sickness?" Zoe asked anxiously, glancing around the plaza for signs of mourning.

Raul shook his head. "That was nothing but berries which we ate, *señora*. They made us sick. Once we stopped eating them, we recovered. We did not send word because we thought you were not coming. It has been so long."

"My caravan was attacked by Indians," she told him in her faulty Spanish, her gaze inadvertently going to Matt.

Raul's gaze swept from Zoe to the four Indians who rode with her. In particular he noticed Matt: the headband, a red cotton shirt tucked into his leather trousers, and moccasins. Around his waist were strapped two holsters and revolvers—American guns. The man may be an Indian, Raul decided, but he certainly wasn't an ordinary one. He must keep his eyes on this one.

"I am Raul Mora, *señor,*" the old man said in heavily accented English, "*alcalde* of Candaleria. I welcome you to our village."

"Thank you," Matt replied. "We didn't mean to scare off your vendor."

Raul shrugged. "You did not frighten him, señor. He was getting ready to leave when you arrived. We had already made our purchases, and he was in a hurry to get to another village before nightfall."

Matt knew Raul was lying, but he didn't know why. He was also aware of Raul's scrutiny, especially concerning his revolvers, and for the time being he would put the interest down as curiosity. A shrewd judge of character, Matt knew that Raul Mora was more than met the eye, more than the jolly little mayor of a sleepy Mexican village in northern Mexico. The portly body and the gentility were deceiving. The eyes weren't; they were alert and aware of all that was going on around him. Making a mental note to be wary of the Mexican mayor, Matt dismounted and moved to Zoe's side, his hand resting lightly on her shoulder, a possessive touch that did not go unobserved by Raul.

170

"This is—" Zoe said, only to be interrupted by Matt.

"I am her husband," he said in fluent Spanish. "Matt Barnabas."

Raul was surprised on two counts—Matt was Zoe's husband, and he spoke fluent Spanish. Most Indians of the Southwest did, but somehow Raul didn't think of Matt as an Indian. Quickly the *alcalde* regained his aplomb and settled into his role as jolly caretaker of the village. He threw back his head and laughed heartily. "Señor Barnabas, you speak my language much better than I speak yours."

"I am Comanche," he said. "We had to learn Spanish many hundreds of years ago, *señor,* in order to trade with your people."

"And to pilfer our people," Raul added.

Matt smiled. "That goes two ways, does it not?"

"It does," the *alcalde* said, briskly rubbing his hands together and dismissing the subject. His gaze swung back to Zoe and he rolled his eyes. "And you, *señora,* are indeed a fortunate woman to have met and married such a man as Señor Barnabas."

"Yes, I know," Zoe murmured, though only Matt could hear her words.

"Come and see what we have for you." Raul flopped his hat on his head, waved one hand across the plaza, and caught Zoe's shoulder with the other one, giving it a tug. Matt walked on the other side of Zoe; the townspeople followed behind, murmuring and giggling. When they stopped, Raul pointed at a newly constructed adobe building.

"This, Señora Zoe, is for you."

Tears pricked Zoe's eyes as she gazed at the buff-colored building and the wooden sign on which were engraved the words *"La Officina de Doctora."* The alcalde pushed open the door and walked into the first of two large rooms.

"Come, come," he said, flinging open the window shutters. "See your office and your home. This is yours while you are in Candaleria."

Dazed, Zoe walked into the room, blinking as her eyes grew accustomed to the cool, shaded interior. She took her hat off and laid it on the table. "It's lovely," she whispered.

Matt stood in the door and watched. At the moment his interest wasn't the house; it was Zoe. She was a beautiful woman, even with her hair pulled into a severe chignon on the top of her head. He wanted to unpin her hair so that it flowed loosely down her back, so that it shimmered like gold in the sunlight. He wanted to take her into his arms and make love to her—to satiate a hunger deep within his body, a hunger that only she could fulfill.

Zoe ran her fingers lightly over the crude shelves that had been constructed in the thick walls, the large table in the center of the room, and the straw-bottomed chairs. She looked at the fireplace built into the corner. When she lifted her hand and brushed the tears from her cheeks, Matt knew how touched she was by the gift.

She was a mystery to him and was becoming more inscrutable with each passing day. After having made love to her, he knew that Zoe was not the superficial or greedy and grasping woman that he had first imagined. He quickly realized she was a woman to whom he could easily open his heart. Because Zoe was different, he had kept his distance: Matt Chandler wasn't ready to offer his

172

heart to anyone.

When Zoe confessed that Weber Fielding was her fiancé, Matt had instantly seen a way to repay the man who had wronged him so many years ago and he had instantly transferred all his hatred and bitterness to the woman. He assumed that she was made from the same mold as her fiancé. Matt had married her to get even with Fielding, not to become emotionally involved with her. Yet after having made love to her only once, that was exactly what was happening: he found himself caring about her, and in a game of revenge, concern constituted a weakness, a flaw that Matt could ill afford.

Her desire to come to Mexico at her own expense to treat the villagers hadn't really fazed him, but her reaction—her heartfelt appreciation at the people's having built this crude two-room hut for her—touched Matt like nothing else could, and he didn't want to be touched. Had he not been so puzzled about Zoe, he would have been irritated with himself. He could only wonder at her being engaged to a man like Weber Fielding.

Yet Matt knew she was a part of the scheme to get his property, to take it away from the Comanches.

"Oh, Raul," Zoe said, her riding skirt flaring around her legs as she turned. Tears blurred her vision. "I can't thank all of you enough. This is truly the most lovely gift I have ever received. I have never had an office to compare with this one."

"We have given you our best," the *alcalde* said. "You deserve that and much, much more, señora."

"That she does," Matt added quietly.

Zoe glanced at the door to see him standing there, his arms folded across his chest. A strange smile touched the corners of his lips, but it really wasn't a smile, Zoe thought. It was warm, not cold, not mocking. She wondered what Matt was thinking, and although she searched his face, she couldn't tell. His expression was inscrutable; his eyes hooded. After lingering a minute on the beauty of his sensual lips and enigmatic smile, she lowered her gaze to the lean, muscular legs that fit so snugly into the leather britches.

Memories rushed forward to wash her in warmth and happiness . . . and a little self-consciousness. She remembered the joy of his ultimate touch. But ever since that first night, he hadn't touched her, hadn't seemed to want to. She remembered the dull ache he'd left her with. Without him, she would no longer be complete. He had stirred a hunger within her that only he could sate. Perhaps she hadn't satisfied him; perhaps she hadn't roused that same hunger within him.

"And this second room, señora," Raul said, breaking the delicate spell by which Zoe was bound to Matt. "It is beautiful, yes?"

Zoe's eyes lifted and she stared once again into Matt's face. As if he understood her thoughts, he really smiled and winked. His hand rose; the tips of his fingers touched those lips that had brought her so much pleasure, and he flung her a kiss. Zoe's blood raced, her heartbeat quickened, and color swiftly rose to her cheeks. Flustered, she turned and followed Raul.

Still smiling, Matt watched her exit in amusement, but he didn't follow. Instead, he turned and walked outside to join the Comanche braves who had traveled with him. Running Horse had chosen to come with Matt; the others had come because of

174

their loyalty to Running Horse.

"You will stay in the house with your woman?" Running Horse asked, respecting Matt's wish that he not speak English in front of Zoe. When Matt nodded, the brave said, "We do not wish to stay in the white man's village. We will return to the creek and make camp there. How many suns will we wait for you?"

"We shall leave on the morning of the seventh sun," Matt answered as he studied the villagers who ambled back and forth across the plaza. Their eyes were constantly darting about, as if they were expecting someone or something to happen. Something was afoot; Matt wondered what.

"What is wrong, Ma-ta-mon-yahu?" Running Horse asked.

"I'm not sure," Matt drawled. "The people here are uneasy about something."

"Do you wish us to remain here with you?"

"No," Matt answered, "I'm not worried about me or Zoe. I'm concerned about the villagers." He shook his head as if to dispel the anxiety. "Let's get those mules unloaded and you can take them to camp with you."

Inside the house Raul was talking to Zoe, but she was too caught up in her own thoughts to hear him. She was irritated that she responded to Matt as she did . . . as if she were a young girl falling in love for the first time. After all, she was a grown woman, twenty-nine years old, well past the age of blushing and embarrassment. But when she was around Matt, she forgot her age, her sophistication, and her poise. She was breathless and giddy, her heart aflutter, her tummy full of butterflies. She did feel as if she were a young girl falling in love for the first time!

"Señora! Señora!"

Raul's call jarred Zoe from her ruminations. With a start she turned to look at him.

"You like your house, yes?"

A warm smile filled Zoe's face and eyes. "Yes," she replied, "I like my house, yes."

A fireplace was in one corner and shelves were built into nearly all the walls. The furnishingly were simple: a wooden cabinet for storage, a dining table with two benches, and a double bed. Zoe's body turned hot as she thought of her and Matt sleeping in the same bed . . . of their making love in that bed. She quickly turned her head, hoping her thoughts didn't show in her face for the *alcalde* to read. In a niche beside the cabinet was a large clay water jug, and wood was stacked by the fireplace. Sitting on each side were the black iron cooking utensils.

The only noise in the room was the creak of Raul's stiff leather sandals as he moved across the tiled floor to the cabinet. He opened the doors and picked up a clay bowl. "Your dishes, señora. I gave them to you. My wife made them herself."

Raul's confession brought tears to her eyes. She wanted to stop crying, but she couldn't. When she had begun coming to Candaleria, she knew the people could not afford to pay for her services. She had come because she loved them and wanted to help them. She had never dreamed that they would do this for her. She moved to where Raul stood and picked up a piece of pottery to hold it lovingly in her hands and to study the vivid design.

"These were the last pieces of pottery Maria made," he said, a sad note in his voice, "before she

176

died." When Zoe's face jerked up and she opened her mouth to protest the gift, Raul shook his head. "I wanted you to have them."

"I can't accept all this," Zoe sniffed. "Really, I can't."

"Then, señora," Raul returned calmly, unconsciously drawing up to his full height, "we cannot accept your services any longer."

Surprised and at the same time disappointed, Zoe stared at him blankly.

"By not allowing us to pay you, you take our integrity away from us," he explained gently. "I will not permit you to do this to my people."

Zoe returned the dish to the shelf and threw her arms around the old man, hugging him tightly and sniffing into his chest. "I didn't mean to offend you, Señor Mora. I gratefully accept the house and office."

"There, there," he said, his pudgy hands patting her shoulders, "I take no offense."

Laughing, Zoe pulled out of his arms and walked to the table to pick up one of the dishcloths to wipe her face. "You know I didn't come for the money."

"*Sí*," he said, "we know."

"By the way," she said, "How is Miguelito? I didn't see him among the children."

At the mention of his only grandson, the old man's face was wreathed in a smile and he nodded his head. "Miguelito is doing *muy bien*, señora. Very good indeed." He measured from the ground with his hand. "He is a tall boy for his nine years. My friends say he looks like me."

"He does," Zoe softly agreed. "I suppose I will see him later."

Raul's eyes twinkled. "Before then, señora. As soon as he learns that you are here, he'll be coming."

"Well," Zoe said, returning to the front room, "I need to get my supplies put away and open my office."

"And I must see about the fiesta," Raul said, his sandals squeaking as he walked to the front door. "Your coming is always an occasion for joy for us of Candaleria."

"Señora! Señora!" a child's voice rang out.

Zoe moved to the door to see a boy racing down the street, one hand filled with a bouquet of wild flowers, the other holding the brim of his sombrero so it wouldn't fly off his head. "Miguelito," she called, bending down and throwing open her arms, "I wondered where you were."

The nine-year-old threw himself into Zoe's arms, his sombrero falling off when his head hit her shoulder. His arms clasped her. "I picked these for you," he said between breaths, pulling back and holding out a flower. "I wanted the house to look pretty for you."

"Thank you, Miguelito." Taking the flowers, Zoe walked into the kitchen and found a vase, which she filled with water. When she set the flowers in the center of the table, she arranged them, then stepped back to say, "There, how does that look?"

"*Muy bonita.*" Miguelito nodded his head and skipped through the house. "Now I will help you set up your office." When he stood outside, he noticed the Indians unpacking the mules. He saw Matt and his eyes widened. His eyes caught and locked to the revolvers. Slowly he inched his way to Raul, and tugging on his britches' leg, asked, "Who is this man, Grandfather?"

"This is Matt Barnabas," Zoe answered. "My husband."

"Oh." The word was fraught with disappointment. The child moved closer to Matt and studied the revolvers a while longer before he finally lifted his face. "I thought perhaps you had come to help the Juaristas in their fight with the foreign emperor."

"Miguelito!" Raul exclaimed.

Matt, watching Raul twist the fringe of his poncho nervously, merely smiled and shook his head. The boy's comment and the old man's reaction to it confirmed Matt's suspicion that the villagers were tense and expectant, perhaps frightened. All this anxiety had something to do with the civil strife in Mexico.

"I am going to join the Juaristas," the boy added with a slight tilt of his chin. "I shall get me a gun and drive the French out of our country."

"Miguelito!" Raul rushed across the room and laid his hand on the boy's shoulder. He smiled apologetically. "Do not mind my grandson, señor. He is a small boy and does not voice the opinions of other people in the village. He hears talk among the young and foolish ones who have refused to accept our new government."

Matt saw Raul's fingers dig into Miguelito's shoulders. "If your grandson is on the side of the Juaristas, Señor Mora, I admire him. I and most Americans admire Benito Juarez and recognize him as the true President of Mexico. I do not respect the French for what they have done to your country."

Briefly the old man's eyes met Matt's to flash his

179

gratitude and appreciation; he nodded. "Miguelito and I will be leaving now. We have much to do. Tonight we have a fiesta in honor of *la doctora.*"

Miguelito said, "Now that you have a husband, señora, you will have no need of my services?"

Zoe bent down and placed an arm around the sagging shoulders. Before she could console him, Matt said, "I am the doctor's husband, not her assistant, Miguelito. She will always need a fine young man like you to gather herbs for her." Matt's head lifted and his eyes caught Zoe's. "I have other duties I perform for *la doctora.*"

Matt's meaning was lost on the child, but not on Zoe. As she stared over the child's head into Matt's sultry brown eyes, she felt limp. Had Matt taken her into his arms to make love to her at the moment, she would offer no resistance. Where this man was concerned, she seemed to have no will of her own. She seemed to want no other will but his.

Totally oblivious to the unspoken messages flashing between Zoe and Matt, Miguelito grinned and reached up to push a shock of black hair out of his eyes. "Until I am old enough to fight with the Juaristas, I will gather herbs for *la doctora.* I will go now." He caught his grandfather by the hand and the two of them left.

Refusing to acknowledge the silent words she and Matt had spoken, Zoe watched Miguelito and his grandfather as they walked down the dusty road. "Aren't they wonderful?" she asked, then turned. "Now you can see why I had to get down here. They need me."

For the time being, Matt also ignored the moment they had shared. "Yes," he answered, "I understand why you had to come."

Smiling, he stepped nearer to tuck an errant curl behind her ear, his finger trailing across a sprinkling of freckles on her cheeks. He only wished he understood her motives better. The more he knew about Zoe, the more disconcerting her alliance with a man like Fielding was. Reluctantly, Matt dropped his hand. If he didn't put some distance between them, he knew that he would take her to bed right now. This irritated Matt; he didn't like to be guided by emotions, especially the baser ones.

He moved to the door and speaking in Comanche, ordered the three braves to bring the provisions inside the house. Once the food was stacked on the floor, the braves slipped out of town to a nearby creek where they were to set up camp.

"Tell me where to put these," Matt grunted, holding several boxes in his arms.

"Over there." Zoe pointed to one of the walls. "Put the larger boxes on the bottom shelves, nearest the door, and the others on the top."

"How long have you been coming to Candaleria?" Matt carefully threaded his way among the supplies to the farthest shelf.

"My first visit was six months ago," Zoe replied, sorting the boxes. "I came with my father."

"Before that?"

"Are we talking to pass the time of day?" Zoe asked. "Or are you really interested?"

"When you've been around me for a while, you'll learn that I never spend my time in idle talk." He turned from the shelf to look directly into her frank blue eyes. "You're my wife. I'm interested in everything about you, including your past."

"I'm not your wife!"

Matt shrugged. "What would you prefer I call

181

you? My lover? My mistress? Or my whore?"

Zoe's face blanched until it was a whiter than the clouds that dotted the sky. "You're despicable," she whispered. "You flagrantly used those terms to remind me of my status—a status that *you* imposed on me."

Matt's hands went to his hips. "No," he replied in the same soft tone Zoe had used, "I called you my wife, the most honorable term I could think of, the most honorable position a Comanche woman can attain. You're the one who refuses the position which I have given you."

"A matter in which I had no choice," Zoe exclaimed bitterly.

"But you did enjoy the results." A teasing grin tugged Matt's lips when color quickly returned to Zoe's face.

"You're despicable!"

"Not really," Matt said. "In time you'll find me quite lovable."

"I might find you many things," Zoe drawled, "but never lovable."

Matt's grin widened and his eyes twinkled with sheer devilment. "I wouldn't count on that, my dear wife. I really wouldn't."

With a sinking feeling that he was telling the truth, Zoe stared at him.

Abruptly he turned. "Now, tell me all about yourself."

Zoe was both relieved and disappointed that he broke the spell that bound them together. Feeling bereft, she stood for a moment, her hands hanging limply at her side. Matt never seemed to operate on an emotional level; he could swing from the passionate lover to the detached bystander so easily

. . . as easily as he manipulated her emotions. This infuriated Zoe; it also frightened her. She must never let him know how much power he held over her.

In an effort to appear as blasé as he, Zoe returned to the unpacking of her supplies. "Before I came to Chandlerville, I lived in Charleston, South Carolina with my mother. We were happy until the war came." Taking the blue and brown bottles out of the container, she lined then meticulously along the table. "I always wanted to be a physician," she said musingly. "I always looked forward to Papa's visits because he would talk to me about being a doctor, about his patients, the medicines, the cures, and new cures waiting to be discovered."

"You didn't live with your father?"

"No," Zoe answered, wiping her hands down the sides of her skirt. "He loved the frontier and Mama didn't. When they first married, Mama joined him in Texas, but she couldn't take the rough life. She was a city girl." A lump formed in Zoe's throat. "If she had loved the frontier like Papa, she might have been alive today. Our home in Charleston was destroyed during the war. Mama died trying to save her heirlooms—things that had been handed down since her first ancestor set foot on American soil. I ran in after Mama to save her, but fire was eating up our home. Part of the roof fell in, separating me from her. One of our slaves saved me. I didn't want to live after that. If only I had been quicker! If only—"

Matt moved to where she stood to cap her shoulders with his hands. He understood her grief. How often did those same words haunt him?

"I'm sorry," he whispered, pulling her shoulders

183

against his chest, and laying his face on the crown of her head.

Grateful for his strength, Zoe rested against him. "I lived, but by the time my father arrived, all the fight had gone from me. But he didn't give up. He nursed me and each day told me about the beauty of his latest discovery, Chandlerville. He had been here for the past four years and loved it; he wanted me to come practice with him. He said women were accepted here. So we packed what few belongings I had and headed west. I've been here ever since."

She lifted her face, and without either of them being aware of what was happening, Matt caught her in his arms. He lowered his head to kiss her forehead down to the tip of her nose, then her mouth, softly, briefly. He raised his lips from hers and gazed into her face.

"Tell me about *you*," she whispered, easily losing herself in the warm, sultry depths of his brown eyes.

"What's there to know?" he parried.

"Who are you, Matt?" she responded, her hand coming up to rest against his cheek. "What are you?"

Matt cared enough about Zoe that a part of him wanted to answer her questions, but he knew his purpose — already it seemed so far away — would not be served if he revealed his identity to her. Yet his quest for revenge seemed to be slipping more and more into obscurity, his feelings for Zoe quickly overriding them.

Eventually he said, "My past is not a pretty one. I'm afraid that if I were to tell you all about me, you'd have cause to feel worse about me than you do now."

184

"What could be so bad in your past that would affect me?" Zoe questioned. When Matt didn't answer, she ventured, "Are you an outlaw of some kind?"

"There are those who have branded me an outlaw."

Something in the quiet admission sounded a warning in Zoe's mind. "A . . . a murderer?" she guessed.

"I promised you that when you got to know me better, I would tell you all about myself. Wait until then," Matt asked.

"I'll wait until then for a full confession," Zoe said, "but I must know if you're a murderer."

"No," Matt answered, "I'm not, but until I prove my innocence, many will brand me as one."

"Something to do with your being part-Indian."

"Something to do with my being part-Indian." He moved his body slightly, brushing his chest against the gentle swell of her breasts, and his head lowered to hers.

"Please don't," she whispered, knowing she didn't have the strength to fight him, knowing that it little mattered to her body if he were a murderer or not.

"You're asking the impossible." Matt's voice was deep and husky. "One taste of your body isn't going to be enough."

"We're so different, Matt. I'm a white woman, a doctor, and I'm needed in Chandlerville. I'll never fit into your Indian way of life. Let me return to what I know; let me return to my fiancé. We'll forget that we ever met. I'll never tell a soul . . . I promise." Zoe was unable to comprehend her own emotions; they were fickle, vacillating from one extreme to the other. One minute she was burning up in her desire to have him, the next she was convincing herself and him that they were incompatible.

A flicker of tender amusement crossed Matt's face. "Can you forget what happened between us?" he asked in a low, husky whisper, his hand descending slowly, tormentingly down her back to cup her buttocks. He gently kneaded them and tugged her closer to his hard frame. He moved closer, his legs brushing hers. As he lowered his head, Zoe turned her face away, but it didn't stop him from kissing the soft, sensitive spot beneath her earlobe. He felt her body tremble and traced the shell-like delicacy of her ear. "Can you forget?"

Zoe's hands slid from his chest to his biceps; they were rock-hard. The entire length of him was rock-hard. The warmth of his breath sent tingles all through her highly sensitized body. His fingers gently hooked beneath her chin and he raised her face.

"I think not," he whispered, irritated because he knew that he would never forget her touch. "Your fiancé certainly won't forget. He may marry you, but every time he holds you in his arms, he'll wonder about your Indian lover. He'll think you're as filthy as the vermin you once slept with."

Zoe kicked Matt, and when he loosened his grip, she twisted out of his arms. Pulling her hand back, she gave vent to the frustration that ran rampant through her and slapped him so hard his head jerked to the side. She saw the imprint of her hand as it whitened on his bronzed features, but felt no regret at all.

"You're not worthy of being called a man!"

His hand going to his face, Matt stared at her.

186

Never had he seen her face so white or her eyes so enormous with hurt.

"Don't you ever touch me again!"

Chapter 11

"Señora, come quickly." A woman, unaware of the tension that saturated the room, rushed into Zoe's office. "My daughter is in much pain, but the baby does not come!"

For a second longer Zoe stared angrily at Matt. Then, pushing her own feelings aside, she grabbed her satchel from the table and rushed after the woman, and Matt followed. When they arrived at a small adobe hut several roads from the plaza, Zoe entered the room to find the young girl, huge with child, lying on a pallet in the corner. She was in the last stages of labor. An examination proved that she wasn't dilating.

"Get me a basin of water and a washcloth," Zoe ordered Matt. "Then put more water on to boil." Sitting down beside the girl, Zoe brushed the wet hair from her forehead; then she picked up a cloth and wiped the perspiration from her face. "What is your name?" she asked in her broken Spanish.

"Consuelo," the girl replied.

Zoe laid the cloth aside and caught the girls' hands in hers. Smiling, she said, "Now we're going to get down to business and have that baby, yes?"

The girl smiled weakly. "*Sí*, señora *doctora*." A contraction began, and Consuelo screamed, her hands clamping painfully around Zoe's.

Zoe waited until the contraction had subsided and the girl relaxed to say, "You are going to continue to have your contractions, Consuelo, but you will no longer feel the pains. It's going to take us a little while to get the baby out because it's turned the wrong way." Quietly Zoe explained the baby's breech position. "Now, to save both of you, you must do what I say. I want you to relax and breathe in deeply."

Squatting in front of the fireplace, where he set a pot of water over the flame, Matt listened as Zoe calmed the girl and put her under hypnosis. He marveled at her skill as she continued to reassure Consuelo while she delivered the baby.

"Clean the table with hot water," she said, "and put a cloth over it. Lay my instruments out and get me a basin of clean water, so I can wash my hands."

Matt quietly did as she said.

Once her hands were clean and dried, she held them out and said, "Tie the apron around me, please." Completely in command of the situation, confident in her ability to deliver the baby, she moved to where Consuelo lay. She slit the tender skin below the vagina to open the birth track and to keep the baby from tearing the girl apart when it came.

Matt stood at her side, his eyes on her face. When her forehead beaded with perspiration, he picked up a washcloth and dabbed at it. He read her expression and watched the movements of her eyes so that he knew when she wanted something and was ready to get it the minute she asked for it. Finally the baby came.

"Here he is!" Zoe exclaimed, holding the squalling boy in the air. The grandmother rushed forward to take the baby as soon as Zoe cut and tied the umbilical cord. The baby taken care of, Zoe quickly sutured Consuelo, then cleaned up herself. Now she sat down on the bed and brought the new mother out from under hypnosis to full consciousness.

"You had a lovely baby boy," Zoe said. "He's healthy and fine. And you're going to be fine also. You will heal quickly if you take care of yourself."

The grandmother, having cleaned and dressed the baby, laid it in Consuelo's arms.

Zoe smiled down at mother and child. "His papa will be proud of him," she said.

"*Si*?" Consuelo murmured, hugging her baby close, kissing the thick black hair.

"Where is your husband?" Zoe asked, wondering why the proud papa wasn't here with his wife.

"Who?" Consuelo asked.

"Your husband," Zoe said, aware of the quick glance between mother and daughter as the older woman slipped into the adjoining room.

"He's—he's out working," Consuelo replied, nervously fidgeting with the baby's blanket. "As soon as he receives word that Manuelito has been born, he'll be home."

"I'm sure he will," Zoe said and laughed when Manuelito began to nuzzle his mother's breast. "Now I will go. I'll be back to check on you tomorrow."

"Señora"— the woman called from the door "one *momento, por favor*. I have something for you."

She entered the room, a skirt and blouse draped over her arm. "I give this to you for helping Consuelo bring her little boy into the world."

"Señora," Zoe breathed, looking at the brightly colored floral skirt and the white blouse, "this is beautiful."

The woman smiled proudly. "Consuelo and I made it for you. You will wear it to the fiesta, yes?"

"Oh, yes," Zoe promised, "I will." She hugged the woman. "Thank you so much."

Matt carried the satchel, and Zoe her skirt and blouse as they left the house. Now that her work was finished, Zoe thought about the argument she and Matt had earlier and determined that she would keep him at bay. Her caring for him placed her in an extremely vulnerable position, and the more she was around him, the more she seemed to care.

"Why are you so quiet?" Matt asked, reaching down to catch her hand in his.

Zoe strove for a casualness she was far from feeling when she moved away from him. "I must keep Consuelo's stitches as dry as I can so that she'll heal without an infection." Zoe shook her head sadly. "I don't have enough money to buy all the medicines that I need."

"Don't worry about it," Matt said. "Tomorrow I'll give you some herbs that will help her heal quickly."

Zoe cut her eyes at him and asked dryly, "Are you a medicine man also?"

Matt chuckled. "Out of necessity, we Indians are taught to be, but I'm not as much a medicine man as you are a medicine woman. The way you handled Consuelo's hysteria today was marvelous."

"Thanks," Zoe murmured coolly, refusing to allow herself to warm under the praise.

"Indians have used the trance method for years. How did you know about it?"

"A seminar I attended at Harvard," Zoe answered. "We were taught to use mesmerism as an anesthesia. Also, while the patient is mesmerized, we reassure them about their condition and their ability to heal quickly and painlessly. We saw an example of this in Boston, and it really worked. I was intrigued by the entire method, but most people were skeptical. No telling how many years it'll be before the medical profession accepts and endorses mesmerism . . . if ever."

"Someday they will," Matt assured her. "But until then, how about my sharing my knowledge of herbs with you?"

"I'd like that," Zoe answered. "I wondered what plants and roots Buffalo Woman was using when she mixed the salve to put on my face."

Zoe and Matt didn't notice the group of men gathered at the end of the road until they were almost upon them. Before Zoe could speak, the villagers scattered in several different direction. Zoe was surprised. During all the times she'd been to Candaleria, she'd never noticed the people being so skittish of strangers before. They hadn't been frightened of her; perhaps they were afraid of Matt and the Comanches.

She reached up to push a strand of hair out of her face. "I wonder what's wrong," she said. "Everyone seems so jumpy."

Matt nodded; he'd noticed it, too. "Civil strife just before a war," he explained. "It's like that when a nation is fighting against a foreign government that has been imposed upon them. I have a feeling that the villagers are really Juaristas at heart, but are forced to profess their allegiance to Maximilian. They're not sure whose side we're on, and they aren't going to take a chance that we could report them to the authorities."

Although she knew of no reason why they should trust her, Zoe was disappointed that they didn't. "I suppose so," she agreed.

Then they turned the corner and entered the plaza. Zoe's face brightened when she saw paper streamers and *piñatas* decorating the porticos. In the middle of the square, children were piling wood for a huge bonfire, and the other women were preparing the food. Delicious odors permeated the air, making Zoe's mouth water. The younger girls had already hurried home to change into their most festive clothes. Consuelo and the Juaristas were forgotten as the carnival spirit snared Zoe.

Grinning at Matt, she said, "An Indian feast five nights ago and a Mexican fiesta tonight. It sounds exciting, doesn't it?"

Before Matt could answer, he heard the rumble of approaching horses and saw troops entering the plaza from the southern side—from the interior of Mexico. Zoe stopped, stared at the riders, then turned her face to Matt in surprise.

"The French," he said. "This may be why the people have been so nervous. Maybe they knew about the visit."

"Why would the French be this far north?" Zoe asked.

"They're after the Juraristas," Matt answered softly. "If the French are here, that must mean the

193

Juaristas are also."

Slowly the two of them walked down one side of the plaza. When they reached the cantina, Raul, adjusting his sombrero with one hand and his poncho with the other, walked out and joined them. Here the three awaited the soldiers. The officer in charge, a young man resplendent in his uniform, drew abreast of Raul to stop his horse and dismount.

"I'm Captain Louis Duprees," he said briskly in Spanish. "I'm looking for the *alcalde* of this village."

The old man stepped forward. "I, Raul Mora, am the *alcalde* of Candaleria, señor."

"Well, Señor *Alcalde,* tell me where El Pantero is."

Raul lifted his brows in question and said, "Señor, I do not know of such a one called El Pantero; therefore, I cannot tell you where he is."

The officer laughed shortly. "Don't lie to me, old man. You—" his wave included the entire village "—all of you know who El Pantero is, and you know where he is. Even I, Louis Duprees, know that he's coming to your village to pick up a shipment of guns from the American gun smugglers."

"I do not know that, señor," Raul replied innocently.

Duprees stared at the *alcalde* for a long time before he said, "I want my soldiers quartered and the horses tended to. Surely you know how to do that."

"*Sí,*" Raul replied.

The captain turned to his subordinate officer and spoke to him in French. After the Lieutenant saluted and departed, the captain returned his attention to the three standing in front of him. The *alcalde* he quickly discounted as being of no importance; he was too old. The other man was truly a barbarian, he thought, eyeing Matt suspiciously. He was dressed like an Indian, but was carrying American weapons. Excitement winged through Duprees. Could this be El Pantero? If so, and if he were to arrest him, he must move cautiously.

"These are not your villagers," Duprees said to Raul.

Before the *alcalde* answered, Matt said in Spanish, "No, we're not villagers. We're Americans."

Duprees effectively hid his surprise when Matt answered and smiled coldly. "You won't mind telling me, then, señor, what you are doing here in Candaleria?"

"Am I under arrest?" Matt asked.

"Not yet."

"Then I mind." Out of the corner of his eye, Matt saw Raul playing nervously with the fringe of his poncho.

The Frenchman inhaled deeply and his nostrils flared. He hated the vulgarity of peasants and commoners; he despised their audacity. He would despise this man even more if he learned that he was El Pantero. That was the one Juarista he wanted to apprehend and execute himself. A merry chase the panther had led him on, but one that was soon to be over.

"You will tell me nevertheless, or you will find yourself under arrest," Louis said in a low voice.

Raul stepped forward and hastily interjected, "La señora, she is a doctor. She comes to our village twice a year to bring us medical supplies and to treat those who are ill."

195

The captain turned to Zoe, and his anger seemed to vaporize immediately. The dark eyes warmed and blatantly swept the length of her body. "Ah, mademoiselle," he said, "may I present myself?"

"You already have," Matt retorted, insinuating himself between Zoe and the young Frenchman. "I'm Matt Barnabas. This is my wife, Zoe."

Smiling at Matt's jealousy, Zoe brushed past him to extend her hand in greeting to the French officer. In her softest and most southern accent, she drawled, "I'm glad to make your acquaintance, Captain Duprees."

Louis' gaze returned to Zoe. He couldn't understand why a beautiful woman would marry such an uncouth man. Taking her hand, Louis flourished a deep bow and brushed the top of her hand with his mouth. "The pleasure is all mine, madame."

Zoe suppressed the grin that threatened when Matt's mouth thinned in anger. She fluttered her eyes and said, "I've visited Mexico often, but this is the first time I've seen Emperor Maximilian's troops, about which I've heard so much."

Louis flashed Zoe a brilliant smile, but his eyes were still suspicious. "Thank you, madame," he said. "I hope what you heard was good."

"Oh, yes," Zoe hastened to assure him, "we southerners are grateful that the Emperor allowed us political asylum after the terrible War between the States."

"Indeed, madame, many of your countrymen are pouring into our country," Louis said. "Rumor has it that Confederate General Shelby and five hundred of his men are marching to Mexico City right now to offer their services to the Emperor." He laughed and waved his fingers through the air. "Of course, we do not need their help. We have enough men to curtail these rebellious Mexicans who call themselves the Juaristas."

"Of course you do," Zoe purred, aware of Matt's thunderous countenance.

The longer Zoe talked to Duprees, the angrier Matt became. Maybe she wanted to forget what had happened between them; he couldn't. Nor could he understand this violent reaction. He'd gone through the entire War between the States without getting so violently angry. He disliked Duprees, but he'd disliked people before without his waging a private war with them. This young pup galled him. The way he was ogling Zoe angered Matt; the way she was flirting infuriated him.

"What is an officer such as you doing out here in the northernmost part of the province?" Zoe affected her most innocent expression.

"Juaristas, madame," Louis answered, his glittering black eyes deliberately sweeping to Matt, "in particularly one called the Panther—and American gun smugglers."

Gun running! Matt thought. He watched Raul twist the poncho more vigorously. Any minute he was going to pull the fringe off the garment.

"We have received word that a shipment of guns is on its way to Candaleria to be received by none other than El Pantero himself," the Frenchman said, clasping his hands behind his back.

Now Matt understood why the villagers were so tense. Somehow they were involved with the Juaristas and the guns.

"Louis Duprees shall not only capture the smugglers," the captain continued smugly, his hand flying through the air, his index fingers pointing, "but

197

he will get the guns and the Juaristas."

"Oh, Señor Duprees," Raul said, horrified that the officer would accuse Zoe of being a gun smuggler, "Señor Matt and Señora Zoe are not Juaristas or smugglers." He pointed to her office across the plaza. "As I told you before, she is our doctor. That is her *officina*. She is here to treat the diseased, not to fight our wars."

Duprees scrutinized the entire plaza — Zoe's office, the decorations for the fiesta, the woodpile, the cooking food — before his gaze came to rest on the revolvers that rested on Matt's thighs. Deliberately he allowed the silence to grow. Finally he said, "I am a suspicious man by nature, Senor *alcalde,* but I accept your word that these two are innocent visitors to Mexico." Again he paused, then said: "But who shall vouch for you, señor *alcalde?*" His lips moved into a cold smile and he stepped out of the street beneath the portico. "Now take me to my quarters."

"*Sí* señor," Raul said. "Come this way, *por favor.* You may have my home while you are in Candaleria."

"What of my men?" Louis asked as the two of them walked away from Zoe and Matt, their voices becoming softer and more indistinct.

"There are plenty of rooms at the cantina," Raul answered and laughed before he added, "plenty of rooms, women, and wine, señor."

By this time the men were too far away for Zoe and Matt to overhear, but Zoe continued to watch them. She saw the French officer stop at the vendor's *carreta* and rummage through the goods until he had selected from fruits and vegetables. He handed these to his aide, who followed him and

Raul down the street.

Matt also stared down the street at the vendor—the same one Raul had said was leaving Candaleria in such a hurry because he wanted to be in a neighboring village before nightfall. Matt wondered why Raul had lied to him about the vendor.

When Louse and Raul disappeared into the *alcalde*'s house, she said, "Captain Duprees is handsome in an odd sort of way, don't you think?"

"He doesn't appeal to me, period!" Matt exclaimed, his hand grabbing her upper arm, jealousy and anger pushing thoughts of the vendor to the back of his mind. "To borrow one of your phrases, he's downright despicable, and you're infuriating. I ought to put you over my knee and spank some sense into you."

Zoe stumbled when Matt gave her a jerk. Grinning into his face, she said, "I seem to have a penchant for despicable men, don't I?"

"From the way you were pawing all over him and flirting, I'd say you do."

"Pawing!" Zoe exploded. "Flirting! I was *not* flirting with him." She yanked her arm out of his grip. "I was being friendly and saving your stupid neck."

"As a married woman you should be less friendly to men, and from now on, let me worry about my own neck."

"How many times must I tell you, I'm not a married woman," Zoe said. "And you're not my father to be giving me orders."

Matt stopped in front of her and caught both her shoulders in his hands, bringing her to a jarring halt mere inches in front of him. "You're wrong about one thing, lady. You're as married as you're

199

ever going to be, and for as long as you live. You're right about the other. I most assuredly am not your father."

Matt, urged on by the demons of jealousy, didn't stop to think of the wisdom of what he was doing or of what he wanted. For four days and nights, he had been tormented by the nearness of her. Today, after what they had shared together on their wedding night, she begged him to let her return to Weber Fielding. She wanted to forget they had ever met. He was going to insinuate himself so firmly into her life, she'd never forget him.

Ignoring the *carreta* that rumbled by on its way out of the village, he hauled her hard against him and heard her soft intake of breath. Zoe's head jerked back and her face automatically lifted. When she saw Matt's face coming toward hers, she opened her mouth to protest, but his lips clamped on hers in a savage, bruising kiss. Zoe's hands spread in protest against his ribs, pressing strongly at first, then more weakly as the kiss turned from punishment into passion, as passion softened the savageness into desperation. Zoe's hands slipped up Matt's chest and around his shoulders. Her mouth opened beneath his to accept the sweet thrust of his tongue.

Later, much later, Matt dragged his mouth away from hers, his breath coming hard and fast, his heart thundering. His body was on fire. "I've never wanted a woman as much as I want you," he muttered.

"I've never wanted a man any less than I do you." Zoe whispered the fabrication. She couldn't allow this man to dictate her emotions like this.

"Tell that lie to someone else," Matt said. "I

know the truth." He laid his hand on her breasts. "Your heart is thudding and your breathing is as quick and heavy as mine."

"Not from your kiss!" Zoe exclaimed. "If you'll remember, you've been dragging me down the street at breakneck speed. Anyone would be out of breath; anyone's heart would be thudding."

Matt swore under his breath as he swept her into his arms and crossed the distance to their house. He opened the door and entered the room, kicking the door shut behind him. Long, determined strides carried them through the house until he stood beside the bed. He deposited Zoe on the mattress and stood for a long time peering through the dusk at her.

Zoe pushed up on her elbows and shook her head wildly. "No," she cried, hurling at him the first accusation that came to mind, "I'm not going to let you use my body again. I won't."

Use her! No words could have stirred Matt more; none could so have braced his resolve with pure steel. These past four days he had hardly been able to keep his hands off her; he wanted to feel her young, supple body in his arms; he wanted to taste the sweetness of her lips, to feel the silkiness of her hair between his fingers. He wanted to hear her growls of excitement, her purrs of contentment. But he hadn't taken her because he'd begun to develop a conscience and to think of how she must feel about the Indian marriage. Earlier her tirade had sliced him to the quick. He'd even been thinking about giving her time to learn him. *Use her!* The words continued to reverberate through his mind.

"No, wife," Matt said softly, "I'm not going to use you. I'm going to set you on fire with desire and make you beg for my possession. When you do finally return to that civilization you're so fond of, you'll never be able to forget the touch of the Comanche warrior Ma-ta-mon-yahu. Forever you'll be branded by him."

"Never," Zoe whispered, unable to take her eyes off him.

His hands slipped under the hem of his shirt and pulled the red material up his muscle-corded chest over his shoulders to drift through the air and land at his feet. Zoe was unable to take her eyes off him, mesmerized by each movement, impassioned anew at the sight of his naked body. She watched as he unconsciously rubbed his palm over his chest in circular motion before he sat down at the table and unlaced his moccasins. They landed on top of the shirt. He stood and quietly moved to the side of the bed to unfasten his gun belt and hang it over the top poster.

"Never," he murmured. "Has no one told you that never is a long time?"

He was so close that Zoe smelled the musky odor of his buckskin trousers; she felt the heat of his body. She saw the bulge of his manhood. Unable to look at him any longer, unable to control her wanting for him, she buried her face in the pillow. Dear Lord, she wanted him. She ached for him, and without his touching her, without his fully undressing, she was ready to beg for his touch. Zoe was ashamed of herself. How could she be such a wanton?

Her body trembled as she heard the trousers slide down his legs to fall on the floor. She felt the mattress sag when he sat down beside her. His hands, ever so gentle, caught each of her shoulders, and he rolled her onto her back.

"No," Zoe begged.

"I promise I'm not going to use you," he whispered, his fingers deftly unbuttoning her blouse as he spoke. Her blue eyes were wide and luminous, a flicker of fear in their depths. "Anytime you wish, you may stop me." He pushed the material off her shoulders and lowered his head to lay his mouth against the soft chemise that covered her breasts. He sought and found the nipple that pressed against the cloth. Taking it into his mouth, he blew his hot breath against her. He felt her body convulse with passion.

Zoe had said no, but she hadn't meant what she said. Not only was the man making a whore out of her, he was turning her into a liar. She moaned, the soft sound coming from deep in her throat. Her fingers spread through Matt's thick black hair; she cupped his skull, her fingertips massaging his scalp.

Her love purrs, her love strokes burned into Matt and drove his passion higher. Still he exercised the most rigid control over his emotions. He slowly withdrew and sat staring into Zoe's passion-glazed eyes.

"You shouldn't do this to me," she whispered thickly.

"Do you want me to stop?" Matt asked.

No! Zoe silently screamed, angry at him because he was so controlled, angry at herself because she wanted him so much she couldn't think straight. *Dear, God, no, she didn't want him to stop!* She closed her eyes and turned her head so that she wouldn't have to look into his face.

"I didn't think so," Matt murmured, a tinge of relief in his tone.

203

He bent down again, his chest brushing against her breasts. His lips lightly moved over hers, again and again, in tantalizing strokes, all promise but no substance. Zoe twisted and tried to turn her mouth away, but he gripped her chin and held her face, settling his lips firmly on hers. His lips, pressing against her, opened her mouth wider, and his tongue plundered and pillaged her sweetness.

Zoe's tongue joined the foray, tentatively at first; then, when she felt the shudder ripple through Matt's body, she became daring. Her hands slid to the back of his skull and she held his head as her mouth began to move across his lips, her tongue exploring the wonder of his mouth.

Her limbs loosened and her body melted into his as he lowered himself over her. Still kissing her, one arm locked around her, he unfastened her chemise and pulled her into a sitting position to slide it from her shoulders. For a moment he marveled at the beauty of her breasts, swaying gently with her breathing; they were swollen, the nipples hard. He cupped the warm, firm flesh in his hands and stroked the tip with his thumb. She shivered beneath his touch. He leaned down to take one into his mouth, and Zoe moaned; her body arched. Instinctively she shoved her breast more fully into his mouth and her hips came against his to create an instant, fiery explosion of sensation in Matt's body. Her skin was smooth and delicious; he sucked strongly, marveling at the shudders of pleasure that made her body tremble.

All coherent thought was gone. Zoe's world was the fiery one she and Matt were creating at this moment. She was compelled to discover and to know it. Her hands moved across his shoulders, down the indentation of his back. Her hands cupped his buttocks. Her lower body aflame with desire, she pulled him against her.

Matt was lost in sensation. He quickly unfastened Zoe's skirt to pull it and her pantalettes down. Zoe helped by raising her hips. When she felt the warm air touch her naked skin, she uttered a soft, almost relieved cry. All thoughts of resistance had long since fled. Matt raised his body, bracing himself on his hands as he guided his roused flesh into hers and smothered any last protest with a devouring kiss.

Drawing back slightly, he massaged her point of pleasure. Her eyes were closed and she turned her head in abandon on the pillow, tendrils of golden hair escaping her chignon to curl around her face. She whimpered, her hips moving in innocent, needful response. He removed his hand and her eyes flew open, her mouth rounded in protest.

"I'm not leaving you," he murmured, his head lowering, his lips taking hers. He situated his manhood against her, pressed and sighed as he felt her warm, moist flesh. Succulent, scented, she opened for him.

When he was buried deep within her, he remained still for a moment, luxuriating in the beauty of their joining. Then Zoe moved; she wiggled her body sinuously and her thighs parted wider. Her hands spread on his back and moved down over the scarred ridges to knead his buttocks.

In synchronized movement he raised his mouth from her and drew back slowly. Zoe moaned her protest and arched her lower body in search of him. He entered her with a deep thrust and again she closed around him, making him a willing prisoner in her velvety sheath of passion. He felt the moist warmth of her maidenhead as it trembled around him. He answered with another hard thrust.

Her fingernails raked his back, and she cried softly, "Oh, Matt . . ."

He pulled away from her. Zoe's eyes flew open and she look around wildly. She reached for him, but he dodged her hands. His fingers lay lightly against her stomach. "Am I using you?" he asked.

Almost nauseated with wanting and totally devoid of pride—the Comanche warrior had stripped her of that—Zoe shook her head.

"Do you want me to make love to you?"

Zoe nodded her head.

"Tell me," Matt insisted. "Say it. I want to hear you say it."

"Make love to me," Zoe said in a low, husky voice.

"Please," he said.

"Please," Zoe begged.

With a groan, Matt was over her, his manhood deeply insinuated in her femininity. He caught her to him and moved with hard, deep strokes, Zoe moving with him, each of them climbing higher and higher toward the pinnacle of ultimate fulfillment. Finally Zoe's body tensed and she tentatively whimpered.

"Oh, yes," he groaned.

She shook violently, her passion rising, hovering on a crest. Her hands balled around the bedclothes. Matt continued to give her pleasure, but strove to hold himself back even as the hot wave was surging. Then Zoe cried out and he felt the shudders of her body. When her cries and shuddering ceased, his own groaning cry filled the room.

Matt, dragging in a heavy breath, rolled over, taking her with him, and pressed her down the full length of his body as he kissed her deeply. Then he held her in a tight embrace. Exhausted from her journey, sated from love, Zoe snuggled into his arms and went to sleep in the deepening darkness of the room. His chin resting on the crown of her head, Matt lay there, listening to her quiet breathing.

Zoe had touched a part of him that had never been touched before, and while it was a new experience, it wasn't an unpleasant one. He had married her to spite Weber Fielding, but now his thoughts were changing. Matt wanted her, and he wanted her to make love to him willingly. He knew that she hadn't come to him of her own volition. He had taken unfair advantage of her, whetting her desire until she wouldn't say no. Her mind and heart would continue to say no, but her body wouldn't. He'd made love to enough women to know how to work them into a passionate frenzy so that he could manipulate their emotional responses. He wasn't proud of himself for having done the same to Zoe.

Whereas his emotion for Fielding through all these years had been bitterness and anger, now he found himself jealous of the man—jealous because Zoe wanted Fielding over him. She preferred a man who was sophisticated and civilized. She admired ambition and wealth.

Matt slowly withdrew from Zoe and slipped off the bed to walk to the window. He unfastened the shutters and threw them open to gaze at the patio behind the house. Even if he were to reveal to her that he was Matt Chandler, educated in the east, son of Uriah Chandler, he knew he would never be Weber Fielding. He wanted to settle down and build a ranch on his father's land, one that was comparable to La Candela de Oro.

He wouldn't be the sophisticated and suave city gentleman; he'd always be the primitive. Maybe that was part of his Indian heritage. He didn't know; he didn't care. Zoe was a genteel lady, born and bred. She would never make it in the wilds. She'd never make it on a ranch, isolated from town and people.

Matt walked to where his clothes lay, picked up his trousers, and slipped into them. He brought Zoe's portmanteau from the office into the living room and set it on the chest at the foot of the bed. Then he stepped out of the house onto the patio and found a wooden tub propped against the wall. He placed this in the middle of the room, then filled it with water. Rummaging through the cabinet, he found a towel, washcloth, and soap.

When he sat on the edge of the bed, Zoe turned over, roused, and smiled sleepily up at him. He reached down to brush the curls from her temples. His large hand rested against her cheek. She was the most beautiful woman he'd ever seen, so delicate and fragile.

"Since the fiesta is in your honor," he said, "don't you think you ought to be present?"

"Un-hunh," Zoe assented as she stretched. Still in the euphoric moment between sleep and alertness, she reached up and ran her fingers down Matt's stubbled cheek. She heard the gentle rasp. "You need a shave."

"So I do."

Matt's eyes wandered down Zoe's body, over her

breasts, the smooth stomach, the gentle flare of her hips and thighs, but he didn't touch her again. They were sharing a wonderful moment and he wanted it to continue. Perhaps in time she would come to accept him as her husband; then he could tell her who he was and explain the reasons for his silence.

As Zoe wakened fully, she was inundated with memories. Her hand groped as she caught and yanked the coverlet over herself.

Shrugging as if it were of no consequence to him, Matt stood and walked across the room once again to stare out the window. "I've poured the water for your bath."

Zoe sat up on the bed, pulling the coverlet beneath her chin. "What about you?" she asked.

When Matt turned to look at her, his eyes filled with gentle amusement. She looked like a little girl sitting in the middle of the bed, bundled up in the covers with nothing exposed but her face, around which strands of blond hair wisped. He walked to where his clothes lay and bent down. "I'm going to check on my braves. I'll bathe at the creek where they're camped and change clothes there."

Zoe was disappointed. "Are you coming back for the fiesta?"

He nodded and said, "I'll be back in an hour."

When he reached the door, Zoe called out, "Matt—"

His fingers closed over the wooden handle, but he didn't turn to look at her.

"Matt, when we get through here in Candaleria, I want you to come back to Chandlerville with me."

"As your husband?"

"As my husband," Zoe replied.

209

Matt hadn't felt such sweet joy flow through his body since he was a small boy. Like honey, it was so sweet and so thick he didn't know if it could pass through his veins.

"As your *ner-co-mack-pe*." The whisper-soft words were a caress to her ears and heart.

"As my *ner . . . co . . . mack . . . pe*," she vowed.

Matt leaned his head against the door and closed his eyes against the bite of tears. He had married Zoe for the wrong reason, but he liked and admired her. They were good together. Surely in time they could come to love one another. Each would have to make some concessions, but that was the way of life.

"Matt?" Zoe scooted to the end of the bed, eager for his answer.

He turned in time to see the cover slip below her breasts, their smooth whiteness a perfect foil for the dark and pert aureoles. She pushed a little higher on her knees, the cover slipping aside to reveal her navel, the smooth expanse of her stomach, and the golden triangle. When she smiled and held her arms out to him, her breasts swaying gently with the movement, Matt dropped his clothes to the floor and stepped toward her.

"It'll be wonderful. You and me." She laughed, a soft expression of her joy. For the first time she had met Matt, she saw his feelings in his face. The smile wasn't large, but it was radiant. The corners of his eyes crinkled and the craggy hardness of his face eased into handsomeness. Zoe was happy with her husband; he was a man of whom any woman would be proud. "We won't tell anyone that you're Indian—"

210

Matt stopped walking, his foot settling on his discarded shirt. "Why not?"

"Because of your past," she answered, her eyes never leaving his face. "We won't tell them so they won't know that you've been accused of—"

Zoe felt as if she were sliding down a steep incline. Her breath shortened; her heart stopped, then pounded furiously, then skipped several beats. She had only uttered a few words, but they had completely transformed Matt. Now he was gray with anger, his features as if chiseled of stone.

Nonchalantly, he stooped down and retrieved his clothes. "I'm not ashamed of my Indian heritage, and I returned to my people so that I could clear my name. I'm not a murderer, much less an outlaw."

"I know that," Zoe said, irritated because she had expressed herself the wrong way. "I didn't mean to insinuate that you were. I merely want us to have a life together, Matt, and I wanted to make it easy for you." She slid off the bed and ran to where he stood. Wrapping her arms around him, she laid her head against his shoulder, her breasts on his chest. "I know the people in Chandlerville wouldn't understand. They don't like Indians, especially the Coman . . . ches. . . ." Zoe stopped. Again she had said the wrong thing.

"The people of Chandlerville don't like Indians," Matt said, grabbing her by the arms and setting her away from him, "especially Comanches, and Doctor Zoe Randolph, one of their leading and most outstanding citizens, cannot bear the thought of being in their disgrace."

Matt had to get away from her. What she said was true; how many times had he rehearsed the

211

same lines to himself? His mind and heart had warned him against caring about Zoe Randolph, but his body listened to no one, to nothing. No matter what the woman said, he still wanted her physically.

"Well, Doctor Randolph, what the people of Chandlerville think doesn't bother me one iota, and I'm not going to play games with you or with them. At least, in a Comanche village the people accept a person for what he is. The Indians aren't as eager to judge others as civilized people are."

"No!" Zoe cried, but Matt had already disappeared into the night, and the thud of the door as it shut resounded through the room.

Chapter 12

Aware of the gaiety as the villagers began their celebration, Zoe hurriedly bathed and dressed, putting on the brightly colored skirt and white blouse. From the bouquet of flowers that Miguelito had given her, she chose a bright red one to pin in her hair, which hung loosely across her shoulders. Matt had told her he would be back in an hour to get her. Well, she smiled smugly, let him come. He wouldn't find her here waiting for him . . . or pining away.

She draped the shawl over her shoulders against the cool night air, and slipped out the door. The fresh air was invigorating and Zoe loved it. She lifted her head and breathed deeply. After her nap today, she was rested. Despite Matt Barnabas, without Matt Barnabas, she would enjoy herself tonight. She smelled the tantalizing odors and realized that she was famished. Pemmican was delicious — with honey, fabulous — but she was ready for a dietary change. She followed the tangy, zesty odors to the huge bonfire that burned in the center of the plaza.

In the blaze of light she stopped and looked about. A hand touched her shoulder. Her head jerked about and she stared into Louis Duprees' face.

"Madame, how pleased I am to see you!"

"Thank you," Zoe murmured, embarrassed when his eyes almost suggestively ran over her bare shoulders to linger over the upper swell of her breasts. Already she regretted her impulsiveness. Instead of punishing Matt, she was punishing herself.

"Your husband," Duprees said, the glittering black eyes skimming the crowd, "where is he?"

"Her husband, monsieur, is right here." Matt materialized from the darkness to stand by Zoe's side. His eyes also raked over Zoe's low-cut blouse, but his look was thunderous. His arm slipped around her shoulders, and his hand bit into the tender, naked flesh. He pulled her to him in overt possessiveness.

While Zoe was angry at Matt's proprietary actions, she didn't pull away from him. She didn't want to give Duprees any hint that she and Matt were not happily married. She had enough on her mind without having to ward off the Frenchman.

"Come, wife." Matt lowered his head and smiled coldly into her face. "Let's move closer so we may enjoy the dancing."

Not for the first time Zoe wanted to slap that smug arrogance off Matt's face. How dare he keep calling her wife! How dare he keep reminding her that they were married. It annoyed her as much as his refusal to come to Chandlerville on her terms.

"Having traveled so far so quickly, *darling*," she said, wrapping an arm around Matt's waist, her hand spreading across his midsection, "I would

214

much rather eat." When she felt the slight tremor in his body, Zoe moved even closer so that her breast brushed his arm. She grinned when Matt cast her a darkening glare. Here in front of everyone, she could torment him as much as she desired with no worry of the consequences. Perhaps in the house he was lord and master, she the slave, but out here she ruled. "Come, *darling*." She caught his hand in hers and moved toward the food stands.

When they were out of hearing distance, Matt jerked her back. "What the hell do you think you're doing?" he grated.

Zoe opened wide, luminous eyes. "Going to get something to eat."

"You know what I mean." His hand lightly brushed across her shoulders. "Wearing this indecent blouse."

Zoe laughed and tossed her head, the golden waves glimmering in the firelight. "Hardly indecent, *darling*," she drawled.

"And don't call me darling in that tone of voice again," he muttered, irritated because he was allowing her to get under his skin.

"Don't call me wife again," she said.

"You're my wife!"

"I have a name," she returned softly, not really offended that he had referred to her as wife, but hurt because he was using the term to affix firmly in her mind and his the position she held in his life. "Perhaps not the name you would have chosen, but the one by which I go. You might try it on for size." They stared at each other for a full second before she said, "Say it, Matt. Call me Zoe. Zoe Ellen Randolph."

The tension and anger drained out of Matt. He

215

reached out to touch the petals of the wildflower that nestled in the golden curls. His fingers lightly traced the outline of her face and chin. She was right: the blouse wasn't indecent. He was simply jealous.

"Zoe," he whispered, his hand curling gently around her neck, his fingertips against her chin. "Zoe Ellen Randolph." *Zoe Ellen Randolph Chandler,* he added his last name silently, savoring the sound of it. He smiled. That would sound much better in a hospital than Zoe Ellen Randolph Fielding.

Zoe found her little game turning on her. She was more affected by Matt's touch than he seemed to be by hers. Already her insides were turning to fire. She didn't care that her desire burned in her eyes for him to read. Since he had taken her to such wonderful heights of ecstasy, she was becoming wanton and lusty. She wanted it again . . . and again.

"Zoe Ellen Randolph," Matt whispered, his face lowering until his lips touched hers in a soft kiss, "you have a beautiful name." His lips firmed on hers as his arms slipped around her body. When he lifted his mouth from hers, he said, "Shall we enjoy the fiesta . . . Zoe?"

Happily Zoe laughed into his face. "We shall, Mr. Barnabas. We shall."

And indeed, Zoe and Matt enjoyed the fiesta. They ate and drank wine and laughed and danced. They celebrated. Finally, however, the arduous journey took its toll on them. Both were exhausted and wanted to go home to bed. Extending their thanks to Raul for such a lovely evening, they gave their good-byes and departed, weaving their way through

216

the festive crowd.

By the time they reached the house, Zoe was almost asleep on her feet. The few glasses of wine she had drunk acted like a sedative. Inside the room, moonlight spilling in through the cracks in the shutters, Matt undressed her, picked her up, and carried her to bed.

"Are you going to sleep here or with your braves?" she asked as she curled into a ball and planted her face comfortably in the pillow.

Already out of his clothes, Matt lay down beside her, the mattress sagging beneath his weight. Smiling, he said, "What's the purpose in having a—" He caught himself before he said wife. "In having a Zoe if you can't sleep with her."

Zoe giggled and snuggled up to him, happy when his arm curled around her. "In certain instances you may call me wife, Mr. Barnabas. Just don't use that certain tone of voice."

"I wish I could promise not to," Matt said, "but when I see other men flirting with you—" He ended his sentence with a shrug. After a long pause, he added, "Zoe, if it were possible for you and me to live in Chandlerville as man and wife, even though the people knew about my being half-Indian, would you really want it?"

When she didn't answer, he moved to look down at her. Without his chest for support, her head rolled onto the pillow. Her face was haloed by golden tangles, the long lashes lay in a crescent on her cheek, and she breathed evenly. Zoe Ellen Randolph Chandler was sound asleep.

In a way Matt was glad she hadn't heard him. Already he regretted having spoken the words. Someday he could tell Zoe who he was and perhaps they could have a future together. First, he wanted to find out why his grandfather sold his birthright to Fielding. Then, no matter what the cost, he must get it back.

Both Matt and Zoe were deep in sleep when Matt was awakened by a noise. He listened: the light taps on the door came again.

"Coming," he called softly. As soon as he slipped into his trousers, he walked across the room and opened the door to look into the uplifted face of Miguelito. In the moonlight Matt saw tears glistening on his little cheeks.

"Señor my grandfather is in trouble," Miguelito whispered, his gaze sweeping all around as if he feared being overheard. "You and señora *doctora* must come with me."

Matt whisked the boy into the room and closed the door. "What kind of trouble?" he asked.

Before Miguelito answered, Zoe shoved up on an elbow and pushed hair out of her face. "Who is it?" she asked, her voice thick with sleep.

"Miguelito," Matt answered. He was sitting at the table pulling his moccasins on.

Holding the cover under her chin, Zoe bolted up. "What's wrong?"

"My grandfather has been hurt," the boy sobbed. "He needs a doctor."

"Run back to the house and tell him I'm coming," Zoe said, sleep and exhaustion gone from her tone. "I'll be there as soon as I dress."

"Abuelo isn't at the house, señor," Miguelito answered.

Matt caught the strange inflection in the child's voice. As he strapped his guns around his waist, he asked casually, "Where is your grandfather?"

218

"He is in the mountains," Miguelito answered.

"What was he doing in the mountains at this time of night?" Matt asked.

"What he was doing there doesn't matter," Zoe returned. "What matters is that I get to him. Now both of you get out of here while I dress. Then we can be on our way."

"The going will not be easy, señora," Miguelito said. "The French have set up guards around Candaleria."

"That's no problem." Zoe dismissed it with a shake of her head. "I'll tell them I must go—"

"No," Matt said quietly, "we can't let the French know that we're leaving, can we, Miguelito?"

"No, señor."

"Juaristas," Zoe exclaimed softly. "Your grandfather is working with the Juaristas."

"Sí"

"Go on in the other room," Zoe said with a wave of her hand. "Let me get dressed and we'll be on our way. You do know a way to get us out of here without the French seeing us?"

Miguelito grinned and nodded his head. "Sí."

Two hours later Zoe and Matt, following Miguelito and his donkey, arrived at a small hut on the outskirts of a small mountain village. Miguelito gave a coded knock and waited; he knocked again.

A whispered voice inquired, "Who is it?"

"Miguelito."

The door opened and the child disappeared into the dark shadows. Matt, moving to Zoe's side and placing a hand on his gun, walked in with her. They heard shuffling and breathing and knew sev-

219

eral people were in the room, but they didn't know who or how many.

Suddenly a match scratched against an abrasive surface and flared to life, revealing Raul Mora's face. The old man lit the lamp, replaced the chimney, and turned to Zoe. "Thank you for coming, señora," he said. "I would not have involved you in our war, but I had no choice." He reached up to clamp his hand on his arm.

Zoe saw the dark stain around the white fabric and the fresh blood that oozed through his fingers. "You're wounded," she exclaimed, moving around the table.

"It is nothing," Raul dismissed. "I did not bring you here to look after me."

Zoe set her bag on the table and opened it. After she pried Raul's fingers loose, she snipped the material away from the wound.

"It is a mere scratch," the old man said.

"But it could get infected," Zoe reminded him.

"I sent for you, Señor Matt," Raul said over Zoe's head, "because I need your help. I must trust you." While Zoe applied antiseptic to his wound and bandaged it, Raul said, "I am too old to ride with the Juaristas, but my heart is with them. Since I speak English, I have been chosen to go into the United States and purchase the guns we need."

"We thought perhaps you were the one who was bringing us the guns," Miguelito interrupted, his gaze inadvertently going to Matt's revolvers.

"Somehow the French learned that we were receiving the guns in Candaleria, and they showed up on the very night that we were expecting the shipment."

"That's why everyone was so skittish today," Zoe

220

said, tying off the bandage.

Raul nodded and reached up to place his hand across his throbbing arm. "I sent word to the Americans that the French had arrived and our rendezvous point had changed. When I arrived at the new meeting place, the Americans were under attack. Two of the Americans were killed, the others were wounded far worse than I. I couldn't bring them into Candaleria, so I brought them here and sent for you."

"Where are they?" Zoe asked, hastily returning her instruments and dressings to her satchel.

Only minutes later, Raul ushered Zoe and Matt into another hut, a lamp flickering dimly on the table. On pallets lay the two Americans. Zoe rushed across the room, kneeling over one of them.

"Why!" she gasped in shocked surprise, staring at the old man. "I know him. It's Wayne Shook."

Wayne Shook. Matt crossed the room and knelt beside Zoe. He knew Wayne Shook. He owned the ranch adjacent to La Candela de Oro. What was he doing running guns into Mexico?

"Check the other one for me," Zoe said, ripping Shook's shirt from his body. "See how badly hurt he is."

Matt crawled to the pallet on the other side of the room, just inside the arc of lamplight. The man's head was turned away from Matt, and his hand covered the wound on his chest. The minute Matt touched the hand to remove it, he knew the American was dead.

"How bad?" Zoe asked.

"Dead," Matt replied. He reached over to catch the man's chin in his hands and turn his head.

Paralyzed with shock, he stared into his younger

221

brother's face. Matt closed his eyes against the heat of tears. Nothing was turning out right. Fielding held a note on his birthright; the Comanches were going to be removed from their home; and Bryan — Matt laid his hand over Bryan's — Bryan was dead. Now his dream of their working together was gone, gone for good.

Matt, turning his head to see what Zoe was doing, was glad that she was busily working with Shook, because it gave him time to compose himself. He walked out of the hut, drawing the brisk air into his lungs as he took a packet of tobacco out of his pocket and with shaking fingers rolled a cigarette. Leaning against the building, he inhaled deeply to fill his lungs with smoke.

He'd often heard people make the comment that a man could never return home, and until now, until this time in his life when he was trying so desperately to return home, he'd never quite understood what the old-timers were saying. Now he did. His dream, to work side-by-side with Bryan and his grandfather, had turned into a nightmare.

He dropped the cigarette stub and mashed it into the dirt with the toe of his moccasin. He and Bryan had shared a few letters through the years, but nothing in them prepared Matt for this. The man lying in there on the pallet was a stranger, a gun smuggler. He wasn't the towheaded boy Matt had left behind, the brother he was coming home to be with.

Matt let his mind wander to the days when he and Bryan had played, worked, and ridden the range together. When Matt had been accused of impregnating Veronica Fielding, Bryan had believed him, standing by his side to defy all of Chandler-

222

ville and Uriah Chandler. When Matt left, Bryan had cried and begged to go along. Matt had refused; he loved Bryan too much and had no idea where he was going or for how long. Bryan had a future at La Candela de Oro. He had his mother and his grandfather, and Matt couldn't take him away from his family.

After Uriah had refused to write, he had written to Bryan to explain his reasons for not taking him along, but Bryan had never really understood. He kept insisting that one of these days he would leave Chandlerville and join Matt. Matt had known differently; Bryan belonged at La Candela de Oro. Through these infrequent letters which stopped with the outbreak of war, Matt had kept abreast of all the goings-on at the ranch.

In the last one Matt received, Bryan had begged him to come home. He had, but now they would never have a chance to ride together again or talk or laugh . . . never!

The door opened and Matt lifted a hand to wipe the tears from his face.

"Matt?" Zoe called softly, peering through the darkness for him.

"Over here," he answered, pushing away from the building and walking back to where she stood. "Just came out for a smoke. Do you need me?"

"No, I've done the best I can."

"Señora—" Raul joined them outside the house. "We must leave now. We must return to Candaleria before Duprees becomes any more suspicious. He will think it strange that all of us are away from the village in the morning. He will suspect that you are working with the Juaristas."

"I can't leave," Zoe exclaimed and turned to look

through the darkness at Matt. "You return with Raul. I'll stay here with Shook."

"You can't do that," Matt replied. "It'll be more suspicious with you gone than with me." When Zoe started shaking her head, Matt caught her shoulders in his hands. "I'll stay here with Shook."

"I'm not going to leave him," she whispered.

"If you don't, you might bring the wrath of the French down on the entire village of Candaleria."

"He is right, Señora Zoe," Raul answered, his head swinging around as he silently kept vigil.

"I'll take care of Shook," Matt told her. "Promise."

Eventually Zoe said, "All right," and walked inside the hut, followed by Matt and Raul. Standing at the foot of pallet, she stared at the dead man. "That's Bryan Chandler. His grandfather owns the largest ranch in Chandlerville . . . La Candela de Oro."

She turned to Matt and murmured, her voice teary, "I don't really know Uriah Chandler. He seems to be such a hateful old man, but I feel so sorry for him. His oldest grandson was killed during the war, and now Bryan. With the exception of his daughter-in-law who lives with him, he's all alone."

Zoe's concern touched Matt deeply. He took her into his arms and held her tightly, pressing her cheek against his chest.

"They had to be smuggling guns into Mexico for the money," she said. "To—to keep their land."

"Señora," Raul said, "we need to be going. We do not have many more hours of darkness to hide us. I will wait for you outside. Be quick, *por favor.*"

Zoe heard the door thud softly as the old man slipped out of the hut. She pushed out of Matt's arms and returned to the table where her bag was. As she sorted through it, she gave Matt instructions on how to administer the medicine she was leaving. After she cut more bandages and laid them on the table, she snapped her bag shut and turned.

"Take care of him, Matt."

"I will, darling," he promised, moving to take her into his arms.

Zoe automatically lifted her face for his kiss, warm and sweet. Finally she pulled out of his arms, picked up her satchel, and walked to the door. Smiling, she turned and waved him a kiss; then she was out the door and running to the horse Raul held for her.

Through the night, Matt sat beside Shook, watching for the slightest change in the man's condition. Finally, when the first pale rays of morning light were creeping in the cracks of the shutters, the rancher stirred.

"Bryan," he mumbled. "Is Bryan all right?"

"He's dead," Matt answered as he pressed a damp cloth against Shook's dry lips.

"Bandits," Shook said. "Ran into bandits."

"Mexicans?" Matt asked, wondering if the Juaristas had double-crossed the Americans.

"Don't think so. No accent. Weren't dressed like Mexicans." Shook lapsed into silence and took several deep breaths. "One . . . of them . . . called . . . Bryan by his name. We stopped the . . . wagons." Another pause: "And they . . . started shooting."

"Why were you smuggling guns to the Juaristas?" Matt asked.

The faded blue eyes stared into Matt's face. "Who are you?" Shook whispered. "You look familiar."

"Matt Chandler."

"Matt!" Shook exclaimed and tried to sit up but coughed and grimaced in pain, quickly lying back down. "Matt Chandler. It's really you."

Matt smiled. "I know I've been gone for fourteen years, but you look like you've seen a ghost."

"I have," Shook said, his hand catching Matt's. "We got word that you died in the War Between the States. Some guy who served with you said he seen you when you took a Yankee bullet. Done buried you, we did."

"I took a Yankee bullet all right," Matt replied, "and it put me down for a while, but I'm very much alive."

"Matt, you got to get to Chandlerville!" Shook's fingers tightened around Matt's. "Things are bad."

Matt listened as Shook talked. The ranchers were in dire straits. The Texas Legislature had passed a head tax of one dollar per head of cattle, and the cost of food was outrageously high. While the ranches were cattle-rich, they had no liquid assets. Confederate money was worthless, and the only ones in town who had United States currency were the carpetbaggers and scalawags. Fielding was taking over one ranch after another. Rather than extending credit to the ranchers, he was foreclosing. If the rancher had no mortgage, but needed money to pay his taxes, Fielding was giving land scrip worth ten cents an acre.

"Uriah needed money so bad that he sold off a parcel of his land to Fielding," Shook concluded with a cough. "He loaned the money to all of us, but it wasn't enough. That's why we was smuggling guns to the Juaristas. Didn't have nothing to do with us taking sides against the French."

"What about the cattle?" Matt asked. "Why didn't you drive the cattle to Kansas and sell them?"

"Didn't have 'em," Shook smiled weakly. "Know this sounds silly, considering we been selling guns to the Juaristas, but when we received news from Shelby that him and his men needed food, we drove our cattle to Mexico. In return, he promised as soon as he had reinforcements from the French, he'd come and drive the Yankees out of Texas. We thought it was gonna be a lot sooner than this, though."

Shaking his head, Matt sighed. "Who did this to you?"

"Had to be Fielding," Shook replied. "He didn't want us coming up with the money."

"Where did you get the guns?"

"I don't know. Bryan made all the plans and told us the less we knew, the better off we'd be. We just came along to drive the wagons." In a few minutes he said, "Promise me, boy, that you'll get Fielding."

"I'll get Fielding," Matt said as Shook's head dropped and his body went limp. It was over.

Hours later, after Matt had buried both Bryan and Shook, he returned to Candaleria, spying French patrols all along the way. He'd done a lot of thinking and had made up his mind that he was going after the men who had killed Bryan and stolen the guns. Although he knew Fielding was behind the murder, he had to have evidence with which to convict him. He was glad that Zoe was in the office when he arrived.

227

"Pack your things," he said as soon as her patient had departed. "We're getting out of here."

"What about Shook?" Zoe asked anxiously. "How is he?" Her eyes searched his face and she had her answer before he shook his head.

"If only I had stayed," she murmured.

"If you had stayed, you couldn't have saved him," Matt returned. "He would have died, no matter what. Now get your things together so we can get out of here."

"I'm not through," Zoe said, slowly rolling her sleeve down. "I haven't been to all the surrounding villages yet."

"You're through for this visit," he announced. "Hell is about to break out in this place. On my way home I spotted several patrols of French troops and the area is swarming with Juaristas. If we're not careful, we're going to be caught in the middle of a second civil war, and this one's not ours. Like I said, lady, we're going home."

Zoe's eyes lit up. "To Chandlerville?"

Matt wished he could say yes, because he wanted to send Zoe to Chandlerville . . . she would be safest there. But until he was sure what happened to Bryan and how he came to be involved with gunrunning, he did not want her to know his true identity, and he certainly didn't want her spreading tales about being captured by the Comanches. Fielding would use that as an excuse to decimate them.

"No," he answered, "back to my grandfather's village."

"To your grandfather's village!" she repeated in horror. "What are we going to do there?"

"The key word is not we; it's you. *You're* the one

who is returning."

"You're sending me back to your grandfather's village alone?" Without waiting for his answer, she said, "How could you, when you know how they feel about me?"

Matt chuckled. "With more confidence than you could take me back to Chandlerville, knowing how the people feel about Comanches."

"I won't go." Zoe crossed her arms over her breasts.

"You'll go," Matt said. The defiant toss of her head didn't affect him at all.

"And what will you be doing while I'm setting up housekeeping in a tepee?"

"I'm going to find the stolen guns."

Zoe's arms dropped and she walked closer to Matt. "Why are you going after the guns? What interest could you have in them? You didn't know the ranchers." As they stared at one another, she exclaimed, "The Comanches! You want those guns for the Indians! You can't. You can't give the guns to the Indians, Matt. They'll use them to kill innocent white people."

"Perhaps," he returned, ready for the moment to let her think he wanted the guns for the Comanches. "Would that be so different from the white people using guns to shoot the innocent Comanches? Either way a human being is dead."

Zoe lifted a hand to her temple. "I didn't mean that the way it sounded," she apologized. "I know that Fielding has ordered them off his land. If they stay and if you give them guns, bloodshed will surely follow. Don't go after them," she begged.

"I must," Matt answered.

"I have no choice in the matter? You're determined to send me to your village?" she asked. When Matt nodded, she said, "As a Comanche wife, do I have the right to ride into battle with my husband?"

The answer was a long time in coming. "As a Comanche wife, you have the right to ride into battle with your husband."

"Then, *my husband,* I exercise that right." She watched the expressions flit across Matt's face. She tilted her chin. "I'm not going back to that camp by myself and that's final."

"All right," Matt finally agreed. Perhaps her going with him was best. This way he could personally watch her and keep his braves with him. "You fully understand that the leader's word is law. You must obey without question any command I give you. It could be a matter of life and death."

Zoe nodded.

"Then, *wife,* come here." Matt's expression remained hard as he gazed at her, but he saw the war that waged within. Finally she took the few steps that brought her within a foot of him. "Closer," Matt ordered.

Zoe glared at him.

"Closer," Matt said again.

Zoe took another step.

"Now put your arms around me."

"What has this to do with life or death?" Zoe asked, refusing to obey.

"This," Matt whispered, his arms closing around her and pulling her against him. His lips claimed hers in a long, deep kiss. When finally he lifted his mouth, he murmured, "I was starving to death for a taste of you, my wife."

Zoe circled her arms around his neck. "Marriage

does have its advantages."

Matt chuckled. "You're not sorry that I forced you into marrying me?"

Zoe stared into Matt's face and knew at this moment that she was in love with her warrior husband. She didn't know what the future held for them, if anything, but she loved him. Still, she couldn't give up her life, nor was Matt willing to give up his.

"What's wrong?" Matt asked.

"I—"

"Tell me," he said.

"I'm afraid," she whispered, *afraid of the power that you have over me.*

Matt caught her in a tight embrace, his hand pressing her face against his chest. "I won't let anything hurt you, Zoe. I promise. I care too much about you."

Chapter 13

Driven by Bryan's murder, Matt doggedly followed the wagon tracks, relentlessly closing the distance between him and the bandits. The trip from the Comanche village to Candaleria had been swift and tiring; this was grueling. On the second day Zoe was so exhausted she didn't know if she could stay in the saddle.

Sending one of his braves ahead to scout, Matt slowed his pace and dropped back to ride beside Zoe. Although she hadn't complained, had eaten her pemmican in the saddle, and had pushed as hard as he and the men, Matt knew she was exhausted. Her clothes and face were dust-streaked; tendrils of hair escaped the perspiration-stained hat she was wearing to wisp around her cheeks. Matt cast her a gentle smile. "Does the Comanche wife wish she hadn't exercised her prerogative to go fighting with her husband?"

"No—" Zoe wiped her gritty face with the sleeve of her blouse before she returned his smile. "I'd rather be here with you than—" She shrugged and left her sentence incomplete. The words weren't said unkindly, but that Zoe considered him the lesser of two evils stung him. Much to his surprise, he wanted her to be with him because she wanted to be. The admission as well as the desire sat uncomfortably on his shoulders. Contemplating, Matt rode beside Zoe in silence.

The scout crested the hill in front of them, his horse moving in full gallop. Immediately Matt tensed; he could tell from Keen Eyes' expression that he had good news.

"Ma-ta-mon-yahu," the Comanche said when he neared, "the tracks are much fresher. Because the wagons are so heavily loaded, they are moving slowly, as you said. I think they have left the mountains and are traveling on the plains. I saw a dust cloud in the distance. Shall I ride on ahead?" When Matt nodded, the young brave turned his horse and galloped away, soon lost behind the shallow cliff.

"The wagons?" Zoe asked.

"I hope so," Matt replied, his spirits lifting. Automatically he quickened the chestnut's pace and eased ahead of the other riders. The foothills made for arduous traveling, but several hours later, they emerged on the flat plain and Matt paused. In the distance he saw the darkened dots and the swirl of dust. For a moment he wished he had his binoculars; he wanted to know for sure that these were the wagons they were pursuing; then he spotted the puffs of smoke spiraling through the blue sky. He smiled.

Zoe pulled Dusty up beside Matt and stopped. Holding her hand above her eyes, she peered into the horizon, fighting the flare of the western sun. "Smoke signals," she murmured.

"Ours," Matt explained. "Keen Eyes is close

233

enough to report. Four wagons and ten men."

"You're outnumbered," Zoe remarked.

"Napoleon always contended that wars weren't won with superior numbers," Matt muttered, "but with superior strategy and a superior confidence in one's ability to win." Because his mind was racing ahead to devise a plan of attack by which he would regain the wagons and take some of the bandits alive, he didn't notice Zoe's quizzical gaze.

She wondered who this man was to whom she was married. He was truly an enigma. Little slips such as this one about military strategies were clues that led her to believe his primitiveness was but a veneer hiding a deep, complex man—a sophisticated product of civilization, who for some reason chose to turn his back on the white community and to live among the Comanches.

Zoe wanted to question Matt about her suspicions, but now was not the time. But she determined to solve the puzzle that was Matt Barnabas—Ma-ta-mon-yahu. Eventually she asked, "Will he keep sending you signals?"

"Yes, but not smoke unless it's something we need to know quickly. One smoke signal won't arouse suspicion or fear, but more will. We don't want to alert the men that we're closing in on them."

"What kind of messages?" Zoe asked.

"Coded rock messages. Along the route will be little piles of rocks that to the undiscerning eyes are little more than piles of rocks. To us they will be messages. I'll point them out to you as we travel."

"What are we going to do once we get the wagons?" Zoe asked, no doubt in her mind that Matt would successfully recover them. Odd, she reflected, that she had been around this man such a short time yet she knew so much about him. She had an innate confidence and trust in him. While she didn't approve of his getting the guns for his people, she couldn't and didn't blame him. She understood his motive, even agreed with it . . . in principle. When Matt didn't answer, she said, "Return to your village."

Matt didn't answer because he hadn't thought beyond finding the men who had killed Bryan. The guns were immaterial to him; the men were not. They knew who was responsible for Bryan's death and Matt wanted to know. He had a score to settle.

"Then what?" Zoe persisted. "Are you going to arm your warriors and send them against the people of Chandlerville?"

"No," Matt answered, seeing in his mind's eye his troopers falling around him during the battles of the recent war, "I'm not going to arm my warriors. Just because I allowed you to come along with me doesn't mean that I'm going to let you dabble in every phase of my life." He glanced down at her and grinned.

Zoe tossed her head impertinently and grinned at him. "I don't want to dabble in every phase of it, but if I did, you'd be a better man."

"And by better man, are you referring to one like Weber Fielding?" Matt asked, egged on by jealousy.

Zoe thought a while before she finally admitted, "Weber has many qualities I admire."

"Wisdom that comes with age?" Matt goaded. "How much older is he than you? Twenty-five or thirty years?"

Zoe turned her head to glare at him. "Twenty."

"That makes you?"

"Twenty-nine," Zoe answered.

"Well past the childbearing years." Matt clucked his tongue, his expression serious. "What kind of wife have I got myself? Most would say you're too old to bear children. Instead of being a dutiful wife who waits at home for her warrior to return from the hunt or from battle, you want to be a warrior at his side." The solemn expression turned into a grin. "You want to give me advice to make me a better man, and the only blueprint you have for a better man is Weber Fielding."

Zoe knew Matt was teasing her, but his reference to her age stung her a little. Age had never bothered her before. Why now? "You think twenty-nine is too old?"

His grin broadened. "Too old for what?"

Zoe felt the heat rising to her cheeks, but she refused to be intimidated or embarrassed. "Too old for your wife? Too old to have your babies? Or would you rather have a young woman?" Zoe looked at him intently, waiting for his answer, realizing that it was important to her.

Matt leaned over to catch Zoe's reins and to stop their horses. Looking directly into her face, he said, "Doctor Zoe, had I been looking for a woman that was obstinate, headstrong, stubborn, and mule-headed, I couldn't have found one that fit the description any better than you." His hand caught her face, his fingers lightly grazing her chin. He saw the pain his words brought to her and realized that his answer was most important. His doctor–wife was a flesh-and-blood person who wanted to be loved and accepted. "But you're also intelligent and have strength of character. You're compassionate and giving. A gifted doctor." He leaned forward to plant his lips on hers in a sweet, breathy kiss. "You're a beautiful woman and a wonderful lover. I'm blessed to have you for my wife."

Zoe's arm lifted, her hand wrapped around his wrist, her fingertips grazing the gold bracelet. "If you could have chosen," she said, her eyes closed against the heat of tears, "would you have chosen me to be your wife?"

"I did choose," he whispered, his lips moving against hers.

"Oh, Matt!" she exclaimed, her eyes opening as she pulled her head away from him. "There's so much I want to say to you, so much I want to know about you. Please," she begged, her eyes intensely blue, "forget the wagons and the guns. Let's you and me think about creating a future for ourselves."

"I can't forget the guns," he answered. "They're part of the future that we're creating for ourselves."

"Matt, you could be killed. I don't want you to do it." Her fingers curled tightly around the wrist, the gold cutting into her tender flesh.

"I won't be killed," he promised. "And we're going to talk. I'm going to find out all about my wife."

"And I'm going to find out about you, my husband, my enigma," she murmured.

He reached up to unclasp her hand from his wrist and held it in his for a moment as they looked deeply into one another's eyes. Then he laid her hand on her lap. "Shut your beautiful eyes and camouflage your enticing body," he murmured, his eyes shifting to the gentle swell of her breasts beneath the blouse. "I must concentrate on other matters now."

"You shouldn't make such a confession, husband," Zoe breathed, deep down wishing that she were more to Matt than a lover. She wanted him to love her. "You give me power over you. Power which I'm strongly tempted to use."

"But you won't," Matt replied, firm in his conviction.

"No," Zoe answered, "I won't."

Running Horse approached Matt and spoke in Comanche. "If we are going to catch up with the wagons, Ma-ta-mon-yahu, we must move. While we remain here in one spot, we give them the edge. They will reach the other range of mountains if we do not hurry. Each day you become more and more captivated by the white woman."

When Matt saw Running Horse's gaze slide to Zoe, he grinned and answered in Comanche. "Yes, the woman captivates me, but I have not forgotten my goal. Nor are we losing any time. The white men have no idea we are following them; they are moving at a leisurely pace. We'll easily overtake them . . . and long before they reach the mountains." He ran his hand over Zoe's cheeks and the bridge of her nose, across the sprinkling of freckles. "Tell me, my friend, do you not think my wife is lovely?"

Running Horse grinned. "I think your wife is lovely, Ma-ta-mon-yahu. Not as lovely as my Wild Summer Flower but lovely." He added, "Do you think she was worth the black stallion, my friend?"

"What are you two talking about?" Zoe asked before Matt could reply to Running Horse's question.

"Running Horse says you are distracting me from my purpose."

"What do you say?" she murmured.

"I asked if he didn't think you were lovely." When soft color tinged her cheeks, Matt laughed. That she was his wife brought immeasurable pleasure to him. "He said you were and then asked if I thought you were worth my prize stallion."

"Do you?"

Matt's and Zoe's eyes locked. Zoe waited for his answer.

"Yes."

Zoe looked at him in wonderment, so full of happiness she thought surely she would explode. When his fingers lightly ran across the bridge of her nose the second time, she asked, "Are you making fun of my freckles?"

"No," he answered, "they fascinate me." Reluctantly he dropped his hand and his expression grew solemn. "The trip has been easy up to now. In order to keep from being detected, we're going to ride through the foothills on either side of the wagons until we're even with them. Remember, you must obey my orders without question." When Zoe nodded, Matt turned to Running Horse and repeated the instructions to him. "You follow Keen Eyes' trail and bring us any news," he said. "When you find him, the two of you join us in the mountains."

The brave nodded and urged his horse into a gallop to relay Matt's instructions to the others. For the next four hours, the small party wound through the boulders until they were parallel to the wagons.

"How close are they?" Zoe asked.

"Farther than it looks," Matt returned, measuring the distance with a glance. "At least a mile."

Zoe hooked the neckline of her blouse with her

239

index finger and fanned it, enjoying the rush of air against her sweat-dampened body. "Are you going to attack now?"

"Yes," he answered.

"Aren't you going to wait for Keen Eyes and Running Horse to join you?"

Matt shook his head. "I want to get to the wagons before they circle for camp and before they get close enough to run into the mountains for safety." He turned to Zoe. "I'm going to find you a place to hide. I want you to remain there no matter what. Do you understand?"

"You're outnumbered, Matt," Zoe said. "Please let me go with you. I'd rather be there with you than—"

Matt shook his head, his eyes hard as flint. "Under no circumstances will you ride out there. You'll endanger me and my men. I can't take that risk. Besides—" the eyes softened "—I don't want to take the risk of losing you."

"What if I lose you?" she countered.

"You won't," Matt promised.

From her hiding place Zoe watched Matt and the two braves as they rode down the side of the mountain toward the wagons that slowly lumbered through the valley. Then she lost sight of them. Clutching the revolver Matt had left with her, she inched forward to peer around the boulder, but the Comanches were lost from sight. She watched the wagons instead, counting the seconds as if they were hours. Finally Matt approached the wagon train, a white handkerchief flying from his lance. She wished she were closer so she could find out what he was saying.

* * *

ACCEPT YOUR FREE GIFT AND EXPERIENCE MORE OF THE PASSION AND ADVENTURE YOU LIKE IN A HISTORICAL ROMANCE

Zebra Romances are the finest novels of their kind and are written with the adult woman in mind. All of our books are written by authors who really know how to weave tales of romantic adventure in the historical settings you love.

Because our readers tell us these books sell out very fast in the stores, Zebra has made arrangements for you to receive at home the four newest titles published each month. You'll never miss a title and home delivery is so convenient. With your first shipment we'll even send you a FREE Zebra Historical Romance as our gift just for trying our home subscription service. No obligation.

BIG SAVINGS AND FREE HOME DELIVERY

Each month, the Zebra Home Subscription Service will send you the four newest titles as soon as they are published. (We ship these books to our subscribers even before we send them to the stores.) You may preview them *Free* for 10 days. If you like them as much as we think you will, you'll pay just $3.50 each and *save $1.80 each month* off the cover price. *AND you'll also get FREE HOME DELIVERY.* There is never a charge for shipping, handling or postage and there is no minimum you must buy. If you decide not to keep any shipment, simply return it within 10 days, no questions asked, and owe nothing.

"I come in peace, señor," Matt said to the beard-stubbled man who was leading the wagons.

The man edged his horse closer to Matt and studied him through squinted eyes. His gaze landed on the revolvers. "Wearing guns?" he countered sarcastically.

"You wear them," Matt pointed out. "Why can't I?"

"I'm a white man."

Matt smiled. "Are you saying that only white men can wear revolvers?"

Matt's cool reserve daunted the man. "Ain't never seen an Indian wearing 'em."

"Now you have . . . and I promise they're for more than decoration, señor. I can use them."

Convinced the Indian told the truth, the man looked beyond Matt, but saw nothing. Not trusting Indians, he was still suspicious. "Whatcha wanting, Injun?"

"Guns," Matt answered.

The man was momentarily taken aback by Matt's straightforwardness. His eyes darted back and forth as he looked around him, and a nervous sweat broke out on his upper lip. He managed a weak laugh. "What makes you think we got guns, Injun?"

Matt kept his gaze on the man's face, but he saw his hand ease down to his revolver. "Rumors fly quickly through Mexico, señor. We know you have guns for the Juaristas. We missed you at Candaleria, but now we have found you."

The man's laughter was shrill, and he lifted his hand to wipe the beads of perspiration from his face. "So . . . you're not an Indian; you're a

241

Juarista."

Matt didn't respond. "We do not want to hurt you, señor, but came to get our guns. We made a deal, and we've kept our part of it."

The bandit was frightened. "Look, friend," he began.

"I am not your friend," Matt interjected. "I want the guns."

"You're pretty stupid to come riding out here by yourself," the man said.

"If I were by myself," Matt answered, "I would have been stupid to do so, but I am not by myself, señor. My men surround you. They are waiting for me to give them word."

"Look, Injun, these here ain't your guns—"

"These are the guns that you stole from Señor Chandler," Matt said. "They are our guns."

The man wiped a grimy hand down his leg. "Why don't you just mosey on, feller? We don't know nothing about these guns being for you Juaristas. These here guns belong to Mr. Weber Fielding. We got to get them back to him." With a slight nod, the man whipped his revolver from his holster and signaled to the other drivers, who did the same, but not before Matt had drawn both of his, shooting him and the driver in the first wagon.

The minute the men drew on Matt, the Comanches came sweeping out of the boulders, their ululations filling the air. The other three drivers were killed, and the only man left alive was the rear guard, who took off toward the mountains.

"I'll get him," Matt yelled. "You take care of the guns."

Remembering her promise to Matt, Zoe hovered in her hiding place, peering over the boulder. When she saw the man riding in her direction, she dropped down and crept farther back into the alcove. She double-checked the revolver. It was loaded. She heard the hooves as they clopped against the hard rocks; she heard loose pebbles clatter across the ground. Then the man rounded the bend where she was hiding. She flattened her back to the boulder and clamped a hand over Dusty's mouth to keep her from neighing. The man stopped his horse, his head turned in the direction from which he'd just come, and Zoe's heart was beating so heavily, she thought surely he could hear it.

He was so close she could see his profile clearly. He was a young man, his face gaunt and pockmarked, his nose flattened unnaturally. A thin scar edged through the black stubble from his temple to the curve of his chin. One at a time he pulled his revolvers from the holsters and reloaded them. Then he pulled the black hat farther down over his face, and slapped the horse across the flank with the reigns.

Not until the sound of the hooves died out did Zoe breathe easily and let go of Dusty's mouth. Still she cowered in the hollow, waiting. When she heard another horse approaching, she slunk farther back. She drew the gun and waited. Closer and closer the rider came. When he passed her by, she saw that it was Matt, chasing the outlaw. Although she wanted to follow to help him, she didn't. She remembered his warnings; she remembered her promise. Nervously she waited in her hiding place, straining her ears until finally she heard the sound of hooves clashing against the rocks.

"Zoe," Matt called out, "are you all right?"

She dropped the gun and raced from the boulders. By the time she reached Matt, he had dismounted and she flung herself into his arms. "I was so worried about you," she cried, lifting her hands to his face, wanting to assure herself that he was unharmed. "I heard the shooting, and then that man—" She shuddered in Matt's arms. "Is he—"

"He got away," he told her, holding her close.

"Oh, Matt, did you see him? Did you see his face? He was so young to be so cruel-looking. He couldn't have been more than twenty, and so hard. A long, thin scar ran along the right side of his face."

"I caught a quick glimpse of him," Matt told her. "He was riding guard on the other side of the wagons and got away before I knew he was there."

Zoe pulled back, her hands now thoroughly roaming his chest and shoulders. "You're not hurt?"

Matt laughed. "Is that the doctor or my wife asking?"

Zoe looked into his face, gladly drowning in those beautiful brown eyes. "The wife," she said softly.

"This is the answer the husband gives to his wife."

Matt lowered his head, knocking Zoe's hat off, and took her mouth, tentatively and softly at first. But when she moved herself so that her body pressed firmly against his from chest to thigh, a feverish heat gripped him. His mouth forced hers open to fill her with the flowing of his soul and to demand the same from her. Zoe arched her back to the gentle pressure of his hand. A warmth spread across her breasts and sank into her belly, tingling downward all the way to her toes before rising again to throb at the joining of her legs.

Finally he broke the kiss, and his lips, warm and firm, nipped hers, moving around her mouth, butterflying across her cheeks and back to her mouth. His hands joined in the loving inquiry to move up her midriff and to cup the fullness of her breasts in the palms of his hands. Her velvety flesh and soft scent wrapped themselves around him to ensnare his heart.

Zoe gasped, lifting her hands to catch him and to still his movements. Her stomach, quivering and tight, drew taut with her desires. She was overwhelmed by those feelings that only Matt had the ability to arouse in her. As always, they were startling and intensely passionate. She placed light, feathery kisses against his neck and snuggled against his sturdy frame.

When her hand slid through the openings on the shirt to touch his chest, an exciting tingle skittered across Matt's flesh. His heart pounded against his ribs and his hand moved in agonizing sweetness up Zoe's arms, over her shoulders, and down her back. He placed hot, searing kisses along the hollow of her neck and along the opening of her blouse.

His touch filled Zoe with an undeniable desire. As his caresses roamed boldly over her body, Zoe moaned softly, surrendering to the passionate spell this man could always weave about her. Gladly she surrendered to the heady pleasure that possessed her flesh.

When Matt finally lifted his face, both of them were breathing heavily. "I wish we could finish what we've begun," he said, "but we better get out of here. These gunshots are going to attract a lot of attention, and most of it isn't going to be friendly."

"Who do you mean?" Zoe asked.

"Juaristas, bandits, Apaches, the French troops," Matt answered as he stooped to retrieve her hat. As she put it on, he walked into the hollow, grabbed Dusty's reins, and brought her out for Zoe.

"Where are we going from here?" Zoe inserted her foot into the stirrup and lifted herself up.

"Home," Matt answered.

"Where is home?" she asked, looking directly into Matt's face.

"We're going to Soaring Eagle's village."

He turned from Zoe's stare and mounted, leading the way through the narrow trail to the valley. As soon as the Comanches were in the wagons, their horses tied to the rear, the group began the slow journey to the Texas border, Matt and Zoe riding lead.

"Did you find out who the men were working for?" Zoe asked, finally breaking the silence but not looking at him.

"Fielding."

Her head jerked in his direction and she exclaimed, "I don't believe that for a minute!"

"Don't believe it," Matt returned, irritated because she always thought the worst of him and the best of Weber. He wondered if she would ever cease comparing him to Fielding. His eyes apprehensively scanned the sky, which was now growing dark with storm clouds. He hoped he could get the wagons across the chain of foothills into Texas before the rain began.

A gust of wind whipped around Zoe, flapping the ends of her bandanna across her face. Planting her hand on the crown of her hat, she asked, "Why

246

would Weber do it, Matt?"

"You tell me." Strands of black hair whisked across his forehead and cheeks.

Zoe inhaled sharply. Matt was determined to be an irritant, and he was. His expression was darker than the sky, his eyes roiling with fury.

"Maybe Weber didn't want the ranchers to get the money," Matt tersely suggested. "Shook said all of them were in hock to Weber up to their necks."

"Of course, they would say that," Zoe replied. "They haven't handled their finances too well and are jealous of Weber because he has. But I guarantee you, Weber has been most understanding since the war." Because she was busy battling the heavy gusts of wind, Zoe failed to see Matt's frown. "He's helped them to keep their land every way he can, even to loaning them money from his personal funds." She turned to Matt and said, "This war has been no kinder to Weber than to others. He's suffered just like the rest."

"Who do you worship, Zoe? God or Fielding?" The low roll of thunder accented Matt's words, and lightning jagged through the blackened sky.

"Look," Zoe exclaimed, dragging the end of her bandanna out of her mouth, "Weber's human just like the rest of us—"

"I'm glad to hear you admit that," Matt interrupted. 'I was beginning to think you'd put up an altar in your home to him."

Zoe bit back her retort and continued with her original thought, "He may have some ulterior motive for loaning the ranchers money out of his personal funds, but why would he kill them?" She glared at Matt. "Give me one good reason. All he had to do was steal the guns. Without their receiv-

247

ing the money from the Juaristas, he has their property. How would he benefit from their deaths?"

That was a question Matt had also been pondering, and one for which he had no answer. In particular, he wondered why Fielding had wanted Bryan dead. "How does the property of these ranchers fit into Fielding's irrigation scheme?"

Zoe reflected a moment before she said, "We didn't really need any of theirs for the irrigation canal. What he needed, he purchased from Uriah Chandler." They rode in silence a while longer before Zoe said, "Come to Chandlerville with me, Matt, and let me introduce you to Weber. I doubt the two of you will get along together, but he's not as bad as you think."

"If I were to come to Chandlerville with you," Matt said, "would you introduce me as your husband?"

"Well, I . . . I . . ." Zoe faltered. "With my being engaged . . ."

"You can't be engaged to one man and married to another," Matt interjected.

"Matt," Zoe pleaded, her hand still on her head, the hat brim flapping in the wind, "you must understand. When I left Chandlerville two weeks ago, I was engaged to Weber. Furthermore, a Comanche wedding ceremony isn't binding."

Matt was disappointed in Zoe's answer, but he understood her quandary. "No ceremony is binding," he told her. "Words said over you, whether they are English or Comanche, religious or civil, don't make the marriage. Marriage is a commitment between a man and a woman. And get this through your head, Doctor Zoe, it'll be better for all concerned if you're married to me. When you

248

return to that civilization you're so fond of throwing in my face, you're going to learn that people have little regard for a woman who's been a prisoner of the Indians."

"It doesn't matter." Zoe swallowed the bitter thought and remembered the adverse way many of the people had acted toward Inez Patterson. "I can't ride into town with a—with you and announce that I'm married to you."

"I can," Matt returned, "and I will."

When the impact of Matt's words hit Zoe, she turned and exclaimed, "Does this mean we're headed for Chandlerville?"

"Yes," Matt answered, riding ahead and calling over his shoulder, "I think it's time we went to Chandlerville. First, we've got to get through the storm."

Matt was taking her home! It was the announcement she had been begging for . . . but she wasn't as thrilled as she'd thought she'd be, and her lack of interest had nothing to do with Matt's wanting to tell the world that they were man and wife. She was a changed woman, and the change was more than physical. Although she wouldn't admit it to Matt, she found herself questioning Weber's motives and wondering if his dream was really for Chandlerville or for himself. She wished she had been paying more attention to the pattern line of the property he had been buying.

Streak after streak of lightning slicked through the sky, and big drops of rain splattered her. Above the thunder she heard Matt yelling orders in Comanche. Whips cracked and weapons creaked as they lurched forward at full speed.

Matt rode back to Zoe and pointed to a shallow

alcove in the side of the cliff. It was large enough to shelter the four wagons. "Over there," he yelled, his words carried on a gust of wind.

Zoe nodded and, lowering her face and putting her head to the wind, followed the wagons to the shelter, then followed Matt to a smaller cave on the other side of the cliff.

"We can have some privacy here," he said. "I'll be back as soon as I get the wagons taken care of."

Her clothes pasted to her body, Zoe walked to the edge of the ridge. While the men were taking care of the wagons and horses, she gazed at the electrified sky . . . so intense, she thought, but so alive and beautiful. Much later, she wasn't sure just when, she happened to look across the hollow and saw Matt as he walked through the rain toward their secret bower.

Zoe's concerns and then the entire world melted away until nothing remained but her and Matt. His red shirt was plastered to his body, his black hair slicked to his head, but he was as vitally alive as the weather around them. The brown eyes looking at her were deep and sultry.

When he began to walk toward her, Zoe's heart pounded against her ribs. Though they hadn't touched yet, a passionate flame burst between them, igniting the wildfire that consumed their thoughts and flesh. He lifted her into his arms and Zoe locked hers around his neck. When he walked from beneath the shelter into the deluge, she lifted her face and he claimed her lips in a hot, searing kiss. As her lips opened to receive his tongue, Zoe clutched Matt's shoulders and pressed herself against his chest. Her senses were dazed with sweet exhilaration.

When he reached a smaller alcove in the cliff, he gently set her on her feet and they stood as if they'd never seen each other before. Matt reached out to push the strands of wet hair from her cheeks; then his hand strayed to the delicate contours of her face.

Zoe felt Matt's hands at the neck of her blouse as he began to unbutton it. Each piece of clothing fell to the floor at her feet. When she stood naked, his hands fell to his side and he stepped back, a look of wonderment on his face. He looked at her as if this were the first time he'd ever seen her.

"Am I pretty?" she asked unpretentiously.

In the flashing light, her body looked as if it were a statue sculpted by loving hands into sheer perfection. "No," Matt whispered huskily, "you're more than pretty. You're beautiful." He moved nearer and leaned down to kiss her forehead, slowly moving his lips over her face, down the soft arch of her neck, back and forth across her collarbone. His lips tasted the skin that smelled so delicious. "So beautiful. Your blue eyes have haunted me all day."

His lips nibbled the fullness of her breasts, his hand gently lifting them from the bottom, pushing the nipple into his waiting mouth. Reverently he sucked the goodness of her body, and Elizabeth felt each tug as it pulled her closer and closer to his frame. Then his hands moved across her stomach to the downy softness at the juncture of her thighs. His fingers touched the moist portal.

"Matt." Drugged with desire, Zoe swayed against him, moaning his name, her hands tangling in his thick hair.

As his fingers worked their magic with her, Matt felt a shudder wrack Zoe's body, and she whim-

251

pered and clenched her hands in his hair. He held her close for a long time before he gently set her aside in order to pull his shirt over his head and toss it aside. He unbuttoned his trousers and stepped out of them.

Mesmerized, Zoe skimmed the bronzed, muscled chest and trim waist and let her gaze settle on his erection. "You're so handsome," she whispered as she moved closer to him, her hands worshipping his chest adoringly, her fingertips touching his nipples, her palms brushing down. She lifted her face and smiled. "So strong. So real."

With a groan of unleashed desire, Matt lowered his mouth to grind into hers in tender abandon. Finally he raised his lips and lowered her to the blanket that he had spread. When they were lying down, his lips, warm and firm, nipped hers, moving around her mouth, butterflying across her cheeks and back to her mouth. His hands brushed up her midriff to cup the fullness of her breasts. Zoe gasped, lowering her face, lifting her hands to catch his and to still his movements. Her stomach was quivering and tight. Daringly she placed light, feathery kisses against his neck and snuggled against his sturdy frame.

His hand moved in agonizing sweetness up her arms, over her shoulders, and down her back. He placed hot, searing kisses along the hollow of her neck before his mouth covered the peak of her breasts, teasing it to tautness.

His touch filled Zoe with an undeniable desire. As his experienced caresses roamed boldly over her quivering skin, Zoe moaned softly, surrendering to the passionate spell that encompassed her. A rapturous tingle ignited a blaze that burned uncontrollably within.

"Matt! Oh, Matt!" She could hardly articulate her thoughts. Her brain was thick and hazy, inebriated from his nearness, from his tenderness. Her tongue was thick from the wine of passion that ran undiluted through her blood.

Matt aroused Zoe until she pulled him close and begged him to become a part of her. As he gently spread her legs, as he lifted himself over her, he kissed her and murmured words of endearment. His hands prepared her for entry. Her pleasure was his pleasure.

Zoe ached to receive him when he brought his throbbing warmth to the moist portal. When he entered, his lips captured hers in another long, deep kiss and he began to stroke her gently with his silken shaft.

Zoe began to move with him. She felt his hands as they slipped beneath her buttocks, his fingers digging into the sensitive flesh, kneading and pulling her tighter to him. All the while he kissed her lips, her neck, her breasts. All the while he fought against losing himself in the pleasure of her hot, velvety sheath. Matt thrust deeply, more rapidly, more fiercely and Zoe's body burst into an uncontrollable blaze of passion. She moved in rhythm to him.

Lost in a magical world, nothing existed except Matt and the soft body beneath him. His entire body ached with the need to release the pent-up desire that surged through him. His thrusts were deeper, more rapid, more fierce, yet always tempered with care and restraint, lest he hurt Zoe. Zoe writhed under his caresses. When she thought she could bear the torment no longer, her blood turned

253

into fiery passion, blazing through her veins. Her heart was pounding; her breath was short and ragged. Every nerve in her body screamed for release. He heard her gasp; he felt her tense, then tremble uncontrollably in his arms. Her dark, moist tunnel of softness pulsated and pushed around him; it clung with each instant, spasmodic contraction. Then Matt buried his face in her shoulder and groaned as he achieved release.

He rolled over. Quietly they lay together in the peaceful afterglow. Zoe pressed her head and palm against Matt's chest. She felt his heartbeat slow down and his breathing normalize.

"I never dreamed that being with a man could be so wonderful." Her voice was low as she ran the tips of her fingers down his chest. She propped up one elbow and looked down at Matt, at the rugged features of his face. Strands of honey-blond hair trailed across his chest. "I feel like my entire body is glowing."

Matt laughed and reached up to cup her face with both hands. "You are glowing," he told her, the brown eyes intently searching her face. "You're more beautiful than ever."

"Are you taking credit for that, Matt Barnabas?" Zoe teased in a love-hushed voice.

"No," he answered, "but I'm glad that I had something to do with it."

"Since you're being so sweet," Zoe said, planting tiny kisses on his lips, "I'm almost ready to admit that you deserve all the credit."

"Thank you," Matt whispered, his hand curling around her skull to culminate the tormenting little kisses with a long, deep one. "It's a humbling experience to know that I've lit the flame of desire within you, my wife."

"Don't get too humble, my proud Comanche warrior." Zoe laughed, her lips brushing erotically against his, the sound washing Matt with a warmth he'd never felt before, a sound that left him completely exposed and vulnerable to her. "It's totally out of character for you. I rather like you at your arrogant best."

Long and leisurely they kissed before Zoe lowered her head and pressed kisses over his chest, moving from one nipple to the other, arousing each to a hard point, then lower down the narrowing swirl of hair. She heard Matt's quick intake of breath when her lips touched the sensitive skin around his navel. She reveled in her power as a seductress when she felt his stomach quiver beneath her gentle ministrations of love.

Her hand touched the thick mat of black hair that pillowed his manhood, and she tantalized him with her touch, so close, yet so far away. A burning fire began in the pit of Matt's stomach, growing hotter and hotter until he moaned his pain, his hands gripping Zoe, holding her, pinning her against his chest. His lips captured hers in a hot, fiery kiss, yet her fingers wouldn't be stilled. When the pressure of his mouth pushed her head back, when his lips opened hers and his tongue invaded the sweet domain of her mouth, Zoe's fingers curled around his masculinity, the soft tips caressing the area of greatest sensitivity.

Matt's soft moans turned into a groan, a blending of pleasure and pain. He was weak with wanting when Zoe pulled her lips from his, lowered her face, and circled his nipple with her mouth. When he could stand the excruciating pleasure no more,

Zoe lifted her face, her hair brushing against his hot skin, and she began to fondle his other nipple with her tongue. The fingers of one hand splayed through the thick hair of his head, the other one gently touched his most intimate parts.

As Matt began to breathe raggedly, Zoe's head lowered, her hair and her lips brushing a path of pure fire down Matt's torso, her tongue flicking excruciating designs on the muscle-taut stomach. She planted a multitude of kisses across his stomach and trailed her fingertips up and down his thighs. Then she pushed herself up and delighted in Matt's adoring gaze on her breasts. She straddled him and slowly lowered herself on him, her moist inner body slipping over his manhood.

Matt wanted to arch; he wanted to thrust himself deeper into the fold of warm, moist femininity, but he didn't want to hurt her. So he let her take the initiative, delighting in the sheathing of his manhood into the scabbard of her inner self just as his soul became sheathed in hers. When she leaned over him, balancing herself on the palms of her hands, she ran the soles of her feet down his legs, stretching her length with his.

Matt, on the brink of insanity from wanting, captured one of the luscious nipples in his mouth, and as he began to tug gently, he caught her buttocks with both his hands, settling her on him as he began to thrust. Crazed with desire to please him and to be pleased, Zoe began to work with him, their bodies moving in matched rhythm.

Zoe's head lowered over his and she murmured, "Kiss me, darling."

Matt released her breast and caught her face in both hands, bringing her lips down on his, gasping

256

and arching as her tongue darted into his mouth. But then, in the duel of love, of aggression, his tongue pushed into her mouth. Filled with her man, Zoe groaned her pleasure, moving frenetically, racing to the summit of joy and completion, carrying Matt with her.

When they reached their climax, Zoe was gasping for breath, but didn't pull her mouth from his. They made the last arch and thrust together, their climax so nearly together that it could have been simultaneous.

Spent, Zoe collapsed on top of Matt, breathing heavily, drawing in deep gulps of air. She closed her eyes and reveled in the sweet aftermath, enjoying Matt's fingers as they pushed dampened tendrils of hair from her face, as they traced the outline of her ears, of her breasts, as they slid down to tickle her buttocks.

"You're quite a lover, sweet Zoe," Matt breathed.

"Thank you," Zoe whispered huskily. "I've had a good teacher." In a few minutes she murmured sleepily, "Matt, I'll climb the highest building in Chandlerville and announce to the world that you and I are married."

"Thank you, my darling."

Sated, they drifted hazily in and out of the sensual world they had created with their love. Vaguely, Zoe was aware of Matt lying next to her, of his hands still lightly caressing and touching her. She was aware of the deep satisfaction of her body. She smiled and stretched, a sigh of contentment escaping her lips.

After Zoe finally went to sleep, Matt stood and slipped into his clothes. Moving to the edge of the alcove, he stared blankly into the rain. She was willing to announce to all and sundry that she was married to a half-breed Comanche. Little did she know that her half-breed was Matt Chandler. He knew that when she awakened, he must tell her who he was. He cared too much about Zoe to let her learn it from someone other than himself, and he cared too much to confess that he had deceived her from the beginning. He wondered how she would react when she heard his confession and learned that he had married her out of revenge, to get even with her fiancé. Revenge tasted bitter.

Chapter 14

Golden rays of early morning light were appearing in the alcove when Matt squatted and set a tin cup and plate beside Zoe's pallet. "Time to get up, sleepyhead," he said, shaking her shoulder.

She turned over, opened her eyes, and looked into his face, smiling. "So early . . ."

"So early," he repeated, watching her stretch her legs so that the blanket covered only her breasts and midsection.

"Seems like I just went to sleep."

Matt grinned. "Well, I admit we did get precious little sleep; however, you seemed to want to—" He stopped speaking and his impish grin turned into a gentle smile when he saw the faint color of pleasure tinge her cheeks.

"Yes," she whispered, reaching out to cup his face in her hand, "I wanted to . . . and I want to again."

Although the words were a perfect reflection of her heart's desire, they baffled and frightened her. Her feelings for this man had created a stranger out of her. The power he wielded over her emotions frightened her. He alone, of all the people in her life, had the power to hurt her.

Matt watched Zoe intently, wondering what she

was thinking—not the passion she was feeling; he knew that—but what she was thinking about him. Although he had had his grandfather perform a special marriage ceremony over them, he knew that Zoe was not bound by Indian law; she knew it too. He hoped she saw him as husband as well as lover. Odd, he'd never had that desire before. A little confused by this revelation, he retreated from his thoughts.

He smiled and turned his head out of her hand as he picked up the cup and handed it to her. "The coffee's going to get cold if you don't drink it. It's not the best in the world hot, so you can imagine what it'll taste like cold."

Zoe nodded and took the cup, lifting it to her lips. Feeling bereft and alone by his having moved a few inches, she wondered how she would feel if he weren't a part of her life at all. Unable to stand the thought, she reached out and laid her hand over his.

Matt looked up and smiled. "I cut you several slices of pemmican and poured honey over them."

"Umm," Zoe sniffed appreciatively, lifting her big blue eyes to take in his face. "I can think of only one thing I like better than being awakened by such a good looking man and served breakfast in bed." Slowly she sat up, the blanket sliding down.

Matt stared at the pale beauty of her flesh for a while, then leaned over to take her breast into his mouth, his tongue flickering over the tip. "So beautiful," he murmured, delighting in the tremor that shook her. "So wonderful." His arms slipped around her and he laid his face against the satin smoothness of her skin.

Zoe wrapped her arms around him and hugged

him tightly to her. She and Matt were sharing something precious, a moment she wanted never to end. No matter what the future held for them, they would never recapture the idyllic moments they were sharing now. Each could be himself without worrying about the strictures of his society. They were not white or Indian; they were simply a man and a woman in love. . . .

No, Zoe thought, correcting herself, she couldn't say they were in love. That Matt didn't love her was her fear. They made love, but Matt had never said anything about being in love, had never given her any indication that he loved her. She wondered about the depth of his emotions for her. Did his feelings go beyond mere physical gratification? She hoped they did.

Another thought nagged her: How would living in Chandlerville affect Matt's feelings for her? For reasons he hadn't shared with her yet and reasons about which she was curious, he preferred the life of an Indian. He had chosen it above that of a white man.

Zoe pushed out of his arms, wishing she could voice her fears and ask her questions, but she wasn't ready for the answer yet. She wanted this beautiful togetherness to last as long as it could. After she had taken several swallows of the coffee, she said brightly, "Just what a weary traveler needs."

"After you eat," Matt said, stretching out beside her, locking his hands beneath his head, "you have time for your toilet, but hurry. I want us to make good time so we can cross into Texas today."

"Umm," was Zoe's only answer. Her mouth was full of pemmican.

Smiling, Matt reached out to wipe a speck of honey from the corner of her mouth. "Before we leave, I want to talk to you."

Zoe stopped chewing and held suspended in air a piece of the pemmican, honey slowly running down her hand. "Sounds pretty serious," she finally said, her heart doing double somersaults.

"It is."

Breakfast was forgotten as the honey cupped in her palm. "You want to talk about it now?"

Matt's smile widened. "No, I'd rather you were giving me more attention than you are your food." He pointed to her palm. "And be sure to wash up. If you don't, you'll be sticking to everything we pass on the way home."

Laughing, Zoe lapped the sticky sweet from her palm. "Can I help it," she asked, cramming the last bite of pemmican into her mouth, "if I'm turning into a good Comanche wife?"

"No," Matt answered quietly, the laughter fading from his eyes, "I guess not."

Neither spoke as they stared at one another, each aware only of the other.

"Ma-ta-mon-yahu," Running Horse called, breaking the oneness of the moment, "come help me with these braces."

"Coming," Matt called. Then to Zoe he said, "Hurry."

She nodded and watched him rise and disappear around the boulder. She chewed the last bit of her breakfast slowly and washed it down with the now-tepid coffee. Setting the cup and plate aside to take to the brook with her when she bathed, she quickly dressed. She ran barefoot to the pool of water at the bottom of the incline.

Draping her towel around her neck, she washed her face and hands, then moved to sit on a large boulder that jutted precariously over the pool, where she could splash her feet. When Matt called, she grabbed her towel and dried off her feet. One of her socks slid to the back of the boulder and she reached for it, losing her balance. As she tumbled backward, she screamed and her head struck against a long, sharp, jagged rock that slashed through the thin material to pierce her shoulder.

She wasn't knocked unconscious, but was only dazed. Her head spun crazily; her shoulder throbbed. She shoved up on her elbows, but pain shot so severely through her chest and shoulders that she collapsed to the ground again. Somewhere in the distance she heard Matt call her name . . . or maybe she thought she heard him. She blacked out and when she came to, she heard an Indian rattle. Odd, she thought dimly that she should hear a rattle out here. Then she felt excruciating pain in her instep. Pure fire burned up her leg.

Zoe's scream had frightened Matt and sent him racing down the mountain to the brook. "Zoe," he cried, climbing over the rock to reach her. "How badly are you hurt?" The words were not even out of his mouth before his hands were making a swift examination. She had taken a heavy blow to the head; it was lacerated as well as bruised. A knot was already forming. He gently probed her shoulder and pulled back his hand to see blood on the fingertips. He put a hand behind her uninjured shoulder, but when he went to move her, Zoe cried out.

"Don't . . . jar . . . me," she grunted. "My back hurts." Quickly she added, "My foot, Matt. Exam-

263

ine my foot. It's burning." Then as he moved to her feet, she asked, "What about my shoulder?"

"Cut and bruised," Matt said. "I'm going to have to turn you over, eventually." His hand curled around the ankle and he saw the two red punctures on her instep. "Good God," he exclaimed, reaching for his knife. "A snakebite!" Over his shoulder he yelled in Comanche, "Running Horse, gather some cactus. Zoe's been bitten by a snake."

"Rattler," Zoe drawled as she fought a wave of nausea. "Heard the rattle."

"I'm going to lance it." Matt's fingers, acting as a tourniquet, dug into her ankle. "It's going to hurt, but it has to be done."

In too much pain to care, Zoe nodded her assent. She closed her eyes and relaxed, breathing deeply, talking to herself so that she wouldn't move when the knife cut into her flesh. She bit her lip, drawing blood, but didn't cry out. She felt Matt's mouth over the wound and the suction as he drew out the poison. Drifting in and out of consciousness, she was vaguely aware of Running Horse's arrival.

Using prickly pear leaves, Matt mixed a poultice which he applied to the snakebite. When he was through, he put his arms around Zoe. "I hate to do this, my darling," he muttered, "but I must move you."

Hovering in the beautiful region of semiconsciousness, Zoe grinned. Matt had called her "my darling," not "my wife." She opened her mouth to tell him, but she didn't want to waste the energy. . . . She felt Matt pick up her hands and loop them around his neck. Then he tugged. Pain shot up Zoe's back and she screamed. Immediately

264

Matt laid her back down.

"Oh, God, sweetheart," he whispered, "I didn't mean to hurt you."

"I'm sorry," she muttered, tears burning her eyes. "I don't mean to be such a baby. They say—" she was gasping in between words "—doctors . . . make the . . . worst . . . patients."

"You're not a baby," Matt gently consoled, "and you're not a bad patient. But I am going to have to move you." He carefully resituated her. Turning to Running Bear, he said, "Her back's hurt too badly for me to carry her. We're going to need a travois in order to get her out of here and up the cliff."

The words were hardly spoken before Running Horse was gone. While he and the other braves made the litter, Matt held Zoe's hand and quietly talked to her. Using a soft monotone—an old Indian method of dealing with pain and one the white man was just learning—he talked her into a light trance so that she was distracted from the pain and felt as if she were floating.

Running Horse brought the travois and laid it beside Zoe. Carefully, Matt and Running Horse lifted her, but even the most gentle of movements jarred her back. Although she hurt abominably, she grimaced and kept from crying out the second time. Sweat beaded on her forehead, and she felt dizzy. When they lifted the travois, the pain was so insufferable, she lapsed into unconsciousness.

For her sake, Matt was glad. After they reached the alcove and set the litter down, Matt turned her over and ripped the bloodied blouse from her body. Once he ascertained the seriousness of the cut, he ran to Zoe's saddlebags to rummage for bandages. Returning, he laid a handful of white strips on the litter beside her and quickly moved to the pile of prickly pears. He picked up one and carried it to the small flame of the morning fire, where he burned off the spines. Afterward he split it and laid it aside, cleaning Zoe's wound before she regained consciousness. Having Running Horse press the two pieces of cactus against the wound, Matt wove the bandages around her shoulders and chest to make a tight compress.

"What are we going to do now, Ma-ta-mon-yahu?" Running Horse asked.

"I need to get her back to Chandlerville," Matt said, "so that her father can take care of her. She's going to need medical attention."

"Do you think her back is badly hurt?"

Matt shook his head. "I'm not sure. I hope it's only bruised." But he wasn't going to take any chances. She would soon be delirious from the snakebite, and he wasn't going to let her suffer the pain of being dragged in a travois over these treacherous mountains. He turned to gaze at the wagons. Riding in one of them would be better for her.

"A wagon?" the Comanche asked.

Matt nodded. "Can we fit the extra guns into the other wagons?"

"No," Running Horse answered, "already they are too full, my friend. We must leave the weapons here if we are to make her a bed."

"Then that's what we'll do," Matt muttered. He realized at this moment that Zoe meant more to him than his own life, than his desire to revenge his own grievance or even his brother's death. He regretted that he had involved Zoe in his scheme for revenge. Had it not been for his selfishness, she would not be here now.

266

Only a few crates of the weapons had been unloaded when they heard bells jingling and a wagon noisily bouncing along the trail. Matt turned to see a donkey coming around the curve, pulling a *carreta* full of hay. A young man whose face was lost beneath a huge floppy-brimmed straw hat walked at the side of the narrow cart, leading the donkey.

Matt's gaze quickly passed the donkey and the man; he saw nothing but the softness of the hay—an excellent mattress for Zoe. He rushed down the incline to meet the Mexican, who stopped immediately upon seeing the stranger.

"Good morning, sir," Matt called in Spanish. "I'm Matt Barnabas, a Texan, on my way home from a trading expedition."

From beneath the brim of the sombrero, the Mexican eyed Matt warily. "Good morning, señor. I am Enrique Garza."

"Señor Garza," Matt said, moving even closer to the *carreta* until he saw the young man's face and his eyes lit up. "You're the vendor who was in Candaleria the day my wife and I arrived."

Enrique dropped his gaze and fidgeted with the burro's harness. Shrugging his shoulders, he said, "I could have been there. I travel all over Mexico with my produce."

Not taking the time to argue, Matt said, "I need your help, señor. My wife has had an accident. She was bitten by a snake and fell, hurting her back and shoulder. We must get her home as quickly as possible without too much jarring. May I buy your load of hay?"

"Surely you know, señor, that your wife will never live to reach Texas," a deep masculine voice called from behind a boulder. When Matt looked up, he

267

saw heavily armed Mexicans standing all around him. Seven he counted in a glance, all carrying rifles that were pointed at Matt and his braves. Each had two revolvers strapped around his waist and ammunition belts crossed over his chest.

"Good morning, señor," the speaker said, lithely jumping from the higher rock until he stood directly in front of Matt. A smile touched his lips and his eyes glittered. He wasn't hostile, but neither was he friendly. "I am Victorio De La Luz."

Out of the corner of his eye, Matt saw more of De La Luz's men rise, a human palisade imprisoning him and his braves. "Juaristas," he said, his brown eyes centering on De La Luz. Matt could tell that he was no more than twenty years old.

Victorio smiled and inclined his head in acknowledgment. "*Sí,* señor."

"Specifically El Pantero."

"*Sí,*" the Mexican answered, "I work for El Pantero. How did you know?"

Matt shrugged. "Call it a lucky . . . or unlucky hunch."

"I shall call it a lucky hunch, señor." Victorio threw back his head and laughed, the mellow sound filling the clearing where they stood. His sombrero fell off to reveal thick, black hair burnished to a midnight blue in the sunlight. "If you know who we are, señor, then you also know why we are here."

"The guns."

"*Sí,*" Victorio replied. "We have come a long way for them."

"What are you going to do with us?" Matt asked, uneasy about Zoe.

Victorio shrugged and held out his hands. "El

268

Pantero has no quarrel with you, señor, if you have no quarrel about giving him the guns."

"Take the guns," Matt said. "Just let me have one wagon so I can get my wife to a doctor. She's hurt."

Victorio brushed past Matt and walked to the litter on which Zoe lay. "I regret I cannot allow you to have the wagon, señor," he said, "but I must have it; otherwise, I have no way to transport the weapons, and we must hurry because the French troops are not far behind us. El Pantero is now waiting for us."

"How can you be so damned cruel?" Matt demanded, his blood boiling. "My wife could be dying!"

Ignoring Matt, Victorio turned his head to shout an order to his men in Spanish, seven of them bounding down the boulders and running to the wagons. Running Horse and the Comanches stepped back to watch the Mexicans as they began to reload the fourth wagon.

Victorio's gaze once again locked with Matt's, and he said, "Since you have delivered the guns to me, I will give you the money."

"You're not giving me anything. You owe me the money for these guns," Matt said angrily. "You can give me one of the wagons so I can carry my wife home. Time's wasting and she's dying."

Smiling, Victorio walked to Matt and stuffed the money into his shirt pocket. "Sí, señor, the money I will give to you. That is the deal I made with the *Americanos*. And while I won't let you have one of the wagons, I'm going to let Enrique take you to the healer in Ciudad de la Cruz in his *carreta*. It is much better-suited to traveling these narrow moun-

269

tain trails, and Enrique knows the trails better than you. Also, your *esposa* is very bad, and if anyone can save her life, *la curandera* can."

"A faith healer?" Matt asked dubiously.

"She has faith, señor," Victorio answered, "but she also has knowledge of many herbs. No one knows more about medicines around here than *la curandera* and her daughter. Besides, you really don't have a choice. Your wife will not live to see Texas. She needs help now."

Matt inhaled deeply and nodded. He had no choice but to trust Zoe to *la curandera*. De La Luz was right: she would never live to reach Texas. "How far to the village?"

"Not many *kilometers,* señor—" Victorio smiled and pointed to the donkey. "The way Rosita travels."

Matt's eyes narrowed. "Enrique is one of you?"

"No, señor, he is merely a vendor, traveling from village to village to sell his goods. Occasionally we run into each other and we exchange goods."

Now Matt understood why Enrique had been reticent to admit he was the vendor in Candaleria. "And I suppose when you're buying his produce, you exchange news," Matt added.

"Si," Victorio replied easily, "we exchange news also, señor. That is the only way we learn about our relatives who live in villages other than our own."

"This is the way you receive your news of the French," he said.

"Since Enrique is simpatico with the Juaristas and happens to be my first cousin, he does tell me where the French are."

"You knew not to come to Candaleria for the

270

guns, didn't you?"

Victorio nodded and said, "And we warned the *Americanos,* señor. I cannot imagine who killed them, but it was not us. Señor Chandler and El Pantero have been business associates for a long time now. We did not double-cross one another." He smiled. "Now take care of your wife, señor, and I will take care of the guns." Victorio spoke to Enrique, then left Matt and moved to the wagons, talking softly to his men.

Enrique bustled to the pile of blankets, picking several up and throwing them over the hay in the cart. "Here, señor," he said, "I have made a bed for the señora."

Two of the braves carried the litter to the cart, and Matt and Running Horse lifted her onto the blankets. Zoe moaned, but didn't regain consciousness.

Victorio walked to the *carreta.* "Thank you for the guns, señor, and take care of your beautiful wife."

"I will," Matt answered, watching as the Juarista nimbly leaped to his horse and waved the wagons forward. Matt then turned to Running Horse.

"Do you wish us to go with you?" the brave asked.

Matt shook his head. "I will go alone, my friend. You and the others return to the village. Tell my grandfather that I shall be there as soon as Zoe is well enough to travel."

As soon as the Comanches rode off, Matt turned from his friend to tie his chestnut to the back of the cart before he hopped in beside Zoe. The *carreta* rumbled up and down the winding trails through the mountains, going deeper into Mexico.

Matt knew they could move no faster, but he was impatient to get medical attention for Zoe. Her fever was soaring, and she was out of her mind with delirium. Every once in a while she would moan with pain. Afternoon glare turned into dusk, and eventually into night. Still they moved on.

When Matt wasn't thinking about Zoe, he thought about Bryan. In particular, he thought about Victorio saying that Bryan and El Pantero had been business associates for a long time. This was the way Bryan earned the money to repay the loan to Weber—the reason why Weber had Bryan killed.

"How much longer?" Matt asked.

"Not much, señor," Enrique called over his shoulder. "Generally I would stop and camp for the night, señor, but I think it is better for the señora if we continue to move. Rosita knows the trails well. We'll be in La Ciudad de la Cruz before the night is over."

"I don't know how to thank you," Matt said as he brushed the fever-moistened tendrils from Zoe's face. He turned his head and in the silvery light of night he saw the Mexican's white teeth flash in a smile.

"When you gave the guns to Victorio, you thanked me, señor."

"Do you want me to drive awhile?" Matt asked, knowing Enrique must be tired.

Another quick smile. "No, señor. Rosita and I are fine. We have traveled the route many times. I will ride on the seat, and if I should happen to go to sleep myself, Rosita, she will take us home."

Exhausted and worried, Matt argued no more. Careful not to jar Zoe, he squirmed around and

272

settled himself more comfortably. As he dozed, Zoe bolted up and screamed, "Matt."

He was up immediately, catching her by the shoulders and gently forcing her into the straw. "I'm here, sweetheart," he assured her. "Everything's all right. I'm here with you."

"Matt," she whispered, turning fever-glazed eyes on him.

"It's me, darling," he said and leaned down to brush his lips against her hot brow. "I'm here with you, and I'm going to take care of you."

As if she understood the words, Zoe settled down in his arms; then suddenly she flung her head from side to side and cried, "Weber? Where's Weber? He's going to come get me. He will, Matt! He will! He won't let me stay with the Indians!"

"It's all right, sweetheart," Matt whispered, holding her close. "It's all right." His heart was so grieved, he could hardly utter the words. Even in her delirium she was thinking about Weber and looking for him to rescue her from the Indians. For the first time in his life he cared about a woman, really cared, and she was in love with someone like Weber Fielding. She needed rescuing from Fielding, not from the Indians.

"Señor," Enrique called, a short while after Zoe had quieted down and was sleeping again, "we are here."

"I wish I had some way to repay you for helping us," Matt said as he scooted up in the wagon and gazed at the mountains silhouetted in the dark.

"I do not want any thanks, señor," the Mexican said. "I receive my reward in knowing that I have helped you and the señora." He was quiet for a long while, then said, "Soon our church will have

273

been here one hundred and fifty years, señor, and we are preparing for our greatest fiesta, a religious celebration in honor of the Holy Mother, Our Lady of the Valley. For the special occasion we are having golden candlesticks made for our altar. These, señor, are going to be identical to the candlesticks that were made for our church on her fiftieth anniversary, one hundred years ago—the original ones were lost when they were shipped to us."

As the *carreta* lumbered through the village plaza, Enrique regaled Matt with the minute details of the coming religious fiesta. When finally they arrived in front of a large house on the other side of the plaza, Enrique jumped from the cart and raced to the gate, pulling on the bell to announce his arrival. Soon the huge wooden door opened, and a tiny face, hidden in the folds of a large scarf and illuminated in the flame of the torch, peeked around.

"Buenos tardes, Corina," Enrique said, pulling off his sombrero. "I bring you news of Victorio, and—"

"Enrique!" The young woman threw open the gate. "We were not expecting you for another day!"

"I would not have been here so soon," he said, his head turning to the *carreta,* "but along the trail, I came across this man and his wife. We hurried because she needs your help. She was bitten by a snake and is delirious. Her fever is very high."

Corina rushed through the gates, her black scarf flying behind her. She handed the torch to Matt and climbed in the *carreta* alongside Zoe, her small hands moving in quick examination. "Get a litter," she called to Enrique. "We need to move her inside to a bed. Also inform Mamacita that we have an-

274

other patient."

When the young woman hopped out of the cart, she looked at Matt. "I'm Corina."

"I'm Matt Barnabas," he said. "This is my wife, Zoe."

"What happened?" Corina asked, glancing impatiently toward the gate to see if Enrique were coming with the litter.

"She fell from a boulder and hurt her back and head. At the same time she was bitten by a snake."

"That explains the delirium," the girl commented, the scarf slipping from her head to fall around her shoulders as she nodded.

In the torchlight Matt could tell that she was hardly more than a child. "Are you the healer?" he asked.

"Sí, I am a healer, but Mama is *la curandera*. She is teaching me, señor." Corina laughed. "You are thinking I am too young to be a healer, no?"

Matt smiled. "Are you a mind reader, too?"

"No, señor, many have refused to let me treat them because I have only sixteen years. They prefer Mamacita."

"I don't mind you treating Zoe," Matt told her. "I was just curious about your age."

"I am old enough to be a good healer, señor. That I promise you. Mama is gone now to tend to a sick woman in the mountains. When she returns, she will look at your wife."

Before Matt could say more, Enrique appeared with three other men and a litter. With Matt's help they moved Zoe from the cart into a small room in the house. Corina gave orders and young girls scurried in all directions, returning in a moment with basins of warm water, washcloths, medicines, and

275

bandages.

Corina hung her scarf over a rack on the wall and turned to Matt. "Enrique will take you to your room. You may freshen up and rest awhile. I'll send for you after I've cleansed her wounds and changed her clothes."

"I'd rather stay with her," Matt said.

Corina shook her head. "I understand how you feel, señor, but you need to take care of yourself so you can take care of her later. She has some bad days ahead of her before she's fit to travel again. Now go." Corina moved across the room, and placing her small palm against Matt's chest, pushed him into the corridor.

The door slammed in his face, and Matt stumbled into someone. As he turned and caught the woman by the shoulders to keep her from falling into the wall, a huge black handkerchief fluttered to the floor, and the folds of her cape swirled around their feet. "I'm terribly sorry," he apologized.

"No need to be," she said with a husky laugh, pulling away and bending down to pick up the handkerchief, which she quickly stuffed into the huge pockets of her dress. "I know how heavy-handed Corina can be when she's tending to her patients. You must be Señor Barnabas." She lifted her hands and to the huge black hood of her cape and pulled it off her head.

Matt was so surprised he could only nod. The woman looked exactly like Corina, just a few years older.

"I'm —"

"You're Corina's mother," Matt finished.

"I'm Corina's mother, Señora Eugenia. I have

276

just returned from the mountains, but no more talking now. Come . . . I shall take you to your room, where you can freshen up and rest. We mustn't cross Corina," she added with a decided twinkle in her dark eyes. "She's much stronger than she looks."

Matt followed Eugenia to his room and was surprised to find his bath already drawn and waiting. Across the foot of the bed lay his saddlebags. "Enrique searched the village for some clothes for you," Eugenia explained, her gaze on the trousers and shirt that lay at the foot of the bed. "I hope they fit and that you like them."

After the woman departed, Matt closed and bolted the door. He shaved first, then undressed and sank into the huge copper tub of warm water. He was glad to have escaped the hustle-bustle of the outside world for a few days. He was sure the tranquility of the house would aid Zoe in a speedy recovery.

Before Matt had finished his bath, he heard a knock and Corina called, "I have bathed your wife, tended her wounds, and given her an herb that lowers the fever and stops the convulsions, Mr. Barnabas. She is resting quite well at the moment, so you do not need to be in a hurry to get to her side. I have left one of our servants to sit with her, with instructions to come get you if there is any change in la señora's condition."

"Thank you," Matt answered.

"Now you get some sleep," the girl ordered. "I'll send someone to get you so that you may join us for dinner."

After Matt bathed and dried off, he slipped into the freshly pressed trousers and blue shirt that

Enrique had brought him. But he shunned the boots, much preferring the comfort of his moccasins to boots of the incorrect size. Even if he had lain down, as Corina had suggested, he wouldn't have slept. He wouldn't relax or rest until he knew Zoe was going to be all right. Opening the door, he hurried down the corridor to Zoe's room, the servant rising when he entered.

"I wanted to see her," he explained to the young girl as he moved to the bed where Zoe lay, her clean hair spreading in golden waves over the pristine white pillow. She was breathing freely and her color was better. He laid his hand over her forehead to find that her fever was still high. Sitting at the bottom of the bed, Matt lifted the sheet aside and looked at her foot, which was wrapped in a bulky compress that was covered with a deerskin. Her leg from the ankle to the calf was swollen.

Sitting down beside Zoe, Matt said, "Honey, are you in pain?" When she didn't answer, he leaned over, his mouth moving closer to her head. "Honey, how are you feeling?" Still there was no answer.

"Don't awaken her, sir. She's doing well." The servant's reassuring voice came from over Matt's shoulder. "She is still fevered, but since she drank the herb *la curandera* gave her, she is no longer delirious and has stopped her jerking. She is in a deep sleep."

He caught Zoe's shoulders and gently shook but couldn't awaken her. "What have you given her?" Matt asked.

"Some herbs to make her sleep," the servant replied, "and we have wrapped her foot in cool clay from the river, which we change often. *La curandera* believes that it draws out the poison."

Hours later, during early evening, judging by the shadows that lengthened against the wall, Matt sat with Zoe, trying to awaken her every so often, but to no avail. The door opened and Corina, having bathed and changed into a beautiful green gown, entered the room.

"Ah, Mr. Barnabas," she said, the black eyes sparkling, "I thought I would find you here."

"I can't awaken her," Matt said.

Corina, near the bed now, laid a comforting hand on Matt's shoulder. "No, I've given her some herbs that have induced a heavy sleep. Don't worry! Your wife is doing fine. It'll be several days before she's over the effects of the snakebite, but she's through the worse. We've given her a little bit of broth and will continue to feed her through the night. By morning the fever should be gone, and she'll be awake."

"What about her back?" Matt said.

"I do not know," the healer answered. "I am hoping that it is only bruised, but until she talks to us, I have no way of knowing. Now Mr. Barnabas, there is nothing more that you and I can do for your wife but let her rest. What do you say that we join Mamacita for dinner?"

Reluctantly Matt followed the young girl down the stairs into a large dining room. Blazing candlelight called attention to a beautifully spread table. A young servant moved unobtrusively in and out of the room as she served wine. Señora Eugenia, dressed in black silk, stood by the fireplace, her hair pulled into a beautiful chignon at the nape of her neck. Her only adornments were a pearl necklace and earrings.

"The wine is from Spain," Señora Eugenia said,

holding her glass in front of the candles to allow the light to flicker through the pale gold liquid. "We buy this especially for our guests, Mr. Barnabas."

Matt took a sip. "It's excellent, Señora Eugenia."

"May I propose a toast, Señor Barnabas?"

Matt nodded and raised his glass as the three of them moved closer.

"To your wife's swift recovery." Señora Eugenia smiled at Matt, her gaze sweeping from the crystal glass in his hand to the bracelet, the design and etchings catching her attention. She unconsciously leaned forward to study it more closely. Then she gasped and her hand fluttered to her chest, clutching at the folds of black material. The wineglass slipped from her limp fingers to fall on the tiled floor, splinters of crystal spraying across the room, the stem rolling to land at Matt's feet.

"What's wrong, Mamacita?" Corina cried in alarm, rushing across the room to her mother.

Señora Eugenia stumbled to the table and collapsed into a chair. Her face was ashen. For the first time her age showed. "The bracelet —" she pointed a trembling hand at Matt. "It is the bracelet, Corina."

The girl moved to where Matt stood and looked at his wrist. "Sí, mama," she answered, "it's the bracelet."

"Madre de Dios!" Señora Eugenia whispered reverently, tears streaming down her cheeks. "This is the miracle we have been waiting for!"

Chapter 15

While Matt didn't deny miracles, he didn't accept that he was one — nor that his bracelet was. Feeling rather uncomfortable and wishing he were anywhere but here, he continued to stare at the dazed woman.

"Please," Eugenia pleaded softly, "take the bracelet off and look at the inscription."

He lifted his arm, three sets of eyes gazing at his wrist, the candlelight glowing brightly against the gold. Ever since his grandfather had given him this bracelet twenty-three years ago, he'd worn it all the time. He didn't have to take it off to read the inscription; he knew the words by heart. *To my beloved husband, Ronaldo, April 15, 1759.* But something in *la curandera*'s expression, that odd inflection in her voice, compelled Matt to take the bracelet off and to look at the words that were almost worn smooth. He felt slightly naked when the air touched the pale skin where the band had been for so long. Turning it over, he looked inside.

"To my beloved husband, Ronaldo, April 15, 1759," Eugenia dictated in a faraway voice as she stared into the blackened fireplace.

So eerie was this confrontation that Matt felt a chill sweep his body. For twenty-three years—ever since his grandfather had given him the bracelet and he had read the inscription for the first time—he had been haunted by this man, Ronaldo, wondering who he was, what kind of man he was. Now, in the most sparsely populated northern province of Mexico, he found quite by accident a woman who knew about the same bracelet.

Eugenia walked to the large ornate chesterfield against the far wall. Opening the door, she withdrew a small wooden chest and returned to the table. After she unlocked it, she lifted another bracelet, a much smaller one, and with trembling fingers held it up, the golden circlet glittering in the candlelight.

"The matching one," she announced in a shaky voice. "Its inscription reads, 'To my beloved wife, Dolores, April 15, 1759.'"

Long, silent strides brought Matt to the table, where he took the bracelet from Eugenia and held it for a moment in the palm of his hand. After he read the inscription, he turned it over and holding it against his bracelet, compared the designs, which were almost identical. He looked up at her in question.

"I believe," she explained, "you are wearing the bracelet which, according to the stories that have been handed down in my family, belonged to my great-grandfather. My grandfather and grandmother made one trip to Mexico City, and while they were there, they saw the bracelets. Each bought one for the other and had it engraved, a lasting token of their love for one another."

Matt listened as the woman began to speak. Over one hundred years ago a group of wealthy merchants had hired her great grandfather to escort a large shipment of gold from Santa Fe to Mexico, but the caravan had never made it. According to the story told by the two brave soldiers who managed to survive, Indians attacked and killed everyone. They didn't know what happened to the gold. Many expeditions went out for it through the years, but no one ever found it. Not a trace," Eugenia concluded, her eyes on Matt's bracelet. "But now—now we have this. Our first clue to over a million dollars in gold!"

A million dollars in gold! The amount staggered Matt. Although he'd heard the story of the golden secret all his life, he'd never thought of so much wealth being hidden in their mountains. He was stunned, astonished, but didn't know why he should be. Indians didn't reckon wealth like the white man; therefore, they didn't place any value on the gold.

"*Sí*, Mama," Corina whispered, a tremulous smile on her lips, tears shining on her cheeks, "we have the miracle for which we have been praying for so many years."

"Perhaps, *mi hija*," Eugenia returned, leaning across the table to fill her a glass of wine and murmuring again, "Perhaps, my daughter."

"—and the gold, Mama," Corina said eagerly, "we can use the gold for the cause. We can give it to—"

Eugenia's husky chuckle echoed through the room, and she waved her daughter to silence. "One thing at a time, *chica*. I think perhaps we were prepared for our miracle, but it's evident that Señor

283

Barnabas isn't. Tell me something about the bracelet. How did you get it? What do you know about my grandfather? Tell me something, anything, that will help me find the gold."

More to have something to do than out of desire for more wine, Matt walked to the table to refill his glass. Eventually he said, "I'm half-white, half-Comanche. When I proved myself as a Comanche warrior my grandfather gave me this bracelet as a badge of honor and valor." He quaffed the drink in one swallow.

"Your tribe is the that who attacked the caravan and stole the gold?" Eugenia persisted.

Matt shook his head. "According to the stories I heard around the campfire as a child, the caravan was attacked by Mexican soldiers who knew about the shipment of gold and wanted it for themselves. Not wanting to be blamed for the murders of their companions and the theft, they staged the scene to look like an Indian massacre. A group of Comanches arrived in time to see what the soldiers were doing. They attacked these men, killing all but two, who escaped to Mexico to tell the story. They buried the gold so that no white man would ever find it."

"Naturally, those who reported the story to us would tell what made them sound the best," Eugenia pronounced, "and people are always ready to believe the worst of the Indians." She clapped her hands together lightly and looked at Corina, then up at Matt, with a bright, expectant smile. "Your people still have the gold, I presume?"

Matt shrugged and set the empty glass on the table. "I don't know. According to the legend the gold was hidden by the medicine man and the

284

chief. Today no one claims to know exactly where it's hidden. I didn't think it really existed."

"I must find it," Eugenia declared, pushing to her feet and pacing around the room. *"I must have it."*

Matt laughed sarcastically and said, "That was the purpose of no one's knowing where the gold was. My people knew the white man would come in droves if anyone should hear such a story."

"I don't want the gold for myself," Eugenia explained.

"We want it for the cause," Corina quickly interjected, her eyes blazing. "We want it to buy guns and supplies so we can drive the French from Mexico."

Eugenia moved to her daughter's side and put her arm around her shoulder. "We have no loyalty to the French," she admitted, "but we are more interested in the candlesticks that Father Suarez was bringing from Santa Fe than the gold." She turned her teary eyes to Matt. "You do not know how much that would boost the spirit of the villagers if we could get our golden candlesticks back, señor."

Matt stared into their expectant faces—first the mother's, then the daughter's.

A series of loud knocks and a call, "Riders are coming," sent Corina scurrying to the window, where she threw open the shutter to peer into the torchlit courtyard as hooves clopped over the cobblestones.

"Paco!" she whispered.

The sound was still echoing in the room as she ran through the salon and foyer, the bolt grating as she slid it through the wrought-iron supports. She threw open the door and a heavy-set, bearded man pushed past her, grabbing the door and slamming it, his spurs jingling as his boots fell on the tiled floor. When he was in the middle of the room, his disapproving gaze settled on Matt and the two men scrutinized each other.

"Paco," Eugenia said from across the room, her gown rustling softly as she moved closer, her eyes searching the gaunt face, "is something wrong?"

"*Sí,* Señora—" He pulled his gaze from Matt to look at Eugenia. "We ran into the French. Several are wounded."

"Victorio!" Corina screamed, running to Paco, catching his arm with both hands and spinning him around. "How is Victorio?" When Paco shook his head, Corina stumbled back, her hand flying to her mouth.

Matt and Eugenia moved at the same time, Eugenia to Corina's side, Matt into the dining room, where he poured the girl a glass of wine. As he reentered the room, he heard Eugenia say sharply, "We have no choice, Paco. We must trust this man. Now, don't stand here disputing my orders. Go get Victorio and bring him here."

Inhaling deeply and casting a disapproving glance at Matt, Paco nodded and walked to the door, his spurs jingling with each step. Silently, in direct contrast to the noisy exit of the Mexican, Matt crossed the huge salon to stand in front of Corina. "Drink this," he said. "It will put some warmth and color into your cheeks."

Corina lifted her grief-stricken eyes and tears rolled freely down her cheeks. "I don't want it, señor . . . I want Victorio. We were to have been married in three months."

"Victorio will be here soon," Eugenia said, taking

286

the glass from Matt and pressing it into Corina's hands, "and we will need our wits about us. Señor Barnabas is right. You'll feel better if you drink some of the wine. Then you must prepare a bed for Victorio. That's right . . . take several swallows."

"Oh, Mama," Corina whispered, rising and swaying against her mother, "what shall I do if he dies?"

Eugenia took the glass from Corina and handed it to Matt as she embraced her daughter. "He'll be all right, *mi hija,*" she promised. "He's going to be all right."

"I hate the French," Corina hissed, pushing out of Eugenia's arms and looking into her mother's face. "I hate them, Mama. If Victorio should die, I will fight beside El Pantero myself."

Eugenia's lips moved into a small, sad smile and she shook her head. "I have lost my husband and son to El Pantero, *mi hija,*" she said. "Must I also give him my daughter, the only child I have left?"

"Yes, if Victorio dies."

"Then we must make sure that Victorio doesn't die," Eugenia said. "Come, let us prepare his room."

Matt was still standing in the living room when Paco and three more Mexicans arrived. The man they carried on the litter hardly resembled the Juarista whom Matt had met the day before in the mountains. A two days' beard shaded his face; his eyes were darkly ringed and hollow, the black eyelashes stark against his pale cheeks. The front of his shirt, saturated with blood, was ripped open, a piece of material, also discolored with blood, wadded up over the wound.

As soon as Victorio was on the bed, Corina sat

287

down beside him, unbuttoning the shirt and pulling it aside. "I will not let you die, my love," she whispered, but when she looked at the gaping, jagged hole in his chest, her words seemed to be an empty promise.

Matt was nodding in a chair at the foot of Zoe's bed when the door opened and Eugenia slipped into the room, a basket of mud over her arm. Setting the candle on the small table at the foot of the bed, she pulled back the covers and unwrapped Zoe's foot, looking at the clay poultice.

Matt stood and walked to the bed to watch Eugenia. Once the foot was clean, she removed and folded the deerskin that protected the sheet from the clay and spread a clean one.

"How is she?" Matt asked.

"Her leg seems to be less swollen, but—"

"But her fever isn't breaking."

"Not yet," she replied. "That will take time."

"She hasn't awakened since we arrived here," he said, worried about the deep sleep to which she had succumbed; it didn't seem natural to him. "Shouldn't the effect of the herbs be wearing off by now?"

Straightening the piece of leather beneath Zoe's foot, Eugenia picked up the basket and placed it on the table next to the bed. "Not quite," she answered, smoothing the mud over Zoe's ankle. "Give them a few more hours."

"Even so," Matt said, "it seems to me that she would rouse when you move her to dress her wounds."

Eugenia looked at the tall man who peered anxiously over her shoulder. "Do not be so anxious, señor. Give your wife time to heal. Sleeping is

God's way of healing the body."

"The few people whom I've seen in sleep that deep never awoke," Matt said flatly.

"She will awaken, señor . . . I promise you that. You must be patient and give her time to heal."

Frustrated because there was nothing he could do but wait, Matt turned and walked to the opened window. "How is Victorio doing?"

"He will live. The bullet missed his heart and lungs."

The room was quiet after that. Eugenia continued to dress Zoe's wounds, and Matt was concerned about Zoe. Abruptly the silence was shattered by quick, sharp raps on the door, which opened before either Eugenia or Matt could move toward it. Enrique poked his head into the room.

"The French have followed Victorio's men to the village," he announced. "At the rate they are moving, they will be here within an hour. We must get him out before Duprees arrives."

Matt spun around. "Duprees?"

"Sí," Eugenia answered, rinsing her hands in the basin, "Captain Duprees has a personal vendetta against El Pantero and will stop at nothing to get him."

"Is Victorio El Pantero?" Matt asked.

"That is a question we do not ask—" Eugenia dried her hands and placed the soiled bandages into her basket "—because we are better off not knowing the answer. But he is the one Duprees would like to capture, because if Duprees has Victorio, he thinks he will either have or will find El Pantero. I must go now; I must see that Victorio is removed from the house before the French troops arrive. Please tie the deerskin around Señora Zoe's leg to keep the poultice in place."

After Eugenia was gone, Matt strapped the deer-skin around Zoe's leg; then he paced the room. Zoe's condition was critical. Although her shoulder was healing nicely, it was bruised and the wound was deep. He wasn't sure how badly her back was damaged. And now she had lapsed into this deep sleep, which if not drug-induced, was a coma. He wanted to get her back to Chandlerville to her father, so she could have the best medical help. At the same time, he pondered the wisdom of moving her.

Louis Duprees' arrival influenced Matt's decision; he couldn't remain at Eugenia's house. He and Zoe had been in Candaleria at the same time that a shipment of guns was expected from the United States. Now they were at the house where Victorio—a known Juarista—was being treated for his wounds. In the right place at the wrong time . . . Duprees had suspected them in Candaleria. How much more suspicious would he be if he found them here after their abrupt departure from Candaleria?

His decision made, Matt turned and walked out of Zoe's room in search of Eugenia. He would buy a wagon and some horses from her, and he and Zoe would leave within the hour.

"Are you looking for someone, señor?" Corina asked when he entered the bedroom where Victorio had been carried.

"Your mother," he said.

"She will be back shortly. She's gone to make preparations for hiding Victorio. You may wait for her in here, if you wish."

Matt shook his head. "Zoe and I can't remain

here with Louis Duprees coming," he told her, quickly explaining the circumstances of their first encounter with the Frenchman. He reached into his pocket and pulled out a roll of money Victorio had given him for the guns. "I would like to buy a wagon and some horses so I can take Zoe home."

"I'm sure Mama would help you," Corina assured him, "but you must talk with her, señor."

Matt had no time to wait; he turned, his long steps taking him down the corridor and out of the house. When he reached the barn, he found them ablaze with light from the glowing lanterns, but to his surprise no servants were in attendance. A quick search produced a *carreta,* which he filled with hay and to which he hitched a mule. He had reentered the barn to saddle his chestnut when he saw a cloaked figure stealing out of the shadows and leading a magnificent black stallion toward the back door.

Matt eased out of the stall before the person could disappear through the exit and softly called, "El Pantero."

The cape swirled in the air as the figure turned around to gaze at Matt, the lantern light flickering dully from the wall behind to cast him in darkness. The part of the face that wasn't hidden by the huge black sombrero was covered with a black mask. Only the eyes were visible, but even they were shadowed, giving the person the obscurity he sought.

"Or should I say La Pantera?" Matt softly asked. He waited a moment before he said, "Señora Eugenia, you are the panther, are you not?"

"Si," a muffled feminine voice said, "I am El Pantero. How did you know?"

"Had I not been so concerned about my wife,"

291

Matt said, "I would have figured it out sooner. Your arrival at the house at the same time as ours, your knowing who Zoe and I were without having spoken to anyone, the black handkerchief in your hand . . . that wasn't really a handkerchief, but your mask."

"My husband was El Pantero," Eugenia explained, walking toward Matt, "but Duprees shot and wounded him. We could not let down the cause, so when Jorge died, my son became El Pantero. He too was killed, and then I became the Panther."

Resolve underlined her words as she said, "I will not rest until the French have been driven from our country. Now that you know, señor, what are you going to do? Turn me in for the reward?"

"I need and want money desperately in order to save my property," Matt said with a shake of his head as he pulled the money from his pocket, "but not this kind of money. Right now, my main concern is my wife's health, señora. While I'm grateful for all that you and Corina have done for her and know that you've done the best of your ability for her, I'm worried that it's not enough."

"You do not have to apologize, señor," Eugenia interrupted. "I understand your concern, and I agree. Corina and I have done all we can for your wife. She needs to be in the care of a physician. Do you know one to whom you can take her?"

"Her father in Chandlerville."

"Then go with my blessings," Eugenia said, refusing the money which he offered her, "but you cannot have my *carreta* or the mule."

"Either you take the money for them," Matt said, "or I'll steal them. I'm getting Zoe out of here."

"I can think of a much better way. Enrique, come here, *por favor*." When the young man rushed to her side, she said, "Go to the church and get Father. We need his help."

"The priest?" Matt questioned skeptically.

"The priest," Eugenia returned.

"I need more than prayers, señora."

"While I'm guaranteeing prayer," Eugenia said, laughter in her husky voice, "I'm anticipating your escape."

"And while I'm escaping," Matt said, "what are you going to be doing?"

"I'm going to lead Captain Duprees on a chase," she answered, unconsciously tilting her chin to underscore her defiance. "If I move Victorio, he will surely die; he has already lost too much blood. At his death I lose yet another child to El Pantero." After a small pause, she added, "I'm not ready for that, Señor Barnabas. So I am going to lead Duprees and his men into a natural trap that will ensnare them for several days, long enough for you to get your wife safely into Texas and for Victorio to get through the critical period of his recovery so we can move him."

Matt twisted the bracelet off his wrist. "Let me return the bracelet to its rightful owner."

"No, you keep it. It is yours."

"Is there anything I can do to thank you for the help you've given to me and Zoe?" Matt asked.

"Yes, señor, there is," Eugenia said, moving closer, her eyes glittering eagerly through the small holes in the mask, her hand curling over his lower arm. "Please find the golden candlesticks and return them to the church in time for our celebration."

After a moment Matt said, "I will do the best I can, señora."

Eugenia stepped back and her husky laughter filled the barn. "When one does his best, señor, he always succeeds. When you return with the candlesticks, I will give you the matching bracelet for your wife."

A voice whispered from the darkness outside the barn, "Father and Enrique are on their way, señora. Now we must be on our way if we're going to catch the French before they reach the village."

Eugenia's cape swirled through the air as she mounted the stallion and galloped out of the barn. Over her shoulder she called, *Vaya con Dios,* señor," and was soon lost to the night.

Dawn was just pushing the gray of night away when a *carreta,* driven by Enrique and Matt, dressed as priests, rumbled out of the churchyard down the street. They halted when French soldiers called out and approached them on horseback.

"Good morning, Father," one of the soldiers said in broken Spanish. "Where are you headed so early?"

"We are headed for the border, my son," Enrique said, a smile on his face. "May I ask what you are doing here in our small village this far north of Mexico City?"

"We are looking for El Pantero."

Enrique laughed. "And you stopped me, thinking I was the Panther?"

"Oh, no," the soldier replied, laughing with him. "We stopped you because we must obey orders, and Captain Duprees said—"

"I know," Enrique said, holding up a silencing hand. "Go ahead, and while you are searching, I'll tell you that I'm on my way to Texas to get a pair of golden candlesticks for our altar. We will use them when we celebrate Mass on the church's 150th birthday."

The Frenchman smiled and bobbed his head. "Ah, yes," he said, "I have heard of the celebration. The 150th birthday of the church."

"Sí," Enrique nodded.

"What are you transporting?" the spokesman asked while the other dismounted and walked to the back of the wagon.

Enrique twisted on the narrow seat and looked over his shoulder at Zoe curled up asleep on the hay. "A small valise of clothes and some hay for the burro. I also have a young parishioner traveling with me as far as the convent."

"She's sleeping quite soundly," the soldier commented, moving even closer in order to peer into her lovely face.

"She's quite ill. We fear that it's a highly contagious disease that will soon spread," Enrique returned, hiding a smile as the soldier jumped back. "Go ahead," he invited. "You may touch her forehead to be certain that I'm telling the truth. She's burning up with fever."

The soldier glanced dubiously at his comrade, who shook his head vigorously.

"That's why we're taking her to the convent," Enrique continued. "Perhaps the good sisters have some treatment for her disease." Looking up, he asked with mild interest, "What makes you think the panther is this far north, señor?"

"An informer." The Frenchman smiled and waved

the priest on, eager to have the ill woman taken away. "Have a good trip, Father. Perhaps we'll see you when you return."

"Perhaps." Enrique's words were lost as the cart creaked into motion. Under his breath he said, "We have done it, Señor Barnabas. You and Señora Zoe will soon be safe in Texas, and I will return to find the one who informs on El Pantero."

Matt ran his finger around the stiff white collar that banded his neck and fidgeted his shoulders beneath the scratchy black wool robe. "We'll soon be in Texas," he agreed, turning his head so that he looked down at Zoe, who still slept peacefully. "I just hope I can keep her alive and safe until I reach Chandlerville."

Keeping on their disguises in case they should meet more French troops, the two men traveled, Enrique keeping up a steady stream of conversation, Matt listening and peering over his shoulder frequently to check on Zoe.

"We shall soon come to the brook, señor," Enrique announced. "We shall stop for some water and food. Señorita Corina packed up a good lunch, no? Tortillas and frijoles! What is it, señor? What do you see?"

Matt's head swiveled around slowly. "Someone's following us and has been ever since we left De La Cruz."

"*Si* señor," Enrique exclaimed, his head bobbing furiously. "That is one of our men. We have nothing to fear."

"I don't fear him," Matt said, "but I don't like being followed."

"It is safer like this," Enrique assured him, pulling the *carreta* beneath the shade of the huge tree that grew on the bank of the stream. "Now we rest awhile and eat."

As soon as he leaped from the seat, Matt rounded the cart to check on Zoe.

"How is she?" Enrique called.

"No change," Matt replied.

"She will be all right—Señora Eugenia is one of the best *curanderas* in all of Mexico. Come now and eat." He swung the basket off the seat.

As soon as they finished their quick meal, the two men climbed into the cart to continue their journey, ever aware of the presence of the unseen observer. At nightfall they arrived at the Rio Grande and forded at a shallow spot. Hastily Matt and Enrique stripped off the black robes and donned their clothes, but still each was wearing a disguise: Enrique was the simple vendor who spent his life leisurely traveling from village to village; Matt was the rugged Comanche warrior.

A slow grin curving his lips, Matt climbed onto the cart. "Take care of my horse. That's the second good mount I've lost over this woman."

"From what I've seen, señor, I would say that you'd gladly lose that many more for her." The Mexican smiled and said reassuringly, "I shall take care of your horse, señor. When you return with the candlesticks, you will find her in better condition than when you left."

"You're so sure that I'm going to return?"

"*Sí.*" Enrique's sombrero fanned the air as he nodded his head. "Now I must go, señor. Paco will be waiting for me on the other side. Have a safe trip. God go with you."

Looking over his shoulder, Matt saw in the bright moonlight a rider move out of the shadows to stand on the opposite shore. Then he heard the splash of water as Enrique crossed the border into Mexico. Alone now, Matt headed the cart for Chandlerville. When he neared town, he was uneasy and felt as if someone were still following him. His head slowly turned and he looked through the darkness, but could see no one.

Laughing at himself for being so jumpy, he threw Enrique's serape over his shoulders and put on a sombrero. He hadn't left Chandlerville under the best of conditions and wasn't sure what his reception would be. Because of Zoe, he couldn't take a chance on being recognized. He didn't have time for the amenities of a welcoming committee. Glad that dawn had not yet chased away all cover of darkness, he eased the wagon down the quiet road.

He heard the soft clop of a horse behind him, and a chill ran up his spine. His right hand slipped beneath the folds of the serape, his fingers curving around the butt of his revolver. Out of the corner of his eye he saw the silhouetted rider as he stopped in front of the hotel and tethered his horse to the hitching post. He heard the dull thud of boots on the boardwalk. Matt breathed easier and his hand slid off the pistol.

Fourteen years had brought a lot of changes to Chandlerville, he thought. Some of the names and places were familiar, but the town was virtually a stranger to Matt. Halstead's was no longer a country general store; it was a three-storied emporium, its sign bold and bright, with glass windows stretching across the front to reveal goods beautifully displayed. Greg Halstead . . . a friend who refused to believe he had gotten Veronica pregnant and who wasn't ashamed to stand up for him.

The Fielding National Bank was a huge, imposing corner building. At the sheriff's office, a lamp burned, the windows opened, and a young man snoozed at the desk. Beyond that were the Lucky Lady Saloon and the livery stables. On down the street and out of town the cart creaked until Matt stopped in front of a large, three-story house and gazed at the shingle hanging from a wrought-iron post. Drs. Quintan and Zoe Ellen Randolph . . . Don't hesitate to knock, no matter what time of day or night.

Matt leaped off the cart and walked up to the white picket fence to push open the gate, his moccasined feet silently taking him to the huge veranda. At the door he found the small chain and pulled, a bell sounding inside the house. He didn't have to ring a second time—in just moments he heard noises from inside. Through the glass panes in the upper door he saw light swaying down the hallway, flaring first low, then brighter as the door opened.

Quintan Randolph, barefoot, his shirt hanging loose over his trousers, stood there, his arm raised, a lamp in his hand. He was about the same height as Matt but heavier, and his brown hair, sprinkled with gray, was tousled from sleep.

"Dr. Randolph?" Matt asked, staring into eyes that were the same color as Zoe's.

Nodding his head, Quintan yawned and raked his hand through his hair. "One of them," he answered, his eyes twinkling. "The other, the younger and more beautiful, is in Mexico."

"Come with me, please," Matt said. "I have someone in my cart who needs your attention. She fell off a boulder and hurt her back. At the same time, she was snakebitten."

"How long ago did this happen?" Quintan asked, racing down the steps and over the boardwalk to the *carreta* in front of the house. In a matter of seconds, Quintan Randolph was utterly transformed: his back straightened, and he was alert.

"Two days ago," Matt answered, his hand banding around Quintan's arm before the older man saw Zoe's face. "Even though she's still running a high fever and is unconscious, sir, she's been treated for the bite. The first day she was delirious; then she went into a deep sleep and hasn't awakened since. That's what worries me."

"A coma," Quintan muttered. In the lamplight he studied the young man who stood beside him. He heard the concern in his voice; he saw it in the drawn features of his face. "Don't worry, son," he promised with that same assurance that Matt had heard so many times in Zoe's voice, "I'll take care of your wife."

"She's your daughter, Dr. Randolph," Matt said, not denying or admitting that Zoe was his wife, and felt Quintan start. "She was bitten by a rattler on her way home from Candaleria."

Quintan jerked his arm from Matt's grasp and ran around the cart to hold the light closer to Zoe's face. "Oh, my God!" he whispered, then shoved the lamp at Matt. "Here! Hold this."

Matt watched as Quintan gently slipped the nightshirt off Zoe and turned her so that he could look at the wounded shoulder and back. Quintan was worried when she didn't cry out in pain. "It's all right, baby," he said. "I'm taking care of you. You're going to be just fine."

"How's her back?" Matt asked after a few minutes of silence.

"I think it's only bruised," Quintan answered. "What she needs now is plenty of bed rest. I need to get her into the house. Stay here with her until I return." In a few minutes Quintan was in the house, banging on a door and shouting as he strode down the hall, "Ezekiel . . . Lou . . . wake up. Zoe's been hurt. We need to get her into the house. I'll get the stretcher."

More windows lit up and soon a middle-aged man and woman opened a door and stepped into the hallway. The man followed Quintan out of the house and the woman disappeared into another room, another window soon glowing with light. Matt eased Zoe into the litter and helped the men carry her into the house and transfer her to a narrow hospital bed. Then he waited in the hall while Quintan gave Zoe a more thorough examination.

Expecting to find her wound inflamed, close to gangrene, Quintan stripped the bandage from Zoe's shoulder. Much to his surprise, he found that it had been cleaned, sutured, and coated with a salve and was healing nicely. After he had redressed it, he examined the ankle and had Lou prepare a poultice, which he wrapped around it. Moments later, with gentle but firm fingers, he probed Zoe's spine, but felt nothing amiss. Quintan thought it was only bruised; still he must wait until she regained consciousness to confirm this diagnosis.

When Quintan pulled the sheet over Zoe, Lou shooed him out of the room. "I'll take care of her now, Dr. Randolph."

Quintan nodded, turning when he heard the door open. Matt quietly entered the room to stand at the foot of Zoe's bed, looking into the pale face of the woman he loved—loved more than his own life. He hadn't wanted to love her, had even been angry that she was thrust into his life. Now he wanted nothing more than to stay with her, to be by her side, to share her suffering as well as her joy. The doctor watched the stranger and wondered what he was thinking.

"Now get," Lou said. "I want to put her into some clean clothes."

"Come with me, young man," Quintan said, his hand capping Matt's shoulder. "There's no arguing with Lou once she's made up her mind, and I'd like to get some questions answered."

"I've put the litter up, Dr. Randolph. Do you want me to go tell Mr. Fielding that Zoe's home?" Ezekiel asked, moving out of the kitchen into the hallway.

Quintan rubbed his eyes wearily and sighed. "I suppose he should be told, Zeke, but I'd just as soon wait a little longer. Maybe after a glass or two of whiskey I'll be able to stomach him better. Right now I think not."

Matt lowered his head to hide a grin. He liked Quintan Randolph, liked him a lot! The doctor was a good judge of character.

"Come on, son," Quintan said, his hand guiding Matt in the direction of the study. "Let's me and you have a few minutes to ourselves before the town comes alive and people start yelling for a doctor."

Quintan's study was a direct reflection of the man himself. It was large and comfortable, done in beige and brown. The walls were covered from floor to ceiling in books. The furniture, though expensive and elegant, was sparse. A mahogany desk reposed in front of the French windows, and grouped to one side of the room were four chairs upholstered in leather. They invited someone to spend pleasant hours in this room.

Walking to a small table, Quintan picked up a whiskey bottle and filled a glass. "This okay with you?" he asked. After Matt nodded, he said, "What happened to my daughter?"

"She fell from a boulder and—"

"That's not what I mean." Quintan crossed the room and handed Matt the glass. "Where are her escorts and her mules? More important, who are you and how did you end up saving her?"

Matt glanced across the room into one of the mirrors that hung on either side of the French doors. He still wore the serape and sombrero. He lifted the glass to his lips and took a deep swallow of whiskey, the liquid fire running from his throat to his stomach. His eyes watering slightly, he gazed at the mirror. *What are you going to tell him?* the haggard reflection seemed to say. *The truth?* But Matt wondered if this were the time for the truth. He had so much to settle, so many questions to answer, and so many riddles to solve.

He took another gulp of whiskey, swallowed, and said, "I'm the man who saved her, Dr. Randolph, when her caravan was attacked by Indians."

"The Comanches."

Matt nodded. "She wouldn't be stopped from going into Mexico, sir, even with her escort dead, so my men and I carried her."

"No," Quintan said, running his hand through his hair, "she's a headstrong woman. Once she's made up her mind, nothing will stop her. Thank

303

God you came along when you did, Mr. —"

"Doc!" Ezekiel's voice sounded outside the study door. "Deputy's on the porch. Wants to know if you need him?"

"Damn," Quintan muttered. "The biggest thing about Bufford is his curiosity. Once he knows, the whole town will know, and they'll all be over here before daybreak." Lifting his voice, he said, "Tell Renshaw — oh, hell!" He walked across the room and jerked open the door. "I'll tell him myself, Zeke."

Matt heard his footsteps as he moved down the hall, the creak of the screen door as it opened.

"Morning, Bufford."

"Morning, Doc. Saw the Mexican driving the cart into town. Wondered if you needed some help."

"Could do with some," Quintan answered. "The Mexican was bringing Zoe home. She's was bitten by a snake while she was in Candaleria."

"Oh, my God, Doc! What do you want me to do?"

"I want you to keep your mouth shut," Quintan answered. "She needs plenty of rest, so I don't want anyone to know about it. Else they'll be over here."

"What about Mr. Fielding, sir?"

"Especially Weber. He'd be upset and over here upsetting me and Zoe. Right now it's better for everybody concerned just to keep quiet."

"Well, Doc, don't rightly reckon we can be quiet about it," Bufford drawled and shuffled his feet apologetically, "I didn't think about Dr. Zoe being hurt, so's I sent Melvin over to tell Weber. I know he's been mighty worried about her and would like to know."

"Thanks, Bufford," Quintan said dryly and

looked up to see a figure striding down the street.

"Quintan," Weber shouted, "What's wrong? Buford told me he saw a Mexican—"

"Yep, Weber," Quintan interrupted, "a Mexican brought Zoe home. She was bitten by a snake while she was in Candaleria."

"I'll tell you one thing," Weber Fielding vowed as he pushed open the gate and walked up the boardwalk, "I'll put a stop to those Mexican visits when Zoe and I get married." On the veranda he whisked past Quintan and opened the door, stepping into the foyer. "Take me to the Mexican," he ordered. "I want to talk to him."

"He's in the study," Quintan said. "You know the way."

Without waiting for the doctor and acting as if the house were his own, Weber strode down the hallway, moving through the opened door into the study, but the room was empty. The only evidence of someone's having recently been in the room were the two partially filled glasses sitting on the small table against the wall.

"He's gone," Weber shouted.

Having followed Weber down the hall, Quintan now stood in the doorway. "Yep, he is."

"Who was he?" Weber spun around.

Quintan shrugged. "We were just about to talk when Ezekiel announced the deputy's arrival. Guess he got tired of waiting and left."

"Did he say why he's the one who brought her back? Where's Snyder and his men?"

"I don't know the answer to that," Quintan replied. "Just know her caravan was attacked by Comanches, and the Mexican saved her."

Weber's face whitened so that his beard stubble

looked stark by contrast. His hands began to shake. "The—the Comanches," he said, his voice strange to his own ears, "did they—did they—capture her?"

"I said I don't know," Quintan replied, walking to the table and pouring another glass of whiskey. Weber hated Indians; he'd never made any pretense about that. Quintan handed the drink to Weber. "Would it make a difference?"

Weber's hand shook so badly that the liquor almost spilled out of his glass. God, but he hated the Comanches! The mere thought of one of them touching Zoe filled him with revulsion. The thought of one of them having sex with her . . . made him ill. He lifted the glass to his lips and drank deeply.

"I asked you a question," Quintan said. "I want an answer." He walked to his desk, opened a wooden box, and extracted a cigar.

Weber returned to the table and poured himself a second drink.

"Damn it, Weber. I want an answer!"

Weber quaffed the whiskey in a swallow. "No, it—it wouldn't make any difference, Quintan."

"Seems like you're mighty concerned about it to me."

Weber walked to the table and refilled his glass. "I'm concerned about Zoe," he said, regaining his aplomb. "About how this is going to affect her. You know how people talk about a woman when she's—when she's—"

"—been a prisoner of the Indians," Quintan finished.

Chapter 16

A lamp, the wick down low, was sitting on a table across the room, the muted light playing softly over Zoe's features, relaxed in sleep. Dark lashes curled against silken cheeks, and her golden hair spread across the pillow to surround her face in a shimmering halo.

Matt sat in a chair at the head of the bed and stared at his wife, wishing he could take her place and buffer her from all harm. Ironically, he felt as if he and Zoe had been lovers all his life; he couldn't imagine a moment without her. At the same time, he felt as if she had just this moment walked into his life; each time he thought of or looked at her, the excitement and exhilaration that comes with that first awareness of sexual attraction raced through him, setting him on fire with desire.

Matt didn't want a life without Zoe. Without her he felt somehow unfinished. He missed her low, husky laughter when she was happy, the spark in her eyes when she disagreed with or was angry with him. He wanted to make love to her, but more than that, he wanted to love her and to have her love him.

This admission left Matt emotionally naked. He rose and walked to the window, leaning a shoulder against the casement and peering into the darkness. For the past fourteen years he had been looking for fulfillment through others. When he was lying in the hospital after the war, wounded and pronounced dying by the physicians, he realized he'd been looking for external evidence that he was someone when all the time he should have been looking within himself. Once he'd learned that worth was measured by oneself, he was ready to face and defeat the hideous monster of his past.

Before he'd accepted that he was responsible for what happened in his life, Matt had shunned a permanent relationship with a woman for fear that he would become dependent on her and she would eventually leave him . . . not necessarily with another man, but through death, the way his mother and father had left him. Then he would be left alone to cope with a world he wasn't sure he understood.

Now Matt had found the woman he wanted, and while Matt believed she loved him, he wasn't sure that she was ready to accept him into the life of Zoe Randolph, doctor and upright citizen of Chandlerville. When two people were thrown together in a life-and-death situation, they naturally turn to one another and clung together. In the Comanche village and in Candaleria, Zoe was free from social stricture and convention and could easily imagine herself in love with him. Matt could deal with coming back home. Being measured by the elite of Chandlerville and found wanting didn't bother him. But he didn't know how that would affect Zoe, and he didn't want to see regret replace the love and happiness in her eyes.

He had wanted to tell her about himself before they arrived back in Chandlerville because he wanted her to have a chance to fall in love with Matt Chandler as well as the Comanche half-breed Ma-ta-mon-yahu.

What would happen when she awoke to find herself home again, surrounded by old friends and situations? Would she hate herself for having fallen in love with the man who was reputed to have gotten Fielding's sister pregnant and to have abandoned her?

No, Matt reasoned, Zoe was an intelligent woman who would listen to him and weigh the evidence. They had reached a point in their relationship where she would believe his innocence. Of that he had no doubt. She would understand his silence.

He pushed himself away from the window and returned to the bed, dropping a hand to touch her cheek. "There's so much I want to tell you. You once asked me who I was and where I belonged. With the white people, or the Comanches? At the time I didn't answer you because I thought it wasn't any of your business. Later, as I came to care for you, I *couldn't* answer. One reason was that I was afraid to tell you about my past. But I'm not afraid anymore because I love you and you love me. Another reason, perhaps an even more important one, is that at the time you asked, I really didn't know. Now I do, and I'd like to tell you."

Matt brushed a strand of hair from her forehead, his fingers trailing beyond the crescent of dark lashes on her cheeks to her chin.

"I don't want you to learn the truth from anyone

309

else," he said, "but your father doesn't know how long it'll be before you awaken. I have so much I must do, my darling, and I must do it quickly. But I promise I'll be back every night to sit and talk with you. I'm not going to leave you."

His other hand caught and held hers, squeezing gently, even though she didn't return the grip. Standing, he pushed the sombrero from his head, leaned over, and laid his mouth softly against hers. A tear running down his cheek mingled with the sweet touching of their lips.

"Whatever else, my darling wife, I love you." Matt's voice broke as he added, "Now I must go, but I'll be back tomorrow night. Sweet dreams."

He slipped out of Zoe's room and quietly moved down the hall, stopping dead in his tracks when he heard Weber speak. He couldn't move; the sound of that man's voice filled Matt with memories—painful, humiliating, and angry memories. Weber's mere presence in the house was suffocating to Matt. He didn't have to see the man to remember what he looked like. Fielding's face was one that time had not erased. Matt remembered Weber's angry threats when he refused to marry Veronica or to claim the baby as his—and it hurt Matt to think of the baby's father not claiming it.

Weber's demand interrupted his thoughts. "I want to see Zoe, Quintan."

Silence!

"I demand to see her."

Again, nothing but silence!

"Quintan—" Weber's voice was rising in anger. "I want to see her right now."

Having no doubt that Quintan Randolph could handle Weber Fielding, Matt pushed away from the

310

wall and quietly moved down the corridor. Before he stepped through the kitchen door, he heard Quintan answer, low and authoritatively, "No, Weber, I think not."

After a moment's silence in which Matt could visual Weber's faced twisted in surprise at the idea that someone would dare refuse to obey his command, Weber said, "She's my fiancée, Quintan. I will see her."

"No, Weber," Quintan repeated quite firmly, "you will not see her until I say so. She's my daughter and my patient. As her father and her doctor, I refuse to let you see her."

"I promise I won't awaken her," Weber said, a hint of pleading in his voice.

"No—" Quintan sighed. "You won't awaken her. She's in a coma, Weber. All we can do is wait for her to awaken."

"A coma!" Weber exclaimed.

"She was bitten by a rattler when she fell over the boulder, hurting her head and back. She received a concussion that resulted in a coma."

"She'll come out of it, won't she?" Weber asked, and even Matt could hear the near-panic in his voice.

Matt waited for Quintan's answer. It was slow in coming. Eventually he heard, "I have every reason to believe she will. She's a strong woman, with an equally strong will to live."

"Dear Lord," Weber muttered, the sound barely audible through the closed door, "I don't know what I'd do if she were to die."

The sincerity in Weber's confession touched even Matt. His experiences with the man had left him thinking Weber was consumed with base emotions

311

and absolutely devoid of such worthy ones. If Weber honestly loved Zoe, Matt could understand her falling in love with him. She would have seen only his good qualities and would have been exposed only to his charm.

"I'm leaving, Quintan," Weber finally said in a low voice, a voice filled with anguish and concern. Matt had to strain to hear. "Send for me the minute there's any change in her condition." The door opened and shut, and then footsteps echoed down the hall.

After Weber left, Matt headed toward the barn for a horse, but stopped when he saw Ezekiel already outside feeding the stock. Matt ducked around the house, wishing he could take off the sombrero and serape, but it was already daylight. If he were seen on the streets of town wearing nothing but his leather breeches and moccasins, he'd attract too much attention. The town was leery of Indians under the best of conditions, and the conditions right now were none too good. He wasn't ready to face another lynch mob. As he crept past the *carreta,* he tossed the sombrero on the seat and hastened down the street to see Weber walk past the Fielding mansion. Curious, Matt skirted into the nearest alleyway and watched Weber walk to the abstract office and bang on the door until it was opened.

Matt moved to the back of the building in search of a way to enter the building unobserved. Totally unashamed of his prying, Matt found a window partially open, raised it, and slipped into the room. Because the door leading into the office was ajar, Matt could easily overhear the conversation between two men.

"Damn it!" Weber swore, jabbing a cigar into the corner of his mouth and lighting it. "Why the hell did Zoe have to go to Candaleria now? I had told her repeatedly not to go. The minute I learned the guns were being delivered there, I warned her."

"Simmer down, Weber," Scully soothed. "We still have plenty of time, and she doesn't know a thing. She'll come out of this-here coma, won't she?"

"Simmer down!" Weber exclaimed. "You're a fine one to tell me to simmer down, Scully Newton. You don't have your life's savings on the line. If I don't get the guarantee on the property, those men back east will send their own agent out here. Then they'll be striking up their own deals, and they've got a lot more money to play with than me. I'll be damned if I'll let them take my land away from me!"

Matt crept to the door to look into the office where Weber and the surveyor sat. Weber hadn't changed much, Matt thought . . . a little gray at the temples. If anything, he looked more distinguished than ever. Although it was only six o'clock in the morning, he was impeccably dressed, black suit and checkered waistcoat, not a strand of hair out of place. His eyes flashed and his chin jutted angrily as he strutted around the office.

"I shouldn't have been so patient and waited like she wanted to," Weber muttered. "If I'd insisted on getting married immediately, I wouldn't be in this boat right now."

"Ah, Weber, you know you couldn't have made her do any different, and you shoulda known she'd hightail it for Mexico the minute you turned your back. She's not like ordinary women. Wants to be a doctor, like a man. Always got her nose in men's

313

business."

"That'll change as soon as we're married," Weber said. "As the wife of Weber Fielding, she'll learn her place."

"Assuming you get married," Scully mumbled.

"We'll be married," Weber promised, chomping down on his cigar. "That I can guarantee you, Scully Newton. I've invested every cent I have in this deal. I'm not about to lose it because of a woman."

Leaning over the desk, Scully traced an imaginary line from Chandlerville to San Antonio. "Whatcha think she's gonna do when she finds out that you need her property for the railroad, Weber?"

"She's an intelligent woman," Weber said in an effort to convince himself. "When she sees how important this is to Chandlerville—"

"—and how much money it's gonna be for all us," Scully slipped in.

"Yes," Weber mused, "when she sees how much money we're going to be making, I think she'll understand and give her approval."

"Anyway," Scully said, "by the time she finds out, it'll be too late for her to do anything about it. You'll already be married. Now all you have to worry about is the line of ranches straight through to central and east Texas."

"I don't have to worry about them any more, Scully. They're mine."

Scully looked at Weber in surprise. "Do you know this for a fact, or are you just speaking your wishes?"

"For a fact," Weber replied absently. "Grisswold got back yesterday. He said they were all dead:

Chandler, Shook, Burns, Monroe."

"Tell you, Weber—" Scully rose and walked across the room to the potbellied black stove, where he picked up a coffee pot and filled a cup. "Want some coffee? No. Tell you, Weber, I don't trust that Grisswold none. A white man who rides with Indians gives me the shivers. That man had just as soon kill you as the next person. He don't have no friends, no loyalty. Don't seem like there's anything in life that he cares about. A man like that ain't no man a'tall."

"You're right," Weber said, one of the few times that he agreed with Scully Newton. "Things worked out for the best—those bandits stealing the guns from them in Mexico. I'm just sorry they killed all my good men. Such a shame Grisswold couldn't have been one of the dead ones."

Scully returned to his chair and sat down, setting the cup of coffee on the edge of the desk. "Yeah. I was a little scared about you letting him have those guns to sell to the Mescaleros. A feller don't know when they gonna turn and use 'em on him. Tell you, Weber, I'm just afraid this whole Indian thing is going to get outa hand. Stirring up the Indians is one thing, but once they get stirred up, there's no telling what they'll do."

"Don't worry," Weber said. "I have it under control. Nothing I do is by chance. Haven't things worked out so far? I have the Burns place, Monroe's, and Shook's, and it's just a matter of time before Chandler buckles. He can't take much more. Both his grandsons are dead. First Matt. Now Bryan."

"Hell, Weber," Scully drawled, picking up the pencil and coloring in large blocks of property that

315

circled the town, "that old man's made of iron. The death of that boy ain't gonna guarantee you his ranch. In fact, I'd bet my bottom dollar that it'll make him all the more determined to keep it, and he sure as hell weren't upset over Matt's death. Hated him, he did. Didn't even come to the memorial service Bryan held for him."

Uriah's absence from the funeral hurt Matt deeply, but why should he have expected anything else from Uriah? Matt knew his grandfather was a man of his word, and in fact, honored it above all else. Uriah Chandler meant it when he disowned his grandson. Come hell or high water, he'd stand behind his words. Matt's resolve to mend things between them flagged a little.

"Maybe," Weber mused, absently pulling at his chin. "One of these days real soon, Scully, I'm going to be the most powerful man in West Texas . . . and after that, the most powerful in all of Texas."

"You sure will be, Weber," Scully said, thumping a finger against the thick dark line that circled Chandlerville, "if you can get all this prime property that surrounds town. Property that the Doctors Randolph own."

"Don't you worry. I'll get it."

"I ain't worried," Scully drawled. "I figure that's your problem, Weber. Anyways, if for some reason Zoe don't marry you, you can always talk Quintan into going along with us."

"Your jokes are running thin, Newton."

Quintan was one of the few people in town who hadn't given Weber his support and had stood in the way of Weber's plans. But when Zoe arrived a little more than nine months ago, a door had

316

opened for Weber. Through her, he could get what he wanted without shelling out a cent. Immediately he had begun a careful courtship of Dr. Zoe Randolph.

While Weber found her to be an attractive woman, he didn't like Zoe's being so independent, nor her thinking she was equal to a man. Those qualities took away from her womanly beauty. Of course, he never voiced these opinions to her. There'd be plenty of time to change her after they were married and the lots were his.

"When does Quintan reckon she'll be coming around?"

"He has no idea," Weber said.

"May be too late," Scully murmured, dropping the pencil. He whistled, then added, "Boy, Weber, just look at this map. Look at how much property Zoe and Quintan own, and all of it surrounding town. Ain't no way you're gonna get that railroad in here unless'en you get ahold of some of it. Old man Chandler knew what he was doing when he doled out these city lots."

"I'll get the land and the railroad," Weber promised.

Scully's words echoed in his ears to remind him of the grave situation. Weber moved to the window and stood looking at the people as they began their usual morning activities. Buggies rattled into town. Shop doors opened, shades were raised; "Closed" signs were taken out of the windows; dusting and sweeping began. "Good morning" rang out up and down the street.

So close to his goal, Weber thought, yet so far . . . so very far.

"The deputy said Zoe was captured by the Co-

317

manches," Scully eventually drawled, squirming in the chair and rubbing his palm over his bald head.

Weber tensed, but answered slowly and very carefully. "The Mexican who brought her in didn't say anything about her being captured by Comanches. The caravan was attacked by Comanches, but he and his men arrived in time to save her."

"Ain't you a mighty lucky man, Weber? I can't imagine how you woulda stood it if'en she'd been taken to a Comanche camp and—"

"Yeah," Weber murmured, "I'm a mighty lucky man."

Already the good folks of Chandlerville had begun casting their pitying gazes on him. God, but he despised Zoe for placing him in such an embarrassing position! If he didn't need those damn lots . . . even if he had the money with which he could buy them. But money wouldn't buy them. The only way he could get them was through marriage. For the rest of his life he would live with gossip and pity. Again his name would be sullied. Eventually he'd have to take care of Zoe as he'd taken care of Veronica and the baby.

Having heard enough to let him know what Weber was doing and how he really felt about Zoe, Matt turned to leave. On the foot of the bed he saw a clean shirt, which he picked up and held against his chest. It was about the right size, and he needed one. Once outside, he headed for the livery stable, where he bought a horse and saddle of sorts, throwing the serape into the bargain for good measure. After an hour of haggling, Matt owned a bay and was on his way to La Candela de Oro.

Matt's thoughts were in a turmoil as he rode.

When he wasn't thinking about Zoe, worried about her health but relieved that she wasn't involved with Weber's schemes, he was wondering what kind of welcome he would receive at the ranch. He hadn't seen his grandfather in fourteen years, and they had parted after bitter and angry words. According to Scully Newton, his grandfather hadn't even attended the memorial service for him. Evidently the old man still harbored ill-will.

"If you walk out of here and turn your back on me and La Candela de Oro, I'm no longer your grandfather," Uriah had shouted. "To you, I'm Uriah Barnabas Chandler. Do you understand me?"

"Yes, I understand."

"Well, what's it going to be?"

"Good-bye, Uriah Barnabas Chandler."

Well, he'd known it wasn't going to be an easy task when he chose to return. He wasn't going to turn tail and run now. He'd come too far for that.

Matt was also concerned about his grandfather's reaction to Bryan's death. By an ironic and cruel twist of Fate, Matt, the returning grandson, the disinherited grandson, must tell Uriah about the death of his youngest, inheriting grandson. Bryan's death could draw him and Uriah closer together or create a chasm between them that would never be closed.

At mid-morning Matt crested the hill, stopped, and saw for the first time in fourteen years La Candela de Oro. His heart was heavy as he guided the bay toward the buildings nestled in the valley, once so beautiful and majestic, now all of them in a state of disrepair. Time hadn't taken its toll; war had.

Looking around him in disbelief, Matt dismounted and hitched the horse to the rickety post out front. Moving up the boardwalk, he looked at the dead bushes on either side that had one time been his stepmother's pride and joy. He climbed the five steps and walked across the veranda. At the door he paused, not sure what to do. Did he just walk in as if he belonged there, or should he knock?

Although his grandfather had disinherited him, he belonged here! He was a Chandler . . . Matthew Barnabas Chandler!

Catching the handle of the screen door, he pulled, the sagging frame grating across the porch, as he stepped into the foyer, where he was instantly assailed by a multitude of memories—joy, sorrow, regret, anticipation—all blended together for an intensely emotional homecoming. He hesitated a moment and considered turning and running, but caught himself. He'd run from the demon of his past for fourteen years. It was high time to face it. Unconsciously, his hand wrapped around his bracelet as if he could draw strength from it.

Matt walked through each of the rooms on the first floor. On finding them empty, he climbed the stairs and moved down the hall until he stood in front of his old room. His hand, damp with perspiration, closed over the knob, but he didn't immediately turn it. He stood for a moment, wondering what changes his grandfather had made after he left, wondering if all traces of Matt Chandler had been erased.

Matt eventually opened the door and walked in to stand in stunned silence. When Eugenia told him the bracelet was a miracle, he had felt uncomfortable, never having associated himself with religion. But right now he felt that he was indeed standing in the middle of a miracle. Although the bedspread and curtains were new and the furnishings were rearranged, the massive golden oak furniture was the same: the four-poster bed, the wardrobe, and the dresser. His desk—the one his father had had specially made for him in New Orleans—was in the corner. Over the bed hung the portraits of his parents; at the foot was his cedar chest.

He walked into the room to stare at the portrait, a sad ache in his chest. Wind-over-the-Water, Soaring Eagle's only child. His mother. Yet he had never called her Mama, only Wind-over-the-Water. Matt was only two when she died, but through the years he'd often lain on his bed and fantasized about her. He pretended that her lips were twitching just before they blossomed into a full smile; he closed his eyes and pretended to hear soft, husky laughter. All these years, and he still missed her.

And Papa . . . Charles Chandler, the only child of Uriah and Florrie Chandler to live to adulthood. Charles was a good man who, like his father, was a part of this rugged, unyielding land. Because of his love for an Indian maiden, Charles had guaranteed them a place to live in peace for the duration of his life and hopefully throughout his son's, possibly longer. His untimely death had prevented this dream from becoming a reality.

When Matt glanced down at the bed again, he saw a golden-haired woman lying there. Dark, curling lashes framed luminous eyes the color of Texas bluebonnets; full sensual lips curved into a beautiful smile.

"Hello, my husband, my *ner-co-mack-pe*," he

imagined her to say. "Welcome home."

Though brief, the fantasy cut Matt to the quick. He had allowed Zoe to come into his life easier than he would allow her to leave. Dear God, he couldn't lose her now. Part of his scheme for revenge had been to marry and get her pregnant, and he still wanted that, but no longer as a means of getting back at Weber, no longer as a means of revenge. Matt loved Zoe; he wanted her to be a part of his life, and wanted her to bear his children . . . their children. He wanted to know that at the end of the day when he returned home, his wife and family would be waiting for him. But whether she chose to share her life with him, he knew she would always share his heart.

Blinking back the tears, angry with himself because any person could touch him deeply enough to cause him to cry, and a little uncomfortable with his vulnerability to a woman, he knelt in front of the cedar chest and unfastened the straps to lift the lid. He smiled and dropped his hand to sort through the childhood treasures. Dora had kept all of them. He picked up his leather ball, one that Uriah made for him, and straightened.

"Drop that toy, mister, and get your hands in the air," a feminine voice shouted, causing Matt to spin around. A heavyset woman in a faded blue dress stood in the doorway, a rifle in her arms, the barrel pointed at Matt. Dull gray eyes, hard and unyielding, squinted in his direction. "What are you doing here in this room?"

Unable to believe this woman was his stepmother, Matt dropped the ball into the chest and straightened. Her vibrant brown hair, now liberally streaked with gray, was severely pulled away from her face and pinned into a tight little bun at the back of her head. Her face was weathered and wrinkled far beyond her fifty years. A scowl replaced the warm smile that had been so characteristic of Dora Chandler.

"Hello, Dorrie," he said, using the pet name he had given Dora years ago when she and his father had first married.

The woman's face suddenly wilted, her body slumped, and the gun slid from her arms, falling to the floor with a thud. She leaned against the door frame. "Matt?" she whispered, her hand fluttering to her throat. "It can't be!"

"Yes, it's me," he answered, a half-smile tugging his lips. "As you can see, I'm well and alive."

"We . . . heard you were dead. Several of the men from your unit, riding through to California, said they saw you get killed during the war. Bryan . . . he had a service for you."

Her voice trickled into nothing and she kept shaking her head in disbelief. Tears filled her eyes, tears of happiness at Matt's being alive and his returning home . . . tears of regret for all the wasted years. And, too, tears of anxiety for what might or might not come of Matt's visit.

"I was wounded and given up for dead," Matt explained, "that's one of the reasons why I didn't get home any sooner."

"You . . . haven't changed, Matt." She sniffed. "A little older maybe; a little thinner."

"I may not look any different, Dorrie," he said, "but I'm a changed man."

Dora nodded her head. "Bryan's changed, too. You wouldn't recognize him. Why—he's probably taller than you. Looks so much like your papa—

blue eyes and blond hair. He's away right now, tending to some business. Just wait till he gets home and sees you!"

Matt's heart lurched and he unconsciously moved toward his stepmother. Why must he be the one to break the news to her? But then, he wouldn't have had it any other way. He loved Dora and wanted to be here when she needed his love and support the most. He wanted her to hear about Byran's death from someone who cared.

The front door creaked open and grated across the porch, the sound echoing up the stairs into the bedroom. Footsteps crossed the foyer and hall, and a deep masculine voice boomed through the house. "Dorrie, I'm home."

"I'm up here, Uriah."

"And Myra?" he yelled back. "I saw one of the livery stable nags out front. Figured she was with you. Well, don't spare any money on getting you a pretty dress for the dance. I want you to be the prettiest woman there. Before she leaves, the two of you join me in the study for a cup of coffee."

Chapter 17

"How is Uriah?" Matt asked.

Dora's expression grew pensive, her eyes shadowed with pain. "He's about the same as he was when you left, Matt. Still stubborn as a mule. But the war's been hard on him. Money's scarce, and we're barely hanging onto the ranch. Guess we're lucky. We've held on longer than most."

"I want to see him," Matt said.

Dora wiped her hands down the side of her skirt. "I've got to warn you, Matt, he doesn't feel any different about . . . well, about—"

"I do," Matt answered with a smile, "and that's all that matters."

"I'm glad," she whispered, picking up the tail of her apron to wipe the tears in her eyes. "You don't know how much we've missed you, Matt."

"You don't know how much I've missed all of you." Matt closed the distance between them, pulling Dora into a warm embrace.

"Oh, Matt," she cried against his chest, "you don't know how glad I am to have you home. When you were a little boy, you must have thought me a mean stepmother—"

"I may have, when I was growing up," Matt

admitted in a low chuckle, "but now I know you did what you thought was best for me, and I appreciate you insisting that I have a proper education."

I so wanted to do what your papa wanted for you!" she said, pulling her face back to look up at him. "For years, your grandfather swore that Charles was partial to you, and at times I believed it myself."

Dora pulled away from Matt's arms and walked across the room to straighten the brushes and combs on the dresser. "But when Uriah began filling Bryan's head with such foolish notions, I realized that your father wasn't partial to you; he just loved you with a different kind of love than he had for Bryan. He knew because of his having loved and married an Indian, life was going to be hard on you."

"Thank you for understanding that, Dorrie," Matt said, looking into the mirror at her reflection.

She turned, leaning against the dresser. "I want us to be a family again, Matt . . . all of us. You and Bryan and Uriah working together to build La Candela de Oro into the ranch it once was."

The mention of Bryan brought with it sadness, but Matt wasn't ready yet to tell Dora about the death of her only son. He stepped to the door, stopped to pick up the rifle, and laid it across the foot of the bed.

"Matt, it ain't gonna be easy," Dora said, moving toward him. "Uriah is a stubborn cuss, and nobody but your grandmother ever saw his heart."

"I know it's not going to be easy," Matt told her as he draped his arm around her shoulder and they descended the stairs. "I never thought it would be, but seeing him again is something I have to do,

326

Dorrie, in order to get on with my life."

Outside the study, her hand closed over the knob. "I'll just announce you, but won't come in."

"You can if you want to."

"No," she answered, "I think the two of you need some time alone to sort out your problems. While y'all are doing that, I'll go to the kitchen and make a pot of coffee." Pushing open the door, she called, "Uriah, you have company."

Uriah Chandler, his hat lying on his desk, his hands in his back pockets, stood in front of the window at the far end of the room and gazed at his beloved land — land he had worked hard for and might soon lose. He turned to look at the tall, bronzed man who entered the room. The cambric shirt, the leather breeches, and the moccasins . . . it was not enough that he had to deal with scum like Weber Fielding, now he had this damned Indian. It was nobody he recognized; yet the man was familiar — most familiar. Uriah squinted in an effort to see better and took a step closer.

"Hello, Uriah," Matt said, a lump in his throat as he looked at his grandfather. The shoulders were a little more stooped, the hair snow-white, but the golden brown eyes were as sharp, as disapproving as ever. "I've come home."

"Matthew!" Uriah stumbled forward, bracing against the desk top with both hands.

As the two men stared at each other, the years seemed to go back in time. On that fateful day fourteen years ago, both had been standing in the study in almost the same positions, Uriah behind the desk, the twenty-two-year-old Matt in front of it.

"But Grandpa," the young Matt Chandler maintained, "I want to inherit my part of La Candela de Oro."

"So you can give it to them damned Comanches," Uriah accused.

"Part of it for them, like it's been for the past thirty-five or so years, but mostly for me."

"Then you'll damn well do as I say," the older man shouted, his fist coming down on the desk with a heavy thud, reminiscent of a judge's gavel. "You're gonna forget about them Indians and be a Chandler. Let 'em be a buffer; that's all they're good for. You don't have to live with 'em. I don't want to hear any more about your Indian heritage. La Candela de Oro is your heritage . . . your only heritage."

"No," Matt shouted, "you're not going to dictate to me like you did Papa, and like you do to Bryan. I love you, but I refuse to be manipulated, Grandpa. I'm my own person, and I demand to be recognized as Matt Chandler, half-white and half-Comanche. I'm no more going to turn my back on Soaring Eagle than I'm about to turn my back on you."

"Those are my terms," Uriah had said, his hand rising, his finger pointing toward the door. "If you don't accept them, then walk out and don't ever come back."

They had stared at one another for long minutes, each silently pleading with the other to give in, but neither did. Cast from the same mold, they had too much pride. Matt put his hat on, turned, and walked to the door.

"If you leave," Uriah warned, "you lose everything. Bryan will inherit everything I have; you'll get nothing."

His back to his grandfather, Matt's hand closed over the doorknob; he twisted and pulled.

"From this day forward, I disown Matthew Barnabas Chandler. I disinherit him."

Today, fourteen years later, Matt stared into Uriah's face and saw no change, no relenting. The eyes were as steely today as they had been long ago.

"Why did you decide to come back?" Uriah demanded, his voice harsh. His weight bore so heavily on his hands that his knuckles turned white. "Things got too rough, so you came back for a handout, hunh?"

"No, I just wanted to come home," Matt began.

"Home! You forgetting, boy, you don't have a home here. You walked away and left it!" Uriah dropped his head to open a wooden box on his desk and to select a cigar. "I seem to remember that home to you was a tepee in a Comanche village."

"Home is where I make it," Matt answered, "and I'd like to make it La Candela de Oro."

Uriah picked up a match and scratched it against the base of the metal lamp on his desk. When it sputtered to life, he held it to the tip of the cigar and said between puffs, "Told you when you left you couldn't come back. So what happened to make you decide that you needed me and the ranch, boy?"

"Matt."

Uriah took the cigar out of his mouth and turned to look at the flint hardness on his grandson's face.

"I have a name, Uriah, and I want to be called by it."

"Never figured out why you didn't want to be called Barnabas," the old man muttered, evading the real issue. "Right good name! Belonged to my grandfather on my mother's side."

While a part of Matt wanted to laugh, the other part was irritated. "Hell, Uriah, why do you demand that I go by a name that you've refused all your life?"

"Plain to see, you haven't changed any," Uriah snapped. "You're as obstinate and ornery as ever."

"I'm obstinate and ornery?"

"Why'd you come back, hunh?" Uriah demanded.

That Uriah was skirting the issue gave Matt hope. His grandfather was thawing: he'd almost joked. Still, Matt knew he must move cautiously and let Uriah have the lead. He answered, "At the close of the war I was wounded, badly wounded. As I lay in that hospital hovering close to death, I realized who I was, Uriah, and where I belonged. I knew then that you, Bryan, Dora and Soaring Eagle were my family, and I wanted to come home to you."

"I haven't changed my mind," Uriah said. "As far as I'm concerned, you're not a Chandler, and not one inch of this ranch will go to you. Everything I have is going to Bryan. He's a Chandler, and he'll get La Candela de Oro."

Matt had never thought the confrontation would be easy, but Uriah was making it almost impossible. At the moment, Matt found it easy to think about walking out of the house and never seeing Uriah or La Candela de Oro again. But Matt knew he had to live with himself, and the only way he could do that was to make peace with his grandfather. In making peace he was going to have to tell his grandfather about Bryan's death. He could

330

imagine how Uriah would blow that out of proportion.

"Did you get the letters?" Matt asked, still not ready to discuss Bryan's death.

Uriah inhaled deeply, then exhaled. "I got 'em."

"You never wrote."

"I never read 'em," the old man lied, in his mind's eyes seeing them tied together and secreted in his wall chest. They had been opened and read so many times, they were tearing along the folds. "I told you that day when you walked out of here that you were no longer my grandson."

"You don't mean that," Matt said, walking toward the desk, his dark brown eyes locking with his grandfather's. "You don't mean one word that you're saying. You're just too damned proud to admit you made a mistake. If you meant it, you'd have changed my room and thrown away my childhood toys."

Uriah's face was twisted in anger, his hand shaking. "I didn't change that room or throw those damn toys away because . . . because Dora wouldn't let me."

"Yeah," Matt drawled, "I know how frightened you are of Dora. I know how you manipulated her just like you did everyone else. How does it feel to be manipulated, Uriah? How does it feel to know that you're on the verge of losing this damned ranch that means more to you than family?"

"What do you mean?" Uriah muttered, finally put on the defensive.

"You used fifty thousand acres of our land as collateral for a loan from Weber Fielding, and right now you're about to lose that land because you don't have the money to make your note."

"You don't know this!" Uriah stubbed the cigar into the ashtray.

"Fielding has already been out to the village to tell Soaring Eagle to move his people. He's already taking over, Uriah. He's acting like the land already belongs to him. He has the Comanches on the verge of war."

Uriah slid into his chair, his fingers gripping the leather arms. "You always were closer to the Comanches than you were to us," he snapped bitterly. "All this talk about a reconciliation, about coming home to La Candela de Oro, yet you went to visit Soaring Eagle before you came to see me!"

"Perhaps I was closer to him," Matt softly admitted. "They were willing to love and accept me as I was. You weren't. You always wanted to change and mold me into what you wanted."

Grandfather and grandson stared at each other. Cut of the same fabric, neither gave. The door opened and Dora entered with a tray in her hands.

"Coffee," she announced, feeling the tension that stretched between the two men as she moved to the low table that sat in front of the sofa. "Mind if I join you?"

"Not at all," Matt said, flashing her a smile; then he returned his attention to Uriah. "I stopped by the village first because it was on the way to the ranch, not because I loved the Comanches more or better."

"It doesn't matter where you went first," Dora said as she set the tray on the desk and poured coffee into three cups. "Soaring Eagle is your grandfather, just like Uriah. Thing that matters is that you came home. Let bygones be bygones."

"I think that's a decision for *me* to make," Uriah

barked.

"Just think," Dora said, "we're going to be celebrating Founder's Day at the end of next week. Wouldn't it be nice to have both your grandsons by your side? How do you take your coffee, Matt? Black?"

"Black."

"I remembered you take it just like your grandpa takes his. Come now, let's sit down and talk about Founder's Day."

"You can jibber-jabber about Founder's Day all you want to," Uriah declared, "but don't include me. I have only one grandson."

For all the outward toughness, the primitive savageness and hardness that Zoe had accused Matt of having, Matt was deeply hurt by Uriah's reception and his refusal to forgive. But Matt had known this was going to be one of the hardest battles he'd ever fought.

"One grandson," Uriah shouted. "Do you hear me? Only one."

Matt moved toward the sofa, but not to discuss Founder's Day. He knew he could no longer put off telling them about Bryan's death. Sitting down next to Dora, he took the coffee pot out of her hand and replaced it on the tray. "You're right, Uriah, you have only one grandson."

Something in Matt's tone caught Uriah's and Dora's attention. He leaned forward, resting his arms on the desk; Dora scooted closer to the edge of the sofa and looked intently into Matt's face as he caught her hands in his.

"Bryan's dead."

"No!" Dora screamed, jumping up from the sofa and knocking the tray off the table, china falling

333

and shattering; coffee splashing on the floor. *Not her baby!* "You don't know what you're saying!"

Matt stood and caught her in his arms, easing her down on the sofa. "Yes, Mama Dorrie," he said, "I know."

"What makes you think Bryan is dead?" Uriah shouted, refusing to accept such news.

"I know he's dead," Matt answered flatly as he held the sobbing woman and comforted her. "I buried him myself."

"You come here and tell me Bryan is dead and expect me to believe it?"

"Yes. You know I've never lied to you."

"No," the old man conceded, slumping down in the chair, "you don't lie, son."

Son. Matt's heart leapt when he heard it. Although Uriah had spoken the word unconsciously, it held a wealth of meaning for Matt.

"Tell me what happened," Uriah said.

By the time Matt finished recounting his story—from his return to Soaring Eagle's village, the trip to Candaleria with Zoe, and his eavesdropping at the abstract office prior to his coming to La Candela de Oro—he was pacing the room. Dora was sitting on the sofa, crying softly, and Uriah still sat behind the desk but his head was lowered.

When Matt sat down beside her, Dora turned to Uriah. "What are we going to do?" she sobbed. "We can't let Fielding have the place now, especially not now."

Like a stick of dynamite exploding, Uriah moved abruptly, his fist pounding against his desk. "Fielding's damned sure I'm not going to be able to pay my note! Well, he's wrong. I'll find a way. I promise you, boy . . . I mean, Matt, I'll find a way."

The two men looked at each other and finally Matt smiled and dug into his pocket to pull out the money Victorio de la Luz had given him in exchange for the weapons. "Here's the money for the guns. We'll start with this. It'll give us a little time to play with. Not much, but enough."

"Any idea how we're gonna get the rest?" Uriah asked.

"Wish I could say the cattle," Matt answered dryly.

Uriah said defensively, "As soon as Shelby gets himself and his men established in Mexico, Matt, he's promised to pay us. He's a fine Confederate officer; he'll keep his word."

"Hell, Uriah!" Matt scoffed, "I thought you had better sense than that."

Uriah drew himself up. "I love my country, and General Shelby promised that he's going to come back and drive the Yankees out. We're not going to be under the rule of them damn blue bellies."

"The war's over, Uriah. We're one nation again, and we better make the best of it. We've got to get on with our living."

"Well, for the time being, we'll do it without the cattle," Uriah muttered. "Always knew Weber had more on his mind than a ditch from the Rio Grande into New Mexico, but I never figured on a railroad. Good thing I used property to lure settlers out here."

Matt chuckled. "Aren't you glad now that Ed Calloway drove such a hard bargain?"

Uriah laughed, recalling fond memories. "Sure am. Before he came out here to do his doctoring, he made certain he had it in writing that he'd get first selection of town lots. The old son-of-a-gun demanded acreage that joined mine and circled town. He said when and if Chandlerville ever did amount to anything, he was going to be the richest and most powerful man about."

"How did the Randolphs get the property?"

"About eight years ago, Ed went to San Antonio and met Quintan. The two of them became partners. Before Ed died four or five years ago, he sold all his property to Randolph. Ain't no way Fielding is going to bring a railroad into Chandlerville without crossing my property and Randolph's, and he sure as hell ain't gonna get mine."

"I've got to save Zoe from Weber," Matt exclaimed, slapping his fist into his open palm.

Hearing the protective note in Matt's voice, Uriah and Dora looked at each other.

"Zoe doesn't know that you're Matt Chandler?" Dora said.

"No," Matt answered.

His curiosity piqued, Uriah stared at his oldest grandson. He'd never really been able to understand Matt; he'd been closer to Charles and the Comanches. Not only did Matt have features like his mother—he had many of her Indian characteristics. That hadn't kept Uriah from loving Matt, but he hadn't known how to express his love. Every overture he made seemed to drive Matt further and further away. After Matt had left Chandlerville, Uriah had realized that his narrow-mindedness and jealousy had driven his grandson from him. He'd read Matt's letters over and over, those he'd written to Bryan, those he'd written to him, until he had almost memorized them, but pride, stupid pride had kept him from answering. This time he would be careful.

Grateful to his grandfather for not prying, Matt changed the subject by asking, "Who was supplying Bryan with guns?"

"I don't know," Uriah answered, rubbing his hand over the nape of his neck. "Bryan said it was better if we didn't know. I shouldn't have allowed him to do this . . . but we did need the money. . . ."

"He was a grown man, Uriah," Matt said. "He did what he wanted to do, and neither you nor anyone else could have stopped him."

"Before it's all over," Dora said, "Weber Fielding will own all of west Texas. He'll see all of us buried."

"No," Matt said, "he won't get La Candela de Oro, and I promise he won't see another Chandler in the grave."

"What about Founder's Day?" Dora asked Uriah. "Are we going to have the big celebration now?"

Uriah, having no enthusiasm left for the celebration, shook his head.

"Yes!" Matt exclaimed. Both Uriah and Dora looked at him as if he were crazy. "We're going to have it. We're not going to let Fielding rob us of our day. We'll whip him at his own game."

"What do you mean?" Uriah wanted to know.

"All the ranches in the area will come to our house for the Founder's Day barbecue."

"Not only the barbecue," Uriah said, "but the ball. We're having that out here at the ranch this year. Me and Bryan were feeling real good about the sale of the guns. Figured we might beat Fielding at his own game, but—" He left his sentence dangling, then shrugged.

"We'll beat Fielding," Matt promised. "The dance

will be an opportunity for us to get together and work out a plan for saving our land. The money I received from the sale of the guns will tide us over for a little while, but we've got to figure a way to get more—and to get it quickly."

Dora sat on the couch crying quietly as she listened to Matt and Uriah plan the Founder's Day dance and barbecue. When there was a lull in the conversation, she said, "Why would Weber kill Bryan, Matt? How does he benefit from his death?"

"It's another part of his plan to get the ranch," Matt answered. "He figures Uriah is all alone now and more defenseless."

"Reckon he was supplying Bryan with the guns?" she asked.

"No!" Uriah boomed. "Weber wouldn't have done anything to help us one tiny bit."

Matt shook his head. "I don't know how Weber knew about the guns, but he wasn't supplying them. Do you know anything about a Grisswold?"

Uriah thought a minute, shaking his head. "Don't reckon I do. Why?"

"He's working for Weber. He's the one responsible for killing Bryan and the others and for stealing the guns."

"I'd like to get my hands on him," Uriah said. "I'd kill him myself."

Remembering the man whom he'd chased in Mexico, Matt said, "He's a dangerous fellow, Uriah. Runs with the Mescaleros. I got the impression that he did this job for Fielding just to get the guns."

Uriah threw back his head and roared with laughter. "Well, at least you messed up that part of

338

their plan."

"I want you to get Weber for me," Dora said thickly, wadding her handkerchief into a tiny ball and shoving it into her pocket. "I mean it, Matt. I want you to get Weber for me." She stood and walked across the room, turning to look at Matt when she reached the door. In a low, dull tone she said, "I'm going to get the mop and clean up the floor. Then I reckon I'll cook us some supper. Since you're about the same size as Bryan, Matt, you can wear some of his clothes. They're upstairs in the wardrobe in his room."

"I guess we'd better break the news to the widows," Uriah said. "The sooner they find out, the quicker they can get their grieving behind them and get on with living. We got a fight on our hands and we'll need our wits about us."

"No," Matt said, "I don't think it's a good idea yet. The fewer who know I've returned, the better. Also, we need to let Fielding play into our hands. He's the one who sent word to the French that Bryan would be smuggling guns into Candaleria. Let him be the one to announce Bryan's death, or let Zoe, when she regains consciousness."

Uriah nodded and after a few minutes chuckled softly as he rubbed his palms together. "Is Fielding going to be surprised when I walk into the office to make the loan payments. I'm going to relish this moment for a long time to come, son. I wouldn't miss the look on his face for anything!"

Dora opened the door and entered the study. "Sheriff Parker's here to see you, Uriah. He said it was real important for him to talk to you."

Leaving Matt in the study, Uriah hurried down the hall into the parlor, crossing the room to shake hands with the sheriff. "Howdy, Lawrence. What brings you out to this neck of the woods?"

"Indians," Parker replied, twisting the brim of his hat in his hands. "The Comanches. They're on the uprising. Got Latcher's place sometime today."

"Anybody hurt?" Uriah asked.

"Both Vonnie and Mabeline killed. Place burned to the ground, and the stock all stolen."

"I can hardly believe after all these years the Comanches would attack us," Uriah said. "Nearly fifty years we've been living in peace with them. I just can't believe it."

"Well, they did," Parker declared. "Sutton saw the smoke and rode over. He got there just in time to see a bunch of them all painted up, hightailing it into the mountains. He went home, packed his family up, and got them into town real quick. Like Fielding says, it's only a matter of time before they attack again, this time killing some innocent white folks. I just wanted to let you folks know so's you could protect yourself, what with your place being so close to Latcher's and all. Give us a few days and we'll have everything under control."

"What are you planning to do?"

Parker shifted his weight from one foot to the other. Clearing his throat, he said, "Well, Uriah, as much as we hated to do it, we followed Weber's suggestion and sent a dispatch to army headquarters at San Antonio to request troopers."

"Damn blue-belly soldiers!" Uriah spat out the words. "We need to have a town meeting and decide if that's really what we want."

"We — we already sent the messenger, Uriah. Reckon we need 'em to take care of these savages," Lawrence stammered, backing away. Even though

Uriah Chandler was in his late sixties, he was a strong man, and Lawrence Parker respected him. And he was a little bit afraid of him.

After the sheriff left, Uriah returned to the study. "Comanches attacked Vonnie Latcher's place. Killed him and Mabeline. Burned the place down and took the stock."

"You're sure?" Matt asked, his incredulity even greater than his grandfather's.

"What Lawrence said. And to top it all off, damn Yankee soldiers are coming!" he exclaimed to Matt. "Now we know why Weber incited the Indians and pushed them until they retaliated. He wanted a reason to send for the troops he intends to use for his own selfish purposes."

Much later that night after supper, Matt picked up a lamp and headed upstairs. He still couldn't reconcile in his mind that the Comanches, not even Bright Knife, had attacked Latcher's place. As much as he thought about it, a reason for the attack escaped him. The minute he opened the door to his room, he knew he wasn't alone. Cautiously he stepped inside, extending his arm in front of him so the light would be projected farther and he could see better.

"Ma-ta-mon-yahu, it is I, Running Horse," a whispered voice said in Comanche, and an Indian materialized from the shadows.

Matt closed the door and set the lamp on the night table. "Why have you come, my brother?" he asked, also speaking in Comanche.

"White men attacked our village yesterday, killing some of our women and children and wounding Soaring Eagle and Buffalo Woman's grandson."

"Is that why Latcher's place was attacked?"

Running Horse shook his head and gave Matt a puzzled look. "No one from our village—not even Bright Knife—has attacked anyone. But if your grandfather dies, the people will follow Bright Knife, who is calling for driving the whites from our country. For the time being, he and his braves are awaiting Soaring Eagle's fate."

"Who attacked Latcher's place?" Matt asked.

"I don't know, but many—too many—Mescalero Apaches' arrows were scattered all over to make sure everyone who came near would know that Indians had attacked. We saw the smoke and rode over to the ranch house to find the man and woman dead. We had to leave quickly because another white man was coming."

"Whites don't know one arrow from another and wouldn't care if they did. All they'll be after is an Indian."

The attacks were too synchronized to be coincidental, Matt thought. Grisswold was behind both of them, playing one against the other. Matt wondered if this was also part of Weber's plan; if it were, he was soon going to find himself being outsmarted. Scully Newton had been right in his assessment of Grisswold: one didn't play around with a man like him without getting hurt in exchange. Weber was way out of his league.

Running Horse untied a leather pouch from his waist and opened it. Holding his hand out, a golden chain dangling from his fingers, he said, "Soaring Eagle sent this. He said you would know what it meant."

Matt reached out, his hand closing over the cross, the sharp edges cutting into his palm. It was a sign that Soaring Eagle did not think he would live.

"Soaring Eagle's magic is strong, my brother, but the wound is bad," Running Horse said. "He had one last request to make: he would like to see his grandson one more time before he goes to the happy hunting ground."

"Tell my grandfather that I will be there."

Running Horse slipped out of the window through which he had entered. Matt opened his hand and looked at the cross, the symbol of leadership worn by every Comanche chief for over a hundred years. Soaring Eagle was telling him that it was time for him to decide which he was, white or Indian. Strangely enough, he was issuing an ultimatum to Matt not unlike the one Uriah had issued fourteen years ago.

As a child, Matt had loved his grandfather's necklace and had often run his hands over the large, solid links, wishing he could wear it himself. He walked to the dresser and stood in front of the cheval mirror, holding the chain over his head. More than his personal interests were at stake here. He closed his eyes, thinking of the tenuous thread that held him and his other grandfather together. How easily it could be severed.

"Matt, I heard voices in your room." Uriah called, fear prompting him to open the door without first knocking. His gaze fixed on the gold cross that gently swung from Matt's hand.

The lamp burned low, its muted light flickering across Zoe's countenance. Her lashes were a dark crescent against her pale cheeks. Her breathing was quiet. Matt, sitting next to the bed, clasped her hand in his. His head was bowed. Time passed very slowly.

The last time he'd sat here in this chair, holding her hand and willing her to live, he'd thought perhaps they had a chance to have a future together. But now he did not know. He found himself too encumbered with the past . . . as was Zoe.

The gold cross sagged in Matt's shirt pocket; its implications weighed on his heart. His heritage demanded so much from him. How much more grief could he go through—Bryan's death; Soaring Eagle; and now Zoe.

His hand tightened around hers; he lifted it and kissed the tip of each finger. Her hand was so warm and soft. He leaned forward and placed a chaste kiss on her cheek. Her breath warmed his face.

He had never thought it possible to love someone as much as he loved Zoe. His love went far deeper than mere desire. A tear trickled down the rugged cheek to drop onto hers. "I love you, my Comanche bride," he murmured. "You are the beat of my heart, the breath of my body. Without you I am not a complete man."

He lifted his head to look at her face. He brushed a tendril of honey-sweet hair from her forehead, his fingers lingering on her warm flesh. The movement jarred the cross; he felt it press against his chest. Its weight was a subtle reminder.

"I promised that I wouldn't leave you, darling, but I must. Soaring Eagle is dying," he told her in a soft voice. "I want to stay here with you, but I must go to him. I must save our people . . . all our people. Yours and mine."

He gazed at Zoe through blurry eyes. He loved

344

her; she loved him. But he wondered if she were ready to accept Matt Chandler and all that he was. He feared not. Again he experienced the same vulnerability now that the twenty-two-year-old Matt had. He wanted to do something for her, but he was helpless to do so.

"I'm entrusting you to the only man who loves you as much as I do. Your father." Matt's voice was thick and husky. Although her hand was limp in his, he tenderly squeezed. "You're going to be fine, *Mah-ocu-ah*. I will return to you soon."

Matt rose and leaned over the bed to press a kiss to her lips. When he straightened, he traced their gentle curve. Tears coursed down his cheeks, but he did not care. This was the woman he loved.

"I'll be back, my beautiful Comanche bride," he promised.

Zoe felt the warmth of the sun on her lids long before she opened her eyes. Slowly she turned her head to the window. A breeze gently rustled the curtain. She heard the door and turned to see Lou entering the room, a stack of sheets over her arm.

"Good morning," Zoe murmured.

Lou dropped the linen and rushed to the bedside. "Good gracious alive! You're awake." Before Zoe could answer, the housekeeper shouted, "Dr. Quintan, Zoe's awake. Come quick." Then she engulfed Zoe in a hug, the two of them laughing and crying together.

Quintan rushed into the room all but dragging Lou away from Zoe. Rather than hugging her, his eyes anxiously studied her face. He stuffed pillows behind her back. "How are you?"

"I'm fine." The sheet slipped down to reveal her pink flannel nightgown. She looked like an extremely young girl in the long, billowing sleeves and high neck. Nothing was exposed but hands and a cherubic face that was framed with riotous honey-gold curls. "Just a little weak."

"You need some good old chicken soup." Lou wiped her eyes with the tail of her apron as she walked out. "I'll go get you some right now."

Quintan rolled Zoe over, and his trained hands probed down her spine. "Does this hurt?"

"It's sore when I move, but I have no aches or pains." She laughed lightly. "There's no serious damage that I can feel."

"Good! I thought you were just bruised."

Zoe reached up and touched the back of her head. "What happened?"

"On your way back from Candaleria, you fell off a boulder and hit your head. At the same time you were bitten by a snake. Had it not been for—"

Zoe's hand went to her forehead and her brow furrowed. Memories rushed in on her, and abruptly she looked around, "Where's—where's . . . where is he?"

Puzzled, Quintan stared at her. "Who? Weber?"

"No." Zoe shook her head and frowned when she was assailed with nausea.

"The man who brought you in?"

"Yes," she said.

"He's gone."

"No!" Zoe pushed the covers aside and bolted up.

"He's not here, baby." Quintan caught her shoulders and laid her back down. "He left the same night he brought you here."

346

Big tears rolled down Zoe's cheeks. "He must have left me a message. He wouldn't have left without telling me."

Quintan's heart hurt as he shook his head, but he did not think it odd she was crying over the Mexican who had brought her in. She was in shock.

"Did he say where he was going?"

"He just told me that he saved you from the Comanches and took you to Mexico. You fell off a boulder on the return trip and hit your head."

"Oh, Papa," she cried.

Tears flowing freely down his cheeks, Quintan gathered his daughter into his arms and held her until her crying was spent.

Later, after she'd eaten, Zoe lay quietly and gazed out the window. Lou sat by the bed darning the clothes and chatting endlessly.

Because her strength returned quickly, Zoe disregarded her father's advice and was up and about in two days. She was cautious, however, to stray no farther than the yard. She sat in the swing on the front porch and stared down the road.

Every time she saw a rider coming, her heart skipped a beat and she caught her breath. She thought perhaps it was Matt; but he did not return. But he would, Zoe thought. Her Comanche husband would return. He loved her . . . she never doubted that for a moment. Matt loved her and would come to her as soon as he could. She must believe in him.

Chapter 18

Wearing a pale blue taffeta gown, her hair hanging in loose curls down her back, Zoe sat in the swing on the veranda, her toe touching the floor now and again as she gave a gentle shove. Quintan, his shirtsleeves rolled up, his thumbs hooked under his suspenders, stood in front of her, staring down Main Street at a wagon loaded to the brim with furniture and people as it lumbered into town. Weber, impeccably dressed in a dark blue suit with a camel-colored waistcoat, set his hat and paper on the table next to the wall.

"People are getting scared," Quintan said, "and that's bad. No telling what's going to happen."

"That's why I thought it was in our best interests to send for some military help. We can't battle these Indians by ourselves, especially with them having guns."

"Guns!" Zoe exclaimed, memories of Mexico crowding her mind, a pockmarked face standing out most prominently.

"We don't know that they have guns," Quintan said. "People are letting their imagination run wild.

348

Every time I hear the story of the raid on Latcher's place, it gets more gruesome. Sheriff found only arrows, and there's some who say they aren't even Comanche arrows."

"You're right, Quintan. There's absolutely too much talk, and it can easily get out of hand. That's one of the reasons why I'm glad that we sent for troops."

"We've sent for the army?" Zoe asked, dazed that she'd missed so much because of her concussion.

"It's not so much that *we* sent for the army," Quintan returned dryly, turning to look at Zoe. "When Sutton rode into town and informed us that Latcher and his wife were dead and the place was burned to the ground, people went wild. Weber calmed them down when he said we needed the army out here."

Gritting his teeth and swallowing his anger, Weber said, "I'm still of the opinion that we need the army. It's much better to let *them* get killed handling these problems than us. After all, they're trained for these purposes. We're not."

Zoe's heart seemed to leap into her throat, pounding furiously. Matt was with those Indians, possibly leading them. He was the one who had supplied them with guns—guns with which they could kill whites. Oddly, Zoe didn't blame Matt any more. She understood that he and his people were only protecting their land. But the guns would bring the U.S. Cavalry after them—eventually bringing his death. She blinked back the tears. She had to go warn him. She had to.

"Zoe," Quintan said, moving to kneel in front of the swing, "are you all right?"

Zoe smiled and nodded her head. "I'm fine, Papa. Memories came flooding back."

"We're not going to have that kind of war out here, honey," he promised, thinking she was reliving her years during the recent war between the states.

"I know, and I'm sorry. I don't mean to be so sentimental."

"It's only natural," Quintan reassured her, patting her hands. "You've recovered physically; now you must give yourself time to heal emotionally. Enough talk now about Indians and soldiers."

A buggy raced down Main Street and pulled to a screeching halt in front of the house. An elderly man shouted, "Doc, I need you out at my place, quick. Dirk's been hurt bad. Figure he might lose his leg. Don't even take the time to hitch your buggy. We'll go in mine, and one of the boys can bring you back."

"Be right with you, Lester," Quintan called, leaping to his feet.

"Papa, do you want me to go with you?" Zoe asked.

"No, you need some time to recuperate. Just because you're feeling well doesn't mean that you can throw caution and good sense to the wind. I want you to relax and take it easy for a day or two longer . . . at least."

"Indians?" Weber called to the man as the door slammed behind Quintan.

"Mountain cat," Lester Fenton returned. "Tore the boy to shreds. We're lucky he made it home."

Minutes later, Quintan hurried out of the house, holding his bag in one hand and his coat in the other. After a hasty kiss that missed Zoe's forehead more than hit it, he ran down the walkway and climbed into the Fentons' buggy.

"Don't look for me until you see me," he yelled as they took off.

As Zoe watched the buggy disappear down the street, Weber said, "You're looking pretty, Zoe, considering how ill you've been."

"Not ill, Weber," she answered, running her fingers lightly over the knot at the base of her skull, "merely unconscious as a result of the concussion." Zoe was surprised to find that after having been separated from Weber for a mere three weeks, she found him to be an absolute bore. She wanted him to leave, and he'd just arrived. She wondered how she could have ever considered marriage to him.

"I'm sorry, Zoe. Not being a doctor, I don't know all the correct medical terms." Although his anger and frustration were growing by the minute, Weber still managed to infuse some sweetness into his words. Marriage to Zoe was his top priority.

"That's the first time I've ever seen you do that, Weber," Zoe commented.

"What?" Weber looked at her blankly.

"Run your hands through your hair and muss it up. Something's worrying you, isn't it?"

Weber's boots snapped against the veranda planking as he closed the distance between him and Zoe to sit down beside her in the swing, his leg crushing the material of her skirt. Taking her hands in his, he said, "My darling little girl."

He was handsome, Zoe thought, the gray at his temples adding a touch of distinction, but his nearness, his touch didn't arouse an answering passion within her. In fact, she found them rather repulsive. They filled her with a great longing for Matt. Dear Lord, how she wanted Matt!

"You have had me worried sick."

Weber's words didn't penetrate Zoe's consciousness; she was looking at his hands as she pulled hers free, remembering and wanting another man's touch. Rather than the soft hands with the manicured nails, she wanted the callused hands that could be so warm and tender, that explored every inch of her body.

"If only I could suffer this illness for you," Zoe heard Weber say from afar, "I would. I hope someday that we know who brought you home; I want to give the man a reward of some kind. He came and went without anyone knowing who he was."

Without leaving a message for me or telling anyone who he was, Zoe added silently, swallowing back her tears. Until a moment ago, she'd thought he did so because he was frightened of the white man. But now she was wondering if it were because he had to deliver the guns to his people.

"Zoe, I love you so much," Weber said. "Please, darling, reconsider, and let's get married right away."

Feeling as if Weber were suffocating her, Zoe pushed away from him, as far back as the arm of the swing would allow. "I don't want to discuss this right now, Weber," she said, knowing she was much too emotional to handle a confrontation just yet. Any intense emotion brought her to the brink of tears. "We need time."

Time was exactly what Weber didn't have. "I don't mean to be rushing you, but I didn't realize how much you meant to me until I thought I'd lost you. Oh, Zoe—" Weber reached for her, but Zoe stood and moved away from him, far away. "I love and want to take care of you."

Anger surged through Weber; the idea of her dodging him, refusing to let him touch her body! At times he thoroughly hated Zoe Randolph. So superior . . . so smug. And now, even after the degrading experience she'd been through, she was still haughty. Look how much he was sacrificing in order to marry her! His name would be sullied by her.

Zoe draped her arms around a porch column and gazed at the squat oaks that dotted the front lawn and shaded the house.

Brought home in a peasant's wagon by a Mexican peasant! Weber thought. No telling what really happened while she was gone to Candaleria. That was the primary reason he wanted to see that Mexican; he would have found out all the details. Knowing them might come in handy in the future; he'd learned that people could be manipulated through their past actions.

My God! He couldn't begin to document how much of Zoe's past he ignored. Her being a doctor was hard for him to accept. Stepping out of her place into a man's world had created a hard woman out of her. She honestly thought she was on an equal basis with men, could think like them, make decisions like them. How that would change, how quickly that would change once they married! He would teach Zoe her proper place in society and dare her to step out of it.

"Zoe, you don't know how proud I am of you, striking out by yourself and going all the way to Candaleria to treat those people."

He stood and walked across the veranda, deliberately brushing his leg against the newspaper that lay in the rocking chair beneath his hat—the newspaper he'd deliberately bought on his way to Zoe's. He knew what the headline story was, but he also knew that Quintan was protecting Zoe and wouldn't let her read it. Weber was of a different opinion; she needed to know. Might make her easier to handle. Smiling, he caught the lapels of his coat in both hands and gazed down Main Street. Oh yes, he would pull the high-and-mighty Miss Randolph from her pedestal.

"Not many men would have done that, much less a woman."

Zoe grinned in spite of herself. How condescending men could be! Even their compliments were insults.

"I stopped in the emporium the other day and Myra said to tell you that the material for your wedding dress has arrived. As soon as you're feeling up to it, she wants to start the fittings."

I already have a wedding dress. Zoe thought of the soft, worked-leather dress with the fringed hem that hung to her ankles. The brilliant patterns and beads had glittered in the sunlight. She could still feel the material gently caress her skin as Matt had slipped it off her body.

"Also," Weber continued, "our furniture arrived while you were gone."

Furniture. Zoe had forgotten about their ordering furniture . . . she couldn't even remember what it looked like. All she thought about was a tepee and buffalo mats and Matt . . . most of all, Matt.

"When you feel like it, love, I'd like for you to come to the house and show Ruby and Lionel how you want it arranged. We're a little crowded now and need to clear out some of the old for the new."

Weber's voice drifted far away, his words nothing but a drone as Zoe lost herself in thoughts of Matt, as she relived all her precious moments with him in Candaleria, memories that might have to last her a lifetime.

Not until Weber moved to stand behind her, his hands gently capping her shoulders, did Zoe come out of her reverie. "Are you getting tired, darling?"

he asked, bending his head to kiss her cheek.

Zoe ducked before his lips touched her. "Yes, I'm extremely tired. I think I would like to rest now."

"Then I'll be going." He turned to the chair, picking up his hat and the paper, which he tucked under his arm. "Do you think you'd feel like having dinner with me tonight?"

"I don't think so," Zoe answered. "I'm just beginning to realize how weak I am."

"I'll check on you this evening." As Weber walked down the steps, he dropped the paper deliberately at her feet, the headlines in bold, black print. When he was sure she'd seen it, he stooped and picked it up.

"Let me see that," Zoe said.

He yanked it out of her reach and tried to tuck it into his coat pocket. "No, Zoe. I don't want you to get upset."

Zoe grabbed the paper out of his hands and read the story: *According to Sheriff Lawrence Parker, Dr. Zoe Randolph, suffering a coma, was brought home from Candaleria, Mexico, by an unidentified Mexican. "No telling what happened to the doctor while she was out there," the sheriff commented.*

"My God," she gasped, "what did Parker tell them? And look—they've resurrected the story about Inez Patterson. How long is that poor girl going to carry the blame for being captured by Indians? They'll be doing this to *me* next, Weber!"

Yes, my dear, Weber thought gleefully, *they will.* "Just consider the source, Zoe," Weber begged. "That's the reason why I took the paper. I didn't want you to read this. I don't care what happened to you while you were gone, darling. We'll overlook it and pretend it didn't happen. I'm just thankful that you're back."

Zoe looked at Weber, really seeing him for the first time. While he was telling her to pay no attention to what the newspaper said, he was saying the same thing himself.

"Weber, I don't think you understand. I don't want to forget what happened to me during the past three weeks; I don't want to overlook one little bit of my life."

Stunned by her confession, Weber stared at her blankly. When he had regained his wits, he said, "I'm terribly sorry. I didn't mean that the way it sounded. And yes, darling, I do care what people are thinking; I care what they're thinking because it's going to affect you and your reputation. You're the woman who wanted to be a doctor. You're the one who has a career to think about. Even you must agree that what people think matters a lot to your profession."

He tucked the newspaper into his coat pocket and caught her shoulders in his hands, forcing her to look up at him. "I've never made any secret about my feelings for you. All Chandlerville knows I love you. I nearly went out of my mind when I thought you might never come out of the coma. Although I resented it, I followed your father's orders to the letter when it came to your care."

"I know," Zoe whispered, remembering when she'd awakened from her nap the day before yesterday. Through bleary eyes she'd seen the masculine figure sitting in the chair next to her bed. When he caught her hand in his, she'd thought it was Matt. Then he'd called her name, and she'd known it wasn't Matt's voice. But Weber had been there with her . . . Matt hadn't.

Her heart broken, she had begun to cry convulsively, and her father had ushered Weber out of the room, returning to her bedside and taking her into his arms to comfort her. Rocking her back and forth as if she were a little girl, he soothed her. Zoe grieved for the senseless deaths of Bryan Chandler and the other ranchers; she grieved for Uriah Chandler and the widows. More she grieved because she had lost her Comanche husband.

"Zoe, please . . . I want us to be married as soon as possible," Weber said, breaking into her ruminations. "I want to take care of you."

Zoe smiled sadly and said, "Weber, I'm not the same woman who rode away from Chandlerville so long ago."

"Of course you are," Weber exclaimed. "You're just feeling bad right now because of your illness."

"Weber, my concussion has nothing to do with the way I feel. My priorities have changed . . . I see everything from a different perspective. I don't even want to *consider* marriage."

"Zoe, we'll discuss this another day," Weber said. "Right now you need to rest."

"Yes," Zoe agreed, "I want to rest now."

Once she'd been willing to settle for second-best, to marry for convenience, but not since she'd met Matt. His coming into her life had caused her to redefine her needs and goals. Strangely, by her own choice, neither Weber nor his causes were any longer among either.

Ma-ta-mon-yahu married me to save me from the Comanches! Zoe thought. *Who's going to save me from myself, from the memories that will haunt me the rest of my life?*

The bitter salt of tears in her eyes, Zoe remembered the Indian ceremony that had united her and Matt in marriage. *It's the living together that makes a marriage, not the words uttered in a cere-*

357

mony, he had said . . . and during the three weeks they'd spent together, she'd lived an entire lifetime.

Weber stood watching as she walked toward the door. When her hands curled around the doorknob, he said, "Zoe, you know the Founder's Day Ball is this weekend?"

"Sure is," Lou's voice boomed from the far end of the hallway. "It's just what this doctor orders for her patient."

Zoe laughed at her housekeeper. "You're prescribing the Founder's Day Ball for me?"

Footsteps brought Lou closer to the veranda and Zoe opened the screen door for her. "Sure am. You need to get out among people again, and it's not that exhausting." Lou looked anxiously at Zoe's face. "Maybe it'll put a smile back into your eyes."

"Maybe," Zoe replied, her head turning, her eyes inadvertently searching the dusty main street of Chandlerville for that one familiar figure who would bring happiness to her heart and laughter to her eyes.

"You know you promised to go with me," Weber said.

"I'll let you know later," Zoe answered.

Irritated, Weber forced a smile, nodded his head, and moved down the boardwalk. Zoe heard his retreating footsteps, but didn't turn to wave goodbye. Rather, she moved for the stairs and the privacy of her room. She needed to get away and think, to decide what she was going to do.

"Lunch is ready, Zoe," Lou called from the kitchen door, where she wiped her face with the tail of her apron. "Are you hungry?"

"I'll eat later," Zoe called as she continued to mount the stairs and walk toward her room. "Right now I want to rest."

"I'm worried about that girl, Zeke," Lou said in an undertone when her husband joined her in the corridor. "She's been depressed ever since she came to three days ago and found out that Mexican didn't hang around after he brought her home."

"Doc Quinn says a person is usually depressed after a coma," Ezekiel said, but he, too, was worried about Zoe. She had been too quiet since she regained consciousness. She spent hours on the front porch, staring down the street as if she was looking for someone. He patted Lou's shoulder. "Don't worry about it. She'll get over it pretty soon."

"Sure hope so," Lou exclaimed with a shake of her head, strands of hair escaping her chignon to wisp around her round face. "Just ain't natural for her to be like this."

When Zoe reached her room, she lay across her bed, blinking back the tears and thinking about Matt. She remembered nothing after the accident, but had no doubt that the man who brought her home, the Mexican wearing the sombrero and serape, was Matt. He was afraid of white people, she decided. That was the reason why he'd left without telling anyone who he was or where he was going. He'd come back—surely he would! He had to know that she loved him.

But what about the guns?

"Zoe." Lou called at the same time that she knocked.

"Come in," she called, hastily wiping her eyes and rolling over as the housekeeper opened the door to enter. "I just wanted to remind you that this afternoon I'm going to ride out to the Hollister place to give Gussie a jar of my chicken soup. She and Bernard have been ailing this week. I thought this would cheer them up. I'll be back in plenty of time to cook supper."

"While you're gone," Zoe said, sitting up and sliding off the bed, "I think I'll walk to the Emporium and see if Myra has my dresses in yet."

"Talking about your wedding dress?" Lou asked.

"No." Zoe shook her head and smiled, her eyes twinkling. "If I decide to go to the Founder's Day Ball, I should like to have something new to wear."

"Now that's what I've been wanting to hear," the older woman exclaimed with a chuckle. "When you begin to talk about spending money, I know you're getting better. But you're not going to walk. No, ma'am. You're far too weak. If you go, you'll let Zeke drive you in the buggy."

"What about you?"

"I'll drive myself. I ain't been hit on the head like you, young lady."

By the time Lou had filled the basket with food and Zeke had brought the buggy to the front, Zoe had changed from her house slippers into walking shoes. Lou was right: she needed to get out of the house. A few hours at the emporium with Myra would do her a world of good. Her parasol and purse in hand, she walked down the stairs to the veranda, where Zeke was helping Lou into one of the two buggies sitting in front of the house.

"Where to?" Zeke called as Zoe approached the second buggy.

"The Emporium first. After that, we'll see."

"Don't reckon you want to tire yourself out the first time you manage to get out of the house," Lou called as she picked up the reins and lightly swatted the horses. "Ezekiel Townsend, you stay right with her. You hear me?"

"Yes, Louella," he sighed, "I hear you."

Zoe grinned. The Townsends had come with her father when he'd left San Antonio to become a partner with Ed Calloway. They were more than employees; they were part of the family.

"The way Louella talks, sometimes, you'd think I didn't have an ounce of sense," Zeke grumbled. "Of course I ain't gonna let anything happen to you."

"Of course," Zoe agreed, enjoying the short ride down the street. She smiled and waved at the passers-by. When Ezekiel stopped the buggy in front of the Emporium, she said, "There's no need on your waiting for me. I'm sure I'll be a couple of hours. You know how these fittings go."

"I sure do," he agreed with a hearty nod. "Lou spends more time in there getting fitted than she does with me. Want me to come back for you in about two hours?"

"Two hours will be fine," Zoe said.

When Zoe first walked into the Emporium, she stood for a moment looking. She loved to come here. The Emporium was one of the largest buildings in Chandlerville and certainly the most elegant. The ground floor was stocked with groceries and hardware and dry goods. The second story belonged exclusively to Myra and the women: here were the patterns, the materials, and all the accessories. Myra was designer and seamstress, creating magic out of each piece of material she cut and sewed.

As Zoe looked around, she noticed two of Chandlerville's biggest gossips, Delma Reeves and Audra Gadding, huddled together. The one was as tall and skinny as the other was short and round. They had always reminded Zoe of vultures, and even more so today. They devoured with relish any bad news or calamity; and they enjoyed regurgitating it to every one whom they met even more. The minute they saw Zoe, they swooped toward her, false smiles plastered to their faces. Inwardly Zoe grimaced, but she tried to appear civil.

"It's so nice to see you about, Dr. Randolph," Delma Reeves said, pressing a bony finger against her cheek and blinking her birdlike eyes at Zoe.

"Thank you, Mrs. Reeves."

"We've really been worried about you," Delma continued.

"Oh, yes," Audra echoed, her round face bobbing up and down. "We've really been concerned — you've been so ill."

"Not ill," Zoe corrected dryly, knowing the only thing these two women worried about was not getting the latest tidbit of gossip. "As a result of a severe blow to my head, I was in a coma."

"Yes, of course," Delma twittered, "a coma. That's what Weber was telling Lloyd this morning when he came into Lloyd's office. You just don't know much we sympathize with you, Dr. Randolph, and all you went through."

Looking around and lowering her voice to a whisper, Audra said, "Sometimes it helps to have another woman to talk to about certain things, if you know what I mean."

"Yes, Mrs. Gadding, I do," Zoe answered.

"Well, honey — " A pudgy hand reached out to pat Zoe on the arm. "I'm here anytime you need a shoulder to cry on."

"That's nice to know," Zoe murmured. "If ever I should need a shoulder to cry on, I'll know where to come." The only shoulder Zoe wanted to cry on was Matt's.

"Why," Delma said, "me and Audra was just talking about you, wondering how you were — and

362

in you walk. We were just wondering about your wedding to Weber."

"Well, don't let me spoil the conversation," Zoe returned lightly. "If I tell you everything, you'll have nothing to wonder about, will you?"

Zoe looked up to see Greg Halstead walking in the back door at the other side of the room, a large sack of flour over his shoulder. Moving in his direction, quickly putting a lot of distance between herself and the women, Zoe called over her shoulder, "Please excuse me, ladies. I'm so glad to have seen you, but I really must rush. I want to speak to Myra about my new gown for the Founder's Day Ball."

"Zoe!" Greg reached up to dust flour out of his dark brown hair. "It's good to see you, girl. How're you feeling?"

Zoe rolled her eyes toward the other side of the store, where Delma and Audra stood, their faces drawn, their mouths pursed in annoyance. "Not so good."

Greg threw back his head and laughed. "I can see how that would get to you. What can I do for you today?"

"I really wanted to get out of the house for a few minutes and I thought I'd visit with Myra."

"Is she gonna be upset!" Greg said. "She's not here today. She's gone to El Paso and won't be back until tomorrow. Said something about exchanging patterns with Mrs. O'Flannery."

"Well, I have a couple of hours on my hands. Do you mind if I walk into the shop and look to see what she's done on the gown that she's making me for the Founder's Day Ball?" Zoe asked, slightly disappointed that she wouldn't get to spend an hour or so visiting with her good friend.

"No, not at all," Greg said. "I know Myra won't mind."

Zoe walked across the room and climbed the steps to the sewing room. At first glance, she saw hanging on the far wall the blue creation Myra was making for her. The neckline was low, with a hint of lace. Evocative, Myra had called it. Brazen was more like it, Zoe had said, wondering what Weber would think of it. He was so conservative. Now Zoe didn't mind. In fact, the dress seemed a direct reflection of her new self—of the woman that had been softened and shaped in love. Not once did she look at the material she'd ordered for her dress. Not once did she think about it.

A little tired from her exertions, Zoe sat on the sofa and whiled away the better part of an hour looking through the pattern books. Finally her growling stomach reminded her that she hadn't eaten anything since breakfast, and she hadn't eaten very much then. Weber had invited her to the Founder's Day Ball with him, but she wasn't going. She would stop by the bank to let him know. She had intimated to him earlier that she didn't want to consider marriage, but that wasn't a strong enough statement. She must break the engagement entirely, and the sooner that was done, the sooner she could get on with her life. She would tell him about it over lunch; surely he wouldn't make a scene in a hotel dining room. Her purse and parasol in hand, she was walking down the stairs when she over-heard several women talking.

"Well, if you ask me, she'll be mighty lucky if Weber does marry her."

"Don't you know it! Why, my husband told me that a woman isn't fit to live with, once she's been with an Indian," another said.

364

"I sure don't want her doctoring me or mine," the first woman said. "Why, Delma Reeves said she saw Zoe Randolph today and she could tell she wasn't the same woman. Had a glazed look in her eyes; you know that look Inez Patterson had when they brought her back in? Looks like Zoe may have been tortured. Delma and Audra figure the Indians hit her on the head. That's why she was in the coma for so long. No telling what those Indians did to her while she was unconscious."

"Poor, poor Weber," the first woman sympathized. "He told Everett just this morning that he was going to marry her, no matter that she may have been captured by Comanches, no matter that they may have . . . well, you know what I mean. He said that he'd already promised to marry her and that he'd stick by his word. She needs him, he claims."

"Can you imagine how hard this is on that poor man? First his sister, now his fiancée. Oh, I do feel sorry for him. But it's a wonder this hadn't happened sooner, the way that woman acts—I never did figure her to be a decent woman, myself. No decent woman would want to be a doctor."

"Well, this just goes to show you. My mama always said what's done in the dark will be revealed in the daylight. Her sins will find her out."

Zoe stood there for a moment leaning against the wall. She hadn't talked too frequently with these women, but she knew them. She'd known they were gossips, but she'd never imagined them to be so vicious. Matt had warned her that she'd be an object of derision when she returned to civilization, and while a part of her agreed with him, another part could never imagine people thinking badly of her. Not when she was innocent.

Well, she wasn't going to take this sitting down . . . or standing up, for that matter.

Zoe straightened her back and squared her shoulders. Although she felt the sting of tears, she held her head high and walked down the rest of the stairs. "Good morning, Mrs. Kelsey, Mrs. Jones. Fancy meeting you here this morning." She greeted each of them with a big smile, but one that wasn't reflected in her eyes.

The two women, horrified looks on their faces, stumbled back, mumbling a greeting.

Softly Zoe said, "It can be quite embarrassing when you meet head-on with the subject you're talking about, can't it? In order to make your conversations a little more truthful and less fanciful, let me clarify a few points for you. I was captured by Comanches who had been ordered off the land they've lived on for the past hundred years by a white man; I wasn't tortured by the Indians; my eyes are not glazed; and I suffered a concussion when I fell from a large boulder and struck the back of my head. Now if you'll excuse me, I'm on my way to meet with poor, poor Weber who's sacrificing so much to marry a tainted woman like me."

Zoe turned, and still holding her head and shoulders up, she walked out of the Emporium before she made a complete fool of herself. She was about to burst into tears. She'd known she'd be sensitive after coming out of the coma but she hadn't expected the depression to be so severe. She'd be glad when she could get decently angry without squalling like a baby. Well, at least she didn't have to worry about crying around Weber . . . he didn't stir up any emotion in her at all. She was completely indifferent to him. However, if she heard much more gossip like this, she'd be hating him! The idea of his talking about her like that!

Nodding and speaking perfunctorily to those she passed on the street, Zoe hurried to the bank, stopping outside the door to blot her eyes with her handkerchief. Then she swept through the lobby to greet the young man behind the counter. "Good morning, Fred."

"Good morning, Dr. Zoe." The clerk looked up and smiled at her. "How wonderful it is to see you up and about! We've been quite worried about you."

"Thank you for your concern," she said. "Is Mr. Fielding in?"

"He had to go over to the abstract office for some papers," Fred explained. "Said he'd be back before he left for lunch. Shall I go get him for you?"

"No, let him take care of his business," Zoe answered, looking out the window at the stagecoach that screeched to a halt in the street.

"Late again," Fred announced, snapping the lid of his watch. "Mr. Fielding is really going to be angry about this. He's really going to rake Arney over the coals. He's been late for every arrival the past two weeks."

As the clerk talked, Zoe watched the people disembark. An elderly man climbed out first, holding a book that looked like a Bible in one hand, his small rounded hat in the other. As he looked up and down the street, he tugged the tail of his waistcoat. A preacher or a salesman, Zoe figured. Following him were a middle-aged woman and a little girl who scurried around the back of the coach into the hotel. Out came two more men.

"Strangers," Fred murmured, coming up to peer over Zoe's shoulder out the window, "and dangerous from the looks of them." His eyes went to the guns that were strapped around their waists. "Headed straight for the saloon," he added.

Zoe didn't notice anything unusual about the men . . . nothing that would set them out in a crowd. Yet they looked dangerous.

"Fred," Zoe said, "if it's all right with you, I'll just go into Mr. Fielding's office and wait for him."

"Fine with me," Fred answered, returning to his post behind the counter, "and I'm sure it'll be fine with Mr. Fielding."

Zoe, moving across the office to lay her parasol and purse on the edge of Weber's desk, which was strewn with papers, as always, noticed that the potted plants lining the window behind it were wilted and yellow. On checking them she discovered they were dry. Moving out the back door, she filled a small can with water from the rain barrel and returned to the office. Once she had watered the plants, she set the bucket in the alley and returned to the office, getting her handkerchief out of her purse so she could wipe her hands.

Inadvertently her eyes landed on the maps, one of Chandlerville, the other of Texas, and she moved around the desk to see better. Smiling, she studied the map of Texas first, tracing the thin red line that stretched from the Rio Grande across the western tip of Texas into New Mexico: the route of the irrigation canal.

Then she looked at the city map to see a faintly penciled line extending from Chandlerville to central Texas. Something was wrong. The line was going directly through part of La Candela de Oro—and not on the 50,000 acres on which Weber held the note, but through Shook's ranch . . . and that of Burns . . . and. . . . Zoe couldn't believe it.

Weber's line was going through property belonging to the three ranchers who'd been killed with Bryan. She sat down in Weber's chair and looked closer. The penciled line originated on her property.

"Zoe—"

The door opened and Weber rushed into the room, his gaze instantly sweeping across the desk to see the tip of her finger resting on the projected rail route. He moved to the desk and as he dropped the brown portfolio he carried, several of the documents edged out.

"What a pleasant surprise!" he exclaimed, happy to see her.

Leaning back in Weber's chair, Zoe saw his gaze once again return to the map. Color flushed his face . . . odd, she thought, how white his skin was in comparison to Matt's, his body soft and flabby, rather than hard and solid.

"What's all this, Weber?" she asked.

Zoe was an intelligent woman and Weber knew it. He also knew only the truth would serve his purpose now. "The red line is the canal route; the one in pencil is the proposed route of the new railroad."

"Railroad," Zoe repeated, her voice a mere whisper. "We barely have a stage line."

Weber moved closer to her, his eyes glittering with anticipation. "Railroads are coming, Zoe. Now that the war is over, the Yankees are going to tie this country together with railroads, and you and I have a chance to be in on it. We can get wealthy from this."

He moved to stand beside Zoe, leaning over the desk, his finger thumping the map as he spoke. "Naturally, people are going to be clamoring for the railroads to be laid in central and east Texas first.

Houston. Brenham. Austin. Waco. Dallas. Sherman. But I've advanced a plan to a group of financiers in the East. We have the one commodity out here in west Texas that the north needs and wants: cattle."

He moved, catching her shoulders in both hands, and peered into her face, his eyes glazed. "Don't you see, Zoe? This is that one chance in a lifetime. We'll own the cattle and the land and have an investment in the railroad. And Chandlerville, not El Paso, will have the railroad. Not only will we be wealthy, Zoe; we'll be powerful."

Zoe was seeing a side of Weber that frightened her. He was obsessed with his desire to be wealthy and powerful. He was looking at her, but not really seeing her. All he could see was his obsession. Zoe gently twisted out of his grip and stood, moving away from him.

"You're sure of getting all this property?" she said.

"It's already mine," he said with more confidence than he felt, recalling Uriah Chandler's visit earlier in the day.

After Weber had left Zoe's and come to the bank, Uriah Chandler had come in and made a payment on all four notes. Weber had been so startled, he couldn't write the receipts for the money. He'd called Fred in to do it. He wouldn't soon forget Uriah Chandler's smug countenance when he personally invited him to attend the Founder's Day Ball at La Candela de Oro and said that he'd decided in the future all of them would be held out there.

"You've already claiming their property," Zoe exclaimed. "How can you do that, Weber?"

"You and I know they have only a few weeks

left, Zoe. Time's running out. Where are they going to get the money?"

"Weber, you can't take the property from those women. Their husbands are dead, and this is all they have left. You must give them an extension. You *must!*"

"I sympathize with them, Zoe, but I can't let sentiment cloud my better judgment," Weber said. "I don't have the money to finance such an extension. Everything I have is tied up in this investment."

As if reeling from a physical blow, Zoe backed up. "Weber, we're dealing with people, not statistics. These women are mourning the deaths of their husbands."

"Zoe, I'm sorry," Weber apologized softly, calculating his moves carefully because he couldn't afford to make one mistake; his plans were too close to fruition. He walked to where she stood and caught her hands in his. "I would have explained this to you sooner, but you were in the coma, and your father — well! I wanted to explain. I was going to explain to you when I returned from El Paso, but you were gone.

"Zoe, don't look at me like this! You yourself said we're dealing with people not statistics, and that's my opinion exactly. I'm doing this for us, for all of Chandlerville. If I don't look after our interests, who will? Think about your dream to build the hospital. Sometimes the few must be sacrificed for the many."

"Not only are you taking the widows' ranches, Weber," Zoe said softly in a faraway voice, "but you have taken Papa's and my property. Your railroad line runs through the land I set aside for the hospital. Without conferring with us, without asking if we approved, you did this. You made all these plans."

"I did," he admitted, drawing her back to the desk. "This is just a tentative plan, Zoe. Here! Look at the site I've proposed for your hospital. Zoe, it doesn't matter where the hospital is located. One spot is as good as another. What is vitally important is the railroad. What matters is our attracting business from the east into Chandlerville, and this is the route they want. Besides, your medical supplies will arrive quicker. Think how wonderful this will be for your hospital, Zoe, and for all of Chandlerville."

One plan is as good as another! The words returned to haunt Zoe. Hadn't she made the same statement to Matt when she was justifying the removal of the Comanches? Now that the move concerned her, she found she couldn't be quite so cold and objective. When it applied to her, it was downright calculating.

But what was the most irritating was that she could see Weber's point. What he was doing was for the benefit of Chandlerville. The railroad would benefit the community more than the canal. And Weber was right: the location of the hospital was second to that of the railroad and the canal.

Unconsciously she reached out to straighten the documents that had slipped out of the portfolio when the name on one of them caught her attention. Weber reached for the packet, but not before Zoe pulled several of the papers out and looked at them. Horrified, she lifted her face and stared at him.

"You've already got the transfer of deeds ready," she accused. "Chandler's, and Shook's, and the other ranchers who were—"

"This is normal business procedure," Weber assured her, speaking quite calmly, taking the documents and shoving them back into the folder. "If the women make their payment, then these will have been drawn up in vain. If not. . . . Zoe, don't act so naïve. You're as ambitious as I am; we see eye-to-eye. That's one of the reasons why you and I are so compatible, why we'll make a perfect couple. You don't understand the world of business, so you must trust me. I do, and believe me, you and I are working for the same end. Come now . . . let's finish our discussion over lunch."

"I don't think I can," she said, her hand going to her temples, which were beginning to throb. Everything was tumbling in on top of her . . . it was too much to assimilate at one time. For Matt to have known so little about Weber, he intuited a great deal.

"What's wrong?" Weber was all concern.

"My head," she whispered. "It's hurting so badly, Weber. I . . . I need to get home. Send for Zeke, please."

"I'll take you home."

"No, I—"

Before Zoe knew what was happening, Weber swung her into his arms. Not wanting to create any more of a scene than she was, she allowed him to carry her out. As he walked through the lobby, he called to the clerk, "Fred, Zoe isn't feeling well. I'm going to take her home. Put all the papers on my desk in the safe for me."

"Yes, Mr. Fielding."

By the time Weber stopped the buggy in front of her house, Zoe's head was pounding furiously. She felt as if the local blacksmith were in residence, swinging his anvil from one side to the other. She allowed Weber to carry her inside and put her on the bed, Zeke following behind, wringing his hands and bemoaning the fact that Doc or Lou wasn't here to take care of her.

"Lou told me not to go off and leave you," he said.

"You couldn't have done anything had you been there. I simply tried to do too much too quickly," Zoe assured the distraught man. "Dissolve some of my headache powders in water, Zeke. As soon as I take that and rest, I'll be all right."

"I'll stay here with you," Weber said.

"I'll be all right," Zoe said, wanting to be alone so she could think, so she could sort through all she had learned today. "I'm just going to sleep."

"Zoe, about . . . well, about . . ."

"We'll talk later. Right now I want to rest."

Weber walked to the door and stopped. "I know what I told you came as a shock, and you might think me rather selfish, but really, I have Chandlerville's interest at heart. Please remember that."

"Yes, Weber," she said, "I'll remember everything."

Chapter 19

After Ezekiel closed the door to Zoe's room, she lay very still, letting the tension slowly drain out of her body. The moment she regained consciousness she'd known she'd never marry Weber, but she continued to believe in his dreams and goals for Chandlerville; she still wanted to be a part of them. Today, when she stood in Weber's office knowing the ranchers were dead, knowing there was nothing their widows could do to forestall foreclosure on their land, she wanted to sever all her relations with Weber whether they were business ones or personal ones. Her dreams and ambitions paled to nothing, replaced by a burning desire to help these people keep their ranches. She'd build the hospital; people needed that. The irrigation canal and railroad were great for Chandlerville, but without citizens, Chandlerville was nothing. A town was people, not buildings. No man should have the power that Weber seemed obsessed with getting.

She didn't know how she could help the widows. Neither she nor her father had any money left; she'd used all her inheritance from her mother to buy medicines and supplies. And their greatest need at the moment was money. Everybody's need at the moment was money!

Zoe discovered today that she hadn't really known Weber, had never seen him as he really was. Although he clothed himself in the garb of humanitarianism, he was greedy and ruthless. She was ambitious, but not to the exclusion of everything else. She wasn't obsessed with ambition. Unlike Weber, she didn't manipulate people or use them to her advantage.

She had awakened to the fact that Weber was using her, marrying her because of the property which she and her father owned. As clearly as if she were looking at the city map on Weber's desk she saw all the shaded blocks that surrounded Chandlerville. Weber couldn't have his railroad without these acres, land to which Chandler, her father, and she held title.

Recalling the glassy look in Weber's eyes when he was talking about his plans, Zoe felt uneasy. When Matt had accused him of having Bryan and the ranchers killed, she'd shunned the idea, but now she wasn't so sure Matt wasn't right.

She must stop Weber, but didn't know how. Matt? She wondered if she could trust him to help her; he was probably the one who'd given guns to the Comanches. But she didn't blame him for that. The white people were declaring war on them, driving them off their land. They had a right to fight for what was theirs.

She would go to Matt. He'd help her; he was the only one who could. The problem was as much his as hers. If they could stop Weber, they could stop the slaughter between Indians and whites. Maybe he couldn't help her; maybe he wouldn't. Even so, she must take her chances. She could never live with herself if she didn't do something to save the people of Chandlerville. If Matt couldn't help her, she'd find a way to help these people keep their land. Somehow she'd find a way. That thought running through her mind, she went to sleep.

When Lou returned later that afternoon, she checked on Zoe periodically, but feeling that sleep was good for her, she didn't disturb her. She wouldn't awaken her until it was time to eat supper. After being up and around today, Zoe's appetite was sure to return by tonight. Dr. Quinn hadn't had time to eat lunch, Lou thought, so he'd be really hungry when he got home, too. Yes, sir, she'd cook a meal fit for the president himself.

Afternoon had turned into evening when Zoe heard the door open and a wedge of light sliced into the darkness. She turned to see an Indian standing in the doorway holding a lamp, his finger over his mouth to silence her. Pushing up on her elbow, she stared at him.

"Matt sent you," she said, slipping out of bed, her stockinged foot touching the floor. "I know he did. You must have a message for me."

Running Horse closed the door and moved to the side of the bed, where he set down the lamp. "You're right," he said, "Ma-ta-mon-yahu sent me."

Zoe's eyes rounded with surprise. "You speak English!"

His lips almost smiled. "Yes, wife of Ma-ta-mon-yahu, I speak English."

"Why did you keep it a secret?" she asked.

"At the time, it was Ma-ta-mon-yahu's wish," he said, "and since we were riding with him, we followed his orders without questions. He was worried about you and sent me to find out how you were doing."

"I'm fine," she cried, her headache not only gone but forgotten. Her surprise over Running Horse's speaking English was pushed aside. Nothing was important but the joy of knowing that Matt hadn't forgotten her. "Where is he?"

"He is with his people," Running Horse answered.

"Something's wrong," Zoe said, her eyes searching the immobile countenance that betrayed nothing. "Otherwise Matt would be here with me. Tell me, Running Horse."

"White men attacked our village three days ago, killing two of our women and five children, and wounding many more. Among those wounded was Soaring Eagle. Matt must stay with his grandfather."

"How bad is he wounded?" Zoe asked.

"A bullet is lodged in his chest," the Comanche replied noncommittally. "Matt will not dig for it because it's too close to the heart, and he's afraid of killing the chief."

"I will go to him," Zoe said.

"Ma-ta-mon-yahu sent me to ask your father if he will come; he does not wish for you to come," Running Horse said.

"He doesn't want me," Zoe whispered, her heart hurting.

"It is not even safe for Ma-ta-mon-yahu to be in the village. The Comanche are angry with the white people, and your life will be in danger. We are deciding now whether we are going to go to war with your people."

"Using the guns he stole from the bandits in Mexico?" she asked, staring directly into the ebony eyes.

"Will the answer I give make you feel any differently toward your husband?" Running Horse countered.

"No, I love him no matter what," Zoe replied. "I simply want to know."

Not accustomed to answering women, Running Horse didn't immediately speak. But he understood Zoe's concern. She knew her husband only as a Comanche; she didn't know him as Matt Chandler. Eventually he said, "Ma-ta-mon-yahu did not bring the guns to his people. The Juaristas took them from us. They are the ones who took him to the village where you received care for your wounds."

"Thank you," Zoe whispered, relief washing over her. Although she wouldn't have blamed him, she was glad that he hadn't been the one to give them guns. She crossed to the armoire and opened it to pull out a riding skirt and blouse. "At the moment, Running Horse, I'm not white or Comanche, man or woman. I'm a doctor who's not at war with anyone or anything except disease. Give me time to change my clothes and get my bag."

"I cannot take you."

"He sent you for a doctor, and you're returning with a doctor," Zoe answered.

"I cannot."

"If you don't, your chief may die," Zoe reasoned. "Evidently you agree with Ma-ta-mon-yahu that he should live or you would not be here. I insist that you take me."

"Ma-ta-mon-yahu will be very angry."

"I will be very angry if you do not take me," Zoe answered, pulling out boots and socks. "As Ma-ta-mon-yahu's wife, I demand that you take me to him."

The brave stared into the blue eyes for a long

379

while before he slowly nodded his agreement. "Ma-ta-mon-yahu will be proud of you,"—again Running Horse's lips softened but didn't quite curl into a smile,—"when he gets over his anger."

Zoe smiled, laughter bubbling up within her for the first time since she'd regained consciousness. "Wait in the hall for me while I change clothes," she said. "It won't take but a minute."

Zoe had never changed so quickly in all her life. Within minutes she tossed the taffeta gown onto the foot of the bed and was pulling on a navy blue riding skirt and a light blue blouse. She tugged on her socks and black boots. She was grabbing her hat from the armoire when she heard Lou's muffled scream.

"Indi—!"

Zoe raced across the room and jerked open the door to find Running Horse holding Lou captive, her back pulled against his chest, his hand over her mouth. The housekeeper's eyes were round with fear and her entire body was trembling.

"It's all right, Lou," Zoe assured her. "Running Horse is my friend. He's not going to hurt you. Do you understand?"

When Lou nodded her head, Zoe said, "Remove your hand, Running Horse. She won't scream again." Her gaze pinned to Lou, she confirmed, "Will you, Lou?"

Running Horse waited until Lou shook her head before he slowly lowered his hand from her face and turned her loose.

"He's come to take me to—to—" Zoe sputtered to a halt before she said Matt's name. She loved her housekeeper, but knew Lou couldn't keep a secret. "To take me to the Indian village. The chief has been injured and needs medical attention."

Lou scooted away from Running Horse and with shaking hands lifted the apron to wipe perspiration from her face. "Dear Lord, Zoe, don't go off with this heathen. You ain't well, girl. Your mind ain't functioning right. You're still suffering from that blow."

"I'm fine, Lou," Zoe maintained, wondering if she'd spend the rest of her life explaining to people that she was mentally competent. "My head has healed, and my mind is functioning better than it ever has. Soaring Eagle needs me and I'm going to him."

"How do you know this Indian ain't trying to get you away from the house so's he can kill you?" Lou demanded. "Why, just last night they attacked Old Man Latcher's place. Good Lord, girl, you can't go gadding around the country with this . . . with this. . . ."

Knowing Matt would have revealed himself had he wanted them to know who he was, Zoe honored his secrecy. "This is the Comanche who saved me, Lou. He's not going to harm me. I trust him."

"Your papa and Mr. Fielding ain't gonna like this none, Zoe," Lou argued. "Besides, what are the town folks gonna be thinking about you running off with a Comanche?"

"I'll tell Papa all about it when I return; he'll understand. As far as Weber and the townspeople, I can't stop them from thinking, and believe me, Lou, they're thinking plenty. Might as well give them some fuel for the fire."

The argument was over. Brisk steps carried Zoe down the stairs into her office, where she lit the lamp, then opened the black satchel to fill it with instruments, medicines, and bandages.

"Please, Zoe," Lou begged, thumping down the

steps behind her, "don't go with him. Wait until your papa comes home at least, or let me send for Mr. Fielding."

"I can't wait for Papa to come home," Zoe answered, whirling around to look at the housekeeper, "and I don't want you to send for Weber. Please, Lou, don't tell anyone where I've gone except Papa. Tell him I'll explain when I come home."

Large tears rolled down the older woman's face and she wrung her hands. "I'm scared, Zoe, scared for your life. The Comanches are on the warpath. How do you know you can trust them?"

Zoe's hands went to Lou's upper arms, her fingers gently gripping the flesh. "I trust the Comanche who saved me with my life. I promise I'll come back unharmed. Promise me you won't tell anyone but Papa."

After a long stretch of silence, Lou promised.

An hour later, as Zoe and Running Horse rode toward the mountains, Zoe asked, "Is this the village Bright Knife carried me to when he captured me?"

"No, we've moved several times since then," Running Horse answered. "We have a main camp where we keep the women and children and other camps where the warriors are."

"Where's Matt?"

"At the main camp," Running Horse answered. "I do not know where he will be when we return. He will be our spokesman at the Big Talk."

"The Big Talk," Zoe repeated.

"Many tribes are meeting to talk about our joining together to drive the white man out of our land."

"No," Zoe exclaimed, "you can't do that."

"I take you to your husband because you are a

Comanche wife," Running Horse said, reproof in his voice, "but I do not talk war with a woman or a paleface."

Properly rebuked, Zoe sat back. For the next thirty minutes they rode in silence, Zoe worried about Matt's being killed if he joined the Indians in going to war against the whites, Running Horse sadly thinking about Zoe's words. It was too late for the Comanche to drive the white man from his land—about three hundred years too late. But this latest attack against their village had united them against whites as nothing else could have. Even when Matt had warned that an army of white soldiers would be coming to drive them away, they had evinced no fear and would not be turned from their decision to fight. They would rather die than be dishonored by their enemy.

When they rode into the camp in the valley hidden in a cluster of mountains, mounted Comanche braves, their faces painted, converged on them. Women and children came running. They said nothing as they closed around Zoe and Running Horse, and even though Zoe could not see their faces or eyes, she felt their hostility.

Zoe was frightened, but didn't allow her fear to show. She straightened her back and held her head a little higher. The first time she had been brought into Soaring Eagle's camp as a prisoner; this time she was entering as a free person, as Ma-ta-mon-yahu's wife, as the doctor who would administer care and treatment to Soaring Eagle. From beneath the brim of the hat she looked for the chief's tepee, the one closest to the water around which others opened. The one with the huge fire burning in front of it. She watched a child dart into the tepee, then come out. He pointed toward her, but turned his head toward the tepee door and spoke to someone who was coming out. A brave . . . Matt?

His black hair glistened in the firelight and his hands rested on his hips, the flames glinting off the bracelet, as he gazed at Zoe. Resting against the bared muscularity of his chest was the gold cross that Zoe had seen Soaring Eagle wear. Matt was dressed in a pair of fawn-colored leather breeches and knee-high moccasins.

Her heartbeat and her breathing quickened. She wanted to leap off the horse, race to Matt, and throw herself into his arms. No longer did she care that he was more Comanche than white. She loved him; his arms were her salvation.

Matt could see no one but Zoe, sitting on her horse so proudly. Tears throbbed behind his eyes. He had been worried about her and had felt guilty because he couldn't be with her. His plan for revenge had died the minute he admitted to himself that he loved Zoe. He didn't care that Chandlerville knew who he was. He cared only what Zoe thought . . . she was his life.

When the scout had arrived minutes ago with the news that the one who rode with Running Horse looked like a woman, he knew that it was Zoe, but had hoped deep down that it was her father. Worried about the volatile climate in the Comanche village, he hadn't wanted Zoe to come here. He wanted only to find out how she was. The camp was a dangerous place for him to be, much less her. But at the same time, Matt was glad that she had come to him. He needed her strength and the assurance of her love. His grandfather was dying — perhaps even calling death unto him because he didn't want to face what lay ahead for him and his people.

Buffalo Woman and other medicine people had tried their potions and magic on Soaring Eagle, but he didn't improve. Matt had been afraid to dig for the bullet; he feared it lay too near Soaring Eagle's heart. If he killed his grandfather while performing surgery, his chances of averting war would be nil. In fact, he would probably be killed himself. During the recent War between the States, he hadn't been placed in such a precarious position. He felt as if he were a man alone against two enemies.

Running Horse and Zoe moved slowly down the main street of the village, the Comanche warriors closing in on both sides and behind them. When she was close enough to be illuminated by the firelight, Matt saw the blue riding skirt and blouse, the dark gray hat that covered her face and the honey-gold hair he so loved. He saw the black bag attached to the back of her saddle.

When she and Running Horse halted in front of Matt, Zoe dismounted. Her eyes—he couldn't see them but knew they were the color of bluebonnets in springtime—settled on him, and Matt fought his urge to grab her into his arms and hug her tight, to make sure she was all right. He stood his ground, his countenance devoid of expression.

"Why have you come, *Mah-ocu-ah?*" The words were gentle.

Wife! Zoe remembered the time in Candaleria when she had forbidden him to call her by that name one more time. Yet now, it was like music to her ears. Behind that one unexpressive word was a wealth of meaning and love.

"I have come to be with you, my *Ner-co-mack-pe.*"

385

Husband! Joy sang through Matt's bloodstream. Zoe had trusted him and had come to be with him.

"You shared my pain and sorrow, my *Ner-co-mack-pe.* I do the same with you now."

"You're looking well," he said.

"I'm feeling well."

"When did you regain consciousness?" he asked.

"Four days ago."

"This is much too soon for you to be up and about," he chided softly, concern underlining his words. "You should be in bed with someone looking after you."

"I'm the doctor," Zoe returned, her heart bubbling over with joy at Matt's concern and tenderness. "Let me make the decision."

Matt smiled. "How are you feeling?"

"I'm fine. Really. I have an occasional headache, and I'm still a little sore and bruised, but I'm all right. Even if I weren't, I would have come, Matt. I would have come even if you hadn't sent Running Horse. I wanted to warn you that the white soldiers are coming to fight you, to drive you off your land. I don't know when they will arrive, but already a messenger has been sent to San Antonio."

Matt had never loved Zoe more than he did at this moment. He could hardly restrain himself from taking her into his arms. How difficult it was to stand there talking so calmly when they wanted to hold each other . . . for him, just to hold Zoe, to be reassured that she was there and was all right. He wanted to give her strength and support.

"I also came as a *po-haw-cut mah-cou-ah,*" Zoe said, turning to her horse to unfasten her medical bag and hold it up for the Tejas to see.

"Medicine woman!" Buffalo Woman charged out of Soaring Eagle's tepee to stand in front of Zoe.

386

The old woman's breasts rose and fell as she breathed deeply. "You are not a *po-haw-cut mah-cou-ah*," she hissed in broken English, pointing a bony finger into Zoe's face. "You are the one who brought our troubles on us. You are the reason why the white men attacked our village, killing women and children, wounding our chief."

"No," Zoe answered quietly but steadily, refusing to cower before such overt hatred and hostility, "I'm not the reason. Perhaps they used me as an excuse, but the reason is far greater than one white woman. Greed prompted whites to attack your village."

Zoe's demeanor and quiet words startled Buffalo Woman, who moved back a step. Matt's eyes warmed as he looked at Zoe; he was proud of her. Yet he kept his expression bland. He was no longer Matthew Barnabas Chandler; until his grandfather recovered, he was Ma-ta-mon-yahu, chief of the *Coth-cho Tejas*.

"I am asking for your help, my husband. The widows of the ranchers who were killed in Mexico are in dire straits. Because they don't have the money to repay their loans, their land is going to be taken away from them. Today I learned that Weber Fielding may be responsible for the deaths of the men who were smuggling guns into Mexico. I don't have any evidence, but I have reason to believe you were right about him. I know these are not your problems, but I want you to help me help these people keep their land and to find evidence to hang Weber."

Matt's love for Zoe overflowed; it was so great, he wasn't large enough to contain it. Had he not already been assured of her innocence, these words would have sufficed. "I will help you."

Zoe knew Matt would say this. He was that kind

of man. Tears burning her eyes, she said, "Now, Ma-ta-mon-yahu, I am asking permission to try my magic on your chief. It is strong. I can make him well."

"No!" Buffalo Woman shouted. "Do not allow this white woman to enter Soaring Eagle's dwelling. Her medicine is bad!"

Zoe heard a horse move through the crowd until it stood close behind her. She felt the heat of a hostile gaze on her back. Goosebumps covered her skin; she knew without looking, without asking, that Bright Knife was behind her.

"I agree with Buffalo Woman," Bright Knife said in an ugly tone. "Do not allow the white woman to see your grandfather."

"The white woman's magic is great," Matt said in Comanche, turning to look at the people who pressed against him and Zoe. "I traveled to the Mexican village with her and watched her treat the villagers there. None of them died, because her medicine was strong."

"You have no judgment when it comes to the white woman," Bright Knife accused, his black eyes raking lustfully over Zoe. He had wanted her from the moment he first saw her, and one day he would make her his. "She has made a fool of Ma-ta-mon-yahu."

"We do not want the white woman to touch our chief," another brave shouted, bobbing his head, which was covered in a buffalo headdress. The crowd, following his and Buffalo Woman's initiative, shouted their disapproval.

Matt raised his hands, speaking when the people grew silent. "Do we deny our chief a chance to live because this is a white woman?" he asked. "Are we going to be so selfish?"

"My people," Running Horse said, "I, too, traveled with the white medicine woman to Mexico. Her magic is great. She can heal our chief."

The people looked at one another in question. They were not sure about Ma-ta-mon-yahu, but Running Horse they trusted. Still Buffalo Woman, the other medicine people, and Bright Knife continued their argument against Zoe's treating Soaring Eagle.

When Matt saw that the crowd was being swayed by Buffalo Woman, he shouted, "I say you do not have the right to make this decision. Take it to your chief and let him decide his own fate."

Absolute silence followed his suggestion. Bright Knife sneered; Buffalo Woman snorted her disapproval.

"Are you afraid of the white woman's magic?" Matt taunted.

"I am afraid of no white woman." Buffalo Woman turned and rushed into Soaring Eagle's tepee. Matt entered next, followed by Zoe. Already the Comanche medicine woman was squatting at the foot of the bed. Her eyes were closed and she mumbled a prayer.

Matt knelt beside the bed and lowered his face to Soaring Eagle's ear. "Grandfather, it is I, Ma-ta-mon-yahu. I have come to ask you a question."

After a long time Soaring Eagle opened his eyes and with fever-glazed eyes stared at Matt. "Speak . . . my son," he whispered, the word ending in a spasm of coughing. A small gurgle of blood came out of the corner of his mouth.

"My wife has come as a medicine woman and would like to work her magic for you. She brings her black bag, her instruments, and her medicine."

Soaring Eagle's head slowly turned, and he

looked at Zoe, who knelt beside Matt. A gnarled hand reached out to touch the cross that rested on Matt's chest. "Did your wife come to bring me her magic, my son, or did she come back to you?"

"She came for both reasons," Matt answered.

Soaring Eagle drew in a deep breath, coughed, and clutched at his chest. He caught the cross in his fist and pulled Matt's head down to his mouth, whispering, "Does she love Matt Chandler, or Ma-ta-mon-yahu?"

"She loves Ma-ta-mon-yahu."

The dull black eyes opened and rested on Matt's face. "She does not knew yet, my son?" When Matt shook his head, his grandfather said, "You must tell her. She is a brave woman and deserves the truth."

"I am going to tell her today, my grandfather. Will you let her treat you?"

Soaring Eagle shook his head and murmured, *"Nei habbe we-ich-ket."*

"What did he say?" Zoe asked.

"He is seeking death."

Zoe scooted around Matt. "Chief Soaring Eagle," she said, "I know you speak English and understand what I'm saying, so listen to me carefully. You have spoken the truth. You are seeking death and are calling it to you. I have strong magic and can treat your wound. You do not have to die. You are taking a coward's way out."

Matt's hands bit into Zoe's shoulders and he grated, "Don't you speak to my grandfather like that! It's disrespectful for a woman to speak so to a Comanche brave."

Zoe turned to glare at Matt. "A man can tell him the truth, but a woman can't—do you want him to live? Then trust me . . . give me a chance."

In the burst of sunlight that spilled through the smoke-hole at the top of the tepee, Zoe and Matt stared at each other. Finally Matt nodded his head and released his grip on her shoulders.

"Chief Soaring Eagle, you have led your people down the path of peace for many years. Now that peace has been threatened and you do not wish to see the outcome because you fear they will go to war. You are dying because you are afraid to face the future."

Soaking Eagle's lids fluttered open. "You are calling me a coward?"

"Yes," Zoe returned. "If you die, you are a coward who is shirking his duty to his people. You do not deserve to go to the Happy Hunting Ground."

"You can guarantee that I will live," Soaring Eagle said.

"I don't guarantee that you will live," Zoe returned. "Only you have the power to call death to you, but I will dig the bullet out and doctor your wound. Only you can heal your wounded spirit."

"Your words are wise, *po-haw-cut mah-cou-ah*."

"I am a wise *po-haw-cut mah-cou-ah*," Zoe returned steadily. "My medicine is strong."

"Work your magic on me, white woman."

Throwing her rattle across the room with a huff, Buffalo Woman leaped to her feet. In accented English she yelled, "I honor Soaring Eagle's decision, but if he dies, white woman, you will give your life in return."

Zoe turned to look at Matt and he nodded. "Weigh your decision carefully, my love," he whispered. "My people are angry at the whites and they mean what they say. I don't know that even I have the authority to protect you."

"I didn't bring any scales with me," Zoe returned

softly, her hand curving around his face, "therefore, I have nothing to weigh. I made my decision before I left the house, my husband. Will you assist me in surgery?"

"I will," Matt turned his face until his lips were pressed against her palm, "my wife."

Chapter 20

Under Buffalo Woman's scrutinizing gaze, Zoe tied off the last suture and bandaged the wound. "The bullet's out, and his heart and lungs are undamaged," she announced wearily, grateful when Matt reached over to blot the perspiration from her forehead with a towel. "I've done all I can. Now we must wait and pray."

The Comanche medicine woman stood, opened her pouch, and brought out a handful of pulverized root, which she began to throw into the air, chanting a song as she circled the room. Although she was exhausted, Zoe leaped to her feet. She had taken Buffalo Woman's insinuations, interference, and threats, but the root dust was too much.

"Get out of this tepee right now," she sputtered between spasms of coughing, her eyes watering, her hands on her hips. "You're destroying my medicine. You tried and failed. Now get out and give me a chance."

Buffalo Woman settled a venomous gaze first on Zoe, then on Matt. "I go," she announced, then said in Comanche to Matt, "Ma-ta-mon-yahu, I hope for your sake the white woman's medicine is as strong as she thinks it is. If your grandfather dies, I do not think either you or the white woman will live very long."

"It is my decision to accept her medicine," Matt answered. "I am the one who determines her fate if my grandfather should die."

Buffalo Woman's lips lifted at the corners, but the smile held no mirth or humor. "You wear the gold cross, but that does not mean you are our chief. Bright Knife is a proven warrior. He and his braves have sworn to avenge our honor against the white man."

"I have sworn to avenge our honor against the white men who did this," Matt assured her.

Buffalo Woman shook her head, coarse black hair swinging around her face. With the fist that held the root dust, she pounded her chest. "No, Ma-ta-mon-yahu, you have sworn revenge against one white man, not against all. You do not have the heart of a Comanche. I go now, but remember all I have said." She walked to the door, her solemn gaze moving from Matt to Zoe and finally to Soaring Eagle. As a last defiant act, she threw the remainder of the dust into the air before she walked out of the tepee, leaving Matt and Zoe alone.

"What did she say?" Zoe asked.

"She's angry because you have so much confidence in your medicine," Matt answered evasively, standing and pulling Zoe into his arms to hold her close and rest his cheek on her head. During his lifetime he'd been in many situations that arose from his being part-Indian, but now he felt the full weight of his birthright. Both grandparents were demanding that he turn his back on one part of his heritage, deny one and claim the other.

Zoe heard Matt sigh as she wrapped her arms tightly around him and pressed her cheek against his chest. For a moment she was content to listen to the rhythmic beat of his heart and to feel the rise and fall of his chest beneath her face. But then she wanted more. Lifting her face to him, she whispered, "I've missed you so much . . . so very much. You'll never know how I felt when I regained consciousness to find that you'd left me."

Matt held her all the tighter when he felt the shudder ripple through her body. "I didn't want to leave you," he murmured, his head lowering to hers, "but I knew your father would take good care of you. I didn't know what would happen to Soaring Eagle—"

"—or to your people," Zoe finished, a smile curving her beautiful lips.

"Or my people," Matt repeated. "Our village was attacked—"

"I know. That's why your people killed the Latchers and burned their house."

Matt stared at her in astonishment; he had never thought about her believing the Comanches had killed the white settlers. He had admired Zoe from the first moment he set eyes on her; in the face of all odds she had been defiant, even with that black ointment smeared all over her face. Soon after, he had become physically attracted to her; then he had fallen in love with her. And his love continued to grow; it knew no bounds.

"You came, thinking that?" he asked with a humility that touched Zoe deeply.

"I don't approve," she whispered, "but I understand why you did it."

"The attack on the village gave all of us a reason to go to war against the whites, but we didn't, not even Bright Knife."

"If your people didn't, who did?" Zoe asked.

"Mescalero Apaches," Matt answered. "I think they and Grisswold—"

"Grisswold?"

"The man who escaped in Mexico. I overheard Weber talking with Scully Newton the morning I brought you back to town, and I have reason to believe Grisswold and the Mescaleros are working together. I wouldn't be a bit surprised if their orders aren't coming from Weber."

"Oh, Matt, what's going to happen?"

"In this move for power and land, Weber is playing both ends against the middle, and he's liable to get caught . . . caught between Grisswold and the Apaches on one hand, and the Comanches on the other. Bright Knife and his braves have already begun their war dances, so it's only a matter of time before war parties depart."

"I'm so afraid, Matt, afraid that you're going to be killed."

Matt's arms tightened around her reassuringly. "I'm going to be all right, sweetheart. I promise."

"And I promise to help Soaring Eagle get well." Zoe cupped Matt's face in her hands and pulled his lips to hers.

Matt accepted the quiet, comforting kiss, finally lifting his mouth from hers to murmur, "I wish I could stay with you, but I must go to sit with the elders." When he saw the pain and question shadow Zoe's eyes, he said, "You'll be all right in here. I won't let anyone hurt you. I promise."

Remembering the venomous hiss in Buffalo Woman's voice and the hostility in her eyes, Zoe said, "It's you I'm worried about."

Matt smiled sadly, his hands covering hers. "Don't worry about me. I'll be fine."

Zoe stood in the center of the tepee long after

Matt was gone, staring at the hardened leather flap that served as a door. Finally she crossed to the other bed and lay down on her side, watching her patient. Time passed and the hour grew late, but activity seemed to be greater with the going down of the sun than before. A huge bonfire burned in front of Soaring Eagle's tent, its arc so large Zoe could see it through the opened smoke-hole in the top of the tepee. She heard the people whooping and hollering to the furious and deafening beat of the drum; feet pounded the earth in echoing rhythm.

The torch that hung suspended on one of the frame poles cast a muted light around the interior of the tepee, and eerie shadows danced on the leather walls. Zoe's lids grew heavy and finally closed, and she drifted into a light sleep. When she awakened later and checked on her patient, his breathing had eased and his body was wet with perspiration—a sign that his fever had broken. As she bathed his face with a damp cloth, he opened his eyes and gazed at her. Before the lids closed, she thought she saw a slight twitching of his lips.

Through the night she sat with him, changing the damp rag on his forehead frequently. When sunlight filtered through the smoke-hole, she pulled the blanket down and removed the bandage to look at the wound. She smiled; it was healing well. No proud flesh. Buffalo Woman came into the tepee and sat cross-legged beside Soaring Eagle's bed, her eyes closed, her mouth moving in prayer. Matt remained with the elders.

Time passed quickly from afternoon to night and Zoe kept her vigil, each passing hour reassuring her that Soaring Eagle would live. A new torch burned to cast a flickering and eerie light through the dwelling. When Soaring Eagle became restless, turning over, groaning in pain as he moved, Buffalo Woman leaped to her feet, shaking her rattles and chanting aloud. Zoe leaned over to hear his whispered words.

"Wa . . . ter," he murmured in Comanche. "I want a drink of water."

The rattles quieted, the chanting stopped, and Buffalo Woman dropped to her knees, pushing Zoe out of the way to press her ear against Soaring Eagle's mouth.

"Water," he repeated.

"Water!" the medicine woman exclaimed in English, her head whirling around, black eyes locking to Zoe's face. "He wants water."

Zoe scooted down the bed and reached into the basin of water, wringing out a cloth which she rubbed over his face and pressed against his dry, cracked lips. She moved to fill a small cup with water and watched as Buffalo Woman dabbed his lips with a greasy concoction. After several small swallows, the lids quivered, the lashes fluttering against the cheeks several times before they finally opened, and the black eyes stared into Zoe's.

"Po-haw-cut mah-cou-ah," he whispered, his lips barely moving. "Your medicine is strong."

Tears running down her cheeks, Zoe nodded her head. "My medicine is strong," she agreed, "but your medicine is stronger, and it's what kept you alive."

"Tell my people that I live," Soaring Eagle declared and closed his eyes agin. "I want to speak with Ma-ta-mon-yahu."

"Do as Soaring Eagle says," Buffalo Woman said, still speaking English. "I stay."

Zoe rushed out of the tepee with a shout, "He's

going to live, Matt. Your grandfather is going to live." She threw herself into Matt's welcoming arms and raised her teary face to him. "He wants to speak with you."

Matt, his arm around Zoe, led her to the circle of warriors who remained seated around the ashes of last night's fire. "Our chief, He-Who-Soars-Like-an-Eagle, has spoken. He says to all of us that he lives. He is waiting to speak with me."

One by one the wizened warriors rose, followed by the younger ones, and departed for their tepees. Soon no one remained but Matt and Zoe.

"Although I did not want you to come to the village," Matt said, "I'm pleased that you insisted on returning with Running Horse."

"I'm glad you sent him to check on me." A beautiful smile curving her lips, Zoe looked into Matt's moon-kissed face and whispered, "I love you, my husband."

"And I love you," Matt said the words to a woman for the first time in his life. His hands were holding her face, tugging it gently to his. His mouth lowered to brush softly against her parted lips, tasting, teasing, making Zoe's pulse race madly.

In Matt's arms Zoe couldn't think properly, couldn't do anything but hold more tightly to him, her fingers digging into his shoulders as he trailed kisses along her arched neck to the wild throbbing in the hollow of her throat. Finally his lips stopped their sensual journey and he simply held her in his arms, his cheek resting on the crown of her head. She felt his chest rise and fall as his breathing normalized.

"We have so much to talk about," he told her, his hands moving up and down the supple curve of her

399

back.

"So much," Zoe agreed. "There's an entire week of my life that I want you to fill in for me." Laughing, she pulled back her head and looked into his face. "I remember I was destined for a serious talk when I fell off the boulder, and we will have that talk and many more, darling . . . I promise. We have all our lives ahead of us for talking, but right now you need to speak to your grandfather." Catching his hand in hers, she led the way into the tepee, both of them kneeling beside Soaring Eagle's bed.

Matt laid his hand over his grandfather's and stared into the gaunt face, the short black eyelashes a dark shadow against the pale cheeks. "It is Ma-ta-mon-yahu, Grandfather. You sent for me."

The eyelids opened and lucid black eyes focused on Matt. The corners of Soaring Eagle's lips twitched a tiny bit as he lifted a hand and touched Matt's face. "You came to me, Ma-ta-mon-yahu," he said in Comanche.

"Yes, my grandfather," Matt answered, "I came to you."

"And if I had died, you would have remained with my people, Ma-ta-mon-yahu." The wrinkled hand slid down Matt's face, the tips of the fingers resting on the bottom of the cross.

"Your people are my people," Matt replied.

"Your heart is touched by my people," Soaring Eagle said, "but your heart does not belong to them."

"Grandfather," Matt began, but Soaring Eagle held up a silencing finger.

"You do not owe me an explanation or an apology, Ma-ta-mon-yahu. You are my grandson, the joy of my old age and a brave Comanche warrior.

400

But you are a man now and must answer to no man but yourself. Life is not easy, my son, when one has two bloods flowing through his veins, and your grandfather Chandler and I have made it all the more difficult by demanding that you choose one or the other of us. To make a choice is difficult, even painful, yet the day is coming when you must." Soaring Eagle lifted his shoulders in order to sit up, but the pain in his chest was too great. "Take the cross off," he grunted, "and put it around my neck. For now I wear it. I am He-Who-Soars-Like-an-Eagle, Chief of the *Coth-cho Tejas*."

Wondering what the old man had said, Zoe watched Matt take off the chain and ease it over his grandfather's head, adjusting the cross on his chest so that it didn't touch his wound.

"Where is Bright Knife?" Soaring Eagle asked.

"He and his braves are in one of the war camps, awaiting word of your recovery or death," Matt answered. "They want to join the Mescalero Apaches and other tribes who are gathering and who declare war against the white man."

"We are so few as to be ineffective against the whites," Soaring Eagle murmured. "Soon we will be on the move again, always one step ahead of them, but never free of them."

"Weber Fielding has sent for soldiers to drive the Comanche from his land, Grandfather. He killed the ranchers who carried guns into Mexico, and he is now planning to take their property away from the widows."

Soaring Eagle sighed deeply and closed his eyes. "Now that the soldiers no longer fight each other, they will be fighting us again, and if they do not drive us off our land, Weber Fielding will."

"If I can stop Bright Knife from attacking any

settlements," Matt told him, "and if I can get some money, Grandfather, I can keep the soldiers from driving you off the land. I can keep Weber Fielding from becoming a powerful landowner, perhaps find evidence to prove that he killed my brother."

Soaring Eagle's eyes opened and he peered into Matt's face. "What are you asking of me, Ma-ta-mon-yahu?"

"I need the money to pay Fielding the loan Uriah and the other ranchers owe him. Then no one can drive you away. You are on Chandler land."

"Your grandfather's land?"

"No, my land," Matt answered. "Uriah and I made a deal before I came here. If I save the land, La Candela de Oro becomes mine."

"Your grandfather spoke with a straight tongue?"

"Uriah is a man of his word," Matt said.

After a long pause, Soaring Eagle said, "You are asking me for white man's money?"

"I am asking you for the gold that was stolen from the white men so many winters ago, Grandfather."

"The Golden Secret," Soaring Eagle murmured, pressing his hand over his cross.

"I have heard the tale many times," Matt said, "but I never knew we captured such a treasure in gold, Grandfather."

"And now you know," Soaring Eagle said, not bothering to open his eyes.

"Now I know," Matt returned. "When I was in Mexico, I met a woman who had a bracelet just like mine. Her great-grandfather was an escort on the caravan, and she told me how much gold was being shipped from Mexico to Santa Fe." Matt paused, but Soaring Eagle made no reply. "I know the reason why the Comanches have never told the whites about the gold, Grandfather. We feared they would come to take our land from us in their search for the treasure. But now they come and the gold will save us. I must know where it is."

"No!" Buffalo Woman abruptly pushed herself in between Matt and Soaring Eagle. Looking into the chief's face, she said, "The Golden Secret belongs to the Comanche."

Soaring Eagle gazed at the wizened face. "You and I have seen the winters come and go, Buffalo Woman, yet we have not shared the same view of the changing seasons. Although it is sad, the Comanche way of life is changing, and we must accept it."

"I cannot," Buffalo Woman said. "I will not. If the white men learn our secret, they will come to our land in herds, running over us in their effort to find the gold. They do not have any money," she reasoned, "so they will soon leave. They will go back to their cities in the east."

"No," Soaring Eagle told her, "the white people will never return to the east and leave us as we were before. Even should they leave, we would not be the same." His head turned and he looked at the fire burning low in the center of the dwelling. "Even now we have grown accustomed to the white man's blankets, his metal pots, and his coffee. Shouldn't we help Matt find the gold if it will help us to keep our land and keep us from going to war against the white man?"

Buffalo Woman took no time to weigh his words. Her "no" was quick and emphatic.

"Do you know where the treasure is?" Matt asked, edging closer to his grandfather.

"My grandfather brought it back to his village and the medicine man hid it in the mountains,"

Soaring Eagle said. "I'm not sure which mountain, but I know the vicinity where he hid it."

"No one knows for sure?" Matt questioned.

Soaring Eagle shook his head and closed his eyes. "I am tired now, Ma-ta-mon-yahu. When I have regained my strength I will talk to you more about hunting for the treasure. Now I must rest. Please go."

"Someone must sit with you," Matt returned.

"Buffalo Woman will stay," Soaring Eagle said, closing his eyes and waving his hand. "Her medicine is strong and we have much to talk about. Now go."

Matt looked at Zoe and said, "He's insisting that we go. He says he wants to rest now."

"That's the best thing he can do," she answered. "Tell Buffalo Woman to watch him, and if his condition changes during the night, to come and get me. Does she know where I'll be staying?" Even in the shadows of the sputtering torch, Zoe could see the glitter in Matt's brown eyes.

"Although she understands English much better than she speaks it, I'll tell her in Comanche to make sure she knows where you and I will be."

Zoe ducked out of the tepee and stood waiting for Matt. When he joined her, she asked, "What were you talking to your grandfather about? Me?"

Matt looked at her in surprise. "No, why?"

"The conversation was intense, almost adamant."

"It was," Matt replied, his arm dropping around her shoulder. As they threaded through the tepees, he recounted all that had happened during their sojourn in La Ciudad de la Cruz, Mexico, concluding with, "If I can find the gold, I can use it to help the Comanches."

"Is your grandfather going to take you to it?" she

asked.

"I don't know. He will talk to me about it when he regains his strength." His fingers tightened around her shoulder, and he pulled her tighter against him as they walked on in silence.

"Where are we going?" she eventually asked.

"To my tepee," Matt answered, his teeth flashing white in the moonlight. "Where do you think?"

"With you so near, I'm not capable of thinking," she confessed. "All I want to do is feel when I'm with you, Matt."

The words were hardly out of her mouth before Matt swept her into his arms and ducked through the flap into a tepee near the river. He gently deposited her on the nearest bed, dropping onto the mattress beside her. Zoe moved into the protective circle of his arms, wanting to be held close, comforted by his warm breath that splayed against her cheek. She never wanted to be parted from him again.

"Zoe," Matt said tentatively, knowing he had to tell her who he was, "we must talk."

"Already we have talked so much, Matt. Please not now," she begged, her hands brushing up his chest, her face lifting to his. "Please love me . . . now."

For one of the few times in his life, Matt allowed himself to be ruled by emotion. Easily persuaded, he pushed aside conscience and good judgment. His confession had waited this long; it could wait a little while longer. He wanted Zoe with a desperate yearning that overrode good intention.

"Yes, my darling wife—" he caught himself.

"Yes," Zoe murmured, "your wife. Once I pretended that I didn't want you to call me that, but now I do. You're my darling husband, and I'm

405

your—"

". . . darling wife."

Zoe's eyes fastened on Matt's face as he unbuttoned her blouse, the material sliding down her shoulders to reveal the swell of satiny skin above the white chemise. For a long minute he looked at her, the gentle slope of her shoulders exposed and silver in the moonlight, her bosom barely covered by the undergarment.

"I love you," he muttered thickly, lowering his face to cover the tip of her breast and blow through the soft material. "I love you so very much."

As if he'd never seen her naked before, as if this was the first time he'd touched her skin, Matt patiently stroked the pearly planes and curves of her shoulders, collarbones, and neck. His fingers unbuttoned her chemise and he pulled it over her shoulders. He felt her tremble beneath his touch.

Zoe reached up and touched his face. No longer were his features harsh and forbidding. How soft his face was! There was no arrogance in it now, only the deep enjoyment of a man who has touched something precious and fragile. How could she have ever thought him a primitive savage without any feelings?

Her hands on his cheeks, she guided his mouth to hers at the same time that his hands cupped her breasts, his thumbs stroking the crests to a throbbing hardness. He held her tenderly and savored the moment in the silvery moonlight, his hands treasuring the feel of her. Zoe gloried in his hungry touch that unleashed the same hunger in her.

Zoe pulled her lips away from his and moaned her desires as his hands worked their magic on her body. Her head rolled back as she gave herself to the richness of his caresses, to the promise of ultimate possession.

Even in the moonlight Matt could see the features of her face filled with passion. Her lashes were dark crescents against silvered cheeks; her lips were parted as she took shallow, quick breaths. He felt his manhood throbbing, thrusting urgently against his leather breeches.

Her stomach shuddering with desire, burning for more than mere caresses, Zoe caught Matt's head and guided his mouth to her breasts. She moaned when his mouth opened and closely warmly over the tips, the texture of his tongue driving her wild.

Matt tasted the luscious flesh that was as tempting as forbidden fruit; he savored the tightening of her nipples in the warm prison of his mouth. He gloried in her passionate whimpers and moans; he reveled in the feel of her hands running up and down his back, cupping his buttocks and kneading them. His rough tongue gently stroked each peak, and his arousal grew as she quaked in his arms.

When he lifted his head later, his lips unerringly found and settled on hers, his mouth tugging gently and sweetly. Wanting to be the aggressor, Zoe cupped Matt's cheeks in her hands and slanted his face to deepen the kiss. Her lips urged his open to receive her tongue. Matt groaned and his hands went around her, sliding down her back, his finger lightly tracing the indentation of her buttocks.

When at last she lifted her lips from his, Zoe was trembling. Her arousal was so intense, so wonderfully intense, she was on the verge of tears. And for the first time since they had been married, she knew that she no longer had to be afraid of the power he wielded over her; she wielded that same power over him. The hunger in his look, his heaving chest, his trembling hands, these proved her prowess as a woman. Just as she wanted Matt, he wanted her.

"Sweet, sweet Zoe Ellen," Matt murmured, "tell me I'm not dreaming. Tell me that at last you're willing to let me take you—"

Zoe laid a finger over his mouth and contradicted softly, "No, my husband, I'm not allowing you to take me. You're not taking me, nor am I giving myself to you. I'm loving you and you're loving me."

Matt's lips fastened on hers. Their kissing contained the heat of the sun and the sweetness of honey, and Zoe opened her lips under his. When his hands raced down her body to the waistband of her riding skirt, she moved her hips and unfastened the catch, helping him to remove the last of her clothing.

In quick movements Matt rolled away from her and undressed, moccasins and breeches flung into the shadows. Naked, he stretched out so that his chest brushed against Zoe's breasts and his legs pressed against the long length of hers. So wonderful was their touching that Zoe felt sure she would splinter into a thousand pieces, but then he was pulling her into the warm circle of his arms, holding her close . . . so close that her scent filled his head, and the fire of her passion became one with his. Her hands went to his chest, gliding over the supple warmth of smooth skin and taut muscle to linger on his tiny nipples. Her hands traced the path of hair that grew down his chest, her fingers boldly moving to his erectness.

Matt caught her hand, removing it and turning her over on her back. He leaned over her, his hands exploring every inch of her body as if he'd never done it before, as if the territory were totally virgin and unclaimed. Zoe's breathing quickened as he ran his hands over her collarbones, down her sides to her waist, over her hipbones, and down each leg to the ankle. She shivered when his hands skimmed up the inside of her legs, brushing lightly over the soft mound again and again.

Heady from her passionate cries, from the writhing of her body beneath his touches, Matt refused to think about Zoe's reaction once she learned who he was. He pushed aside the hurt and grief he could visualize in her eyes when she asked him about his reticence in admitting who he was once he'd learned she loved him and wanted to be his wife. For the moment, he allowed himself to be totally ablaze with passion, letting it burn away all thoughts and regrets. He lived only for the moment . . . he might not have many more.

"For days I have dreamed of touching you like this," he muttered huskily. "I have never been separated from you."

His mouth roved from the throbbing pulse point in her throat over her breasts, down her midriff to her navel.

"Please, Matt. I love you," she whispered again and again.

Matt eased up and over, lowering his weight full on her. With his knee, he urged her legs apart and touched her femininity with his firm virility. Unable to endure the pleasurable torment any longer, Zoe opened her legs and thrust her hips to receive him. Matt laughed throatily.

Zoe gasped with pleasure when she felt his hard male strength ease into her, stretching, filling and satisfying. Matt stroked slow and deep, then stopped to let her warm flesh open and pulsate tentatively around him.

Matt's lips captured hers in a long, deep kiss as he began to stroke her gently with his silken shaft. Zoe moved with him. She felt his hands as they cupped her buttocks, his fingers digging into the sensitive flesh. His lips moved from her lips to her neck and then her breasts.

When Zoe thought she would die from sheer pleasure, her blood turned into molten passion. Her heart pounded; her breath was short and ragged. Every nerve in her body screamed for release. Matt, spurred on by her whimpers and her thrusting, plunged deeply, rapidly, fiercely, and Zoe's body burst into an uncontrollable blaze of passion.

Matt's entire body ached with the need to release the burning desire that licked through him. He heard her gasp and felt her tense, then tremble convulsively in his arms. The soft flesh that surrounded his manhood quivered and pushed around him; it clung with each instant spasmodic contraction.

Quietly they lay together afterward, both on their backs. Zoe laid her head on Matt's chest, where she felt his heart beat slow and his breathing normalize. Matt stroked her hair.

"I love you," she murmured.

"I love you," Matt whispered, his eyes staring through the smoke-hole at the star-studded sky.

Chapter 21

Moonlight cast Zoe in a halo of hazy light as she lay on the mattress on her stomach, her shoulders protruding from the blanket. Her cheek nestled against the pillow and her golden hair lay tangled around her face. Naked, Matt sat beside her out from under the cover, leaning against the frame headboard.

He reached out and brushed a curl from Zoe's cheek, his fingers lingering on the silken softness of her skin. After they made love he carried her to the river, bathed with her, and brought her back to the tepee. He wanted to make love to her again, to possess her, to be possessed by her in love. But he couldn't . . . he'd already taken unfair advantage of her many times over. Now was the moment of reckoning. Matt could put it off no longer. He must tell Zoe who he was. He hoped the bonding of their love was strong enough to endure its first test.

"I'm so glad Running Horse came to get me," Zoe murmured, nuzzling her cheek against the wonderful touch of his hand.

Matt flipped over. "Me, too."

Zoe scooted up on her knees in front of Matt and slid her hands up his chest to his face. She caught his head and brought his face down on hers, their lips touching and melding into a long, hot kiss. She felt the smooth motion of callused hands up her buttocks and back. His fingers gently capped her shoulders and he pushed her slightly away from him, his gaunt face peering through the moonlight into hers.

"There's nothing I would rather do, sweetheart, than spend the night making love to you, but we must talk."

"Talk, my darling, if you must," Zoe murmured. "I'll do what I must do."

As she pressed her breasts against his chest, her palm slid down the flat stomach, below the navel to the pubic hair. Her fingers curled around his manhood and she gently stroked, delighted when she felt the surge of his arousal. Her mouth closed over one of his nipples, her tongue encouraging it to a hard crest.

If Matt's resolve had not been so great, the sheer pleasure that raced through his blood would have diluted it, even decimated it entirely. "There's nothing I would rather that you did, my darling wife," he said huskily, "than make wild, passionate love to me, but we *have* to talk. And what you're doing is absolutely not conducive to conversation."

His hands caught Zoe's shoulders and he set her away from him. Standing and moving away, he found his breeches and slipped into them. Afterward he reached for his shirt, which dangled from one of the tepee poles. Digging through his pockets, he found his sack of tobacco and papers and

412

rolled a cigarette.

Zoe heard the match scratch against one of the stones that rounded the fire pit, then saw his face reflected in the sputtering light. "Must be serious," she said softly.

"It is." He took a deep drag and exhaled, watching as she squirmed on the mattress until she was leaning against a stack of pillows. Her skin glowed like polished silver in the moonlight, every inch of her sculpted beautiful and perfect.

Zoe intuited that his confession was going to mar the beauty of their relationship and didn't want to hear it. She was happy with Matt; she loved him and wanted nothing, absolutely nothing, to take away this happiness or to come between them. When she had regained consciousness, she realized that Matt meant more to her than anything else in the world. He was her life.

"When we first met, you wanted to know who and what I was," Matt said.

"Not now," Zoe said. "I don't care who or what you were. Isn't it enough that we love each other?"

"Because we love each other, I must tell you who I am," he said.

Because the moon was to his back and his face was in the shadows, Zoe couldn't read his expression, but felt the deep sadness that underlay the words.

"My full name, Zoe, is Matthew . . . Barnabas . . . Chandler. Uriah Chandler is my grandfather."

Matthew . . . Barnabas . . . Chandler. The words slowly tumbled around in Zoe's mind. From somewhere came the thought from so long ago: she had been right—Uriah's oldest grandson was different from either Uriah or Bryan. Matthew Barnabas

Chandler was his own man, even different from the Matt Barnabas she had known. Uriah Chandler's oldest grandson wasn't the man she'd fallen in love with; he was a stranger.

Even though the night was warm, she curled up and covered herself with a blanket. Somehow she felt less vulnerable now.

From afar she heard Matt say, "During one of the last battles of the war, I was wounded, but didn't die. I was on my way to the ranch to patch up things between Uriah and me when Bright Knife brought you to the village."

She listened as Matt talked about himself and his life as a child, caught between two diverse cultures. She heard his side of the story concerning Veronica Fielding. Although he kept his voice emotionless when he described the beating and branding given to him by Fielding's men, Zoe felt his humiliation and pain; she felt and understood his savage desire to get even. When he recounted his argument with Uriah that culminated in his being disowned, Zoe suffered with him.

She wanted to go to him and wrap her arms around him, but this wasn't Matt Barnabas or Ma-ta-mon-yahu speaking. This man was a stranger, far away from her. He wasn't the one with whom she had been living. This was Matt Chandler, a man who hated Weber Fielding as much as Weber Fielding hated him, a man bent on revenge.

While Zoe understood Matt's sorrows and grievances, while she hurt for him, she also hurt for herself. Matt could have . . . he *should* have told her. She had poured her heart out to him, had confessed to him, yet he had told her nothing about himself. She remembered his strange reaction

414

the night of Bryan's murder, but even then he hadn't said a word. His own brother dead, and he hadn't shared it with her. He'd suffered; she didn't doubt this. But he'd kept it bottled up inside and had allowed her to think he was chasing the men for the guns. Her most poignant sorrow was the knowledge that he'd left her in Chandlerville without telling anyone—not even her own father—who he was. To the very end he'd kept his identity secret, and at the moment she thought it was extremely self-serving on his part.

Like Weber, Matt had used her.

After a lengthy silence in which she watched him tap tobacco out of the pouch onto the tiny sliver of paper, she asked, "Why did you marry me?"

"Initially, to save you from Bright Knife, but I fell in love with you."

"Something you hadn't counted on," Zoe said.

He lit the cigarette and took a long drag, saying as he exhaled, "Something I hadn't counted on. But I married you forever, Zoe. I want it to last."

Holding the blanket over her body, Zoe gathered her clothes, her hair falling around her face. Whereas before she had enjoyed sharing her nudity with Matt, she now felt embarrassed. "You know, Matt, in a lot of ways, you and Weber are alike. He wanted to marry me for my property; you married me in order to have your revenge against him."

"I married you for all the wrong reasons, but I love you." Matt watched as she slipped into her pantalettes and chemise, then her blouse and skirt.

"Love me or want me, Matt?" She laughed, the sound bitter, and turned to look at him, all the while buttoning up her blouse. "I thought you were different from the other men I've known. Your

415

taking me to Candaleria to tend the sick, bringing me back home when I was hurt, and promising to help the widows keep their land . . . I had no idea that you were a Chandler and that you'd already applied the money you got for the guns to your grandfather's note at the bank. I was worried about the soldiers killing you. How funny!"

Matt stubbed the cigarette out; all of a sudden it tasted bitter. "You have a right to be angry, Zoe—"

"Thank you," she snapped sarcastically. "I'm glad you think so, because I plan to be mad for a very long time, Matthew Barnabas Chandler, and I'm going to enjoy it. How do you think I feel, knowing that I've been used by both you and Weber? A doormat for two men. A whore for one. What's the matter, Matt? Is the truth going to bother you?"

"Damn it, Zoe!" Matt exclaimed, goaded into anger by what he considered infantile behavior. "I admit part of my motive for marrying you was wrong, but part of it was good. Had I not married you, Bright Knife would have made you his whore, raping and torturing you . . . and more. For God's sake, can't you understand, I love you and I'm sorry for not telling you who I was sooner."

Zoe said, "I want to go home, Matt. I want to be by myself for a while to think things through."

Understanding, Matt nodded and stared at her. Finally he asked, "Have you told Weber about us?"

Zoe licked her lips, suddenly gone dry, and folded her arms across her chest. "I broke our engagement."

"I'm a good judge of character," Matt said, his brown eyes narrowed as he scrutinized the woman in front of him. "I knew you'd do that. What I want to know is, did you tell Weber about me and you?"

"No," Zoe murmured, her anger turning into misery as she realized that she was as guilty as Matt was. But she hadn't known whether Matt wanted his identity known or not. No, her reason was totally selfish. She hadn't wanted a confrontation with Weber. "I didn't — I wasn't — "

"It doesn't matter," Matt said, but it did: it hurt him deeply, but he couldn't blame her. She had no way of knowing who he was or if she'd ever see him again. And she had so recently regained consciousness. He was expecting too much from her.

"Let one of your braves take me home," she said.

Yes, Matt thought, he could easily order a brave to escort her home, but his heart constricted painfully at the thought of her leaving.

"Ma-ta-mon-yahu," Running Horse shouted from outside the tepee, "Soaring Eagle sends for you."

"Please, Matt?" Zoe urged him.

"We'll discuss this later. Right now I need to see what my grandfather wants." The whoosh of the flap echoed through the tepee as he ducked through the door.

He could have sent her home with Running Horse; that's the way he brought her here. But he didn't want her to leave. He was afraid that he was going to lose her. He had suffered a similar fear when she'd lapsed into the coma, but his consolation had been his knowledge of her love for him. If she left him now, he had no consolation at all.

He reasoned that if she left while she was angry and hurt, he'd lose her forever. He recognized that she needed time to accept his confession; he wanted to give her this time to get over her anger and to think clearly about their marriage. But he wanted her thinking to be done on his territory. If after careful consideration she still felt the same way, if she wanted to return to Chandlerville without him, well. . . . He wouldn't even consider such a thought.

Speaking Comanche, he said to Running Horse, "Stay here with Zoe until I can post a guard."

The brave hiked a brow. "Your wife came of her own free will, my friend, but I take it she's not staying of her own free will. She has much spirit."

"Either that or I'm getting old, as Bright Knife accuses," Matt answered dryly.

"Maybe a little of both," Running Horse conceded.

When Matt entered his grandfather's tepee, he found Soaring Eagle sitting up, forming a circle with the elders, Buffalo Woman, and Bright Knife. "You sent for me?" he asked.

"I did," Soaring Eagle replied. "Please sit down. I called the council and have spoken to them about your request to know more about the Golden Secret."

"The white people have brought us nothing but death and destruction," Buffalo Woman exclaimed, her ebony eyes glittering venomously through the maze of makeup. "I say we should give them the same."

Sharp Claws, one of the elders who was highly respected for his judgment, said, "Once the whites learn about the gold, no matter that you have taken it, Ma-ta-mon-yahu, no matter that it is all gone; they will keep coming, searching, and digging in our mountains. They will never believe it is gone, and we will have no peace."

"Even if you should not let me have the gold,"

Matt said, "there is no guarantee that the white men won't come, Sharp Claws. When the woman in Mexico saw my bracelet, she recognized it. She knows the story of the gold and will tell others. You'll have more protection if the gold is found."

"If the gold is given to you," Bright Knife said, "you can give it to the whites. Always you have been more white than Comanches."

"If the gold is given to me," Matt said, ignoring Bright Knife's inflammatory words, "I will have the money to repay the loan that my grandfather owes Weber Fielding, and I shall have enough to give to the other ranchers until they get on their feet and have a chance to sell their cattle in Kansas. We shall make a blood covenant between us, and I promise that your land will be recorded in my name, and no one will be able to take it away. The land will belong to the *Coth-cho Tejas*."

"I don't trust a blood covenant with a man who is neither white nor Indian." Bright Knife spat the words contemptuously at Matt.

The hours passed as the council argued. Sharp Claws and Soaring Eagle, leading one faction, favored helping Matt find the gold; Buffalo Woman and Bright Knife, heading the other, violently opposed it. At the end of the conference they were as far from a consensus as they had been at the beginning.

Eventually Bright Knife said, "I go now, Soaring Eagle, but I say this before I leave. Because of your promise to attend the Big Talk, my braves and I have not gone on the warpath yet. We did not join the Mescalero Apaches when they raided the whites who lived out from Chandlerville; we did not pay the whites back for attacking our village. The other

chiefs are waiting for you to get strong again so w
can meet and talk. I ask that you give Ma-ta-mon
yahu's request careful thought. Wait five suns be
fore you give Ma-ta-mon-yahu your answer abou
the gold."

Soaring Eagle nodded his head. "You are right
Bright Knife. I have promised that I will meet wit
the council of tribes. I will continue to weigh al
that I have heard but won't give an answer to Ma
ta-mon-yahu until five suns have passed."

Bright Knife and Buffalo Woman filed out of th
tepee after the elders, but Matt remained behind a
his grandfather's request.

"I do not know if the council will agree to tel
you where the treasure is buried, my grandson. I
the decision were mine alone to make, I should giv
it to you and be done with it. But I have only on
part of the story of the Golden Secret . . . the par
that was painted by my great-grandfather, Blue Sky
Buffalo Woman has the other. She received it whe
she was a young woman and her magic was th
greatest in the village. No one can take it from her
she must give it away willingly to someone who i
worthy."

The old chief's voice died away and he closed hi
eyes for a few minutes. A smile twitched his lips
and his lids fluttered but didn't open. In a dream
voice he said, "As a very small child I rode with m
grandfather through the mountains and he woul
tell me about the great victory and the golden se
cret. But I do not know the exact spot where th
treasure was buried."

"You're tired, Grandfather," Matt said, noticin
the lines of strain around Soaring Eagle's mouth
"You must lie down and rest. I'll bring Zoe so sh

420

an take care of you."

"Yes," Soaring Eagle said without argument. He as tired and wanted to rest.

As soon as Matt helped his grandfather to lie own, he fetched Zoe, who examined Soaring Eagle nd changed his bandage before he went to sleep. Your fever is down and the wound is healing quite ell. Right now you're tired because you've overex- ted yourself."

"I do what I must do," Soaring Eagle answered earily in English, his lids closing. "Ma-ta-mon- ahu, have you told her?"

"Yes, Grandfather," Matt answered, surprised hat his grandfather was talking so Zoe could un- erstand them.

"That is good. You will go with me to the Big alk."

"Yes," Matt answered.

Scooting to where Matt sat cross-legged, Zoe sked, "What's he talking about?"

"Indians believe there is strength in numbers; iey think if they can band together, they will suc- ed in driving the white man off their land. Sev- ral of the tribes are meeting to discuss such a bining."

"Will Soaring Eagle agree to join them?" Zoe sked.

"I don't know," Matt answered. "That's what he's eciding now."

"Does he have an alternative?" Zoe asked, her eart going out to these people and to the man ho now slept quietly.

"We have a slim chance," Matt replied, leaning ack on the buffalo robes.

For a long time he and Zoe talked about the

legend of the Golden Secret, and inevitably th
discussion returned once again to their sojourn i
La Ciudad de la Cruz. Although she had heard th
story once, Zoe was curious to hear it again. Sh
wanted to memorize everything that had happene
to her and Matt while she was unconscious. Whe
he related the part about the bracelet, he took hi
off and handed it to her. Patiently he answered al
her questions and sated her curiosity.

"Eugenia not only saved your life," he concluded
"but she may have saved Chandlerville from Webe
Fielding. I had heard about the Golden Secret al
my life, but did not know that it really existed o
the value of it until Eugenia recognized the bracele
and told me. If only I can find the gold. . . ."

Zoe turned the bracelet over in her hand and ra
her fingers over the design. "Eugenia had one jus
like this one?"

Matt smiled and nodded. "A smaller one tha
was identical in design. She promised she woul
give it to you when I returned with the golde
candlesticks. Then each of us would have a match
ing bracelet."

"With half a map," Zoe said, "do you reall
think you'll be able to find a treasure in gold that'
been hidden for over one hundred years?"

"I have a much better chance with half a ma
than with none, but either way I shall look. It's m
only hope of saving La Candela de Oro an
Chandlerville."

"What are we going to do in the meantime? Sta
here? You know we can't do that. As soon as Papa
gets home, Lou's going to tell him that I left with
Comanche, and both he and Weber will come afte
me. It's best for everyone if I go home."

Matt pulled her close to him, pressing her cheek against his chest. "It probably is, but I don't want you to go. I want you here so I can take care of you. If you're gone, I'll worry."

As with her suggestion that he send her home with an escort, Matt recognized the validity of Zoe's argument, but was afraid to let her go. His primary concern was her overexerting herself. But he was also afraid. His fear wasn't her telling We-er that Matt Chandler had returned; his fear was that she wouldn't want him, that she didn't love him. He knew he couldn't make her love him; yet he couldn't let her go either . . . not just yet.

"Ma-ta-mon-yahu," a runner shouted from outside in Comanche, his voice growing louder by the time he pushed the flap aside to enter the tepee, "many white men are hunting the woman."

"Are they close to the village?" Matt asked.

"No," the brave answered.

Matt stood, strapping his guns on. "We must lead them away from here."

"What's wrong?" Zoe leaped to her feet. "What's he saying, Matt?"

"I have a little matter I must attend to," Matt answered, evading her question and walking around her. "You stay here with Soaring Eagle until I return."

"Matt," Zoe exclaimed, flinging herself against him, "I demand to know what's happening. It concerns me, doesn't it?"

"Stay here until I get back," Matt said, his hands banding around her arms as he set her aside. He disappeared through the door only to reappear again. "Guards are posted, so don't try to escape." The leather flap whooshed down.

423

"Matthew . . . Barnabas . . . Chandler, at times I really do despise you."

"It is not good for a *po-haw-cut mah-cou-ah* to speak with a forked tongue. It will give her bad magic," Soaring Eagle said, but Zoe made no reply. "Ma-ta-mon-yahu loves you."

Zoe sighed and said, "Maybe . . . in his way."

"I should think that is what you would want," he said. "Would you have him love you in another man's way?"

"He married me out of revenge," Zoe said, a tinge of petulance in her voice.

"The reason why he married you is no longer important," Soaring Eagle reasoned. "What is important is that he loves you. You must believe that."

"Where has he gone?" Zoe changed the subject.

"One of our scouts saw many white men riding."

"They've come after me," Zoe whispered. "I knew they would."

"You are glad?"

"No, but I told Matt they would come after me, and they won't give up until they find me. Weber won't let them."

Matt wanted me to get even with Weber. Weber wants me for his railroad. Neither wants me for myself. But even as the thought ran through her mind, she knew that no matter why Matt married her, he loved her. That's the reason why he refused to let her go. He thought he would lose her for good.

"You wish to marry this man called Fielding?"

"No."

"Then why do you care about him?"

"I don't," Zoe replied, scooting close to the old

424

chief. "I'm worried about you and your people. Weber is determined to get you off this land, and he doesn't care how he does it. When he finds out that Matt's alive, he'll be out after him. Please, Soaring Eagle, you must let me go. Matt has too many things on his mind to be worried about me. If I leave, I promise you the white men will return to Chandlerville."

Digesting Zoe's words, Soaring Eagle was quiet for a long time. Finally he opened his eyes and looked at her. "Do you hate my grandson so much?" the old man asked.

Zoe didn't answer Soaring Eagle; rather, she crossed her hands over her breasts and paced the tepee, wondering when Matt would return. When she heard the flap whoosh, she turned to see Buffalo Woman entering the tepee.

"I have come to ask your help, *Po-haw-cut mah-cou-ah,*" the Comanche said in slow and faltering English.

Astonished, Zoe only stared.

"I want you to bring your magic to my tepee. My medicine is not strong enough to make my grandson well. His flesh burns to the touch. He is a small warrior who has seen only four winters, and I do not want him to die."

"I will come," Zoe answered, knowing how much it cost the Comanche woman to ask for help in curing her grandson. Zoe picked up her bag, gathering her medicines, bandages and instruments. To Soaring Eagle she said, "I will be back as soon as I can."

"Go," he said, then called out in Comanche to the guard to let Zoe pass.

When Zoe arrived at Buffalo Woman's tepee, she

found the child lying on the bed with an ugly gash running down his left leg. The cut wasn't too deep, but it was badly infected. If it wasn't cleaned and treated properly, he could easily develop gangrene. Delirious with fever, the child thrashed about.

"What's his name?" Zoe asked as she knelt beside the bed and opened her bag.

"Yellow Sun," his grandmother answered. "Can you make well?"

"Yes," Zoe answered, "I can make well. Get me a basin of clean water. Yellow Sun," she said as if he understood English, "I'm going to doctor your leg and make you well."

Continuing to talk to him about anything that came to mind, her voice low and soothing, Zoe cleaned the wound, then searched through her bag for the bottle of whiskey which she always carried. A smile tugged the corner of her lips when she remembered the last bottle she'd opened in a tepee.

"Hold him," she told Buffalo Woman. "I'm going to pour this on the cut and it's probably going to burn."

"Why you pour firewater on him?" Buffalo Woman asked. "Why you no pour it down throat?"

"To pour it on the wound helps the wound to heal; to pour it down the throat only . . . only . . ." She stopped her explanation as she groped for the right words.

"Man gets *loco,*" Buffalo Woman finished.

"Yes, he gets *loco.* Now hold Yellow Sun's leg, please."

"Him brave. No need for me to hold."

Drawing a deep breath, but refraining from arguing with the old woman, Zoe caught the child's ankle firmly in her hand and poured the whisky on the cut. She felt Yellow Sun's body tense, but he didn't move his leg or cry out. When he went limp, she knew he'd passed out. Quickly she sutured the cut.

"He's going to be all right," she said to Buffalo Woman as she bandaged the wound.

"Thank you, *po-haw-cut ma-cou-ah*," the Comanche said. "Someday I will repay you."

"You don't owe me anything," Zoe replied. "I'm a doctor. Tomorrow either my father or I will be back to examine him."

Turning from Buffalo Woman, Zoe walked out of the tepee.

As Matt and the ten braves riding with him topped the hill, they saw a lone rider galloping toward the group of white men. Matt made no mistake that it was Zoe; her blond hair, unfurling like a flag behind her, shone in the morning sun. His face was immobile, and his eyes, although a little bright, were unreadable. She had wasted no time leaving the camp and returning to them . . . to Weber.

"Do not grieve yourself, my friend," Running Horse said. "No matter what this looks like, the white woman loves you."

"I have never grieved over a woman," Matt said coolly. "I'm not going to start now. Come . . . we must return to the village. We have much to do before the Big Talk."

They turned and moved down the hill, returning to the main camp. They hadn't ridden far when they spotted another rider approaching. His rifle was held high in the air, a white kerchief attached to the end of the barrel.

"From the way he rides," Running Horse said, "I would say he's white, but he's not one of the others."

Matt had his braves spread out to form a single line on either side of him, and they waited, watching the rider as he slowly approached, the white handkerchief blowing in the morning breeze. Something was familiar about the man, something about him nagged at Matt, but he couldn't place him.

The man stopped about ten feet in front of the line of Comanches, looking each of them in the face and giving no evidence of fear, his gaze finally coming to rest on Matt. "I want to speak with the one called Matt Barnabas."

"Either you are the most foolish white man I've ever met or the bravest," Matt said.

The man smiled, a mere twist of the lips. "Certainly not foolish, and more intellectual than brave."

"Who are you?" Matt asked, the feeling of familiarity growing stronger.

"Paul LeReaux."

"I don't recognize the name."

"It isn't important enough that you should," LeReaux replied. "I work for the American government."

"How'd you manage that? You sound like you're a Southerner. From the sound of your accent and your French name, I'd say Louisiana . . . probably New Orleans."

"Originally, I was from there," LeReaux admitted, "and I'm still a Southerner in heart, but one who's not accepted or appreciated. You see, I—"

"I know," Matt replied. "You went North and

fought for the Yanks."

"And now I'm tracking down some stolen guns."

"I bought mine," Matt replied.

Paul grinned and reached up to push his black hat farther back on his head. "I'm not talking about your revolvers or your rifle. I'm talking about army-issue rifles. Four wagons of them, recently. I traced the guns to Bryan Chandler, who was killed in Mexico."

"Are you saying Bryan stole the guns?" Matt asked.

"I don't think so," LeReaux returned. "I think he's just the middle man, the one who finds a buyer, delivers the guns, and collects the money. He probably gets paid so much for each run into Mexico. On this last trip, I understand a Comanche by the name of Matt Barnabas got the guns and sold them to the Juaristas."

Now Matt grinned slow and easy. "If you were to meet this Matt Barnabas, he would tell you that your 'understand' is wrong. The *Juaristas* stole the guns from *him*."

"If I were to meet this Matt Barnabas, would he tell me who was supplying Bryan Chandler with the guns?"

"Why would a Comanche know the answer to this?" Matt parried.

"I have reason to believe that Matt Barnabas is Bryan Chandler's half-brother. And, no, I'm not a mind reader or a magician. I've been investigating Bryan and his activities for a long time now, so I knew he had a half-brother who was part-Comanche. The rest was easy to figure out. This trip to Candaleria was the first time I caught Bryan with the goods. I think Matt Barnabas might be interested in finding the man who's ultimately responsible for Bryan's death."

"Matt Barnabas knows who's responsible for killing his brother."

Silently the two men stared at each other for a long time, each measuring the other. LeReaux lowered his rifle, took off the handkerchief, and stuffed it into his shirt pocket. Then he slid the rifle into the saddle holster and lifted a hand to tug his hat lower on his face.

"Reckon I've made a mistake," he said, yanking the reins and turning the horse around. "Guess I'll just mosey along."

Matt saw the profile and knew the man . . . the one who'd followed him into Chandlerville the night he brought Zoe home. It wasn't mere coincidence.

"How long have you been following Matt Barnabas?" Matt asked.

"Since you buried Bryan Chandler and Wayne Shook. We knew your brother was smuggling guns across the border and who he was selling them to. What we don't know is the name of his supplier."

"Sorry, I can't help you on that count," Matt replied. "I don't know either. Quite by accident I discovered that my brother was a gun runner. When I did, he was already dead. The only piece of information I have in regard to the guns is this: one of the men who killed the ranchers is still alive. His name is Grisswold, and he works for Fielding. If he's not already in Chandlerville, he will be soon. I have a strong hunch this man doesn't know who the supplier is, but would like to."

"What does he look like?"

After Matt quickly described Grisswold, LeReaux

said, "Basically, our government supports the Juaristas and wants to see them helped, but we draw a line on selling weapons stolen from the American government. I'm sorry about Bryan's death. For selfish reasons we didn't want any of the Americans killed; only they could have told us what we wanted to know. As long as the supplier's alive, he'll find someone else to buy his stolen guns and remain in business."

"One of the men, Wayne Shook, lived, but he didn't know anything," Matt said. "According to him, Bryan told them they were better off knowing nothing."

"Remember everything the man told you," LeReaux said. "If anything seems important, let me know. I'll be staying at the Chandlerville Hotel, Room 5. And I appreciate your help."

As they watched LeReaux ride off, Running Horse said, "What are you going to do now, Ma-ta-mon-yahu?"

"I'm going after my wife."

431

Chapter 22

Colorful Chinese lanterns, hanging along the edge of the veranda, from the trees, and from the overhead ropes, swung gently in the evening breeze and set La Candela de Oro ablaze with a rainbow of light. Music coming from the house blended with laughter to fill the air with festive gaiety. Young couples strolled on the lawn, and older ones sat in chairs, talking low and sipping their punch.

"Oh, Papa, it's all so beautiful," Zoe breathed as she climbed out of the buggy. "I just hope that Mr. Chandler doesn't lose his . . . that Weber doesn't . . ."

"Chandler won't lose it," Quintan assured her. Looking quite distinguished in his new suit, which he'd bought expressly for the occasion, he tugged on his waistcoat and straightened his hat before he offered Zoe his arm. "Seems to me this is the best way to celebrate your broken engagement to Weber. In fact, I shall be drinking to it all night long."

"Papa, you're incorrigible."

"Only on certain issues," Quintan defended with a jaunty grin. "I just hope Weber concedes his loss

432

gracefully."

"That, Papa, is a problem," Zoe sighed, remembering only too well Weber's reaction when last night in the privacy of her parlor she'd told him she wasn't marrying him, now or ever. At first, he'd refused to believe her, and he'd treated her like a child. When he saw she was adamant in her refusal, he'd run the gamut of tactics from anger to pleading. His last words had been, "We'll talk about this when you're feeling better."

As Quintan and Zoe followed a pathway lined with more bright lanterns, Quintan said, "Weber will have to accept that you're not going to marry him, but he's not going to give up on the property. He can live without you, but not without his schemes for wealth and power."

"I'm afraid of Weber, Papa," Zoe confided, a shiver running down her spine. "Ever since he told me about the railroad, he's been different."

"Not different," Quintan said. "You just opened your eyes and saw him for what he really was."

When they entered the bright parlor through French doors, Dora and Uriah were there to greet them.

"Good evening, Drs. Randolph," Uriah said. "Welcome to La Candela de Oro."

"Good evening, Uriah," Quintan greeted him, his gaze immediately going past Uriah to the hostess. Sweeping his hat off, he took Dora's hand and held it up to his lips, brushing his mouth across it. "Mrs. Chandler, how delighted I am to see you!"

Entranced by Dora Chandler, Quintan was only vaguely aware of Uriah's taking his hat and hanging it up. He couldn't believe this was the same woman he'd seen in town. That one was nondescript; this one was a handsome woman indeed. Her hair, lib-

433

erally streaked with gray, was brushed back in soft waves and pinned up in a chignon of curls. The blue gown enhanced the color of her eyes and showed her figure to advantage. He was certain he wanted to get to know Dora better.

"We're so glad you and Zoe could come," Dora said, her heart fluttering.

"And we're very happy to be here, Mrs. Chandler. Thank you for inviting us."

Zoe, delighted that her father was enamored with Dora, admired the house. "You've done a wonderful job with the decorations," she told Uriah. "Everything is beautiful."

"Yes," Quintan agreed, his eyes never leaving Dora's face, "I must agree with Zoe."

"Thank you," Uriah and Dora said at the same time, but Uriah spoke to Zoe, Dora to Quintan. Uriah's eyes twinkled when he realized that they were using the same words to carry on two different conversations.

Pleasure hotly colored Dora's cheeks as she reluctantly withdrew her hand from Quintan's clasp and turned to Zoe. "We had a lot of help this year with the decorations. Everyone is so excited about its being our fiftieth Founder's Day celebration."

"Zoe Randolph!" a woman's voice called above the music. "Just the woman I want to see. Come over here. I've been saving you a chair."

Zoe turned to see Myra Halstead sitting across the room waving at her. She turned to Dora. "Excuse me, Mrs. Chandler, Mr. Chandler. Let me see what Myra wants."

Uriah nodded his head and stuck his cigar back into the corner of his mouth, turning to stroll once again through the crowd.

"I'll be right back," Zoe promised.

"Take your time." Quintan flashed Dora a smile. "Don't hurry on our account. I'm quite sure Mrs. Chandler and I can entertain ourselves, can't we, Mrs. Chandler?"

Feeling as excited as a young woman who was being courted for the first time, Dora smiled. "I'm sure we can, Dr. Randolph."

Zoe grinned as she looked from her father to Dora; then she turned and walked to where her friend sat.

"Oh, Zoe," Myra gushed, "even if I did make it myself, your dress is gorgeous. That shade of blue is the exact color of your eyes, and only you can wear it so low without seeming indecent. Didn't I tell you? What does Weber think of it? God, he must be so proud of you! I'm so envious of the way you can wear your hair pulled back like that, leaving little curls to wisp around your face. Oh, look, here comes Greg."

"Here you are," Greg said, a lock of hair falling across his forehead, "one cup of punch. Zoe, would you like one?"

"If you don't mind," Zoe answered. "I'm really thirsty."

As Greg walked away, Myra craned her neck to look over the crowd. "Where's Weber?"

"We didn't come together," Zoe answered. "Papa brought me."

"Do you want to tell me about it?"

"Nothing much to tell," Zoe said. "We—we decided not to get married."

"Oh, Zoe," Myra drawled, placing her hand over Zoe's. "Don't worry about all this gossip . . . Weber's not going to listen to it. You've just had a lover's quarrel. In a couple of days you'll both be laughing over all this."

"No—" Zoe began, but Myra cut her short.

"I know Weber was angry because you went to the Comanche camp and treated that old chief, but he had a right to be, Zoe. You should have known better. *You* know how much Weber hates those Comanches. Lord, how well I can remember—" Myra leaned closer to Zoe and lowered her voice "—how Weber reacted when Matt Chandler got Veronica pregnant. God, he hates Comanches."

"I'm a doctor," Zoe said, resenting Myra's comments. "My job is to heal people. I don't ask who or what they are before I treat them. I dug a bullet out of an old man's chest and tended to a child—both of whom were wounded as a result of a white men's raid. If I had it to do over again, I would, Myra, but Weber and I didn't quarrel. We simply parted company."

"Oh?" Myra's eyes widened.

"I broke the engagement because I don't love Weber. I don't want to be his wife."

"Well," Myra said, hiding her mouth behind her hand, "I don't think Weber feels the same way as you do."

Zoe followed Myra's gaze to see Weber coming directly toward them. He looked quite handsome in a new black suit with a pale green waistcoat. He smiled and greeted people as he walked toward Zoe.

"Here you are, my dear," he said sweetly, as if they had come together. "Sorry I'm late."

"I wouldn't know, since I arrived only minutes ago," Zoe said. "I had a last-minute patient."

"You really work too hard," Weber chided gently. "You need to lighten your load, darling. I trust you're feeling much better than you were when you arrived home yesterday afternoon."

"I felt quite well when I arrived home yesterday,"

Zoe said, striving to keep the irritation out of her voice. She wished Greg would hurry up and return with the punch. Her throat was dry and raspy.

"Zoe, may I talk with you, please?" Weber asked, pulling up a chair and sitting down uninvited. Then he turned to Myra and said, "Please excuse us . . . I want to talk."

"Of course, Weber." Myra immediately rose. "I was just thinking about asking Greg if he wanted to dance."

"Please don't leave, Myra." Zoe reached out and caught Myra by the hand. "Weber and I have nothing personal to talk about."

In danger of losing everything he owned, Weber pushed all pride aside and cried, "Zoe, I've never begged for anything in my life, but I'm begging you . . . please marry me."

Zoe's face flushed with embarrassment as the people closest to them turned to see what the commotion was all about. "I gave you my answer yesterday, Weber. It's final."

"Do you want me to go down on my knees in front of my friends and business associates?" Weber asked, desperation causing his voice to quaver. "Well, I will."

"Weber," Zoe whispered, "please don't make a scene."

From the landing a masculine voice, quiet but authoritative, said, "You may have business associates, Weber, but you flatter yourself if you think you have any friends. Now turn the lady loose. I don't like to see women manhandled. And this is my party. I don't want someone like you making a scene and ruining it."

The voice was familiar, but too many years had dimmed Weber's memory; his head jerked up.

When he saw Matt descending the stairs, he blanched and turned Zoe loose so quickly that she stumbled and fell against Myra.

"Matt Chandler!" Weber's words were nothing more than a croak.

"Matthew Barnabas Chandler in the flesh," Matt said.

The hush that fell over the crowd was as deafening as any noise Zoe had ever heard. Every eye in the room was on Matt. Zoe felt a wonderful warmth sweep over her. For the first time since she'd met Matt, she saw him in tailored clothes. She couldn't believe the transformation. As an Indian, he was devastatingly handsome, rugged, and primitive. But tonight, dressed as he was, Matt was suave and urbane. He exuded a cultured sophistication that put every other man to shame.

"Don't let my coming spoil the party, folks. We're here to sing and dance and have a good time. Musicians, strike up a tune. I think we'd like to dance."

Matt's eyes caught Zoe's and she saw the laughter in the sultry brown depths. He was well aware of the sensation he was causing, she thought, and he was thoroughly enjoying it. He slowly descended the stairs. Again he paused, his eyes still on her. Then a few long, leisurely strides marked the distance between them. The easy lines of his dark blue suit and the gray shirt disguised a lean, hardy body. No muscles bulged, but anyone looking at him knew that he was a man in prime physical condition. He moved with a feline grace.

"Dr. Randolph," he said, bowing in front of Zoe, "may I have the honor of this dance?"

Of all the scenes Zoe had imagined when Matt first met Chandlerville society, this was not the one.

Intuitively she knew he wasn't going to announce their marriage; he was going to wait for her.

Breathlessly she said, "You may, Mr. Chandler."

Zoe wasn't aware that she was in Matt's arms until he was swinging her onto the middle of the floor in rhythm to the music. She felt as if they were floating on a cloud somewhere in heaven. Around and around they twirled in perfect step. For such a tall, muscular man, Matt was a smooth dancer.

Hatred boiling in the depths of his cold eyes, Weber watched them. The hatred he'd felt for Matt Chandler fourteen years ago was nothing compared to the feelings that coursed through him now. Revenge wouldn't begin to appease Weber.

Completely oblivious to those malevolent thoughts, Zoe looked into Matt's face and said, "I didn't expect you."

"Surely you knew I was coming after you." His mouth was closer to her ear.

"Why?" Zoe asked, her heart pounding so furiously she knew Matt could hear it above the music. "So you could get even with Weber?"

"No," Matt returned, "because you're my wife and I love you."

Zoe stumbled, pulled back her head, and looked into his face. "Matt," she whispered, tears sparkling in her eyes.

"I would have come to La Candela de Oro whether I met you or not—" they stopped dancing and stood in the middle of the floor—"because I was coming home. I've come back to save my grandfather's property, but I came to this party specifically to be with you."

"Thank you," Zoe murmured, her face warming with pleasure. Her hand spread over his muscular shoulder and he whirled her around the room again.

"You're a beautiful woman, Dr. Randolph."

"You're a handsome man, Mr. Chandler."

"I rather thought so," Matt said, "when all the women were ogling me."

"You're too modest," Zoe teased.

"Maybe not modest," Matt said, "but fair. I came tonight to tell you that you were right."

"About what?" Zoe asked.

"About our marriage. A Comanche wedding isn't recognized in a white community, and you're not bound by it. You and I are not married and have never been. You're free to marry Weber. I set you free."

Zoe reeled from the blow. She didn't want to be set free. Matt's change of attitude surprised and bothered her. "I've already told him that I don't love him. I'm not going to marry him."

"Did you tell him about me?"

"No," Zoe whispered, watching the brown eyes grow darker. "Matt, I—I didn't—"

"It's all right," he whispered. "You said you needed time, and you do."

Neither said another word as they danced, but the magic of the moment was broken. When the music stopped, Matt led Zoe back to where she had been standing.

"Matt Chandler," Myra said, "I didn't think you'd ever dare show your face in Chandlerville again."

Matt rested his hand on Zoe's back, his touch light but proprietary. "You're not the only one who thought that, is she, Weber?"

"To tell the truth, Chandler," Weber said, having regained a certain amount of his aplomb, "I am surprised to see you here . . . for several reasons."

"I'll bet you are," Matt replied easily.

Greg Halstead pushed through the crowd and caught Matt in a bear hug. "You old son-of-a-gun. I'm glad to see you home again. It hasn't seemed right with you gone."

"I'm glad to be home, Greg."

"Sorry about Bryan."

Matt nodded.

"Now, folks," Uriah shouted, climbing midway up the stairs, holding out his hands for quiet, "I want to tell you some great news. My grandson is going to help us get the money to save our homes. No scalawag or carpetbagger is going to get what's ours."

Thunderous applause followed the announcement.

"Just how do you propose to save the property?" Weber asked Matt.

"Not by running guns, Weber."

Weber and Matt stared at each other for a long time before Weber said, "I congratulate you on your audacity, Matt, but your timing is off. I don't think you know just how much your grandfather owes me or how soon he owes it. There's no way possible you can save La Candela de Oro. I'll get it if I must take it piecemeal."

"The only way you'll get it," Matt replied, "is to take it, Weber, but I don't advise your trying that if you want to live."

"Are you threatening me?" Weber asked.

"No, just promising."

"Zoe, get your things," Weber said. "We're leaving."

"No, Weber, I'm staying, and I'm going to do something I should have done days ago." Zoe caught Matt's hand in hers and ascended the bottom two stairs, Matt following. She said loudly and clearly, "Ladies and gentlemen, I would like to make another announcement. Four weeks ago on my way to Candaleria my caravan was attacked by Comanches. My escort was killed, and I was taken captive to their village."

A murmur went through the crowd. Those who were seated edged forward in their chairs. Stunned, Weber stood still as a statue. Quintan, standing to the side with Dora, chuckled.

"I was rescued by a brave named Ma-ta-mon-yahu, who was half-white and half-Indian. We were married in a Comanche ceremony and lived together for three weeks as man and wife. I would like to present my husband. Ladies and gentlemen, Ma-ta-mon-yahu."

Zoe cast Weber a smug smile as the crowd clapped and cheered for her and Matt.

Turning to her husband, she said, "If it's agreeable with you, Matt Chandler, I should like for us to continue living together as man and wife. I find the Comanche ceremony quite binding and legal myself. And I'd rather live with you outside wedlock than with any other man in wedlock."

The world quietly melted away until only Zoe and Matt were left. They turned to each other, caught each other's hands, and stared into one another's eyes, enjoying one of their most sublime moments together.

Matt's voice was deep and husky when he said, "I'm of the same opinion, Mrs. Chandler, and there's nothing I should like better than for us to live together."

"A toast to my grandson Matthew Barnabas Chandler and his bride, Zoe Randolph Chandler,"

Uriah shouted.

"A toast to Mr. and Mrs. Matt Chandler," Quintan shouted, smiling into Dora's face when they raised their glasses.

"To my son and daughter," Dora whispered, tears glimmering in her eyes.

Enraged, Fielding quietly retreated into the darkness, nursing his hatred.

Matt strapped his guns around his waist, then slipped into the black leather vest. Picking up his hat from the dresser, he walked out of Zoe's bedroom. As he walked down the stairs, he heard the chimes from the clock announce the hour: six o'clock. Then he heard a knock.

In a few minutes he heard Lou open the door. "Yes?" she asked.

"I know this is mighty early, ma'am," a masculine voice said.

"Sure is," Lou returned. "Ain't had breakfast yet."

"It's important, ma'am, that we see Matt Chandler."

Lou raised her brow in surprise. Funny how fast word got around that Matt Chandler was staying with Zoe.

"I'm Toby Jones," the man continued. "This is Sammy Smith."

"Wait out here on the porch," Lou said. "I'll see if he's up yet."

Before she could turn away from the door to summon Matt, he walked past her to see the two men who were no more Smith or Jones than Matt was Brown. At a glance, he recognized them as professional gunmen. Their weapons were as necessary to them as their arms or legs.

Curious about their visit, he said, "I'm Matt Chandler. What can I do for you?"

In an undertone Smith said, "We're business associates of your brother. Could we go somewhere private and talk?"

"Where?"

Smith grinned, exposing a mouthful of straight, white teeth. "Scared, Chandler?"

"No, careful—and extremely picky about whom I'm seen with in public."

"How about the saloon?"

"Too early for a drink," Matt counted. "How about the hotel dining room?"

"Fine. Say half an hour?"

"Half an hour."

Minutes later Zoe came out of her surgery, slipping into her white overall. Giving Matt a quick kiss, she twirled in his arms and said, "Tie this in the back for me, darling. Who was that?"

"Two men who want to talk with me. They said they were Bryan's business associates. Do you know them?"

Zoe pulled away from Matt and ran to the door, gazing at the two men, immediately recognizing them. "They're not from around here. I saw them getting off the stage earlier in the week."

"If you don't stand still, I'm not going to get this thing fixed," Matt said, following her to the door. When he had tied the sashes, he lowered his head and nuzzled her neck.

"How can I stand still when you're doing that?" Zoe murmured, leaning her head over to expose even more tender flesh.

"Are you suggesting that we go back upstairs, Mrs. Chandler?"

Zoe turned and looped her arms around his neck. "I would love nothing better, but—"

"Me, too," Matt said, kissing the tip of her nose. "I promised those fellows I'd meet them at the hotel dining room in thirty minutes."

"They're dangerous, Matt . . . be careful."

"I will."

After a long farewell kiss, Matt left and walked to the hotel, joining Smith and Jones in the dining room. They invited him to join them for breakfast, but he ordered only coffee.

"Well, Mr. Chandler," Smith said after he had finished eating and pushed his plate away, "we're here because your brother has caused our company a great deal of concern."

"In what way?" Matt asked, leaning back in the chair and pulling the pouch of tobacco from his vest pocket.

"Well, you see, we offered him a chance to make some big money."

"Hauling freight." With a dexterous twist of his fingers, Matt folded the tobacco in the paper and ran his tongue down the edge.

Jones said, "Well, you might say that. Now, he's supposed to give us so much of what he makes, and he hasn't sent the company their share of his last load. The boss has been patient with him, but his patience is wearing thin. So he sent us to collect. We've been waiting for him, but he hasn't shown up at the ranch."

"Not likely that he will," Matt said, dragging a match across the bottom of the table. Holding the flickering flame to the tip of his cigarette, he said, "You see, gentlemen, Bryan was killed on his last trip and the merchandise was stolen from him."

"This could be a lie," Smith said.

"You know it's the truth because you've been here in town long enough to have questioned people about Bryan. You've heard about him being killed running guns in Mexico."

"What we figure is that you were in on this with him."

"Sorry, Mr. Jones and Mr. Smith, you need to go back to school. You figured wrong. After having spent the last four years of my life shooting men and boys with guns, I sure as hell don't want to be peddling them to someone to kill with. So you lost some money. That's business. You have to be willing to take the risks."

The waiter neared the table with the coffeepot, but Smith waved him away. "How would you like to join our organization, Mr. Chandler. We'll give you the same deal we gave your brother."

"Not me, gentlemen," Matt said. "I'm going prospecting myself. But I'll tell you what. My brother has a friend who's in town and who'd be mighty interested in your organization. This fellow was with Bryan on this last trip into Mexico; he might be able to tell you what happened."

Jones and Smith looked at one another. Finally Smith leaned both arms on the table. "How do we know we can trust this man?"

"You don't," Matt answered. "But it won't hurt for you to meet him. Then you can decide if you want to include him in the deal. Shall I send for him?"

"Who is he?"

"Paul LeReaux."

"What do you know about him?"

"Just what I told you," Matt answered.

"Let's go."

The three men pushed away from the table,

walked across the dining room, through the lobby, and up the stairs, stopping when they reached Room 5. Matt knocked.

"Who is it?" LeReaux called.

"Chandler."

"Come on in . . . the door's unlocked."

Matt opened the door and led the way into the room. LeReaux, clad in trousers and an unbuttoned shirt, sat on the bed smoking a cigar.

Matt said, "I have two men here, Smith and Jones, who are interested in talking business. They're Bryan's business associates and are interested in learning about the freight business between here and Candaleria."

His gaze slid past Matt to the two strangers. "Good morning, gentlemen. Just what do you wish to know?"

"How long have you known Chandler?" Smith asked.

LeReaux's gaze flitted back to Matt, and he wished he could read eyes. "I've known him only a short while. Knew his brother longer. Made the last four trips into Mexico with Bryan."

"Give me the dates of the past four shipments," Jones said. "And what kind of merchandise was he transporting?"

Matt moved across the room and sat down to listen as the interrogation continued, the men bombarding LeReaux with question after question, the answers coming without any hesitation.

"With regard to the last shipment," Paul LeReaux concluded, "I believe Weber Fielding was the informer. Somehow he learned about our taking the guns into Mexico, the delivery date, and the rendezvous point. The men, who shot and killed four others who were riding with us, called Bryan by name."

"Would you recognize any of them?"

"One of them was young, in his early twenties, I'd say, with a flat nose, like it had been broken several times. His face was pockmarked, with a long, thin scar running from his temple to his chin on the right side. He rode a black roan horse, the admixture so unusual, I'd know it at a glance."

"You'll recognize the man as easily?"

LeReaux smiled and waved his hand toward the window. "I'll recognize him, and you will, too. All we have to do is wait for him to show up at Fielding's. From here, gentlemen, I have a wonderful view of the bank, the front entrance, and the alleys on both sides."

Matt stood. "If you're finished with me, I'd like to be on my way. I have work to do before the sun goes down today."

"We wouldn't like word of our business to get around, Chandler. Could mean a shortened life span."

"I doubt it," Matt drawled, leisurely moving to the door. "But to set your minds at ease, I'll let you know that I support the Juaristas and their cause. Be seeing you around, LeReaux. I wish you success in all your business dealings, and may these new associates prove to be . . . exactly the ones you were hoping for."

A frown creasing his brow, Greg Halstead stood in front of the window in the Emporium, his fingers still clutching the drawstring of the shade as he watched Matt walk into the Chandlerville land and title office. Seeing his old friend last night had brought back a lot of memories for Greg; he hadn't been unaffected by what happened to Matt fourteen years ago. Pulling the shade back down, twisting the sign to read "Closed," and making sure the front door was locked, he walked into his office at the rear of the building.

He went directly to the cabinet on the far wall, opened the door, and pulled out a whiskey bottle and a glass. Without moving from the spot, he poured a drink and quickly quaffed it. As he drank the second, he walked around the room, finally sitting down in his chair. Brooding, he hunched over his desk. He was on this third drink when he heard the knock, an insistent knock that didn't go away. Sighing, he took a last swallow, stood, and walked through the store to see Weber Fielding standing at the front door, his hand and face pressed to the pane so he could see into the dim interior.

The minute Greg unlocked and opened the door, Weber demanded, "What's wrong? Why are the shades drawn and the door locked?"

"I didn't feel like opening right now," Greg said, rounding his shoulders when he stuffed his hands into his pockets.

Close enough to catch a whiff of Greg's breath, Weber exclaimed, "My God, Greg, you've been drinking!"

"Yes I have, and I'm going to have a lot more," Greg said, walking to his office.

"What's the occasion?" Weber asked as he and Greg weaved through the store displays.

Greg refilled his glass and waved it through the air. "The return of Matt Chandler, as if you didn't know. Want a drink, Weber? No."

"Are you crazy?" Weber said.

"That's the exact question I've been asking myself

since I learned about Bryan's murder, and since Matt returned last night."

"What's Bryan's murder got to do with the way you're acting?" Weber asked, looking disdainfully at the half-empty whiskey bottle, then at Greg.

"He was my friend," the store owner shouted, his eyes wild. "My friend, Weber—and you sent your thugs after him. I just as good as killed him."

"Not for the first time, I seem to recollect," Weber replied suavely, not one whit perturbed by Greg's accusations. "When you arrived in Chandlerville, you were an escaped murderer who'd been sentenced to hang."

"I was framed and you know it," Greg said.

"You and I may know it," Weber returned, walking over to Greg's desk and stuffing the cork in the bottle, "but in the sight of the law, you're still guilty. Regardless of your past, I took you in and furnished you with the wherewithal to make your dream of this emporium come to fruition. And I don't intend to let you destroy yourself because of misplaced loyalty and sentiment."

Greg raked his hands through his hair. "Blackmail is what you call it. Because of you, I've betrayed two of my best friends."

Weber slid into Greg's chair, leaning back and twining his fingers behind his head. "Don't play the victim with me. You were perfectly willing to let me persuade Veronica to accuse Matt Chandler of being your bastard's father. All you could think about at the time was protecting yourself and Myra. I had to think of what was best for everybody."

"I never thought it would get so far out-of-hand," Greg mumbled. "I didn't dream you'd get people so riled up they'd try to brand him."

"I didn't make those people do anything they

450

didn't want to do," Weber pointed out. "The masses are always waiting for someone to come along and encourage them to give free rein to their base desires and emotions. They're willing to commit the most heinous deeds in the name of justice."

"So are you, Weber. Don't you think I haven't been haunted by the idea of you using an innocent baby as a pawn in this game of power you've been playing with the Chandlers for so long. Thank God Veronica and the baby died. At least they escaped."

"Greg, for God's sake, shut up," Weber said. "We have enough trouble on our hands without your going loco."

But Greg wouldn't be quieted. Like a boil that has finally erupted, all the poison within spilled out. He raged back and forth in the small room. "All these years I've supplied you with information. Pay Greg, and he'll find out anything you want to know. God, I make myself sick! Those poor women pouring out their hearts to Myra and me, and I trot right over to you with the news, and you buy their property right out from under them for nothing. And I'm the one who told you Bryan was taking a load of guns into Candaleria. I should have known! I should have known you'd kill him."

Weber had always known that Greg wasn't a strong man, but he'd never seen him this distraught. He was on the verge of hysteria, on the verge of ruining everything Weber had spent a lifetime building. Weber knew that he must calm him down.

Speaking quietly but firmly, he said, "This is business, Greg. When are you going to learn to separate your emotions from business?"

"As long as it was land grabbing, I didn't mind," Greg answered. "But murder is something else. I won't stand for it."

"Don't play the self-righteous hypocrite with me. You've been aware all along what we've been doing. You're just having to get your hands dirty now, and you're afraid somebody's going to find out what you really are."

Hearing the pounding on the front door, Weber stood and moved out of the office, calling over his shoulder, "You've got to open this place up, Greg. You're attracting too much attention, and this isn't good for business. Yours or mine."

As soon as Weber cracked the door, Scully slipped in. "Thank God, you're here, Weber. Matt Chandler's —"

"My God! Both of you!" Weber threw up his hands, completely exasperated. "Matt Chandler's been in town less than twenty-four hours and the two of you are falling apart."

"Weber —" Scully nervously pulled at his chin "— I'm worried. Things ain't going as planned. Matt Chandler's been in the land office, going through all my records and maps. Won't tell me what he wants 'em for. Drawing maps and trails and looking."

"Where is he now?"

"Randolph's. Looks like he's getting ready to go somewhere."

"Where?" Weber murmured to no one in particular.

"Don't know," Scully said, "but he sure was interested in the area around the Comanche Mountains. Wanted to find everything he could about it. Old records, Weber. Real old. Going back a hundred years or so."

"You know him better than any of us, Greg. Why would he be going to the Comanche Mountains?"

"That's where the Comanches live," Greg retorted.

"No," Weber said, "there's more to it than that. He has a reason for being in the land and title company, going through old records. A specific reason. Think, Scully! What could he be looking for?"

"For God's sake, Weber, I don't know why he's out there, other than to see his grandfather."

"We've got to follow him and find out what he's up to," Weber said. "I have too much invested to lose it now."

"This ain't good, Weber," Scully said. "We don't have time to go chasing after Matt Chandler. We've got enough problems without creating a new one."

"All the more reason for following Matt Chandler, gentlemen. With him dead, we've solved all our problems."

"Kill Matt?" Scully and Greg said in unison, both staring at Weber as if he'd lost his mind.

"Yes, gentlemen, kill him. I always remove obstacles," Weber informed them coolly, a peculiar gleam in his eyes. "Permanently. There's no better time than the present and certainly no better place than out in those godforsaken mountains."

"I don't want to be in on this," Scully said, shaking his head vigorously. "I remember only too well what them Indians did to the fellows who beat Matt and branded him. No siree, not me."

Greg said, "You may try to kill Matt, Weber, but you won't succeed. He's smarter than you."

"He's right, Weber," Scully added, swiping at his head nervously. "Matt's Comanche. Don't'cha forget it. If we follow him he'll know it, and he'll get us out there and kill us. With you dead, ain't no one to foreclose on the ranches. Your death is good as gold to them. They won't need no money. Let's get out now, Weber, while we're ahead."

"I've always called the shots," Weber said, "and I shall continue to do so."

"You can call them for yourself and Scully as long as you want," Greg said. "But you can count me out. I'm no longer a player. The stakes are absolutely too high."

"Yes," Weber drawled, looking at Greg, "I think perhaps you're right. You're no longer a player in this game. You never *were* a visionary. Scully, you get back over to the land office and stay there. If you hear anything, let me know. In the meantime, I need to find Grisswold."

After Weber and Scully left the Emporium, Greg stood in front of the window and watched until Weber disappeared into the bank, Scully in the land and title office. Weber's words tumbled through his mind. *You are no longer a player in this game. I always remove obstacles . . . permanently.* As the full meaning of the statements hit Greg, he began to tremble. Just like Matt Chandler, he was a marked man. Weber was going to kill both of them. He was responsible for Bryan's death, but he wouldn't have Matt's on his conscience. He was getting out. Yanking down the shade, he walked out the door and across the street.

When he crossed the alley between the saloon and the newspaper office, he heard someone call his name. He turned to see Grisswold standing there, a sinister grin on his face, his revolvers aimed straight at him. Before Greg could run, shots rang out and a bullet pierced him in the chest. Intense heat seared through his body. Gasping and clutching at his chest, blood oozing through his fingers, he staggered up the steps and crawled to the door of the *Daily Voice.*

People flocked around and from far away he heard someone call, "Get Doc Randolph."

"Lloyd," Greg mumbled, calling for the editor of the Daily Voice. "Got a . . . story . . . for you."

"Who did this, Greg?" Lloyd asked, putting an arm beneath Greg's shoulder and holding him. "Who shot you, man?"

"Get . . . Zoe," Greg whispered. "Got to . . . warn . . . her."

"Don't worry," Lloyd said, "she's coming."

Zoe, her medical bag in hand, pushed through the crowd to kneel beside Greg. "What happened?"

Capping the back of her head with his hand, Greg pulled her face close to his mouth and whispered for her to hear only, "Weber hired Grisswold to kill me. Going to follow Matt . . . and kill him. Get out of here and warn him."

"I will as soon as I've taken care of your wound."

Greg coughed, spitting up blood, then pushed her hands away from his chest. "I'm taken care of. Weber saw to that. Get me a pen and paper, Lloyd. I have a confession to make before I die. I want to put it in writing."

Chapter 23

Sunlight radiated through the smoke-hole to spotlight Zoe, who sat opposite Soaring Eagle. "Haven't you heard a thing I've said? Weber Fielding is going to kill Matt if he finds him! Please, you must do something to help him!"

"Ma-ta-mon-yahu is a warrior. He can take care of himself," Soaring Eagle replied, his face immobile, only a flickering in the depth of those ebony eyes to reveal his anxiety.

"How can you say this? He's doing all of this for you. He's out there hunting for that damned gold so he can buy this property and allow you to live here in peace. That stubborn old woman sitting out there like a bump on a log, refusing to give him her half of the map."

"It is up to Buffalo Woman and her Spirit to make that decision," Soaring Eagle said without rancor. "The council was undecided about sharing our knowledge of the golden secret with him. I gave Ma-ta-mon-yahu my deerskin on my own. I saw no other way to save my people after I decided that my people and I would not join the other tribes and go to war with the whites."

"At least you could have one of your braves help me find him, so I can warn him."

"You will stay here," Soaring Eagle said. "You will be safer here. This is what Ma-ta-mon-yahu would want."

"I'm not a Comanche," she said, sweeping her hat off the floor onto her head and jumping to her feet, "and I won't be treated like one. I'm his wife, and I intend to go out there and find him."

Her palm slapping against the leather door, Zoe rushed out of the tepee and mounted her horse. Soon she was climbing the mountains, following the narrow trails, her fear superceded by her desire to find Matt before Weber did. Once her anger abated, she realized the folly of her impulsiveness. She didn't know the country, and there was no way she was going to find Matt. Still she rode, refusing to turn back.

The sun relentlessly beat down on her. Rivulets of perspiration ran down her face and between her breasts; her underarms were ringed. The afternoon glare was so bright that she squinted as she searched the horizon, always looking for Matt and the black stallion—the one Uriah had given him last night as a welcome-home gift and a wedding gift.

She stopped the bay and lifted her field glasses to sweep the horizon, but saw nothing. Nothing! She untied her bandanna and drew in a deep breath as she mopped the perspiration from her face. She heard rocks clinking against the mountain, spraying around her. Then she heard the steady clop of a horse; someone was on the trail behind her.

Frightened, she guided the bay behind a small formation of rocks and hid, pulling her rifle from

457

the scabbard. Minutes stretched into hours, but she saw no one. She grew so tense that her shoulders and neck began to hurt; her head began to ache slightly. Then she felt a hand on her shoulder. Her heart pounding in her throat, she turned to see Buffalo Woman.

"What are you doing here?" Zoe demanded, frightened, relieved, and angry at the same time.

"You go in wrong direction," the woman said. "Sacred Mountain no that way."

"At least, I'm going," Zoe returned. "That's more than any of you are doing for him."

"I take." Buffalo Woman turned to disappear into the rocks behind Zoe.

"Why?" Zoe called as she put her rifle up.

When the medicine woman appeared on her mule, she said, "I owe you. Your medicine strong. You save Yellow Sun. Now I help you."

Soaring Eagle's decision to refrain from joining the other tribes in their declaration of war on the whites angered Bright Knife and his braves. Yet they remained in camp under Soaring Eagle's authority until Soaring Eagle gave Matt the deerskin with one-half the map to the cave where the gold was hidden. Now the tenuous thread binding them to their people was broken. Bright Knife and his braves declared themselves renegades and broke their allegiance to the tribe. Leaping on their ponies, they rode out of camp with the promise never to return. Relentlessly they had tracked Matt.

Stopping at the brook to water the stallion which Uriah had given him, Matt saw them coming. But he wasn't surprised; he'd known they were following him for several hours. No need to run from them, he thought. Now was the time of reckoning.

When the lance had sliced into the dirt in front of Matt's boots, he had accepted the challenge knowing that it was to be a fight to the death. No less would suffice. As Bright Knife's followers dismounted and circled him and Bright Knife, Matt unfastened his gun belt and hooked it on his saddle horn; then he unbuttoned his shirt and slipped out of it, draping it over the horse. Wearing only his trousers and his boots and grasping a knife in his right hand, he turned to look at each of the Comanche warriors before his gaze came to rest on their leader.

"If I win," he said, "your braves will return to Soaring Eagle's camp and remain loyal to him."

Bright Knife stared at Matt a long time before he said, "They will."

"Then I fight you to the death."

The gleaming blade of his knife in his right hand, Bright Knife threw back his head, a battle cry ringing from his lips, piercing the air—a battle cry that was meant to demoralize his opponent, but Matt had blocked out the sound. Reverting to his training as a Comanche warrior, he closed his mind to anything but fighting and defeating Bright Knife. Before he could find the gold and save his land, he had an obstacle to overcome.

Flexing his fingers as he adjusted his grip on the hilt, Matt crouched and moved in a circle, his eyes locked on the Indian, his movements leading and compelling obedience from Bright Knife. Round and round they went, and slowly their hands lowered; quickly one of them moved, his arm swinging, the blade singing through the air. One slashed, then the other. They swayed in and out; they jumped to avoid the sweep of the sharp blades;

they circled some more. Smaller and more agile than Matt, Bright Knife moved in closer and with an abrupt forceful lunge hit Matt's arm, knocking his knife out of his hand. A wicked grin on his face, the Comanche's leg swished out to kick Matt's weapon out of reach.

Now he was coming in for the kill; his opponent was unarmed and worn down. Bright Knife could see the lines of fatigue around his lips and eyes. Ma-ta-mon-yahu was an old warrior. Around went the young brave's knife, slicing in a wicked downward sweep. The steel sang through the air, missing Matt by a slender margin, then whipping upwards again. Up went the knife, and Matt, now winded, knew he had to depend on quick thinking to outmaneuver Bright Knife. The young brave was quick and highly skilled; he was in prime physical condition. Matt moved as if to try to block it, really a decoy to throw Bright Knife out of rhythm and to cause him to make a mistake.

Bright Knife didn't underestimate his opponent. Having witnessed Matt's speed the first time they'd fought, Bright Knife hurried his roundhouse cut just as Matt hoped. Checking his forward motion, Matt sucked in his breath and swayed his torso out of the radius of the knife's swing. Unable to stop himself, Bright Knife bent over, and the knife pointed toward the ground, away from Matt.

Even as the Comanche prepared to cut up again, Matt pivoted into a snapping kick that thudded home against the other's rib cage. Bright Knife cried out in pain as two ribs broke, and the kick propelled him into a large boulder. Despite the pain, despite the force of the blow, Bright Knife hung onto his weapon and sprang to his feet, his eyes glazed, and lunged toward Matt, the knife pointed directly at Matt's stomach. Matt's fingers closed around Bright Knife's wrist. Still the point slid across Matt's stomach to graze the skin; Matt's hand, like an iron band, clamped around Bright Knife's wrist, slowly twisting until the blade pointed at Bright Knife and only the hilt rubbed Matt.

Using all his strength, Matt butted his body against Bright Knife, the blade sinking into the Comanche brave's flesh. Bright Knife gasped and staggered back, both hands clutching the hilt of the knife that protruded from his stomach. For a moment he looked at Matt, opening his mouth, but no words came. Then he fell dead, facedown in the dirt.

Breathing deeply, Matt turned to the other braves and said in Comanche, "I have fought Bright Knife fairly, and the golden secret is mine if I find it. The deerskin is mine to use. I have kept my honor. Now keep yours . . . take Bright Knife's body for burial, and return to Soaring Eagle's camp."

Matt turned and walked to the brook. While he was washing and redressing himself, the braves slung Bright Knife's body over his horse and rode away. Sitting down, Matt unrolled the deerskin and studied the faint markings.

In the distance Zoe saw a man sitting beside the brook. Grazing close by were a black stallion and several mules strung together. At first she thought she was dreaming, but as she and Buffalo Woman rode closer, the blur of color and figure became more defined.

"Matt!" she called, racing the bay toward him.

Surprised to see both women, Matt dropped the deerskin and stood up. "Zoe . . . what are you

461

doing here? How did you find me?"

"Buffalo Woman brought me," she said, answering the second question first. As she jumped off the horse and ran to throw herself into his arms, her words tumbled out almost incoherently, "And I came because Greg's dead. Weber killed him, and he's after you. And Grisswold."

"Whoa . . . slow down," Matt said. "Tell me one thing at a time."

Sitting down with him, Zoe recounted all that had happened since he'd left Chandlerville earlier that day. She told him about Greg's confession before he died.

"I never dreamed that Greg was the father," he said. "Never. I thought he was my friend, and all the time—"

"It's over, darling," Zoe said, holding his hands in hers and squeezing gently. "Don't think about it anymore."

"Because of Greg," he said, his eyes shadowed with grief, "Bryan is dead. Greg's really the one responsible for his death."

"Weber would have killed Bryan with or without Greg," Zoe said.

"You're right," he agreed and both of them stood quietly, holding hands. After a long while, Matt said, "Zoe, I don't know what we're going to do. You were right—half a map is no better than no map. I don't know where to begin. In fact, I can't even understand some of these marks."

"I have the answer," she said. "Buffalo Woman came along to help us."

The Comanche woman, sitting a few paces from Matt and Zoe, held a rolled-up deerskin in her lap. In Comanche she said, "I brought this to you, Mata-mon-yahu. Now you can find the golden secret."

"Why did you change your mind?" Matt asked.

"I give you this because your wife has strong magic. She saved my grandson's life; I will save yours. Bring that to me, and I will read."

Matt brought his map to Buffalo Woman and she spread both deerskins in front of her and read them, her gnarled fingers tracing lines that ran here and there. She mumbled as she studied the drawings, but finally rolled up the maps and lifted her head.

In broken English, she said, "I take. I know place."

The deerskins safely in her possession, Buffalo Woman rode lead and Zoe followed, Matt bringing up the rear with the string of mules. Anticipation was high and the ride grueling. Heat and exhaustion were forgotten.

About an hour later Buffalo Woman stopped. Unrolling the deerskins, she checked once again and nodded. "It is here."

The three of them dismounted and hobbled the horses and mules, and Buffalo Woman knelt on the ground to spread the skins out once again. For several long minutes she pored over them, then motioned to Matt and Zoe. As she ran her fingers over the drawings, she explained them, first speaking in broken English. Tiring of that, she reverted to Comanche. When she finished talking, Matt stood and glanced around.

"Where is it?" Zoe asked, unable to keep up with the garbled words.

"Here somewhere is about all I know," Matt replied. "The landmarks have changed since they were first recorded. Or perhaps by the time they made the maps, their memories had dimmed. Let's spread out and see if we can find a cave."

463

Hours passed and the three searched the entire area. Once . . . twice. Zoe didn't think they left a stone unturned or failed to look behind a single bush. Every nook and cranny was investigated. Exhausted and disappointed, she sat down on a small boulder and untied her bandanna to wipe the sweat and grime from her face.

"We may not be in the right place at all," she said.

"This place," Buffalo Woman adamantly maintained. "We find."

Matt pushed his hat back on his head and dropped his hands to his hips. "I don't know where. We've looked everywhere. Given time, we could find it, but we don't have that much time. Probably an avalanche has covered the cave entrance."

"Maybe a Comanche-made avalanche," Zoe suggested. When he turned and walked away, Zoe called, "Where are you going?"

"Back over here," he answered. "This looks like the mark on the map. I thought I'd move a few of the rocks, just in case."

Though exhausted, Zoe and Buffalo Woman followed, all three of them heaving rocks. Despite her cut and bleeding hands and her broken nails, Zoe dug and dug some more. Then she saw the small opening, a hairline crack.

"Matt!" she screamed, "I've found it. I've found the cave!"

Like madmen, they clawed through the rocks and debris until finally they had an opening wide enough for them to slip through. While Matt was making torches, Zoe checked on the horses and mules to make sure they were secure and got the weapons and gunnysacks. Refusing a weapon, Buf-

464

falo Woman rolled her deerskins together and tucked them under her arm.

"I'll lead," Matt said, "and the two of you follow close behind. We don't want to get separated."

By torchlight they moved carefully and slowly because the floor of the cave was wet and slippery. At intervals Matt attached the torches to the wall so they would have light when they came out with the gold. The flickering flames cast eerie shadows on the walls around them. The farther they walked, the larger the cave, until finally it burgeoned into a large cavern, a waterfall rippling into a large, clear blue pool. All three caught their breath in awe. Through a tiny opening in the roof, sunlight splayed into the room and danced over the water. On a flat rock formation in front of the pool were four large trunks, the lids fastened.

Zoe pushed around Matt and raced into the room, extending her arms as if to grasp and hold the beauty she saw around her. "Oh, Matt," she cried, "what a beautiful place to hide the treasure. It's almost as if this is a holy place!"

"It is a holy place," Buffalo Woman said.

Zoe turned to see her standing in the darkened part of the cave. "Aren't you going to come in and look at the golden secret?"

"No. I bring. I pay debt of honor. I go now."

"Thank you, Buffalo Woman," Zoe said, thinking how differently she felt about the woman now than she had when she'd first met her. "You have saved your people. Your medicine is great."

Buffalo Woman nodded, then turned to Matt to say in Comanche, "I have brought you to the sacred cave, Ma-ta-mon-yahu, and revealed to you the golden secret. Please be careful; I do not know if the spirits will be angry or not. Even if they are not

465

angry, Bright Knife will be."

Answering in Comanche, Matt said, "Thank you for bringing me here, Buffalo Woman, and I will heed your advice because you are a wise woman with great medicine. But I have no fear of Bright Knife. He challenged me today when he learned that my grandfather had given me his deerskin. We fought to the death."

"I go now." Accepting the challenge as part of their code of honor, Buffalo Woman said nothing about Bright Knife's death. Tonight she would wail for him; he had died like a Comanche warrior. Her deerskins clutched protectively to her side, Buffalo Woman turned and soon disappeared into the darkness of the cave.

Matt joined Zoe and the two of them walked farther into the cavern to stand in front of the chests. Both were quiet because the room seemed to be filled with a reverent silence. They unfastened the chests one by one, unable to believe the riches they saw. Strings of pearls . . . jewels of all kinds. And golden coins . . . hundreds, thousands of them all gleaming in the sunlight.

Pearl necklaces dangling from her hands, Zoe danced around the room, finally falling against Matt. Deliriously happy, she threw her arms around him. "You've done it, Matt. You've saved La Candela de Oro. You've saved Chandlerville."

"Not quite," he said. "We've only found it. Now we have to get it home. That's going to be the difficult part."

"Do you think Fielding knows we're here?" Zoe dropped the jewelry into the nearest chest.

"Probably, but he doesn't know what we have. Now, let's put that out of our minds. We have to get this out of here and on the mules. Let's start filling these bags, lady."

Quickly Matt and Zoe worked to empty the trunks, one holding the bag open, the other filling it. As a bag was filled and tied off, Matt set it next to the cave.

"Only one more bag to go," Zoe announced, straightening up and rubbing the nape of her neck. "We'll have to make a second trip for what we can't carry on this one."

"What's wrong?" Matt asked, wondering if her head was bothering her.

"Bent over too long," she answered, then realized he thought she was suffering from her wounds. "My head's fine, Matt," she told him. "Really. But I'm worried . . . we haven't found the candlesticks yet. Nothing that even resembles one."

"Well," Matt said, "we have that small chest still."

Zoe unfastened the straps and opened it, bringing the jewelry out by the handfuls, but she found no candlesticks. Then, as Matt set the bag by the cave, she searched through the cavern. When she uncovered nothing else, she asked, "Do you think Eugenia could have been mistaken?"

"Could have been," Matt answered. "The candlesticks may be part of their family folklore. But now that we know where the cave is, we can come back and search for them later. Right now we want to get these out of here and loaded before dark. I want to get back to the ranch with them as soon as possible."

Several trips later, Matt was loading the mules and Zoe was making one last search through the cavern for the candlesticks. As he cinched the last bag in place, Matt heard the snapping of a twig and the clinking as loose pebbles sprayed down the side of the mountain; he knew someone was out there. Automatically his hand went to his revolver.

"You're a mighty hard man to follow, Chandler. The Comanches taught you well," a man called from somewhere above Matt. "Okay, Weber, you can come out now. We have 'em covered."

A sinister smile curling his lips, Weber stepped from behind a large boulder. He had discarded his suit coat and had strapped a revolver around his waist. "While you rely on brawn, Chandler, I rely on brain. I hired me a man who thinks like you do. Let me introduce you to Grisswold."

Matt eased away from the mules as Grisswold leaped down from one boulder to the next until he stood on the ground beside Weber. Grisswold's blue eyes were the color of ice; they were just as cold and hard.

"Seems I get a chance to repay you for what you did to me and the boys in Mexico," he said, his voice low and gravelly.

"Let's just say you'll get the chance," Matt said. "You were lucky that time; you won't be now."

Weber laughed. "You're remarkable, Matt. Even now that you're breathing your last, you're cool and collected."

"Just because you say it, Weber, doesn't make it so," Matt said. "I've managed to miss two death sentences you've passed on me. I have confidence that I'll miss this one also."

"If it was Weber you were dealing with," Grisswold said, "I would agree, Chandler. But it's me, and you're not going to walk away from me."

Matt stared at Weber and Grisswold. He could draw down on one of them for sure . . . maybe both.

"He's mine, Fielding," Grisswold said. "You

promised."

"Yes," Weber answered, "he's all yours. As I said, all I want is to have Zoe and to see him dead."

Cool chills ran down Matt's spine when he heard Weber. He couldn't let him have Zoe; he wouldn't.

"But I must confess, Grisswold, I'm curious about these," Weber said, walking over to the mules and untying one of the bags. He brought out a fistful of jewelry. He opened bag after bag. "Good God! Look at this. He must have a small fortune here!"

Weber was so excited he could hardly contain himself. A smile radiated his face; his eyes lit up. The gods—if there be any gods—were smiling on him, he thought. He was going to see Matt Chandler killed, he was going to get Zoe, and he had found himself a personal fortune.

Impassive features hiding a raging anger, Matt watched the expressions flit across Weber's face. Hatred, that bitter hatred that he'd felt for Weber so many long years ago, welled up within him to poison his system once more. His fingers ached to curl Weber's throat, to squeeze the very life out of his body. He was a parasite, sucking the life out of others so that he could live.

"This is a pleasant surprise, isn't it, Fielding?" Grisswold said, glimpsing out of the corner of his eyes the gold bracelets and pearl necklaces that spilled out of Weber's fist.

"Uh . . . yes," Weber agreed, abruptly reminded that he was going to have to share his booty with Grisswold. Greed prompted him to alter his plans somewhat. He couldn't stand the thought of dividing these riches with someone like Grisswold.

"Half and half," Grisswold said, shifting his weight and moving, his icy blue eyes never leaving

Matt.

"You'll get your share," Weber promised. After he returned the jewelry to the bag and retied it, he moved out of the way. "Right now, let's take care of Chandler. We want him out of the way once and for all."

"For sure," Grisswold agreed.

Matt breathed deeply, drawing in air, breathing out tension. Inhale . . . exhale. The brown eyes refused to be intimidated; the features failed to give way to anxiety or nervousness. Matt detected a small muscle twitching at the corner of Grisswold's right eye and saw the right arm bend ever so slightly, his hand poised at gun level. Matt's was hanging loosely by his side. Grisswold moved so that he was standing directly in front of Matt, not more than ten feet between them.

Perspiration beaded Matt's upper lip and trickled down his spine. Grisswold's blue eyes were unreadable and frozen; he showed no emotion. Matt was leery of this kind of man because he merely existed. Grisswold had no great desire that compelled him to live; therefore he had no fear of death. Yet Matt refused to break the gaze; he knew the man had a weakness. He had only to find it.

Grisswold's hand began to inch toward his revolver, the side of his face twitching slightly, the scar growing more pronounced and colored. In fluid motion, the smoothest coordination Matt had ever come up against, almost simultaneous action, Grisswold's hand clamped over the revolver, whipped it from the holster, and started firing. By the time the barrel was level and aimed at Matt, three shots rang through the air.

As quickly and with an even smoother blending of muscle and motion as Grisswold, Matt drew his gun, his legs slightly bending, and fired. Matt felt the slug as it hit his thigh; he staggered and fell to his knees. Out of the corner of his eye he saw Weber duck behind a boulder. Grisswold remained where he was, firing both revolvers. Another bullet hit Matt in the chest, and he crumpled to the ground.

"So long, Chandler!" Grisswold's farewell shout was followed by maniacal laughter.

Although his body was racked with pain, Matt pulled himself up. On his knees, his wound causing him excruciating pain, he took aim and fired at Grisswold before his revolver slipped out of his hand; then he fell to the ground.

Having heard the shots, Zoe came racing out of the cave, covered with dirt, and fell over Matt's prone body. Screaming, her hand went to his back, where she felt the warm, sticky blood.

"Matt, are you all right?" she cried, oblivious to everything else as she turned him over. She laid her head against his chest and heard the faint beating of his heart. Then, frantically, she ripped the shirt from his body and used it as wadding to stem the flow of blood.

"No need to do that, lady," Grisswold said, "He's a dead man."

Zoe looked up to see Grisswold standing in the open, his legs apart, an ugly smile on his face. He clutched his chest and blood oozed through his fingers. He threw back his head and laughed.

"I thought you were going to be such a challenge, Chandler. Fielding kept warning me about how dangerous you were, but you weren't. Look at me . . I came out of this with only a scratch, nothing but a flesh wound."

Another shot rang out. Grisswold, screaming out

in pain as blood spurted from his forehead, stag
gered backward and fell to the earth, his opened
eyes staring blankly at the boulder behind which
Weber hid.

"You bragged a little too soon, Grisswold. Surely
you didn't think I was going to share all this wealth
with you," Weber said, revealing himself. Dropping
his revolver into the holster, he turned to Zoe.
"Hello, my dear. How nice of you to meet me
here."

"Weber," Zoe whispered.

"Come on, Zoe," Weber said, crooking his finger
at her, "you and I are going to take the gold and
get out of here."

"No."

"If you know what's good for you, Zoe, you'll do
as I say."

"I'm not coming. Please, Weber, you can have the
gold. Let me stay with Matt. He needs me."

"Ah, my dear," Weber droned, "that's exactly why
I want you. Do you think I want you for yourself?
I want you because Matt Chandler wants you."

Frightened, Zoe laid Matt on the ground and
slowly rose. For each step that Weber took toward
her, she backed up one. "You're not going to get
away with this, Weber," she said.

"Oh, yes," he said, his voice menacingly quiet as
he backed her into a boulder and stood directly in
front of her, "I will. Now come on. We don't have
all day."

"I won't," Zoe cried, dodging to the side.

"No one is here to defend you, Dr. Randolph."
Weber's arm flew through the air, his hand cracking
across the side of her face.

Tasting the blood, Zoe reached up to rub her
hand over the cut at the corner of her mouth. "

don't need anyone to defend me," she said, so quietly that Weber could hardly hear her. In a move that surprised Weber, her arms shot out, her hands pressed against his chest, and she toppled him to the ground. She had to stop him. He was a maniac.

"You shouldn't have done that, Zoe. You're getting me angry."

A gun . . . she wanted a gun. Running, stumbling, falling to the ground at Grisswold's feet, she saw Weber walking toward her, his hand on his revolver. She pushed herself into a sitting position, her hand brushing against Grisswold's weapon.

"You've forced me to do this, Zoe. I would have enjoyed letting you live, but now I must punish you. You really deserve it, you know? You're the one who has done all this to me . . . caused me to lose everything I've ever worked for."

Weber drew. In one continual motion, a fluid economy of motion, Zoe's fingers slipped around Grisswold's revolver as if it had been crafted for her hand. She raised it and aimed at Weber. Tears streaming down her face, she fired again and again, watching as he crumpled to the ground, his fingers clawing in the dirt as he tried to crawl to the mules. When she had no more bullets left, when Weber stopped his convulsive movements, Zoe dropped the gun and crawled to Matt.

Sitting beside Matt, the two of them illuminated in the flickering torchlight, Zoe wiped his face with her wet bandanna. His wounds were serious, but not fatal, and she had cleaned and bandaged them. Fevered, he slept fitfully. Now she could only wait.

Hours passed. Throughout the night she continued to wipe his face with cool water. He tossed and turned; he muttered incoherently. Then he broke out in a cold sweat. His temperature slowly returned to normal; his breathing seemed less labored. Only then could Zoe nap beside him. Finally thin spindles of light shot into the cavern through the tiny hole in the roof. *Morning.*

She checked on Matt. His forehead was cool and he was sleeping soundly. She rose and stretched her stiff limbs. She crossed the cave and knelt beside the pool to wash her face. Staring at her reflection in the water, she hand-combed her hair and re-pinned it into a knot at the top of her head.

The play of light in the crystal-clear pool caught her attention. It was so beautiful that she could hardly believe it. She was surrounded by a golden nimbus. It was so real that she turned. It was real! And it was coming from a corner of the cave that was touched only by the morning sun.

She sprang to her feet and raced to the source of light. She climbed over the rocks, then suddenly stopped. There in the middle of a clearing was what appeared to be an altar. Sitting on the square, hand-hewn boulder were the golden candlesticks.

This was the miracle they had been waiting for!

Zoe crawled over the last of the rocks and walked up to the altar. Slowly she reached out and grasped the two candlesticks. Her heart was singing. This was a good omen.

"They were here after all."

Zoe looked up to see Matt waiting on the other side of the mound for her. She smiled brilliantly. "You shouldn't be up."

"I woke up, and you were gone."

"I saw the light. It was reflecting off the jewels."

"I guess this means we're going to have to return to Ciudad de la Cruz," he said.

"Eugenia will be so happy, Matt."

Weak, Matt returned to the pallet Zoe had prepared for him and sat down, leaning his back against the cave wall. She packed the candlesticks and sat down also. Putting his arm around her shoulder, he drew her close.

With all her love shining in her eyes, she smiled up at him and laid her hand on his cheek. "I love you, my Comanche husband."

"I love you, my Comanche bride."

"Are we going to live in a tepee?" Zoe asked.

Matt grinned. "How about La Candela de Oro?"

"Anywhere, so long as it's with you."

He lowered his head, his lips touching hers in an infinitely soft kiss.

TURN TO CATHERINE CREEL — THE REAL THING — FOR THE FINEST IN HEART-SOARING ROMANCE!